# THE SHAAR PRESS

THE JUDAICA IMPRINT
FOR THOUGHTFUL PEOPLE

# TIME

A SHAAR PRESS PUBLICATION

# BOMB

## A NOVEL BY
## YAIR WEINSTOCK

### TRANSLATED BY MIRIAM ZAKON

© *Copyright 2002 by* Shaar Press

First edition – First impression / May 2002

**ALL RIGHTS RESERVED**

*No part of this book may be reproduced* **in any form,** *photocopy, electronic media, or otherwise without* **written** *permission from the copyright holder, except by a reviewer who wishes to quote brief passages in connection with a review written for inclusion in magazines or newspapers.*

This is a work of fiction. Names, characters, places, and incidents are either the product of the author's imagination or are used fictitiously. Any resemblance to actual persons, living or dead, or locales is entirely coincidental.

**THE RIGHTS OF THE COPYRIGHT HOLDER WILL BE STRICTLY ENFORCED.**

Published by **SHAAR PRESS**
Distributed by MESORAH PUBLICATIONS, LTD.
4401 Second Avenue / Brooklyn, N.Y 11232 / (718) 921-9000

Distributed in Israel by SIFRIATI / A. GITLER
6 Hayarkon Street / Bnei Brak 51127

Distributed in Europe by LEHMANNS
Unit E, Viking Industrial Park, Rolling Mill Road / Jarrow, Tyne and Wear, NE32 3DP/ England

Distributed in Australia and New Zealand by GOLDS WORLD OF JUDAICA
3-13 William Street / Balaclava, Melbourne 3183 / Victoria Australia

Distributed in South Africa by KOLLEL BOOKSHOP
Shop 8A Norwood Hypermarket / Norwood 2196, Johannesburg, South Africa

ISBN: 1-57819-770-8 Hard Cover
ISBN: 1-57819-771-6 Paperback

Printed in the United States of America by Noble Book Press
Custom bound by Sefercraft, Inc. / 4401 Second Avenue / Brooklyn N.Y. 11232

attribute of preserving memories and records of exper
ences for the use of subsequent generations.
**time•bomb** (tīm´ bom´), *n.* a bomb so arranged as to explo
at a certain time.
**time•bomb** (tīm´ bom´), *n.* a situation, condition, etc. having
disastrous consequences resulting from long preparation.
**time•capsule** (tīm´ cap´sule), *n.* a receptacle containi
documents or objects typical of the current period, place

# PROLOGUE

The last rays of the sun lit up the room with a golden glow that grew dimmer from moment to moment. Then it was gone completely, and the room descended into darkness.

A motionless figure lay on the bed. An onlooker would have found it difficult to detect any signs of life. Suddenly Shmuel Bilad awoke with a confused start. He shivered; his body was covered with goose bumps. The terrible scream heard in his dream seemed so real to him. For a full ten minutes he lay in his bed trying to compose himself.

*What time is it?* He sat bolt upright and grabbed his watch. *I haven't davened Minchah yet! Who knows if I've missed shekiah!*

He leaped out of bed and hurried as quickly as possible to prepare himself for prayer. His mind was in a whirl. It had been years since he had slept so heavily, a sleep much deeper than a normal night's slumber. It is said that sleep is one-sixtieth of death; undoubtedly it was this kind of sleep that was meant.

Even after he had finished praying and had once again fallen into bed, still trembling, he could not understand what had come over him, and why he was feeling such a deep weariness.

How fortunate that the necessity of *davening* was so deeply ingrained in him that he managed to remember it amidst the chaos that had overtaken his brain. He usually *davened Minchah* at 1 o'clock in the afternoon, in yeshivah; the habit had almost caused him to miss the afternoon prayers today.

Yeshivah. That was it.

His mind began slowly, ever so slowly, to clear, like water whose sediment sinks to the bottom, leaving transparent liquid. Now he could remember well what had sent him to sleep in the middle of the day, something almost unheard of. It was the telephone conversation this afternoon.

For two weeks he had nervously awaited the call. What wouldn't he do to get the coveted position of *maggid shiur* in Yeshivas Masuos Avraham? He knew the students in the top class of the yeshivah, and the desire to teach them burned within him like a flame.

At noon the much-anticipated call finally came through. The ring caught him when he was in the kitchen. He anxiously lifted the receiver. He knew what he was expecting: "Rabbi Shmuel Bilad, we've decided to take you on as a lecturer in the yeshivah. Prepare to give a *shiur* in *Perek 'Lo Yachpor.'*"

He had already prepared ten classes, on credit so to speak.

But instead, the words came upon him, sharp as thorns. Every word pierced: "Rabbi Bilad, this is Efraim Levi, the secretary." (He should have realized that if the *Rosh Yeshivah*, R' Isser Zalman Samet, had not made the call himself, that was a sign that something had gone wrong.) Efraim stuttered and seemed to be having difficulty in choosing his words. "We don't need proof of what is well known; we're all aware of your tremendous ability in Torah."

Shmuel realized he was breathing heavily. He cut him off impatiently. "*Nu* — and so —"

Efraim was truly pitiful. The task of being the bad guy had fallen to him. The words seemed to stick in his throat. "We had a special staff meeting on the issue. Don't think, Heaven forbid, that we're in any way criticizing you, but — but —"

After that stammer, nothing else had to be said. Shmuel could feel a rock, cold and hard, settle upon his heart. His jaws tensed, and he felt paralyzed by pain. Efraim Levi muttered something about special suitability needed for the students in the current class: "They're overstimulated, and need someone young and effervescent, like they are." (*With all due respect,* Shmuel thought bitterly, *you yourself are approaching 50, and your beard is partly white. The students had obviously discussed the fact that they were learning in a yeshivah for young people, and not in an old-age home.*)

"But the current *shiur beis,* that is, next year's *shiur gimmel,* is another story entirely. It consists of incredible boys, much more stable and mature. We hope that next year we'll call upon you to do a marvelous job as teacher of *shiur gimmel.*" That was Efraim's feeble attempt at bandaging a bleeding wound. "The main thing, R' Shmuel, is for you to continue to do great things. We'll be in touch."

The conversation left him drained and despairing. The disappointment was terrible; his exalted mood had shattered into shards of pain and bitterness. He ate his lunch listlessly, without appetite, and then fell apathetically into his bed.

He had awaited this call for two weeks. Waited? Every few minutes he had wandered over toward the phone in his home, or gently padded the cell phone in his pocket.

And then he had fallen into a very deep sleep.

That was when the black nightmare began. A nightmare, not a dream. The nightmare that had begun to recur again and again.

Dark skies, threatening, almost black. Frightening rain clouds, cold and biting rain pounding down upon Jerusalem. A boy standing, wailing in the gloom, completely drenched. Shmuel recognizes the boy. The boy lifts dark eyes accusingly towards him; suddenly Shmuel sees himself reflected in the boy's pupils. He sees himself as he looks today, and he stares into his own eyes and sees, again, the boy's accusing eyes, and within those eyes he sees himself and within himself he sees the boy, two mirrors reflecting each other endlessly.

The boy cries and cries. His weak sobs grow stronger, turn louder and louder, like a screaming siren.

The siren takes on words. "Shmulik, you are guilty. Shmulik, why?"

The terrible echo of the siren, the wail of the words, "Shmulik, why?" always awakens him, no matter how deep his sleep.

*Time Bomb* / 9

How many years had passed since then? Thirty-six.

*What's the matter with me? Why should something that wasn't my fault at all, something that happened when I was just a child, why should such an event turn my life into a nightmare?*

How could it have happened, that terrible thing?

The memories overwhelmed him.

## Prague, 5598 (1838)

It was late at night when he decided to do the deed. The decision had been preceded by months of doubts, sleepless nights, long days filled with persecution and hatred. He had been beset by fears and misgivings. Several times he had decided to act, only to back down at the last minute.

But tonight he was going to cross the Rubicon, to do a deed from which there was no turning back. Finally he was at peace with himself. There had been just too many persecutions. He was at the end of his tether, having fallen from the giddy heights to the lowest depths. He was a strong person, but he could not bear the degradation any longer.

"They've made the decision for me," he muttered with bitter anger as he donned his clothing in the darkness of the room. "The good L-rd can't have any complaints against me, can't ask me why I've done this. Am I guilty? Or perhaps the guilt rests upon Your sweet children who have harassed me, humbled me, all but struck me. Me, who helped everyone in this 'incredible' community. They've left me no other choice."

Silently, he left his house in the ancient Jewish Quarter of Prague.

The Altneushul stood out in the dim starlight. The sloping roof seemed to split the dark sky with its sharp spires, rising like a challenge into the blackness. There was no moon on this night, with the lunar month coming to an end; this fact, too, became a part of his calculations. Better that no one witness his deeds.

*With all this, I'm ashamed of what I'm doing,* came the depressing thought. *Is that surprising? This is extremely difficult.*

The Jewish community building, near the Altneushul, was also dark, but a large clock on the spire told him the time, marked in Hebrew letters. Prague Jewry, which had always felt threatened by the vast number of churches in the city, the thousands of gilded crosses that pierced their vision from every spire and tower, took great pride in the clock. With its square Hebrew letters and a movement that circled counterclockwise, the clock provided a warm and pleasant air to the Jewish ghetto, intimate, a community encircled, a lone island in a stormy Christian sea.

He walked between winding streets and alleyways, trying to trad quietly upon the cobblestones, not to make any noise, not to draw attention to himself. His shadowy figure blended well into the darkness as it crept silently through the Jewish Quarter which, ten years hence, would see its walls destroyed by order of Josef II and which would be named for him — Josefov.

He took a deep breath. Now he was no longer in danger of being found, yet even here in the Old City he was known by many men. He was, after all, not some anonymous person. But here, at least, he could find some justification for his presence. He had no intention, in any case, of retracing his steps. He had burned his bridges behind him.

He stopped for a moment, trying to remember where Cardinal Matthias Bilcav stayed when he was not in his luxurious residence in the great Hradcany Castle that looked down upon Prague. During the day he could find his way around here, more or less, but in such darkness how could he remember whether to turn right or left, go forward or back?

His head moved back and forth, turning from side to side. Suddenly he felt both frightened and panic stricken. A drunk emerging from his saloon might well honor him with a swift and brutal blow, solely because of his obviously Jewish appearance. He took a deep breath to compose himself and forced himself to think with icy calm. Again he examined his surroundings. All around him rose buildings with sharp steepled roofs, beautifully designed in a variety of architectural styles. Some were gothic and ancient, relics of the days of Charles IV, others baroque, in the style that characterized the city over two centuries earlier, during the days of the Reformation of the Roman Catholic Church. The cornices of the windows were decorated with bas-relief images of delicate flowers; carved statuettes stood in niches built into the walls; entranceways were decorated with wide arches. Craftsmanship was evident in each and every building, and none resembled the next: each one had been given its own individual imprint. What a difference between these fashionable buildings and the tasteless ones of the Jewish ghetto! A short distance away, the Vltava River streamed placidly, like some ancient and mighty serpent snaking its way through Prague, its calm green waters coursing pleasantly downstream.

All of a sudden he recalled, with startling clarity that the Cardinal actually lived quite near to here, next to the old town hall, the "Staromestska radnice." He had to walk in a straight line until he saw the council headquarters, which looked like a row of private homes with a tower at one end. Immediately after, stood a large home with a giant golden cross on its facade. Another cross, this one next to the entrance, served as a second indication.

He walked quickly and confidently and in a short while stood before the Cardinal's home.

A carved wooden door met his eye, a heavy knocker in whose center was carved a cherub with a turned-up nose that had been worn down by thousands of blows to the wood.

He gave a few subdued knocks, hoping the Cardinal was a light sleeper who would awaken quickly.

His hopes were fulfilled, or perhaps the Cardinal had already been awake. The door opened a crack, that immediately widened. The Cardinal's eyes gazed in shock when, by the light of a flickering oil lamp held in his hand, he recognized his honored guest. Impossible to mistake that small, burly figure, that red face and the narrow eyes that emitted an expression of wisdom. That expression, now, seemed to have been extinguished.

"Getzel Fernbach! The wealthy banker and head of the Prague Jewish community. What brings you to my house at this hour of the night?"

Getzel Fernbach put his finger to his lips. "Sssh, speak softly; no one knows of this visit."

The Cardinal rapidly recovered his composure. He threw his arm around the banker's shoulders and pulled him inside. The door was swiftly slammed shut.

They walked through the darkened foyer and entered a large room. The oil lamp trembled in the priest's hands, giving off a weak reddish light, revealing heavy antique furniture. There was a comfortable wide bed meant for guests, large oil paintings on the walls, and an immense wooden closet in a corner.

They sat down near a large table. The lamp was set down on the floor, illuminating the faces of the two, casting giant shadows upon the walls.

"Getzel, what brings to my house the owner of the Bank Fernbach, head of the Prague community, and number one resident of the Jewish ghetto?" the Cardinal asked, his curiosity evident in his voice.

The banker shuddered; his eyes were cast down and his hands played nervously with the edge of the tablecloth. His voice trembled as he said the words, "I want to convert."

"What?" the Cardinal shouted in consternation.

Getzel took a deep breath. How hard this was, despite the fact that he had thought of it a hundred, a thousand times in recent days. But his voice grew steadier as he said, "I want to change my religion. To convert."

The Cardinal, too, had gotten over the initial shock. His voice sank to a hoarse whisper. "What's happened? What brings a respected Jew, of high position, to change his beliefs and his religion in his old age? Have you finally recognized Christianity's superiority over Judaism?"

"Apparently you haven't heard what's been going on in the Jewish ghetto." The banker's eyes flashed with hatred. "I've been pushed out of my job as community head and excommunicated. Everyone shuns me. My bank is beset with financial difficulties and has almost collapsed as a result of the excommunication. I have huge debts and I can't get out of them unless I join the Christians of Prague."

The Cardinal was disappointed. The wealthy Jew had gone bankrupt, and had lost his prestigious position as well. The Cardinal's sharp mind swiftly went over the facts. Every situation had to be assessed and used to the best purpose. He glanced at the Jew shrewdly.

"Getzel, I have a wonderful idea. But first let me clarify one thing: Why did they excommunicate you?"

"My enemies are slandering me," Fernbach's voice trembled with rage. "Absolute baseless slanders! My community, which over the years

*Time Bomb* / 13

I've supported with enormous sums, has betrayed me without making the tiniest effort at discovering the truth. No one bothered hearing my side of the story. If these are my brothers, it's time for me to look for different ones."

Yes, the situation was good, excellent in fact. It had been many years since such a juicy bone had fallen onto the Cardinal's plate. He swallowed a laugh that threatened to burst forth and forced himself to speak coolly and serenely.

"Getzel, my friend, let me suggest an excellent deal to you," the shrewd spark in his eye now burned with fervor. "You don't have to convert. I wouldn't suggest you take such a step at your age. You won't feel comfortable in your new world and in the end you'll be frozen out of both worlds."

Fernbach was taken aback. "But what should I do? Stay among those who've betrayed me? Happily thank them for spitting on me, those who enjoyed my generosity all these years?"

"I didn't say that. I can restore your former position," Matthias spoke with the confidence of one who has planned ahead and knows what lies before him.

"And what about revenge? Wouldn't you want to take vengeance?" he asked after a brief silence.

"Certainly." The banker jumped up from his place. "I want to punish each and every one of them. Vengeance doesn't begin to describe what I wish to do."

Matthias grinned inwardly. Probing the wound had yielded good results. "You will have your revenge upon them, Getzel, a revenge so sweet that Satan himself couldn't imagine such a thing. None of them will know what happened, and how their entire wonderful community was destroyed; only you, my dear Getzel."

"How will you do it?"

"I have a plan." His voice sank into a whisper, a hiss. "Listen."

*Chechnya, the Caucasus Mountains, 5760 (2000)*

Night fell on the mountains, a darkness illuminated only by the stars. Winter's chill, a cold that crept into the bones, hung heavy between the peaks.

But in the secret headquarters of the Chechen rebels it was not cold; the atmosphere prevailing there radiated hot anger, fear, and panic. The burning hatred was like something out of a nuclear furnace, hatred for anything or anyone Russian. A few days earlier the Chechen rebels had been dealt a terrible blow, with the capture of Salamon Radeyv, "The Gray Fox," taken into Russian custody. Vladimir Putin, the Russian president, had been so proud of the feat that he had personally informed his people of the deed. He made the dramatic announcement immediately prior to the elections, and it was possible that as a result he had risen from acting president to the actual, official president of Russia. He had, indeed, cause to be proud: Salamon Radeyv, son-in-law of Dzhokar Dudayev, one of Chechnya's greatest leaders, was considered one of the most dangerous, sought-after terrorists, and his forces had inflicted heavy losses upon the Russian occupiers.

All of Russia could see the prisoner with their own eyes. It was hard to recognize him: his short beard had vanished, as his captors had forced him to shave. The sunglasses that he always wore, even in dark rooms, had been removed. One mystery was revealed: a glass eye had been hidden behind those dark glasses. Beneath the beard the terrorist's face was riddled with scars, a reminder of a Russian whip from the not-so-distant past.

Radeyv's face had changed almost unrecognizably, but the real transformation had taken place within. The incredible self-confidence he had radiated, the well-known arrogance, the mouth that had voiced such terrible threats toward Russia, the personality that seemed to know no fear — hardly any of that remained.

The broadcast ended and the picture metamorphosed into the face of the Russian narrator. In the rebel headquarters someone rushed to turn off the set. The atmosphere was heavy. Chatav, another leader of the Chechen guerrillas, ground his teeth in rage as thoughts raced swiftly through his mind.

The war of the tiny Chechen nation seemed all but lost. Grozny, its capital city, had been captured by the Russians after being turned into a pile of rubble by the heavy air and artillery strikes. Russia had fought a brutal, uncompromising war in Chechnya. It had committed atrocities there — and the world had stood silent, with the exception of a few human rights organizations, and some media people, particularly in the United States, who had protested the mass murders and the slaughter of innocent civilians. The American government kept its peace and said not a word in the face of the horrifying scenes.

The entire Caucasus region hung in the balance, and Russia wanted desperately to hold on to it, thus ensuring access to the Caspian Sea with its vast oil reserves. In Russia's eyes the Caucasus was nothing more than its backyard, as it had been for all of history — or at least since the days of the great czars in the 18th and 19th centuries. The United States had no objection to Russia protecting its interests in the Caucasus.

"Have you seen what they've done to our Salamon?" Chatav asked, his pain kept carefully in check. "It was hard to recognize him."

His mobile phone vibrated in his pocket; he put it to his ear. "Quiet," he said, his voice tinged with awe. "Our esteemed leader, Aslan Maschaduv, wants to speak."

He placed the phone next to a microphone that stood upon his desk. The voice of President Maschaduv could be heard clearly, despite some static.

"We cannot remain silent," Maschaduv said. "We must hit the Russians with such a blow that the entire world will tremble. But not only them. The hypocrisy of the Americans pains me even more than the cruelty of the Russians. We will hit both of them together. They have captured the 'Gray Fox,' but many other foxes lie in wait for them, waiting for their prey. Chatav, you will surely be meeting with members of the media. You will tell the world that our *mujahideen* are prepared for battle, and not only in Chechnya. We will take the struggle right into Russia. Our war for an independent Chechnya will shock the world. Sitting next to me is one of the best of our men, Selim Yagudayev, who has given me an incredible idea for how to return Chechnya to our hands. Just wait and see."

*Jerusalem, 5670 (2000)*

The three-story house in the elite neighborhood of Savyon Beit HaKerem had not changed in the past decade, since the Talmi family had come direct from Argentina, land of their birth, to live there. In 1990, it had been lovely by any standards, and the ten intervening years had simply enhanced its grace.

This was not a house for millionaires, and Talmi had no ambitions to be one. But it was clearly beautifully designed, spacious and modern with much air and light and furniture that displayed no ostentation. This was a house where everything flowed naturally and quietly. This was meant to be a place that inspired thought and contemplation by its distinguished residents: the regional judge Professor Dori (Doriel) Talmi, his wife, the law professor Ariella Talmi-Sturm, and their journalist daughter, Nufar Talmi, who came there on the few days when she was not staying in Gaza. The residents of Savyon Beit HaKerem respected their notable neighbors. Judge Talmi was a well-known figure, a brilliant jurist who had been educated in the ivy tower of Argentinian academia and had burst like a thunderbolt coming down from Olympus into the political life of the State of Israel when he snagged one of the top legal-political posts in the nation. He stubbornly insisted that all of his judgments were absolutely free of the taint of politics and were completely professional.

Dori had a pleasant personality, shy and reserved, but beneath his shining bald pate lay an acute legal brain. He held controversial views on almost every issue, particularly in the matter of the judicial authority upon Israeli society. His views were unusual even within the left-leaning judiciary itself, and more than one colleague had remonstrated with him on them. Professor Talmi heard them out, gave his shy smile, and declined to reply. "I'm no debater," he would say laconically, when asked why he did not argue for his beliefs.

No one knew the true answer. Dori Talmi scorned argument because he believed in deeds, not words. He had a clear goal: to be appointed one day to the Supreme Court, and from there to become its Chief Justice. At that point he would be able to put his legal and philosophical views into practice and to imprint his radical beliefs onto every issue, whether the people liked them or not. He knew better than the rest what was good for human society in general and Israelis in particular and he would rewrite the norms and mores of behavior for them.

Professor Dori Talmi was absolutely convinced that he and a small group of enlightened judges were the elite among the elite in society. They represented the ultimate of human development, the purity of human genius; it was they who were the torchbearers of an ethical vision. He looked at the six billion inhabitants of the globe and saw the majority of them as trained monkeys. Only in the universities, in their schools of humanities, and in the temples of the law, were there those who could answer to the designation "human beings." It was a small number, but ultimately those "human beings" would create the norms and ethics for the entire world.

There was one more place where this pure enlightened understanding dwelled, but Professor Dori Talmi did not want to think about it.

# 1

*Jerusalem, 5724 (1964)*

A large stone house stood in the Old Katamon neighborhood, its windows enhanced by wide arches; it was one of the buildings whose Arab owners had fled during the War of Independence. Jewish refugees from the Old City of Jerusalem, fleeing their homes when they fell into the hands of the Jordanian legionnaires, had appropriated these buildings for their homes.

Two arms sneaked out of the window on the second floor. Here, one could see the lush leaves of the house plants lovingly tended by Hadassah Levin. Now the leaves were being pulled off the stem, one by one, as Moishy Levin attempted to assuage his grief and despair.

Shmulik Bilad cast a frightened glance out of the window. From the floor above him came the voice of Hadassah Levin; a wailing voice, a voice that broke hearts. She gave a wordless sob, a reedy sound that seemed to pierce his soul anew. How long would she continue to cry this way? If the nightmare did not end, he would have to run away from here.

"It's your fault, Shmulik," he whispered to himself. "If you had been a more responsible boy, Mrs. Levin wouldn't have to cry all night."

"But I just forgot," an inner voice answered in his defense.

"To forget is to sin," a prosecuting voice declared sternly in a mantra that echoed over and over.

And to think that he and Dudy Levin were best friends.

Dudy Levin was younger than Shmulik by nearly a year, yet they were in the same class, the closest of friends and soul mates. Shmuel Bilad was a tall, well-built lad with clear eyes. Dudy Levin was short and slight of build and his sparkling eyes were black. Two dark *peyos* descended from beside his ears, giving his sensitive face an unkempt look. Dudy was a bright lad, mischievous and yet a bit of a coward. His sharp witticisms kept everyone laughing; his family adored the boy and were very proud of him. Shmulik was more restrained. Together, the two were an inseparable pair, involved in every adventure and excitement, both in their own neighborhood and out of it.

That past Tuesday they had been sitting in the yard of their local yeshivah. Dudy was unusually quiet and thoughtful and his eyes, always sparkling, were dreamy, with a touch of melancholy.

"Dudy, what's the matter?" Shmulik demanded.

"It's my birthday today. I'm 12 years old."

"Mazal tov," Shmulik said.

"In another year I'll be bar mitzvah," Dudy said, pronouncing each word slowly, like a child sucking on a candy and trying to make it last. "I'm thinking about it. It's time to starting learning the *halachos* of *tefillin*. Shmulik, I'm going to take on *ol malchus Shamayim*, Hashem's Kingship! Think about it!"

Shmulik gave him a long, measured look. "What's with you, Dudy? There's still plenty of time, a whole year. It's not like you to be so serious."

"To take on *ol malchus Shamayim*, for that there's still time?" Dudy seemed almost angry, again not like his usual self. "In another half an

20 / *Time Bomb*

hour we'll be *davening Ma'ariv,* and when I say *Krias Shema* I take upon myself *ol malchus Shamayim.* Besides, I hate to tell you this, we always have to feel we're accepting Hashem as our King; *Krias Shema* just reveals what's going on in our hearts."

Shmulik did not know what to say. Dudy had never spoken this way before. Shmulik lapsed into silence and Dudy also held his peace. They left yeshivah and walked down Chizkiyahu HaMelech Street, entering Bustenai Street, where they lived, one above the other.

When they were ready to part on the stairwell, and Shmulik had already opened the door to his apartment, Dudy seemed to awaken from his dream. "Shmulik, my parents will be away all day tomorrow. The twins have an appointment with a bone specialist. Let me leave our key with you; you know they won't let me have one." He spoke almost defiantly: Dudy's parents, Hadassah and Shalom Levin, did not depend on their son for anything to do with keys or, for that matter, any personal property. Dudy was notorious for losing things, though he refused to admit it himself.

"No problem," Shmulik answered, encouraged by the sign of normalcy in his depressed friend. Shmulik then burst into the house. "Hi, Imma, what's to eat?" But Imma was not home; only Tzipi, his older sister, was there, locked in her room, studying reams of papers for a major upcoming history exam.

As he sat down to a meal of schnitzel and mashed potatoes he heard a knock on the door. Dudy was bringing him the key. "Tomorrow after school I'll pick it up." He left as suddenly as he had come; again, unlike him. Usually Dudy loved to hang around to chat.

The next day everything went wrong. Shmulik overslept and when he raced out of the house, half an hour late, he did not remember that Dudy was to pick up his key and did not say a word about it to his family. Had he only known that his parents were going to be out of the house all day, had he only known that Tzipi, after her big history test, planned on spending the afternoon with friends. Had he only woken up on time, to hear all of this. But he had overslept.

And he did not know.

In the morning during a *shiur* in Gemara a mischievous spirit suddenly overcame him. When the rebbi stood with his back to the class, pointing

*Time Bomb* / 21

to a chart illustrating certain complicated laws, Shmulik stood up and mimicked the rebbi in a way that set the whole class laughing.

The furious teacher managed to catch a glimpse of Shmulik sitting down hastily at his desk, its surface decorated by dozens of the boy's doodlings. In a rage, he ordered Shmulik out of the classroom with the threatening words, "Don't come back tomorrow without your father."

Shmulik pointed to the black skies. "But Rav Guttman, there's thunder outside and it's raining hard and I haven't got an umbrella."

As if to emphasize the truth of these words, a bolt of lightning lit the sky. The blast of thunder that followed it caused the windows to rattle. The rain, which had been coming down strong, intensified even more. Rav Guttman handed the boy his umbrella. "Take this and go home, Shmulik."

Shmulik, surprised at his rebbi's unexpected sign of humanity even while he was furious, said, "But what will the rebbi do without his umbrella in this pouring rain?"

"By the time we go home the rain will have stopped," Rav Guttman answered, adding in acid tones, "And don't forget to bring it back to me when you get here tomorrow, an hour late as usual."

Shmulik deliberately took his time as he gathered his things and carefully fastened his coat, button after button.

"Go home already," his rebbi thundered.

Shmulik stood in the doorway of the classroom, his eyes pleading as they stared at his rebbi, who continued to write on the chart. "Shmulik, don't stand there. Close the door and go already!"

The door closed. Shmulik found himself in the deserted corridor. This was not the first time he had disturbed the *shiur*, but this time Rav Guttman had really gone too far, to throw him out in the rain!

He held his brown briefcase in his hands. The shiny brass metal corners that were supposed to keep it from fraying bumped into his legs with every step, but he was so enveloped in a wave of self-pity that he did not pay attention to the pain.

The bus drove slowly through traffic-packed streets. Shmulik was cold and wet and he thought about what he would tell his mother, how he would explain why he was home two and a half hours after he had left.

The bus stopped near the Edison Theater, on Yeshayahu Street, parallel to Strauss. Not far from here was the B'nai Brith Library.

In a split-second decision, Shmulik jumped up and managed to get off before the narrow back door had slammed shut. Fortunately the library was open. Inside it was warm and pleasant. He put the dripping umbrella in a corner, next to his briefcase, picked out a thick book from a shelf, and began to read.

Rav Guttman had been completely wrong. The rain did not stop that day. The thunderstorm raged for many hours, but Shmulik did not hear a thing. He was deep in a gripping adventure story and had forgotten the entire world.

Dudy Levin went home without an umbrella. Somehow he managed to avoid the worst of the downpour, by sprinting from one awning to another, until he finally reached the stairway of his home. He knocked on the door of the Bilad family, waiting for Shmulik to hand him the key. Moishy and Ahrele, his 10-year-old twin brothers, were identical in everything, both good and bad. The two of them were bright and mischievous, with eyes that sparkled with fun. They each excelled in their classes. And they shared a weakness of the bone structure, and suffered from similar motor disabilities. It took them until the age of 2 to master how to walk, and holding objects in their hands was difficult for them. They should have undergone physical therapy but the research into their problems was not yet advanced and in any case their impoverished parents had no money for such things. When their parents heard of a doctor in Haifa who specialized in these problems and who came highly recommended, they made an appointment. That was where they were today, and that was why Dudy was standing here facing a locked door.

Much to Dudy's anger and chagrin, no one opened the door to the Bilad home even after he banged against it with all his might and shouted Shmulik's name. No one heard him. Only two families lived in the large Arab house, and neither was home. Dudy's stomach growled; he was really hungry. Occasionally he went out to the street to impatiently look for a sign of Shmulik. The rain lashed out at him with its huge drops and quickly coiled its cold way down beneath his thin clothing. The Levin family, like the Bilads, was not very well off, but while the Bilads still managed to make ends meet, the Levins were truly impoverished, and the children dressed accordingly: a coat that had known better days, a frayed sweater whose time had come and gone, patched pants, and thin-soled shoes.

Dudy had no idea what time it was, but the darkness of the sky told him that the day was coming to a close. Still no sign of Shmulik. His anger and panic turned into a sob. He stood and blubbered in the rain, calling Shmulik's name again and again beneath the windows. Perhaps Shmulik had fallen asleep, perhaps that bookworm was absorbed in reading and did not hear his, Dudy's, despairing cries.

Shmulik was, indeed, sitting and reading, surrounded by thick walls, in a well-lit and heated room; Dudy Levin, meanwhile, stood and soaked up the rain, half out of his mind with impatience.

Finally the adventure story came to a close. Shmulik glanced at the large clock on the wall. "Oh my, it's already 5 o'clock." Five hours he had been sitting here, barely noticing the time go by. Suddenly he felt hungry. He quickly put on his coat and raced outside toward the bus stop, forgetting both his briefcase and Rav Guttman's umbrella.

When he reached Katamon three-quarters of an hour later, night had fallen. He climbed the five steps to his apartment in the dark. Suddenly his foot hit some kind of bundle. He jumped back.

"What's that? I mean, who's that?" he cried anxiously.

The dark form slowly stood up. Even in the dimness Shmulik could see the gleaming eyes belonging to Dudy Levin. "Thank you very much, Shmulik, you're really very responsible."

"Who's that? Dudy? I completely forgot." Shmulik nervously clasped his hands together. "Don't tell me you've been waiting outside all this time."

"I won't tell you anything. I will be angry with you forever."

"Dudy, forgive me," Shmulik was almost crying. Dudy remained silent.

Now the two of them were facing the same problem. The Bilad home was locked. They waited for two more hours in the freezing cold, not exchanging a single word. Dudy coughed ceaselessly. Shmulik believed that he was doing it on purpose, to make him feel worse about his lack of responsibility, but the cough seemed to grow worse and worse. Tzipi finally came home at 8 o'clock in the evening and opened the door for them. Dudy grabbed his key, coughing, his face pale, and raced home.

Even after the door was closed Shmulik could hear his friend coughing. A terrible, heavy feeling descended upon him.

During the night Shmulik heard, from the mists of sleep, the sound of footsteps racing above him. He turned over and went back to sleep.

That night the lights did not go out in the Levin home. Close to midnight Dudy's coughing became so bad that he nearly choked. His temperature shot up until, "the mercury almost broke the thermometer," as Hadassah Levin told the nurses in the hospital emergency room at 2 o'clock in the morning.

The doctors examined the shivering boy and looked concerned. They sent him immediately for an x-ray of the lungs.

"Let me explain what's happening, Mr. Levin," the chief doctor said after he had seen the x-rays. "Your son has a very serious case of pneumonia in both sides of the lungs. We're putting him on a penicillin drip immediately, but you must know that the situation is not simple."

Shalom Levin turned white. "What do you mean?" he asked weakly. "Won't the penicillin work?"

The doctor put an encouraging hand on his shoulder, trying to sweeten the bitter pill. "The antibiotic is fine. But I've hardly ever seen such a serious infection. If your son was more robust, I would be more optimistic. But your son — "

"His name is Dudy," the father interjected.

"That's right, Dudy. He's a thin and weak child. Let's hope for the best, but you must pray very hard for his recovery."

The tone of his voice was closer to despair than to hope. Shalom burst into tears. The doctor patted him on the back, but his eyes, too, were moist.

The doctor's prognosis proved to be all too accurate. The frail body was no match for the illness. The doctors did all they could but Dudy slipped through their fingers. The funeral took place on Friday morning, and the boy was laid to his eternal rest.

Shmulik Bilad would never forget the broken cries, the horrifying wails that came from the Levin home that afternoon. Shalom Levin's groans of pain blended in with the heartbroken screams of his wife,

Hadassah, while the 10-year-old-twins, Moishy and Ahrele, sobbed in unison. Neighbors came to try and strengthen the family in their sorrow. Shmulik, though, sat terrified in his room, not daring to go up. Clearly, he felt, he was responsible for his close friend's death. He was an honest and ethical boy, and even if he had wanted to somehow escape blame for his negligence, he could not. The librarian from the B'nai Brith library had appeared the next day in the Bilad home, the briefcase and umbrella in his hands and a pleasant smile on his face as he returned the lost objects. Rabbi Guttman would not allow Shmulik to return to the classroom without his father, who would be forced to shiver in the icy frost of the rebbi's criticism of his son. Shmulik was absolutely ensnared in a tangle of troubles, but everything paled before the terrible bitterness of self-flagellation: "How could I have been so irresponsible; how could I have forgotten what Dudy told me?"

He sat in his room and blamed himself, casting judgment in a repetitive monotone: "It's all your fault, Shmulik. All your fault. If only you hadn't been such a terrible student, if only you had thought of someone besides yourself."

His agony grew worse when he heard from his parents how several of the people who had come to visit the Levins had spoken of this blow as a "tragedy upon a tragedy." Only two years had passed since Aryeh Yissachar Levin, Dudy's older brother, had drowned in the sea. Aryeh Yissachar had truly earned the honorific name of *"ilui,"* genius, in the full sense of the word. He knew ten *masechtos* by heart and was as familiar with the "*Ketzos HaChoshen*" as one is with his own room. He had something worthwhile to say on almost any topic, and a bright future was projected for him by all who knew him. After his tragic death Shalom Levin had comforted himself in his second son, Dudy, a sensitive boy whose wit, like his bright eyes and impish grin, warmed the father's broken heart during those dark days.

Now the Levin family had been struck once again, and the pain was too much to bear. Shalom sat, stonelike, his head bent, sighing ceaselessly as visitors came and went. In the second room was Hadassah, the bereaved mother, her sobs piercing right through Shmulik's heart as he sat, tormented by unbearable pangs of conscience.

On the last day of the *shivah* he finally found the courage to go up the stairs. He sat across from Shalom Levin, wondering what to say.

Shalom gazed at him with empty eyes. In his inexperience and youth, Shmulik did not comprehend the melancholy and bereavement; instead, he was certain that the father was thinking: *Shmulik didn't even get a sniffle, and only my Dudy had to die.* No such thoughts went through Shalom's mind. Descended from a family of chassidim, he had been raised with the dictum: "To say, if only I had done such and such everything would have been different, borders upon apostasy." He accepted G-d's judgment upon himself and Shmulik was, to him, nothing more than a young boy who had been chosen, for whatever reason, to be one of the emissaries who had taken Dudy away from them at such a tender age. True, punishment was exacted by one who merited punishment, so apparently Shmulik had been liable for something, but that was not for him, Shalom, to understand. Go try and figure out Heaven's reckonings. "Hidden are the ways of Hashem," he told all who had come to comfort him. "Dudy must have been a reincarnation of a soul sent to earth to rectify something from a former life, and having corrected what was lacking he was sent back to his source."

He tried valiantly to get over the loss, to return to his affairs, but the awful pain seemed to overpower his very body. Day and night he wept; he could not recover his composure. Half a year passed, and one day he went to sleep and never woke up.

Three times death had passed through the Levin home in less than three years. The family was left beaten and miserable. Friends and neighbors flung up their hands in despair. No one had an inkling of how to deal with the triple tragedy.

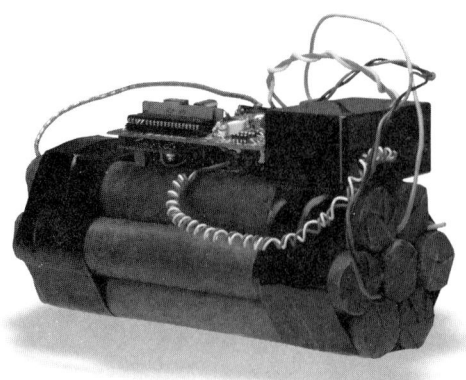

# 2

One of the visitors during the week of mourning for Shalom Levin was a red-bearded, well-dressed man with sparkling, friendly blue eyes. He introduced himself as Yehoshua Cohen and explained that he had been a close friend of Shalom Levin since their days in yeshivah. The brokenhearted widow made an effort but could not recall the name. Still the man was insistent, even bringing up many forgotten incidents. He spent more time than normal in the house of mourning, spoke to the twins and tried to cheer them up and take their minds off the tragedy. Moishy and Ahrele, who were by nature happy children, were grateful to the man who had given them a few blessed minutes of forgetfulness during this black week. After an hour he said goodbye and left. Hadassah Levin stared at the closed door, thinking how strange it was that he had not uttered the customary farewell sentence: "May the Omnipresent comfort you among the other mourners of Zion and Jerusalem; may you know no more sorrow."

The thought vanished in an instant. There were others who did not know quite what to say, and in any case she was too caught up in her own agony to give the matter much attention.

28 / *Time Bomb*

The last day of *shivah* was the most difficult. In the morning the neighbors gathered in the house for the final *Shacharis* service. After *davening* the mourners sat down on the low benches and the neighbors comforted them with the traditional phrases, telling them, as is customary, to stand up on their feet and sit no more.

Hadassah Levin's tears, frozen the entire week, suddenly dissolved. The symbolic act and words — "Enough of your sorrow, may it be His will that you need not mourn and suffer more" — seemed to pierce her wounded heart like a sharp arrow, brutally opening it. She almost suffocated as the tears flowed. She fell backwards upon the couch, her arms around the twins. Her body was wracked with sobs that seemed endless. The wails grew worse as she stood by the fresh grave of the one who had been at her side for twenty years, the one who had left her here, alone and hurt, to care for sickly twins who needed all sorts of special therapies, without a coin in her pocket.

The wonderful phenomenon that would become common in later days, when philanthropists and managers of charitable funds make every effort to help families in need, and particularly families who had experienced tragedies, did not yet exist in the years between 5720-5730 (1960-1970). The Levin family was left alone on stormy seas, their ship wrecked beneath the waves, and no one was there to throw them a life preserver.

When they returned home they found a warm meal waiting for them, fresh from the Bilad kitchen. So it was during the next days, particularly on Shabbos. But the next week Tova Bilad returned to her job. She had told no one that she had taken time off from work in order to help the Levins during their days of mourning. Every good deed has its price: next month, she would see its cost in the diminished paycheck she would bring home. This had been a luxury of *chesed* that she could afford only this one time. That *Motza'ei Shabbos* Mrs. Levin came to thank her from the bottom of her heart for her efforts and her kindness, and to beg her at the same time not to do more. "You don't have to take my suffering upon your shoulders."

Tova Bilad shrugged her off, explaining that it was no hardship, but each knew that this was only a show. The truth was, the burden was too heavy for her.

Hadassah Levin tried to get back to normal, but nothing was normal. The twins returned to their studies; that was the only thing that remained of the past. The kitchen shelves were empty, the larder bare. Only a hard piece of leftover challah remained in the breadbox. This challah provided sandwiches for the twins, while she herself ate one dry slice.

For lunch on Sunday there was a little leftover soup from Shabbos; Monday, they ate the remains of the chulent, down to the very last bit of barley.

Tuesday, there was nothing left to eat.

The grocery owner agreed to sell her bread, milk, and a few dairy products on credit, though she did not know where she would get money to pay the bill. Breakfast and dinner, then, were taken care of, at least partially.

For the first time the children ate bread and cheese for lunch as well. At night, the widow would go to the Machaneh Yehudah *shuk* after closing and join the legions of impoverished men and women scrounging through the piles of fruits and vegetables that were no longer salable.

The humiliation was unbelievable. Mrs. Levin was a refined woman who had never been pushed in a crowd, never had to deal with loud, ill-mannered people and their wild shouts — "Why are you grabbing that tomato from me?" She sometimes suffered ringing blows as well, from common, coarse women who were much stronger than her. The results were not worth the effort: the fruits and vegetables that she brought home, choking back tears, were half rotten. There was no reason to continue.

On Wednesday the twins ate bread and cheese for lunch; on Thursday they enjoyed a cup of leben. On Friday they hungered, waiting for Shabbos, and on Shabbos once again Tova Bilad came through for them and brought them a full meal.

Hadassah Levin often wondered why, other than Tova Bilad, none of the neighbors did anything for them. The answer was really quite simple; fortunately for her, she did not know it: behind their backs the Levins were known as the "sour lemons." Shalom and Hadassah had always walked around with bitter, sour faces. Though it was a result of their hard lives, still, inevitably it had built a wall between them and their neighbors, a wall created by mutual antipathy. Even after the tragedies had struck the family, no one knew how to change the situation. The Bilad family's help was just a small drop in a great sea of want. Food was not the only thing lacking. The twins' clothes were in tatters; they were ashamed to wear them to *cheder*. Hadassah would cut pieces from her dead husband's clothing and put patch upon patch, until the clothing looked like some kind of madman's creation.

Nights, the widow would give vent to her misery with heartrending sobs. Ahrele would look at her fearfully and join her in crying. Moishy was more introverted and reserved and expressed his grief by quietly pulling leaves off the plants in the window boxes. Leaf after leaf went flying down, until there was nothing left but bare stems silently shrieking in their emptiness.

After a month the grocery owner's patience ran out. The widow's debt had grown ominously large, and there was no sign of any payment. There was the previous card as well, tucked securely into his cardboard box, with a large balance still owed from before her husband's death. No one was even talking about paying up that bill. On Sunday morning, when Hadassah took her bread, cheese, and milk, the grocer took her to the side and told her icily that his own financial situation would not allow him to continue to sell to her on credit. If she wished to make any further purchases, she would have to bring cash.

Two days later Moishy and Ahrele went to school with their lunchbags empty. They walked to the bus stop, Hadassah's anxious eyes accompanying them. How she longed to go with them, but she was afraid that she would give in and burst into tears. She did not want them to see her cry. Once she had turned away, the two continued to walk, passing the bus stop. They made their way to the old eucalyptus tree whose wide trunk had broken through the ruins of an old stone fence in the yard of the Aharanov house. With no strength left, they fell upon the moist ground.

A pair of eyes was watching them carefully from the other side of the street.

"Aren't we going to *cheder*?" Ahrele, the more passive of the two, asked his brother.

*Time Bomb* / 31

"No, we're not going," Moishy, the aggressive twin, declared. "Look at our clothes; rags, not clothing! We've got shoes in our holes, and the rain is coming in for a visit in every puddle!" he added with bitter humor.

"We've got holes in our shoes," Ahrele corrected him innocently.

"No," Moishy was adamant. "The holes are bigger than the shoes. We've got nothing to eat; we're starving." He looked upwards in entreaty. "Our Father, in *Gan Eden*, have mercy on us! Dudy, you were a *tzaddik*, why don't you throw down some money from Heaven? You see everything that's going on!"

The two wept a little and then sat down quietly, depressed and frightened. They had no idea what to do next. They knew just one thing: the situation could not go on as it was any longer.

A red-bearded man crossed the street and approached them. "Don't I know you from somewhere?"

Moishy remembered him instantly. "Of course! You came when we were sitting *shivah* for our father."

"That's right," the man said with a melancholy smile. "I'm still mourning for your father; I was his friend. His good friend. My name is Yehoshua Cohen. Has something else happened? You look so sad, even more than you should under the circumstances."

The two exchanged glances, as if asking, twin to twin, if it would be permitted to ignore Imma's warning and reveal to someone that they were hungry. Moishy gave a little nod of assent; in any case, their ragged clothing gave them away.

"We don't have anything to eat. We're hungry," Moishy muttered brokenly.

Yehoshua looked stunned. "Hungry? Oh, no! How did that happen? Didn't you eat anything at home before coming out?"

"Our home is empty." Now it was Ahrele who was confiding. "There's not even dried-out challah left from Shabbos."

"I understand." Yehoshua nodded his head in sorrow. The two of them told him how they had decided by themselves not to return to *cheder* until they had new clothing and something to eat.

Yehoshua stood silently for a few seconds. "You mean to tell me that no one is helping you?" he asked unbelievingly.

"No one," Ahrele repeated.

"Except for the Bilads," Moishy corrected him. "But they have also stopped, because they are poor, like we are."

"We can't let two children starve," Yehoshua whispered, checking through his wallet. "Good, I've got enough money. Come with me to the grocery."

The two cautiously followed him, grinning at each other. Dudy, the *tzaddik*, was showering them with candies from *Gan Eden*.

Yehoshua took them to a distant grocery. Moishy understood why: "So that they won't ask him to pay back our debt." He bought them two large rolls and a chunk of halvah. Then they went to the greengrocer; when they walked out each child was holding a ripe, juicy orange and a shiny red apple in his hand. From there the three rode to the city, to a large clothing store. Yehoshua outfitted them, from head to toe — and put everything on his bill. There were warm flannel undershirts, black woolen slacks — "just like yeshivah *bachurim*" — sturdy shoes, thick sweaters, and winter coats of a quality they had never experienced.

They were embarrassed by the overwhelming kindness of this stranger, who came upon them in their darkest hour, but they accepted his generosity with the natural joy of youngsters who had yet to learn from the adult world the secret of hidden motivation and hypocrisy. When they reached their *cheder*, some two hours late, their friends hardly recognized them. The others touched the new clothes in awe and asked where they had come from, but the two children held their peace, loyally following their benefactor's request that they say nothing in *cheder* about what he had done.

After dropping them off at school, Yehoshua again traveled to the city center and bought a wealth of things for them. After a few hours he knocked on Hadassah Levin's door, his hands full of heavy packages containing priceless treasures: large and succulent fruits in season, ripe vegetables just waiting to be eaten, a large bag of broken wafers sold by weight, luscious cakes from a well-known kosher bakery. There were masses of canned goods, cleaning supplies, even a few packages of cotton swabs to clean out dirty ears.

Hadassah stood before him, embarrassed and scarlet faced. "Why have you brought this?" she asked, humiliated. The house behind her was absolutely empty. Shalom Levin had been a man who had lived frugally, and his family had never felt the taste of such luxury before.

Yehoshua Cohen blew his nose with a trumpeting blast, and muttered something about the terrible Jerusalem cold. He reminded her that he had been a close friend of her late husband, and told her that this morning he had met her two children, who had decided not to go to school because they had had nothing to eat. Hadassah, upset, gave a deep sigh. "*Oy*, my poor *tzaddikim*, my poor boys. They never said a word to me." Yehoshua waited for her to regain her composure and then helped her put the groceries on her bare shelves and to make an impressive pile of fruits and vegetables in a metal basket that had, until now, contained only two small onions and a dried-up orange. When he had completed his task he apologized for having caused any unpleasantness and left the house, a marvel of courtesy and delicacy.

When the twins returned home, running to tell their mother the incredible news of the *tzaddik* who had helped them in the morning, they found that their barren kitchen had turned into a veritable restaurant. "I love that man," Moishy announced, carefully peeling a fresh banana. Ahrele grabbed a handful of lemon-flavored wafers and hungrily stuffed them into his mouth. "These wafers are so fresh. I wish he would come every day," he murmured through a crumb-stuffed mouth.

Hadassah felt a stab of discomfort. The gift was certainly a welcome one, a kind of "*mishloach manos*" come to save them, but the niggling doubt just would not leave her: From where did such rare generosity spring? She skimmed through her husband's notebooks, kept from his yeshivah days. He had written down notes of all the lectures he had heard from his *rabbanim*, together with his own *chiddushim* (novellae). Occasionally he mentioned the name of one or another of his friends, writing down their comments on his work.

But the letters were small and cramped and the widow's eyes were tired. She fell asleep, a notebook in her hand.

The next day she continued the task. Suddenly she noticed the name Yaakov Cohen. Perhaps that was him?

But a week later she could not have cared less if his name was Yaakov or Yehoshua, or anything else for that matter. The house was once again empty and the children were hungry. As she walked out of the house, determined to ask the neighborhood *gemach* for a loan, she met Yehoshua Cohen walking up the steps, his hands once again full of bags. Her eyes lit up: this time, he was an angel bringing salvation, an angel that had turned up at just the right time.

He was not alone, and the woman who came with him had also not come empty-handed. "Let me introduce you," he said courteously. "This is my wife Miriam."

This time the treats included two chickens, freshly slaughtered. "From the Meah Shearim slaughterhouse," Yehoshua did not neglect to mention the fact. "Do you know how to *kasher* a chicken?"

"What a question!" Hadassah shrugged her shoulders; in truth, she had almost forgotten, it had been so long.

She cut the birds, took out their innards, and left them in water for half an hour. Then she pulled out the "*zaltz breitel*," the salting board, from the closet, salted the birds with coarse salt, and left them for an hour until rinsing them. She put the *kashered* birds on the top shelf of her refrigerator, as close as possible to the block of ice that stood in a special spot on top and slowly melted into a flat, faded blue shelf. The refrigerator was nothing more than an ice box, really, kept cold by a block of ice purchased once or twice a week when Herzka rang the bell on top of the cart pulled by his old, tired horse.

During the entire time Miriam Cohen, Yehoshua's wife, helped clean the house, while Yehoshua chatted with the children, who had taken to him like an old friend. Hadassah rinsed the salt off her hands and turned to Yehoshua, who was busily playing "bulls-eye" with the boys.

"I found a notebook of my husband's, from his yeshivah days," she said suddenly. "He mentions there 'my clever friend Yaakov Cohen.' Do you think he meant you?"

Yehoshua Cohen furrowed his brow for a few seconds in an effort of memory. "Certainly. That's my second name; my full name is Yehoshua Yaakov Cohen. I'm just wondering why Shalom would have used my lesser-known name."

*Time Bomb* / 35

While the conversation ensued, Miriam Cohen continued cleaning and organizing the house.

When the couple was ready to leave, Hadassah escorted them out. She was endlessly grateful, deeply indebted to them. "I don't know how to thank you for all you've done," she said, her voice breaking with emotion, as they boarded the bus.

Endlessly grateful. Deeply indebted. Almost literally indebted: she felt for the first time how the words "thank you" could build walls, prison walls, around a person. Prison walls: Yehoshua would visit periodically, each time bringing something new for the house. On his sixth visit he wordlessly left an envelope on the kitchen table. When he left she eagerly ripped it open.

It contained two hundred lirot; half a month's average salary. The sum enabled her to repay a portion of her debt to the grocer and even send the twins for two treatments for their long-neglected physical problems. Yet, occasionally, dark thoughts beset her. She had once heard, from a wise rabbi well versed in human psychology, that everything a person does has some kind of motive. There is no one who does something without some motivation behind it. *What is your motivation, Yehoshua — Yaakov — Cohen?*

# 3

**S**lowly, determinedly, Yehoshua became a part of the Levin family circle; by the time six months had passed he was no longer subject to the scrutinizing eyes of the anxious widow. With his connections he managed to find her employment in a sewing workshop on the other side of the city. The salary was a joke, really, but getting out of the house gave her the opportunity to clear her head and regain her self-confidence. On Tuesdays and Thursdays she worked until 7 p.m.

It never occurred to her that the workshop owners were working hand in hand with Yehoshua in order to get her out of the house and take possession, piece by piece.

The first time that she worked late, the philanthropist awaited the children when they returned from school. In his hand was a package containing hot, tantalizing meat, of a sort they had never seen before, together with two side dishes, "that my wife sent." The hungry children fell on the special treat ravenously, praising the extraordinary taste. A spark danced in Yehoshua's eyes. On Thursday he brought them sausages, the likes of which they had never eaten in their lives. The boys trusted him completely and never asked him where the food had come from. For six months Yehoshua had regularly brought them foodstuffs with a top *kashrus* certification. Could they have realized that this same man was now feeding them meals that were absolutely *treif*?

The laws of Torah are also the laws of nature: Poisoned food poisons the body, unkosher food poisons the soul. The boys' hearts began to be closed to all things holy. Their natural fear of Heaven melted away, growing colder day by day. They observed the mitzvos unenthusiastically, only with outward show. They continued going to *cheder* but occasionally brought home notes from the teacher announcing that one or the other was sitting, staring at nothingness, not working. Their mother assumed that the teachers did not understand the poor orphans.

Three more months passed. Hadassah could not comprehend what had happened to her children, who began to exhibit hatred for their Jewish traditions. Now Yehoshua began to drip his venom into the innocent children's hearts. He told them about the founder of Christianity, and his apostles, and read them portions of the New Testament. Yehoshua brainwashed them with hatred for their Jewish heritage, and drove a wedge between them and their friends.

"But the Bilads did help us," Moishy protested during one of their conversations.

Yehoshua opened his eyes wide. "Shmulik Bilad's conscience, and that of his parents, is bothering him, because he caused the entire tragedy. Don't you defend the Satan."

The next time Yehoshua "explained" to them that G-d had abandoned the Jews and exchanged them for the Christians. If they would only look around, he said, they could see clearly that the Christians were the blessed people. Why should you suffer so much during your lives? Yehoshua asked sweetly. Go to the true religion and see how your lives will become like Paradise.

The boys wondered between themselves how a man who looked like a religious Jew could have converted to Christianity, and during one of their meetings they found the courage to ask him. Yehoshua, who was certainly one of the most clever of the Christian missionaries of

Jerusalem, began to laugh at the innocent questions. In order to allay their suspicions he assured them that he was just as Jewish as they were; he simply wanted to give them food for thought.

In addition to this "food for thought" came food for digestion. *Treif* food. Yehoshua was very wary of Hadassah, and thus only brought his "meat" — ham — on Tuesdays and Thursdays, when she was still at work. But his wily mind did not rest, and he trapped Hadassah herself, by offering her chicken that came from a nonkosher butcher, and that had not been ritually slaughtered. He explained that he had asked the *shochet* in Meah Shearim to remove the chicken's head and neck because otherwise the blood would stain his cloth basket. In her worst nightmares Hadassah never dreamed that she was *kashering* a chicken that had been bought in a *treif* store, the same place where Yehoshua purchased ham and sausages. He had won her confidence and she followed him like a blind person in a maze. And so she, like her children, imbibed the poison into her soul, eating food that was absolutely nonkosher.

Just when she had finally managed to find a workable daily routine, everything fell apart. The apartment in Katamon did not belong to them; they had rented it for a nominal monthly sum. When she requested that her lease be extended for another year she was astounded at the negative reply. The owner requested that the Levin family leave the place within the month. Two days later the owners of the sewing workshop regretfully informed her that because of financial difficulties they could not keep her on any longer.

Hadassah Levin's eyes were circled with black rings as she returned from her job for the very last time. Mechanically she boarded a bus and took a seat. She saw nothing, she heard nothing. Her head seemed about to explode with pain, with sorrow, with fear of what tomorrow would bring. Every day was worse than the one before, every day more bitter.

Her sole comfort was the thought of Yehoshua's visits, each time bringing so much good food with him. But he came only once a week, and this morning the kitchen had been bare once again.

When she came into the house she imagined hearing her children call out excitedly, "Imma, Yehoshua was here!" As always they would pull her into the kitchen to show her all the goodies. Instead, she heard her learned Moishy tell Ahrele, "You know? In our house it's the opposite of *Seder* night."

"Why?" Ahrele asked. Moishy explained. "On *Seder* night you first eat bitter herbs and then a good dinner; here, we ate the dinner first and now we've got nothing but bitterness."

She gave a melancholy smile.

---

The supplies in the house were dangerously low. The hungry children had eaten everything that was edible; only the paint chips remained to chew upon. Hadassah sat and cried, her eyes swollen and red. She awaited some kind of dramatic revolution that would come and save them. If all this was not enough, a new worry had cropped up: Moishy could not move the fingers of his right hand. The doctor at the clinic told her that only a doctor abroad could handle the problem. The next bit of news was even worse: if the problem was not dealt with, he would lose the use of the hand entirely. Paralysis. To cap it all off, because the boys were identical twins, it was almost certain that the same problem would eventually beset Ahrele.

There was a knock at the door. Ahrele ran to answer it.

"Yehoshua!" They heard Ahrele's happy cry. "What have you brought us?"

"Nothing." Yehoshua wrung his hands in sorrow. "Absolutely nothing. Not even gum."

Hadassah lifted depressed eyes. "What happened?"

Yehoshua spoke sadly. "My money is gone. I've used all my savings on you. I'm left with my last few coins."

Hadassah burst into tears. "You're an absolute *tzaddik*, and I always suspected you of ulterior motives. Please forgive me, but I'm lost — completely lost."

Yehoshua looked thoughtfully at the two pale boys sitting on the creaking sofa, books in hand, listening to the conversation taking place.

"Look," he said, after ostensibly having given the matter some thought. "I've lost my financial backing, but for your children I'm prepared to do everything." He pulled a few bills out of his pocket. "Take this as a loan. Go to Rechavia. There's a private doctor there, Dr. Wilhelm Crusa. He's a specialist in children's motor difficulties." He pulled out another bill. His voice broke. "And here's something more to buy groceries with. I can't bear to see this plight."

His eyes glittered with suspicious moisture. He wondered inwardly if these were what they called "crocodile tears." Or perhaps it was something to do with digestion.

※

That day Hadassah and the twins went to Dr. Crusa, who saw his patients in a private office in a stone-fronted home in Rechavia. It was a single-story building with a large garden that boasted chrysanthemums in a wide variety of colors. A green lawn had been carefully maintained. A housekeeper named Hilda ushered Hadassah and the twins into a waiting room, beside a well-lit fireplace, and asked them to wait. She pointed to a pile of brightly colored magazines written in a foreign language that lay in a basket beside them but Hadassah forbade her children to touch them. "We're careful with what we look at," she reminded them.

The doctor, an elderly German whose eyes were shrouded behind thick lenses and whose white mustache almost covered his upper lip, gave Moishy a thorough examination, and heard from Moishy's mother the litany of pains and troubles that he and his twin brother had gone through since their birth.

The doctor's assessment was crisp and clear.

"Frau Levin, here in this country there is nothing to be done for your sons."

"*Oy vey!*" She crumpled into the chair and suddenly looked old and tired.

The doctor ignored her distress. "Didn't they tell you?" he asked coldly. "There are only a few places in the world which have this kind of experience with children's hands. This is certainly not the place."

"And where is?"

The doctor spoke with authority. "The best place is in Caracas, the capital of Venezuela. There is a special clinic just for children with these problems, with the best doctors available."

Hadassah spoke — not speech, exactly; more like a cry of pain. "So what — should we do? Travel abroad? I don't have the money to buy a loaf of bread!"

The doctor remained still in the face of the stormy outburst. A deep silence filled the room. Moishy looked with interest at a heavy glass container that contained wooden sticks used to check people's throats. He knew that he was the subject of the conversation and he turned into himself, using the only armor available to children. Ahrele jumped onto the scale and moved the weights around, right to left, trying to figure out his accurate weight.

From the other side of the heavy door they could hear the monotonous ticktock of an antique clock. Suddenly it chimed six times. "I'm very sorry, Frau Levin," Dr. Crusa said with as much warmth as his frosty voice would allow. "I can only give you a professional opinion. Because of your difficult financial situation I will forego my usual fee of 80 lirot. I must emphasize that if you don't take care of these children now, they will be paralyzed for life."

Yehoshua arrived that evening to hear the results of the doctor's visit. Hadassah was out of ideas. "What should we do?" she asked him in increasing panic. "On one hand, I have nothing to lose by taking this trip; there's nothing left for me here. No apartment, no job, no money. On the other hand, I haven't got the money to travel abroad, I haven't got the money for treatments, I don't know anything about Venezuela, I don't speak Spanish, nothing — I shouldn't sin with my mouth, but the only thing I can do is jump off the roof!"

"Heaven forbid! How can you speak that way? To jump off the roof?" Yehoshua protested loudly. "Life doesn't belong to us, it is a gift from the Creator. I understand your sorrow and distress and know from where it comes." He said gently, "With the help of G-d everything will work out."

"Work out? How?"

"If Dr. Crusa had sent you to the United States or Europe I wouldn't have anything to suggest, but actually in Venezuela I have good friends.

I'll loan you the money for three plane tickets. Don't worry about paying me back; we'll work something out."

"I have no words to thank you. You're a *tzaddik*," Hadassah burst out. "Like an angel from heaven you were sent to me during my hardest times."

Yehoshua kept an embarrassed silence. "I have only one request," he said modestly. "There's no need to tell anyone about the trip and my contributions."

---

One day the Levin family disappeared. The apartment in Katamon was suddenly empty. No one knew where the widow and her two children had gone. After about a week a rumor started circulating that they had gone to a country in South America.

The terrible news of the Levin family's conversion to Christianity came from Saadyah the greengrocer, known as "the radio" by the neighborhood children because of his tendency to retail news together with vegetables. "Those villains, the missionaries, came to this broken family like vultures on a corpse," Saadyah told his enthralled customers. "They came hidden, masked, pretending to be religious Jews. That's how they managed to confuse their minds and brainwash them into converting."

Housewives standing in the pale winter sun of Jerusalem, baskets in hand, stood frozen as their potatoes and carrots were weighed, listening to the dreadful news. Someone remembered a red-bearded Jew who had often visited the twins; another mentioned that she had once seen the same man riding in a car on Shabbos in a different part of town, but that she had assumed she had been mistaken. A third furiously added that such things should not be accepted quietly. The neighborhood residents somehow managed to find a clear picture of Yehoshua Cohen and circulated it throughout the city beneath the headlines: "Danger! A kidnapper lives among us!" As in the well-known cliche, they firmly locked the barn door after the horses had been stolen. For at that moment Pedro Marchio, once known as Yehoshua Cohen and who had been, himself, a Jew who had converted, was far from Israel. He laughed to himself whenever he thought of the success of his mission. In Venezuela he reaped the fruits of his Jerusalem efforts.

*Time Bomb* / 43

The news of the family's conversion was actually exaggerated and a little premature. When Hadassah Levin reached Caracas, members of the mission, suitably disguised, met her. They put her up in a large, nicely decorated apartment. The twins were taken for treatment in a medical center located outside the city, staying there all day. Hadassah occasionally tried to walk through the city and get to know it, but generally she preferred to stay in her warm, secure shell. She did not know the language and the natives and their customs puzzled and alarmed her. She sat in her home and waited. She had little to do other than wait, hope, and pray. Yehoshua's friends took care of all their needs, and kept her away from her children with all sorts of crafty schemes and excuses. Her influence on her children lessened and lessened. Their motor skills improved from day to day; but their Jewishness diminished likewise. Hadassah watched hopelessly as her Jewish children melted away, with two gentiles totally taking their place. When she finally recovered and tried to flee back to Israel it was too late: Moishy and Ahrele had been converted to Christianity in a formal ceremony in the church, with Yehoshua Cohen serving as godfather.

Too late, Hadassah Levin realized that she had fallen into the claws of a slick and dangerous rogue who had stolen her children from her. Yehoshua Cohen had lain in wait for them from the moment their father had died, patiently and cleverly weaving an unbreakable snare for them.

But how had he known about them at all? Who had told him of their dire poverty, their awful situation that enabled him to destroy a chain of endless Jewish generations?

She vowed to take vengeance against the one who had revealed her secret to Yehoshua and had brought her to such a terrible fate. There would be a sweet and unique revenge, too, against the kidnapper himself; the day would come. She would not rest and not be silent until she had made him pay the final reckoning.

And in the meantime, Hadassah Levin decided, she would stay in Venezuela to do battle against the Christian missions that now dominated her sons — and to return them to Judaism.

# 4

**B**ecause of the Levins' cool ties with the neighborhood, the news of the family's conversion did not cause more than a temporary stir. Only Shmulik Bilad remained wounded and mournful. He was beset by feelings of guilt and for a long while suffered from a deep depression. While his friends went through the usual teen ills of acned faces, he felt the scars of a broken heart for the part he had played in the destruction of an entire family; those who had died and those who had converted. He knew, too, which was the worse fate: "More terrible is one who causes another to sin than one who kills another," he would tell himself occasionally on a dark night, as he lay sleepless on his bed, and fear would chill his heart. "The day will come, Shmuel Mordechai son of Tova Gittel, when the soul of your friend Dudy Levin will come to take revenge. The day will come."

After repeating those words of dread for what seemed the hundredth time, sleep would elude him. At other times he suffered from nightmares and dreaded the vision of demons and wraithlike souls; his eyes burned in the darkness of the room until a bluish light heralded a new morning.

Only then would he finally doze, waking up a few short hours later when his father shook him from the bed, growling, "Every morning you wake up late. What's going to become of you?"

Shmulik, introverted and reserved, balled his fists and never revealed to a soul what was troubling him. The sufferings of a tortured spirit were reserved only for himself.

Years of study and progress in yeshivah were what saved Shmulik Bilad from falling prey to a destructive depression. He put all the power of his agony into Torah and became a true *masmid* who spent every free moment learning, in addition, of course, to his daily classes. He became an expert in many areas which are not usually familiar to yeshivah students, certainly not at his young age. His reputation preceded him in *yeshivah gedolah*, and students argued over who would be privileged to learn with him *b'chavrusa*, as a study partner. As an excellent student, when the time came the matchmakers ran after him with the best of suggestions.

After his marriage to Shoshana, daughter of R' Avraham Mendel Klein, a well-known *Rosh Yeshivah* in the south of the country, Shmuel Bilad joined a *kollel* in Jerusalem, starting a family in the capital city. The children came, one after the other. He was helpful in the home and played a major role in their rearing and education, but the main portion of his thoughts were always in his Gemara. "A *ben Torah* can be recognized through his dreams," he used to say. "The dreams attest to the true internal desires of a person's heart. If someone dreams about worldly vanities, it means that he is really interested in them. If someone dreams about a difficult Rambam, he is a true *ben Torah*!"

Shmuel Bilad dreamed almost exclusively about his studies. For nearly ten years he hardly left the tent of Torah study. Intensive, nonstop learning in his *kollel*, uncompromising effort in the forty-eight ways in which one obtains Torah wisdom, earned him the reputation of a *talmid chacham* of great stature.

After a decade in *kollel* he was invited to become a *maggid shiur* in Yeshivas Chochmei Minsk. The agreement was for him to work for three months without salary as a trial period, in order to assess whether he was up to the task. The trial period was shortened to one week. R' Chaggai Sovovitch had taken over for the *Rosh Yeshivah*, R' Gad Koziner, who was abroad for medical treatment. He listened to the novice's initial classes from behind a partially opened door and smiled in pleasure. R' Shmuel Bilad was a success story, if one could judge from his stunning start. First of all, he was interesting. To keep young, energetic students attentive for two solid hours was quite an accomplishment. Everything worked out: R' Shmuel explained things clearly, making even the most complicated topics seem fairly simple. His vocabulary was good; he knew the "yeshivish" parlance but varied it with a wealth of fascinating images. "You could lick your fingers," is how R' Chaggai described the class as he listened. But he did not make a final decision until he saw the students leaving the classroom. More than that he did not need: the shining eyes, the great enthusiasm and excitement and, most important, the circle of students who surrounded R' Bilad as they walked out said it all. The excitement continued through the coming days; if anything, it grew even greater. This was more than success; this was triumph.

After a week R' Bilad was officially installed as the *maggid shiur* of the second-year students. He put great efforts into preparation and, at the same time, worked hard to develop the students and teach them to become scholars. "From others you'll hear tons of commentaries," he used to tell his pupils. "From my friends, you might even come to understand them. But from me — you yourselves will learn to write commentaries."

Yeshivas Chochmei Minsk was proud of its new treasure, who came to represent the yeshivah. R' Shmuel's year was a happy one; the yeshivah, too, was pleased — until the *Rosh Yeshivah*, R' Gad Koziner, recovered and returned from the United States, together with his father-in-law, R' Simchah Blark, the founder and administrator of the yeshivah.

When R' Simchah returned he found, much to his chagrin, that the students were not particularly interested in his son-in-law, R' Gad. Their attention and loyalty were given over completely to the new star, R' Shmuel Bilad.

The yeshivah administrator bluntly told his son-in-law, "It's either you or him." He realized that though his son-in-law possessed a unique personality, R' Bilad's charisma was a threat, not only to Gad, but to the entire staff. The students were not content to admire R' Shmuel. They worshiped him and had built a cult of personality around him. Within a short while all the other lecturers would the yeshivah, and only R' Shmuel Bilad would remain. R' Simchah was a clever and learned man with broad-based experience in life. He could hardly believe that his son-in-law, who should have been the prime mover in the effort to dislodge his competitor from the yeshivah, would, instead, fight fiercely on behalf of R' Shmuel. R' Gad patiently explained that because of the conflict of interest, he, R' Gad, had to do the opposite of what inclination would have him do.

"Our *tzaddik* will destroy everything," R' Simchah complained to his wife, Treina Blark, who served as housemother for the yeshivah. "I'm trying to save our naive son-in-law from himself. I'm not going to give up the yeshivah that I created with my two hands."

R' Simchah called R' Bilad to his office the next day and spoke bluntly to him. "You're too successful," he told him frankly. "I think you're a great treasure for the yeshivah world, but you're taking over the institution that I created through great efforts. It's not right that ten teachers should feel threatened because of you, and that students should spend the day comparing who is closer to R' Bilad."

"And what do you suggest?"

"Here you are like Adam in *Gan Eden*. Everything's been prepared for you; angels roast your meat and pour your wine," R' Simchah said in friendly tones. "Go and start a yeshivah for yourself. Make your mark in the yeshivah world. Fulfill the verse, 'Let your hands work so that you shall eat.'"

R' Bilad was offended and shocked. He had never heard of a person being fired for being too successful. "Have you discussed this with any *gedolim*?" he asked.

R' Simchah looked at him dismissively. "In our yeshivah, my son-in-law is the *gadol*!"

One month later R' Bilad left the yeshivah. Perhaps R' Simchah was right, and he should open his own yeshivah. On the other hand, he did not know how to go about it, nor was he equipped to do so.

For two years he sat in the *kollel*, waiting for something to happen. He felt disgruntled and angry: here he was, perfectly capable of inspiring and teaching young men, turning them into real scholars, and yet unable to do so.

And then his luck turned. A good friend used his influence to get him a job in Yeshivas Meoros Elimelech. It was a comedown for him: from second year in an advanced yeshivah to the top *shiur* in a *yeshivah* high school, but it was better than nothing. He bit his lips and began to deal with the younger students. The main thing was the goal: to build scholars!

Eleven happy years passed in Meoros Elimelech. He had finally found his place.

Or so he thought.

Over the course of the years, R' Bilad slowly became burned out. His light seemed to dim; his students no longer ran after him with the same fervor and enthusiasm that they had during his first seven years in Meoros Elimelech. New lecturers came and drew the admiration once reserved for him. The most galling of all was the fact that in other yeshivos the position of older lecturers improved; as they aged, they were more and more respected, like old wine growing more valuable with time. As their beards grew more and more silvered, his peers, men the same age as he, were already revered as rabbinic leaders. It was only he, it seemed, who got the kind of looks cast upon one whose time has come and gone. The new lecturers, the "new guard," were men of high caliber, scholars, clear thinkers, with elegant explanations and fluent language. He tried his best to compete with them, but with little success. The *Rosh Yeshivah*, R' Michael Pankovaski, was loyal to him for a long while, standing by his side when someone tried to undermine him; a heroic effort that attested to the fact that R' Michael had indeed internalized the *mussar* books that he had learned.

Finally, though, R' Bilad came to the conclusion that the contest had been decided long before. R' Pankovaski could support him for another year, two years, but something whispered into Shmuel's ear that he was doing an injustice to the *Rosh Yeshivah*, taking endless advantage of his good heart, by preventing him from injecting new blood into the staff; a young, exciting lecturer, product of the next generation, who would understand the youngsters under his tutelage and speak their language. Of R' Bilad they undoubtedly said that he was an antique, speaking an archaic tongue that belonged to yesteryear.

R' Pankovaski fought like a lion on his behalf, begged him not to pay attention to what the others were whispering about him. But just when he had managed to persuade him that this was just some temporary wave that would undoubtedly pass away, an anonymous letter somehow turned up in R' Bilad's desk drawer. "The students would be very grateful," it said, "if you would take early retirement."

In his tense state he did not need anything more.

With a bitter taste in his mouth he quit his job. His heart wept. When he walked into his house he went to the mirror and examined what he saw. True, his beard was now gray, actually almost white. So what? He felt as young as he had twenty years earlier; his abilities were as great. He could prepare a lecture so exciting it would explode like fireworks, a *shiur* that would astonish the heads of the great yeshivos. But he did not want to astonish anyone, he simply wanted to contribute something to the Torah world in Eretz Yisrael.

But perhaps that Torah world did not need him. Perhaps his place was in an old-age home?

The thought broke his spirits. He spent his nights tossing on his bed. The Eskimos used to bring the aged, no-longer-productive members of the tribe to ice-covered tundra and leave them to their fate. Did the Torah world do the same to its old people? Did it, too, have its ice-covered tundra?

During those periods the old nightmares returned. Images from the past that he had thought buried forever resurfaced. Dudy Levin ran after him, night after night, asking in his delicate voice why he had forgotten about him on that cold rainy day, leaving him to die in his youth, before he had even begun to taste life. Behind Dudy's stabbing question lay something else, something that did not surface in the dream, something that R' Bilad could not avoid: the matter of the Levin family conversion, for which he was also partially responsible. Mrs. Hadassah Levin was undoubtedly an old woman now, if she had not passed alway already. But what of the twins, Moishy and Ahrele. They were 11 years old when they had left the country. Their Jewish future had been stolen from them; their lives looted by the despicable missionaries. Where were they today? What were they doing? Were they still alive? Did they have children? Three generations of Christians! Woe to him, to his soul! *HaKadosh Baruch Hu* demanded of Kayin the blood of Hevel's progeny: "The bloods of your brother" — written in the plural form, bloods, for it was the blood of the murdered man and those generations murdered, the generations that should have been born in the future. All of those Christian generations, all those generations that could have been fine Jews! The thoughts tortured him, kept him awake night after night.

The nightmares grew, bound up in the terrible disappointment he experienced from Yeshivas Masuos Avraham. While awaiting their reply he had not sat with hands folded. He had used every connection he had, put on pressure where he could, phoned dozens of men who might be able to influence the staff that administered the yeshivah; in the end, they had given him the knockout punch through the telephone, using the secretary. That was followed by the deep sleep that afternoon, when the dream had appeared more vividly than ever.

If this were to go on, he would go mad. What could he do?

※

Shoshana Bilad watched hopelessly as her successful husband wilted and drooped like a neglected houseplant. Plants and flowers were her specialty, as a healing therapist working for "Bach Flowers Remedies," where she investigated the homeopathic healing properties of vegetation. In the Bilad home they often referred to the names of the popular Bach remedies, remedies such as "Rescue," manufactured from the dew that fell on certain herbs; "Star of Bethlehem," that was used for first aid, particularly in cases of shock and trauma; "Mimulus," that helped in cases of fears from known causes; "Honeysuckle," used for tension; and "White Chestnut," helpful against negative thought patterns. She knew all about the thirty-eight essences of herbs that were discovered and named for Dr. Edward Bach.

Shoshana Bilad knew clearly that her husband's problem stemmed from his soul, but she had no way to help. "He's just fine, but in the yeshivos they think he's past his prime," she explained on the telephone to a friend who wanted the medication "Impatiens" for her son, who suffered from hyperactivity, and who had then asked, with some curiosity, why R' Bilad had looked so depressed at a recent wedding.

"How foolish," her friend objected. "Your husband is still young and energetic. A man of 50 doesn't belong to the past."

"I wish everyone thought as you do," Shoshana said in tones of despair. She thought of her husband, spending the last month at home. Soon he, too, would need natural medications to improve his spirits.

The next day it became clear that there were others who thought as her friend did, that a man of 50 did not belong to the past. Yeshivas Taharas HaTorah came looking for R' Bilad. When he came for a meeting with the *Rosh Yeshivah* it became clear, both to his joy and perturbation, that they wanted him to work as a *"meishiv"* (one who answers students' questions) in the yeshivah.

"And a lecturer I can't be anymore?" he asked, wounded.

The *Rosh Yeshivah* made a gesture with his hands, as if to say, "That's what's available."

Shmuel grabbed the opportunity; the alternative was to sit at home.

He was familiar with the *sugya* being learned in the yeshivah. The following day he came to the yeshivah, sat at one of the back benches with great deference, and began to shake back and forth behind the *shtender*. After five minutes he noticed others looking at him, heard whispers. "That's the great R' Bilad." "He's come to help us with questions." "What an honor." Immediately afterwards two young men came to ask him something, then two others, then still more.

On his way home R' Bilad felt his spirits soar. So he was not unnecessary in this world. Someone needed him. You did not have to be a lecturer in a yeshivah in order to give to the Torah world; someone like him could also contribute.

The next day a long line formed in front of R' Bilad's *shtender*. He grew excited and answered questions at length and in great detail. He would run to the bookshelves, pull out commentaries, and he brought to the yeshivah a fire of enthusiasm.

That's how it seemed to him, at least.

After a week one of the lecturers came to him and delicately explained that he was taking too long, missing the most important aspect of the *"meishiv's"* job, which was to give succinct answers. He had to leave time for everyone, not to get involved in a *"moyradig vort"* with two or three of the top students, leaving a long line of others waiting for replies.

"He doesn't understand a thing," R' Bilad mocked the lecturer to himself, and he continued with the same behavior.

After a month it became clear to him that the young lecturer was correct, and even had meant the advice for his, Shmuel's, own good. Now here he was again, sitting at home, marked "not fit for the job."

Thus R' Bilad moved from one place to the other, from one job to the next. He was the head of a *kollel* for *ba'alei teshuvah*, but did not enjoy it and left of his own accord. When he told his superiors of his decision to leave, he was astonished to see that they breathed a sigh of relief.

From there he went to a *yeshivah ketanah*, this time as *mashgiach*. After two months he was told that he did not understand the students; he was meant to be a *rosh yeshivah* or lecturer.

When he was invited to become a teacher in an eighth-grade class he was deeply affronted. "I, who could be a *rosh yeshivah*, should be a *cheder* rebbi?" he asked angrily.

But his wife, Shoshana, practical as always, would not let him be, and he went to the *cheder*.

He managed to hang on for a year and succeeded (he thought) but, shockingly enough, at the end of the year the principal hinted that perhaps he should rethink his suitability for the task.

"So what's left for me?" he asked one of his friends bitterly. "To be a substitute in a *cheder*? And to wait until they show me the exit door, even from a job like that?"

The friend, too, did not understand. A man of such a variety of talents such as Shmuel Bilad, what had happened to him? What could be the cause of his lack of success in every job that he filled? Behind his back he had already been labeled a "loser." He began to suffer from a very poor self-image.

It seemed that some hidden hand was constantly keeping success away from R' Bilad. It was the hand of Dudy Levin, of that he was certain, Dudy who knew no peace in the grave and had continued to persecute him until this very day.

How could he appease him?

*Time Bomb* / 53

# 5

Shoshana Bilad put a new strip of paper onto the narrow therapy cot. In ten minutes her first patient would arrive for half an hour of reflexology treatment. Shmuel hurried to leave the house, his brain still full of the complaints his wife had made during their argument. Shoshana, who, in addition to her work in Bach Flowers, reflexology, and healing, was also a trained psychologist, had told her husband that in her opinion he was caught in a cycle of self-destruction: inappropriate job, failed attempt, firing, new job (again, inappropriate), and on and on. "You've got to break the cycle, or else you will one day find yourself in a mental hospital."

"How do you break cycles?" Shmuel asked. "I certainly don't want to wind up in an institution where they strap you to the bed and come at you with needles as big as barrels."

"It's not funny," Shoshana said, pulling up a stool next to the cot. "You only make jokes about mental institutions when you're not in them. There's not much humor in the wards."

"So what do you suggest?" Shmuel asked, growing serious.

"Go abroad. Get a little rest, a breath of fresh air. See the world, you will feel refreshed." She shot the suggestions at him, almost like orders. "When you come back we'll think together about what job suits you, and then use all our available connections."

"You know that I've never in my life left Eretz Yisrael, and I have no plans to do so now," Shmuel objected.

"Let's decide not to decide now. We'll ask our Rav." Shoshana ended the conversation.

He went down the steps lost in thought. A *kollel* composed of senior citizens met in the neighborhood *beis midrash* where he had his morning learning *seder*. The youngest one there was 70 years old. Among them Shmuel felt like an elderly man; every day he came home a little more depressed.

In the building's lobby he glanced at the mailboxes. Lately he had become interested in the mail; partly out of boredom, partly out of some kind of fantasy that he would receive a letter from a yeshivah, asking him to come and be its head.

There was, indeed, an envelope in the box, from a foreign country, if one could go by the stamp. His name was written in large, awkward letters. His eyes tried to make out the postmark. "Caracas, Venezuela." He looked, unsuccessfully, for the name of the sender.

His heart missed a beat. In the past days he had been thinking more and more about the Levin family. Could there be some connection between these thoughts and this letter in his hand? He opened the missive slowly, careful not to lose a single printed letter.

His breath came quickly as he read its contents. It was written in Hebrew, in large, black letters:

"Hello Mr. Shmuel Bilad. Do you remember your neighbors in Katamon, Dudy Levin and his family? How do you feel after you helped an entire family convert to Christianity? Do you think that *HaKadosh Baruch Hu* will ignore it, after 120 years? And maybe even before that? If you think that it's not right, come and meet me in Caracas. (Here a date was written in.) I have something to discuss with you. I will wait for you in the entrance to the building that houses the offices of the B'nai Brith Anti-Defamation League, on Avenida Altameira. So do we have a deal? Wednesday, less than three weeks from now, at 10 o'clock in the morning."

He was stunned. Was there someone on the other side of the globe who still remembered that long-forgotten and painful affair? He had difficulty breathing, as if someone had kicked him hard in the ribs. Whoever had written that letter was cruel, merciless, probing the festering, open wound, even prescribing the cure: where he should travel, and when. Even the words "B'nai Brith" brought up old sins. The anonymous writer had touched upon Shmuel's sensitive and uneasy conscience, knowing that he, Shmuel, could not refuse.

Could not refuse? Hadn't he just now made his declaration, stating that he would never leave Israel to travel abroad?

But curiosity burned within him. He just had to meet whoever had written this letter, and finally discover the fate of those twins, Moishy and Ahrele Levin. Then, swiftly, came a second thought: Should he actually travel to far-off Venezuela only out of some childish curiosity and unjustified guilt feelings? Great rabbis had long ago explained to him that he was not guilty for what had happened to Dudy Levin. And what hadn't he done in order to atone? He had fasted many days, given large sums to charity, gone to the *Kosel* for forty days in a row, saying all of *Sefer Tehillim* there daily. He had learned entire *masechtos* to eradicate the blot on his soul. Now, suddenly, the genie was out of the bottle, and his feelings of guilt had returned in full force. Self-flagellation, it seemed, was a particularly Jewish trait that one could not escape.

He jammed the letter into a suit pocket. "Let me sleep on this for a night or two," he whispered to himself, walking into the sun-drenched courtyard.

In the *beis midrash* he found himself ceaselessly daydreaming in front of his open Gemara. The mysterious writer wanted to meet him in two weeks. He did not even own a passport. If he was going to go to Venezuela, he had better start planning, and quickly.

In the Interior Ministry they told him that he would receive his passport in a few days. His impatient haunting of the mailbox was finally justified: after three tense days he found two large envelopes inside. One was stamped with the words "Ministry of the Interior." The other bore a Venezuelan postmark.

The dusty alcove near the garbage cans in his building hosted him once again; he concealed himself inside the recess in order to be able to read the letter in privacy.

This letter, too, was brief, a few lines in English. Shmuel was fluent in five languages. His father had been born in Munich and spoke an elegant German, his mother had been born and raised in Brooklyn, moving to Israel as a single woman, and she had spoken to him in English. His grandmother, Bronia, spoke to him in Arabic. Yiddish and Hebrew were the necessities of life, without which he could not converse with a soul in his neighborhood.

He looked at the letter. Two lines in all, but chilling nevertheless. The words were made up of letters cut out from a newspaper and pasted together. "Mr. Bilad," said the headlines. The remainder was the stuff of nightmares. "Warning. If you come to Venezuela you will return to Israel in a coffin."

On the side of the letter were several clippings from newspapers published in Caracas. He could read the names of the newspapers — El Nacional and El Universal, but he did not understand the Spanish. Another cutting, though, from a local Caracas English-language newspaper, *The Daily Journal,* gave him an idea of what the articles were about. The subject of the reports was a series of assassinations of figures from the world of organized crime that had taken place not long before. The photographs were graphic and bloody. On the bottom of the page more letters had been pasted: "This will be your end if you come here."

R' Bilad mulled the probable reaction of his son Yanky, a young and adventurous lad. Yanky would doubtless see this as a wonderful challenge. The first letter, with its dire threats regarding his entry in the next world, would not have impressed him, but warnings of coffins would stir his imagination and sharpen his senses. For Yanky, threats always had the opposite effect; he had been like that since childhood. But R' Bilad was no young firebrand, he was a responsible and mature individual.

At dinner with Shoshana that night, he startled her. "I've decided that you are right."

"I'm always right," his wife laughed. "The question is, about what?"

"About my traveling abroad, to relax a little. I've changed my mind. I'm going."

"Mazal tov," Shoshana said happily. "You're doing something very wise. But you'll have to go yourself. I can't leave my patients. Go, clear your head a little, and come back. Where are you going to go?"

"I don't know. You have any ideas?"

Shoshana gave him a curious look. "What do you mean, you're going with no idea of where to go?"

Shmuel explained himself. "I've made the decision in principle, but I don't know where to go. I know the world like a little Japanese boy who has never stepped out of Tokyo. You're a woman of the world."

Shoshana glanced at the newspaper lying open on the table. Her eyes fell on an advertisement that called upon the public to join Gold Travel on an unforgettable trip to Czechoslovakia.

"Why don't you go to Prague?" she said, showing him the newspaper. "Some of my friends traveled there last year, and they said that you must see the city. It's like going back to the 17th century."

R' Bilad grinned. "That sounds good. Everyone always says we're living in the Middle Ages."

※※※

One week later Shmuel Bilad left with a large group of religious tourists. The staff of Gold Travel took care of all the problems of kosher food, and found them a good hotel and an experienced tour guide.

On the airplane he read through a pamphlet that the tour organizers had given him. He learned about the history of Prague, beginning with the second half of the ninth century. He got fundamental information on the various kings that had ruled, the Duke of Bohemia who had proclaimed the city his capital, Holy Roman Emperor Charles IV, the king of Bohemia, who ruled there from the year 1347-78. He skipped several centuries and jumped to the end, to the days of the "Prague Spring," the uprising led by Alexander Dubcek that was cruelly put down by the Russians, who invaded the city on the night of the 20th of August 1968. Then he moved on to contemporary times, when, after the "Velvet Revolution" that brought down communist rule in Czechoslovakia, the union of the Czechs and Slovakians came apart, in 1993, with Prague becoming the capital of the Czech Republic under the leadership of Vaclav Havel.

He was familiar with the Jewish history of Prague since the days of his youth. That is, he knew of the Maharal, R' Yehudah Loewe, who had lived there. Now, looking in the pamphlet, he learned that the community of Prague was the first *Kehillah* in Bohemia and one of the most venerable of all of Europe, and of immeasurable importance in the history of European Jewry. He learned about R' Avigdor Kara, *rav* of Prague six hundred years earlier, who wrote the elegy, "*Es Kol HaTila'ah*," after the majority of Prague's Jews were slaughtered in the riots of 1389. Prague's Jewish Golden Age was undoubtedly during the days of the Maharal, who was recognized even by the gentiles as a spiritual giant.

He waited impatiently to see the city itself. "One of the world's most beautiful cities," it was called by most people. Still, he could not forget that this trip to Prague was nothing more than camouflage, a cover-up for the real thing: his trip to Caracas, capital of Venezuela.

---

The Prague Castle (Prazsky Hrad), that stands up on the Hradcany Hills, looks down upon the city, and is a source of pride to the entire Czech Republic and one of the best-known tourist sites in the world. The enormous fortress is a collection of ancient fortifications, the oldest among them standing over 1100 years, from the time Prince Premsyl set up a fortified settlement in the ninth century. For many years the fortress served as the palace for the kings of Bohemia, and each of them added something — a fact that explains the jumble of styles within the different parts of the fortress. The site is one of Prague's most popular ones, and every day hordes of tourists come to visit, with the majority planning their trip at noon in order to see the ceremony of the changing of the guard that takes place precisely at that hour.

Shmuel and the members of his group had not planned their visit for noon, but their guide had taken it into account, wanting them to enjoy the colorful ceremony that was an example of Prussian etiquette that had long since vanished from the world.

The ceremony took place in the western courtyard of the fort. One minute before noon the large crowd that filled the area grew silent in anticipation. From far off came the sound of soldiers marching in perfect unison. The tourists watched the splendid scene for a full hour. Groups of guards exchanged their posts to the sound of trumpets. Their arms glinted in the rays of the sun. On the second floor of a nearby building an army band played marching songs, adding another dimension to the magical atmosphere. The departing guards marched in long lines, their legs in perfect rhythm. Their blue uniforms shone in the sunshine. The crowd applauded enthusiastically.

"A Czech trick to encourage tourism," was the general consensus of the group at the ceremony's conclusion. "In the modern world, there's no place for such pomp. But if that's what the tourists want, why not? The Czech tourist industry certainly loses nothing by it."

For many hours they wandered through the fortress, which resembled a miniature city in size and scope. They bypassed the churches and instead gathered at certain major points in the ancient fortress: the Imperial Stables, the ancient summer palace (Kralovsky Palace) and other sites. They took pictures of one another next to the tall, statuesque guards standing adjacent to their narrow sentry boxes. One mischievous boy from the group tickled a guard with a small feather, but did not manage to get even a blink from him. "They're copying the Queen's Guards in London," one tourist explained, as he stood before the sphinxlike guard. "But the British original is better."

The boy could hardly bear to leave the impressive figure, with his impressive blue uniform so reminiscent of another era. But the tour guide's threat to leave all the stragglers behind accomplished the task: the boy's father dragged him away. From there they took the subway to their hotel in the center of the city for lunch.

This was an organized tour for religious Jews, whose primary interest was to see the wonders of Jewish Prague. But their tour guide had chosen to change the route. "First you should see all of Prague; then, with that as background, you will better understand the history of the Jews in the city."

After lunch they went down Vaclev Boulevard, the city's main thoroughfare. A huge complex of buildings soared over one end of the long street. This was the Narodni Museum, a science museum that was of no particular interest to them, except for its unusual architecture and lovely winding staircases. From the museum they proceeded along the main street toward the city. They passed sword swallowers and metal workers who soldered iron on open flames. Shoeshine boys offered their services for a few stray koronen. Sidewalk peddlers offered crystal at incredibly low prices.

In the evening they crossed the Charles Bridge that spanned the Vltava River. From the bridge they could see the city's illuminated skyline, wonderful in its profusion of spires that seemed to reach toward the heavens. Unlike most of Europe's cities, Prague had not been destroyed during the Second World War. While the Nazis were destroying all trace of any culture not stemming from the Aryan race, they had not touched ancient Prague and thus the city was saved, looking much as it had three centuries earlier. Its beauty was indeed breathtaking. Its houses were built in a variety of styles and colors, an urban museum of a millennia of architecture — towers and castles, turrets and gates, bridges and stone-edged arches. The tourists' heads spun from the profusion of beauty that they saw in every corner. There were hardly two houses that were alike; each had its own unique style, the personal seal of whatever architect had planned it.

They walked in a group over the bridge, keeping their eyes carefully away from the sculptures and crosses that edged both sides.

"I've never seen anything like this," one of the tourists, who had toured Europe extensively, remarked. "This city is so full of crosses and sculptures, even more than the Vatican." Not quite accurate, but certainly close to the truth. It seemed that the city had more dead statues than living men; more crosses than stray cats.

No one had prepared them for the astonishing sight that was awaiting them as they continued.

A huge crucifix rose above them in the center of the bridge, on a tall pillar. Suddenly they saw Hebrew letters written in gold on a black background. "*Kadosh, kadosh, kadosh Hashem*...Holy, holy, holy is Hashem of the Hosts..." They almost shouted the words of the *pasuk*. There, also, they saw Hashem's Name, in its four letters, written in this almost impossible intersection of holiness and impurity.

Shmuel's blood surged to his temples. "What a desecration of holiness!" he shouted, his fists balled in wrath. "Who is responsible for this abomination?"

"Quiet. Silence!" the tour guide hissed. "Don't let anyone hear you. It's because of a fanatic such as you that this horror is standing here."

With the placid waters of the Vltava flowing behind him, the guide stood in the center of the teeth-gnashing, furious group and told them the tale of the statue.

"A Jewish visitor by the name of Eliash Bakofen, who was in Prague 150 years ago, was, like you, walking on the Charles Bridge. When he saw the crucifix he spit on it in disgust.

"To his misfortune at the very same moment a group of Jesuit priests were passing. They were furious at what they considered a desecration of their holy form. They grabbed the Jew and dragged him to the police. The force of law, naturally, was on the side of the powerful Church and not the weak Jew. The court not only sentenced the Jew to a harsh punishment, but they levied a fine on the entire Jewish community. The satanic punishment that the judge — who, by the way, was a Jew who had converted to Christianity — decreed was to decorate the crucifix with Jewish letters, and especially with the holy words that the Jew says every day during *Kedushah*. The wicked mind that conceived of such a thing was not satisfied with that alone; he also decreed the weight of the golden letters and the exact size they had to be.

"You can imagine," the guide continued, "the terrible humiliation that any Jew feels when he sees his holy words in a desecration that shrieks up to heaven, and the stinging shame of the Prague community, forced to give up its money in order to appease the anti-Semitic church.

"The story doesn't end here. During World War II the Nazis looted the letters, which were worth a fortune because they were pure gold. The greatest absurdity of all is that the city of Prague, out of a cold and heartless reckoning that it will bring in tourists, Jews and gentiles alike, returned the letters to their place, this time made of gilded bronze —"

"Who was that converted judge?" Shmuel broke in, the pain leaving him troubled and upset. "He should be pulled out of his grave, his bones should be ground up and sent to the four winds."

"Who knows?" the guide gave a bitter grin. "We've always been our own worst enemy. The apostate Jews have always made us the most trouble."

"Vile convert," Shmuel spat viciously at the sight, checking first to make certain that no Christian eye was watching.

Vile convert? And what of the Levin family that had converted to Christianity — and how much was he, Shmuel Bilad, responsible for that conversion?

*You've come to Prague to forget your troubles, but they're running after you. There's no place where you can find peace.*

At 1 a.m. they returned to the hotel. The guide informed them that the next morning after *davening* and breakfast they would tour the ancient Jewish quarter of Prague, the Josefov Quarter, with its vast treasures, the Altneushul, and the Meisel, Pinkus, and Spanish synagogues.

Shmuel lay sleepless in his bed. The image of the crucifix and the gilded letters seared his brain, took away any hope of rest. He felt anew the surge of anger. He wondered again and again how so many Jews could come and visit Prague, many of them men of position and influence, all of them passing that filthy abomination, feeling moved and upset and then forgetting. Why didn't any Jew utilize his connections in order to remove that terrible shame? Where were those community activists who seek mitzvahs? Why didn't such a provocation toward Heaven rob them of sleep? Today — as always — anything could be achieved with enough money. Why, then, did an activist or organization not pressure the Prague authorities or bribe the proper official to get rid of that abomination? It had been there for more than enough years.

"The *Shechinah* is in *galus*," the revelation suddenly came upon him. "There's no other explanation; the *Shechinah* is in *galus*. The holiest of words are in captivity."

*Time Bomb* / 63

Only with dawn's breaking did his fatigue finally overpower him, sending him into a short and restless sleep.

He never dreamed of what an adventure he was going to become entangled in the very next day.

# 6

Judge Doriel Talmi believed with all his heart that he deserved to sit on the highest bench in Israel's judicial world — the Supreme Court. He was a very smart man, brilliant in legal affairs. His religious friends, and he had them, used to pat him on the back and tell him mournfully, "What a waste; if you were observant you would have surely been one of the great *roshei yeshivah* of the generation."

Indeed he had all of the signs of a genius: the ability to master enormous amounts of legal and academic material, and the talent to write lengthy and brilliant works. He was on familiar terms with the ruling elite of Israel, but he wanted more; he wanted to be a ruler, to feel and use the power.

It was in the court system that he wanted to rule, a huge and complex world in itself — and from there, to go on and rule the academic and communication aspects of the judiciary. He wanted to leave his personal imprint on the entire judicial world. Dori Talmi had a step-by-step plan. The second step called for him to become the head of the Supreme Court, and from there to set in place his own ethical values, the ones that seemed so correct to him, on all aspects of Israeli life. Perhaps if he succeeded in holding on to the coveted position for many years, he would turn the State of Israel into a lighthouse of judicial ethics for the entire world.

His progressive beliefs saw no difference between one person and the next. Everyone was equal, regardless of religion, race, or gender. In these wild days, when Arabs were stabbing, attacking and murdering Jewish soldiers and civilians alike in almost every place in Israel, it was Professor Talmi who stood at the forefront of those who spoke so fervently of the evil that Israel was perpetrating against the Arab population in the country, and of the backwardness and lack of equality in Israeli society. He had the unfortunate habit of declaring his views on days when some unfortunate Jew had been stabbed to death by a young Arab or after a car bomb had gone off in a market, leaving innocent passersby maimed or dead. With the sound of mourning Jews and their guttural shouts of "Death to the Arabs" playing on a radio in the background, Dori Talmi would stand before his students and enunciate his thesis: that we are still a primitive nation under the sovereignty of unenlightened forces. Everyone has the same rights, including the Arabs, and if it happened that some murderers had sprouted among them, it was we, the Jews, who were responsible: our oppression and our occupation had caused this discontent and hopelessness. Second, the murderers were a minority among them, with the vast majority interested in living quiet and lawful lives. Third, are there not, then, Jewish murderers as well? Just look at Yigal Amir.

Dori Talmi did not hide his views; conversely, he trumpeted them whenever he found a way. To all who knew him it was obvious that he believed that the law and legal values took priority over all other standards. Dori's friends, and various journalists, had often asked him: Don't you think that this is a judicial dictatorship that you envision; won't your path bring the judiciary into boundaries where it doesn't belong; will the judiciary not take upon itself to decide matters of faith and belief, matters which only the Knesset is permitted to decide?

Dori Talmi would smile that pleasant, modest smile of his and answer in measured and intelligent tones: "In his work on government, Plato suggested that government power be vested in a group of wise men who have received education preparing them for it. I believe that the judges of the Supreme Court are that group of wise men who should have total and absolute sovereignty in the state."

The fact that the judges, unlike the men of Plato's dream, had never received the authority to govern, but only to judge, did not stop him from moving further in his ideas. He envisioned the Supreme Court as higher than the parliament that had been elected by the people, though the judges were selected by a small committee whose decisions and deliberations were more classified and secret than the discussions made by the Atomic Energy Commission.

But whoever thought he knew the real Dori Talmi was mistaken. Dori had two faces. One profile was enlightened and tolerant, known to the public by its perpetual, sympathetic, and modest smile. The other side, dark and threatening, was familiar only to his wife, Professor Ariella Talmi-Sturm, and a few close friends of the respected judge.

In his inner sanctum one could meet another, completely different, Dori Talmi. A hard man, conceited and impatient. A man who, facing one opposing word, could flare up like a torch and burst out into a flame of anger and fury — and sometimes violence.

*Winter 5761 (2000-2001). The intifada is at its height.*

Beginning on the first day of the Jewish New Year, the nation of Israel found itself in the midst of a guerrilla war thrust upon it by the Palestinians. A new name could be heard in the air: Tanzim — the Fatah Youth. Another murderous arm began to emerge from the multitentacled, bloodthirsty octopus, Yasser Arafat, who instructed his men to go out into the streets and begin a second intifada. The first intifada, twelve years earlier, was populist in character, and was generally carried out by stone-throwing youths. This second intifada was armed and much more dangerous. It began with throwing stones and Molotov cocktails and continued with shooting attacks throughout the land. Gilo, Jerusalem's southernmost neighborhood, became a target for snipers every evening, and occasionally during the day as well: they would take their positions on the roofs of houses in the adjoining Arab-Christian village of Beit Jalla, aiming at the neighborhood that had, until the beginning of the year, been one of the city's quietest, despite its dangerous proximity to the Arab-held city of Bethlehem.

The Israelis found themselves gritting their teeth in the face of the country's weak, inconsistent, and helpless policies, by a government that seemed anxious only to survive politically. Its only determined actions were to tie the hands of the Israeli army, hardly allowing the IDF soldiers to respond to the provocations of the Palestinian "policemen," whose bloodthirsty faces were now openly revealed. The members of the Palestinian National Council (an innocuous name for the murderous command of the Fatah organization), despite their negotiations with the Zionist enemy, had never planned, not for a moment, to give up on their goal of ruling the entire territory of the State of Israel, and to oversee a complete ethnic cleansing of the region; that is, the slaughter of every Jew in Israel. It was just the same treatment that Mohammed had given the Jewish tribe known as Quraish. He first signed a cease-fire agreement with them, a treaty that bore his own name, and then, when they were no longer wary of him, he slaughtered every one of them.

Chairman Arafat often mentioned his signed agreements, but at the same time at every opportunity he spoke of jihad, Moslem holy war. The government of Israel closed its ears and its eyes; its spokespeople explained again and again, with smiles fixed grimly to their faces, that it was all talk, just for internal consumption. When he spoke of jihad they insisted he meant a jihad of peace.

The truth was revealed at the beginning of the year 5761 (September-October 2000). From day to day the situation grew worse. One of the most horrendous moments came two days before the holiday of Sukkos, when two reserve IDF soldiers mistakenly passed a Palestinian police roadblock near Ramallah. They were forcibly pulled from their jeep, dragged to a police station in the city, with the policemen inviting the rabble and the mob to come and lynch the two unfortunates.

Every person in Israel heard and saw how the barbarians, lacking in the least bit of humanity, tortured two innocent men, pulling at their very flesh, desecrating their bodies while wildly shrieking jungle cries. The people demanded vengeance. Even top American journalists said at the time, "If you erase Ramallah from the face of the earth, the world will understand your pain."

But Israeli policy used a secret weapon: "toy soldiers." The reaction would have been funny, if not so very painful: a few helicopters threw some bombs on empty buildings in Ramallah, three hours after they had been evacuated by the residents, who had been warned.

The policy of restraint of the Israeli government, which had become synonymous with dreams and fantasies, threatened the sanity of every citizen. Wise men from around the world asked how an entire nation, that had accomplished so much, was willing to commit suicide in real time. Men asked each other, "Who is keeping this country from acting like any other country in the world would act in such a situation?" Among the people the sorrow grew and the bitterness blossomed. Men known for their patience in the past spoke harshly of the government and its policies, until there were actually questions asked about where the leadership's loyalties lay: Are you with us or are you our enemy?

---

Deputy Prime Minister Max Landau was busy that day. He jumped from one broadcaster to the next, called several press conferences. Every two hours or so he had something to say, or, rather, a threat to make, and journalists raced after him, believing each time that he would finally announce an operative move.

When he went outside following one press conference, the participants burst into laughter. "Forty-eight hours. Again, Mr. Potato Head has given them forty-eight hours."

"Mr. Potato Head" was, of course, Max Landau. A bespectacled, tall man whose white hair and wrinkled face testified to his advancing years: he was in his late 70's. Max had made aliyah to Israel forty years earlier from Belgium, and he had immediately gotten involved in the young state's political life, becoming a party functionary who slowly moved up in the ranks. His lack of military experience — he had never served in the army — was a major disadvantage; he did not know how to manage a battle. From the time that the troubles had erupted he had been constantly giving the Arabs forty-eight-hour ultimatums, forty-eight hours that never seemed to end. With every new wave of violence he announced, parrotlike, his forty-eight-hour deadline, coupled with nonsensical threats that had turned him into the laughingstock of the world.

Journalists love nicknames, and Max Landau had quickly been dubbed "Mr. Potato Head" because of his resemblance to the toy so beloved of American children. Anyone who looked at his beady eyes and frozen face had little reason to wonder who was responsible for the infuriating restraint that the political and diplomatic sector had placed upon the army, in the face of pogroms and lynchings. It was clear that only in the event of a major escalation on the part of the Arabs would there be a change in the degrading response of Israel, and even then only with endless limitations and restraints upon the soldiers, leaving them mere scarecrows in the battlefield.

Once, when the heads of the government had been terrified by the demographics of the *chareidi* world, which threatened to turn them from a minority into a majority, they had decided to bring a million Russians to Israel, knowing full well that one-third or perhaps even half of them were non-Jews. Bloating the population with Russian gentiles was their answer to the *chareidi* threat.

But beneath that motivation lay an even more serious reason, one more terrifying, for the import of huge numbers of gentiles into Israel and the creation of a non-Jewish character in the land, with shops selling pork, the breaking of all laws and mores of modesty, and the transformation of Shabbos into a normal business day.

Many hands had secretly mixed this dreadful pot, and when it became impossible to stop the immigration from Russia, when it was clear that not even 20 percent were Jewish, these covert forces aided and abetted the non-Jewish wave of immigrants to Israel.

It was Max Landau who was behind these policies. But, unlike the other leaders who sought merely to minimize *chareidi* power, Max had an additional reason for it.

※

Like all the other ancient buildings in Prague, the Altneushul had a pointed roof. But unlike the other slanted roofs, the events that had taken place beneath the once-red tiles, now blackened with time, of the Altneushul, had become swathed in mysterious tales told of the famed Golem, he who had been created — or, depending on whom you spoke to, not created — by the Maharal of Prague. Metal beams on the outer wall, the one facing the street, were used as makeshift steps that led to the mystical roof where legend had it the Maharal had buried the Golem after having taken away the holy Name, which had given it the breath of life, and turned it back into a mound of dirt.

The synagogue itself was as interesting as the roof. It was a somewhat dark building with very thick walls. In the entranceway stood a security officer to check all visitors. There was a small foyer which held a large bowl and a metal cup for *netilas yadayim*. "Here, in this synagogue, the incredible genius, the Maharal of Prague, prayed," the guide told them reverently. They saw the Maharal's seat on the eastern wall. A metal chain surrounded the area, keeping people away. The *bimah* was circled by intricately carved bars. Above it hung a red flag that King Charles IV had presented to the community in the year 5117 (1357), with Hashem's Name embroidered upon it.

They wandered through the synagogue, gazing at the high ceiling, the arches, breathing in the damp air that seemed to have been frozen for centuries, from the days of the Maharal, imbibing the unique atmosphere, trying to catch some echoes of the lost past, of the greatness that had characterized the Jews of Prague, greatness that was no more. The guide told them of a massacre of the city's Jews that had taken place in the synagogue a century before. For more than one hundred years the congregants had refused to clean the large bloodstains on the synagogue walls, stains that seemed to give off a scream of pain: "Avenge the spilled blood of Your servants..."

"Have you ever heard of a time machine?" One of the group surprised them with his question.

"What are you talking about?" Shmuel answered, his eyes scanning the letters engraved all over the walls. There was an entire history etched into these thick walls.

"I would give a fortune to get into a time machine and be here in this synagogue the way it was four hundred years ago," the man said wistfully. "To see the holy Maharal *davening* here, to live in history."

"To forget a little of our present troubles," the man's wife interrupted with a hearty laugh. "The mortgage, the overdraft in the bank — "

"We are now going to the Meisel Synagogue," the guide hurried them out. "We won't wait for anyone."

---

The Jews of Prague had lived with complete autonomy. They even had their own mayor, mayor of the ghetto as he was called. One of these mayors, perhaps the best known, was Mordechai Meisel. Meisel was Prague's richest citizen, and King Rudolf's finance minister. He used his wealth and position to do much for the Jews of his city. In approximately 1590 he helped renovate the ghetto. At the same time he built the large synagogue that bears his name. Its outer walls were pale, almost white. It had round windows decorated with the geometric figures that characterized Prague's synagogues, particularly the Spanish Synagogue, that boasted eastern motifs.

Today the Meisel Synagogue serves as a repository and home of the Jewish Museum. A portion of the exhibit, "The history of Jews in Bohemia and Moravia," is on display there.

Behind thick glass windows one can see Judaica treasures that span the 900-year history of the Jews in those lands: cantorial clothing, equipment for circumcisions, gravediggers' instruments, knives for ritual slaughter, Seder plates and Kiddush cups, menorahs, porcelain cups for *mayim acharonim* decorated with delicate miniature drawings. There was an embroidered hat for a cantor, a shoe used for the *"Chalitzah"* ceremony, and a "wimple," a piece of cloth first used at a *bris* that the German Jews would then convert to a belt to tie around a Torah scroll. An embroidered *chuppah* and marriage contracts were also on display. Here was the daily life of the Jewish community, their Sabbaths and their holidays, their family life with its birth, *bris*, bar mitzvah, marriage, and divorce customs in all its aspects.

The display was unusually beautiful, and the guide told them that all that they saw here was nothing compared to what was found in the huge storehouses in the Meisel Synagogue's lower floors. The Nazis, who captured Prague, had planned on changing the Jewish ghetto there into a massive museum of the lost race. They brought to Prague Jewish possessions looted from all over Europe, put them into giant warehouses, and began to catalog them, but then the war overtook them. All the Judaica, worth billions of dollars, could still be found in Prague.

"Are you serious? Billions of dollars are lying beneath our feet?" one of the group asked in wonder.

The guide backed off a little. "Maybe not billions, but certainly many millions are under us. And, I have to say, the security is very lax. There is an alarm system that with a little know-how is easily circumvented; someone could empty the storehouses without much effort. He would just have to prepare a large truck near the ghetto gate — I might be exaggerating a bit, but that really is the unfortunate situation."

"It's begging to be stolen," a tourist declared.

The guide's last words aroused much interest among the tourists, and among members of another group standing nearby. Shmuel noticed two of them exchange glances. They looked like Arabs. But what interest could Arabs possibly have in Judaica?

A lot. If you were talking about money.

"Will they be taking advantage of the information they just heard?" Shmuel wondered. He decided to stick close to the pair. The two wandered to a quiet corner and conferred in low tones near an exhibition of a Jewish family's Shabbos table of 300 years ago. Shmuel stood nearby, displaying a sudden interest in the exhibit. Shmuel understood Arabic well, thanks to his grandmother Bronia, born in Old Jerusalem, who had learned the language from her Sefardi neighbors and who had insisted on speaking to her grandson in that language. The two were busy with their planning and paid no heed to the bearded Jew standing dangerously close.

There were a few words that he did not quite catch, but the main thrust of the conversation he understood well. They had decided to come back, at 2 o'clock in the morning.

# 7

**D**inner garnered praise from all. Mrs. Gold, of Gold Travel, stood next to vats filled to capacity with salads and huge aluminum pans brimming with chicken, meat, and a variety of side dishes. Her face was shining like the noontime sun. As the members of the group passed her on the way to their tables, each of them stopped to give her a compliment. She certainly knew how to prepare tasty food and relished the many kind words, which provided enough energy to sustain her to the next meal.

Shmuel, though, ate absentmindedly, hardly noticing what he was putting in his mouth. He was in a serious quandary. Should he try to prevent the planned burglary — or not? It seemed that it would be better to sit tight and do nothing. He had no proof, nothing tangible to show to the Prague police force other than his own testimony. At best the police would send him back to the hotel with a polite smile and thanks for his efforts, but no one would do a thing.

At the table were several men and women who had separated from the group in the afternoon and visited the square in the Old City, the heart of

Prague. After they had had eaten to their hearts' desire, they discussed their impressions of the excursion, loudly voicing their appreciation of everything they had seen: street musicians, trained dogs, horses with carriages decorated in the style of the Middle Ages. What they spoke of most of all, though, was the ancient seasonal clock, one of Prague's most famous attractions. "Every hour on the hour the clock chimes and then ten figures appear in two windows in the clock tower, nodding down at the onlookers. Finally a rooster crows and a bell rings the hour," Yekutiel Sharabi, a schoolteacher on a sabbatical, told the others excitedly. Enthusiastic and lively was the man know as Kuty, much beloved in the group, due to his good cheer and contagious enthusiasm, though he was quite unfamiliar with the religious world.

"The clock was created in 1410 by the expert clockmaker Mikolas Makdania, and was renovated after eighty years by another clockmaker, Hanosh," Kuty continued to rave. "He's the one that created the wonderful scene we saw today. Legend has it that the king of Bohemia gouged out the eyes of the clockmaker so that he would not be able to duplicate his work anywhere else. In revenge, Hanosh sneaked into the clock and broke it. It didn't work for a century, until it was finally repaired. Gilded plates on the clock show the times of sunrise and sunset, the astrological signs, the placement of the stars — "

"And the ten sons of Haman, while you're at it," Zerach Britman, chassid of the group, broke in, as he cut a piece of cake. "I suggest you rein in your enthusiasm. The clock also shows four vices, and in the past included the figure of a Jew lending out money at high interest, as a display of the vice of greed. And if you knew who those ten figures were nodding down at you, worse than the ten sons of Haman — "

"Who are they?" asked Kuty curiously.

"They are the holy men of Christianity — men who did no good at all to the Jewish nation," Zerach explained, his mouth full of cake.

"This city is chock full of idols, it's unbelievable," a third man interjected, pouring himself a drink.

"And what do you have to say about Prague, R' Bilad?" Kuty suddenly turned to him.

Shmuel carefully wiped his mouth. "Prague has helped me say the prayer '*Aleinu*' with more devotion, and for that I'm pleased."

"What do you mean?" a chorus of voices asked.

Shmuel smiled. "I've never before understood the words, 'To remove idolatry from the land and the idols will be completely destroyed', the way I understand them now."

"You're right," Zerach Britman agreed. "This is the first and last time I will be visiting Prague. It seems that we've come to a factory that manufactures crosses. The *tum'ah* this city radiates could almost explode an 'impurity meter.' If you took that meter, for example, to Yerushalayim, the needle would hardly move. In Bnei Brak it would stay at zero; in the Chazon Ish *Kollel* it would go into the negative numbers."

"What's an impurity meter?" Kuty, totally unfamiliar with Zerach Britman's style of speech, asked.

"A small watch manufactured in the Ruhak factory."

"Ruhak? What's that?"

"*Ruach HaKodesh*, my friend. *Ruach HaKodesh*."

✼

Zerach Britman sat in his room, preparing for bed. A light knock on the door interrupted a huge yawn.

"What's up, R' Bilad?" he asked his visitor courteously. "Have you come to share your adventures?"

"I've come to share some doubts."

Shmuel then told Zerach what had occurred that day in the museum.

Zerach glanced at his bed longingly. "To tell the truth I don't understand what you want from me. I'm a teacher in a *cheder*, not a hotel security guard."

"That's true," Shmuel agreed, "but you have your wits about you and sharp eyes and, in addition, you are the only one in the group, except for me, who's come without family. You and I can go there and watch to see what happens."

Zerach sighed. "I'm tired, and tomorrow, early morning, the group is traveling to the mikveh of the Ba'al Shem Tov near Pilsen. You want to make me into a detective for a night?"

Shmuel grew persuasive. "All the great luminaries of the chassidic world will be grateful to you if you prevent the theft of Jewish holy objects that have already been stolen once by the cursed Nazis, and that may now fall into the hands of our enemies, the Arabs."

Zerach sighed once again. "I was about to say *Krias Shema. Nu*, let's go."

On their way to the subway Shmuel told him that the Arabs had spoken about meeting at 2 a.m., but since everyone had warned him against traveling so late on the subway he was setting out two and a half hours early.

"Maybe we should go by tram," Zerach suggested.

Shmuel aggreed. They walked through unfamiliar streets, feeling strange and unsure of themselves. With his English and German, Shmuel could manage fairly well, but many Czech citizens spoke nothing but their native tongue. Much time elapsed until they found the correct tram line. Only a few people were waiting at the stop. Two men and a boy of about 8 sat on the sidewalk. The tram approached and stopped. As they were boarding a few more people jumped out from the darkness. Shmuel suddenly felt someone's hand in his pocket.

*They warned me about pickpockets in Prague,* he remembered, pushing the hand away with all his strength.

He turned around and saw one of the men who had been sitting on the sidewalk standing behind him now, staring at him ruefully. With one arm he held onto the small boy, who had obviously been used as a decoy. Shmuel and Zerach burst into loud cries as the gang of pickpockets melted away into the darkness.

"At least I saved my wallet," Shmuel said, patting his pocket. "What insolence! A nice, innocent-looking young man holding on to a little boy."

After their adventure on the tram they decided to try the subway instead; better to have to walk to a faraway station than fall into the hands of crooks!

Not long afterwards they realized they had gone from the fire into a very hot frying pan.

The subway was almost empty. Only four sinister-looking men, in their 40's, entered their subway car. Shmuel and Zerach did not take their eyes off them and waited with beating hearts to reach their destination.

*Time Bomb / 77*

The subway stopped at a station. There was a trickle of traffic into and out of the train, and on the public address system they could hear the announcement that had become the ultimate symbol of transport to the Prague tourists. Shmuel and Zerach whispered the words together with the polite mechanical voice: *"Ukonczeta vistup ah nastup, deberzhe sa zabirai."* (Please stop entering and exiting; the doors are closing.")

"I'll never forget those words," Shmuel laughed. Zerach nodded, not taking an eye off the foursome, who were standing in front of the subway doors on both sides of the car. There were two by each door, two on each side. There was no way to avoid them.

The doors closed. The train began moving through an underground tunnel. The tinny, pleasant voice spoke again. *"Parzhisti staniza, Pankara."* ("Next stop, Pankara Street.")

They continued until they reached the station near the Josefov Quarter. The thugs had despaired of them, it seemed, and had gotten off before them. Shmuel and Zerach left the train, following the sign to the *vistup*, the exit.

At 1 a.m. they were standing near the *"Beis HaTaharah,"* at present a museum of the Prague *chevrah kaddisha*, in the past used to prepare the dead for burial. At the entrance was a white sign with the words, *"Chevrah Kaddisha,"* and *"gomlei chassadim."*

They whispered to each other, trying to decide what to do if the Arabs would arrive, and where they should hide. The area was quiet. No sound emerged from the cemetery where the Maharal of Prague was buried. "I think we should go to the Meisel Synagogue and wait for them there," Zerach suggested.

"Don't you think maybe we should stay here?" Shmuel replied, feeling all his courage suddenly melt away. "They won't come this close."

"My friend, if we've gotten into this, let's get in up to our necks," Zerach hissed, though it seemed to Shmuel that he, too, had grown paler.

With hearts pounding, the two of them walked between the ancient buildings toward the Meisel Synagogue. The lovely building was enveloped in blackness and the courtyard was locked. In the darkness of night they could just make out its silhouette, looking like some kind of medieval castle.

They sneaked among the shadows, hugging the main gate. "We'll wait for them here," Shmuel said. Suddenly he felt Zerach's hand cover his mouth. "Quiet," Zerach hissed. "Don't ruin everything."

Shmuel felt somewhat offended. What kind of behavior was this? Zerach gestured toward a narrow window at the left side of the gate.

Shmuel looked in that direction and felt his heart racing.

From the darkness of the synagogue he could see a thin ray of light, the glow of a small flashlight. He listened intently and heard what sounded like a box being dragged along a floor. The noise seemed to grow closer. "They're already here," Zerach whispered. "Looks like they've managed to neutralize the alarm. If they hear us we're sunk."

Shmuel understood what had undoubtedly happened. The Arabs in the museum had noticed him, and when they realized that he understood what they were saying, they had tried to deceive him by giving him the wrong information. At 2 a.m. they planned to be far away, their loot stashed safely. They had not taken into account Shmuel arriving so early.

He thought quickly. "What do you think, Zerach? Should we wait for them here or go in and surprise them?"

Zerach shook his head emphatically. "Go in? Are you crazy? And if they're armed and decide to shoot?"

They waited in the courtyard. The sounds of moving boxes grew louder. The door opened. Zerach and Shmuel lay prone on the floor and then cautiously raised their heads.

Two shadows walked through the courtyard not far from them. They were holding large cartons in their hands.

Suddenly it became clear to Shmuel what he had to do. Before Zerach had a notion of what was going to occur, Shmuel leaped to his feet, his fingers forming the shape of a gun. "Police! Police! Hands up!" he shouted.

The two figures exploded into mad action, racing toward the street. One of them stopped for a moment, put down the heavy box, and slammed a fist into Shmuel's face. Shmuel fell to the ground with a thud, his nose bleeding. The thief once again picked up the carton, put it onto his shoulder, and ran after his friend. Zerach saw that a car was waiting for them, parked nearby, its engine running. He bolted after

*Time Bomb* / 79

them, but his physical inferiority was immediately evident. Though he ran faster than he would have believed possible, the two reached the car before him. Without thinking, Zerach jumped onto the automobile. A beefy hand came out of the window and struck a solid blow to his head. Zerach slumped down onto the sidewalk, and the car drove swiftly away.

---

The tiny telephone in Judge Doriel Talmi's pocket rang during the speech. Apologetically he looked at the display and identified the number.

"I'm so sorry," he said, his face scarlet. Some of the students were snickering; lecturers routinely ignored university rules that demanded that cellular phones be turned off during classes. Dori heard the whispers, stopped on his way out the door, and again apologized. "You know me already, and know that this doesn't usually happen. I always turn it off, or put it on 'vibrate.'" His face grew redder at that slip: University rules banned "vibrate" during lectures as well. He slipped out of the room.

In the lecture hall, after his exit, his students sang his praises. They were impressed by Professor Talmi's sensitivity. "Did you see how he blushed?" one young student said. They all knew that beneath Professor Talmi's shinning bald pate lay the sensitive soul of a noble and aristocratic poet.

That noble and aristocratic poet stood in a quiet corner of the hallway, a comfortable distance away from the classroom, and spoke intently on his cell phone to the journalist Boaz Avneri of Israel Television's Channel 2.

Boaz had brought him the news that caused him to shudder. "Have you heard that they are appointing Regional Judge Dan Katzir to be a Supreme Court justice?"

"No! A thousand times no!" His face paled. Dan Katzir was his, Dori's, chief competitor for the Supreme Court justice position that would become available after the resignation of aging justice Akiva Maimon.

80 / *Time Bomb*

Boaz chuckled nastily. "A thousand times, yes! I've checked the report. I'm relying on reliable sources in the justice system."

"Reliable sources" was journalistic jargon for routine leaks in the system. Judge Dori Talmi was quite familiar with those reliable sources; usually he was one of them.

"And the Chief Justice is ignoring the Emil affair?"

"What's that?" Avneri asked, surprised.

Dori swallowed a triumphant cry. "Dan Katzir was involved, twenty years ago, in a bribery case concerning a police officer named Emil, in order to get a file closed on Dan's wife, who'd been involved in bank fraud. But that just slipped out. Forget it: I haven't said a thing."

Boaz grabbed the bait like a carp that had been fasting for a year. "You've got to tell me more."

"Impossible." Talmi argued with him. "That file is classified."

But with Boaz's increasing pressure Talmi gave in, making an appointment to meet him in the upscale restaurant Atlantis that evening.

After they had enjoyed a lavish and expensive meal on the journalist's tab, Boaz knew that the outrageous cost of the dinner had been worth it. Dori had told him everything about the bribery offer. He had also given him detailed advice as to how to make the juicy story public knowledge.

The next day the Israeli street buzzed with nasty rumors that linked Dan Katzir's name with corruption and fraud charges. No one knew the source of the stories, but after a week of nonstop buzzing it was Boaz Avneri who came out with the scoop, revealing all the details together with incriminating documents and assorted testimonies.

Dan Katzir's journey to the Supreme Court came to a grinding halt. He found himself sudddenly working ceaselessly to clear his name, without any idea of how that old affair had been dredged up.

Dori Talmi laughed quietly in his home and carefully prepared the next sensation in the event that this was not enough. He had connections in many places and knew how to use every dark moment in the lives of his competitors to his own advantage. In his pursuit of the post of Supreme Court justice he did not flinch at using any means, foul as they might be, and was quick to make use of his ties with top people in the Israeli media.

*Time Bomb* / 81

He would get to where he wanted to be, even if he had to step on a thousand bodies in order to achieve his goal.

※

"What do we do now?"

Zerach Britman managed unsteadily to get back on his feet. He had fallen heavily upon the stones of the sidewalk and a nasty bruise was forming on his temple. Shmuel had gotten up and he ran toward him in an effort to assist. He stood near him, still holding a tissue to his own nose in order to stanch the flow of blood.

Unexpectedly, Zerach burst into laughter. "Take a look at the two heroes. I think the Prague police force will be happy for us to join its ranks. You with a nose that's turned into a tomato, me with a bump as big as a challah roll."

Shmuel did not crack a smile. He examined the tissue. "*Baruch Hashem*, the bleeding's stopped." He was both disappointed and furious. "How did they manage to neutralize the alarm?" he said, looking forlornly down the street where the thieves and their getaway car had disappeared.

"Leave that to someone else to figure out," Zerach said as he sat down on the gate. "You yourself heard the guide say that the security arrangements were worthless. Should we call the police?"

Shmuel glanced across the street. To their misfortune — or perhaps their good fortune — no one had seen the incident. The car had left without leaving a trace. What could they tell the police? Perhaps they would suspect them, Shmuel and Zerach, of the theft.

"Let's get out of here," he said to Zerach, who was rubbing his ribs, which were still aching from the force of his fall. "In the hotel we'll try to get the swelling down. And don't forget, you're traveling to the Besht's mikveh tomorrow in the mountains near Pilsen."

Zerach looked at him. "Before we rush off to the hotel," he said thoughtfully, "let's go through the courtyard. Maybe something's left here, some clue. At least we'll know we've done all we could."

Shmuel agreed, and they carefully retraced the route the two thieves had taken. The small stones gleamed like pearls in the glow of their flashlights. There was nothing in the street, and they turned to the courtyard of the synagogue.

Zerach was the first to notice it. "Look over there," he whispered excitedly. Shmuel turned to gaze at a dark object that was lying, as if abandoned, near the metal gate. In the darkness it was hard to make out what it was.

Shmuel stooped down and picked it up. It was a leather-bound book that emitted the musty smell characteristic of aged objects. "When I frightened them, they were standing right here," Shmuel said, replaying the night's adventures in his mind. "The book must have fallen out of the box. Let's take it to the hotel."

"And what about the police?" Zerach asked cautiously.

Shmuel's eyes gleamed like diamonds in the darkness. "Let's first see what it is. Then we'll find a way to return the book to its owner. As a matter of fact, I'm not so convinced that the management of the museum are the legal owners of the things in their possession. They just have them now, given to them by the Germans in the war or by whoever decided they should keep them. Don't forget that the Nazis stole the things from their rightful owners."

The pair returned to the hotel by cab at 2 a.m., for the exorbitant cost of 800 koronen. Their nocturnal adventure was at an end. Zerach hurried to Shmuel's room, where the two treated their various cuts and bruises. Then they turned their attention to the ancient book.

Zerach took a deep breath. "First of all it's a *sefer,* written in Hebrew letters. Second, I can recognize the language. Can you?"

Shmuel looked closely at the words. "It's Hebrew letters, but of an ancient kind, full of points and curlicues. The *alef* and the *mem* are drawn very sharply and some of the letters are attached. The language looks to me like some ancient Germanic Yiddish."

"You're right," Zerach agreed. "I recognize that Yiddish. You won't understand a word of it, even half a word. It's full of long-forgotten phrases, made up of dialects that characterized that era. To you, it could be Turkish."

"And not to you?"

Zerach grinned. "I have dozens of books in my home that I inherited from my grandfather. They are written in this same Yiddish. I read them like you read the newspaper."

"Let's see," Shmuel dared him.

Zerach did not hesitate for an instant. He read the title: "*Die Yudische Geschichte fun Kehilla Kedosha Prague — The Jewish Story of the Holy Kehillah of Prague,* by Avraham Abba Schriftgisse, community scribe, Prague."

He leafed through the ancient crumbling pages. "Listen, this sounds like a real historical find," he said in wonder. "Do you want me to read you the first chapter?"

"You're not tired?" Shmuel looked at Zerach's bloodshot eyes.

Zerach gulped down three cups of water. "All the fatigue is gone," he announced formally. "With a find like this, who can sleep?"

## 8

*Prague, 5598 (1838)*

The tops of the trees bent as if bowed in prayer, humbled before the shrieking wind that brought fierce waves to the usually tranquil waters of the Vltava River. Prague seemed to curl into itself like one bundling up into a heavy winter coat. Only a few carriages ventured to cross the Charles Bridge. Here and there a solitary figure walked over the bridge, holding his hat with curled fingers. Despite these precautions, the occasional hat went flying into the swirling waters of the river, quickly swallowed beneath the waves that hammered at the banks.

Two men walked on Narodni Trazhida Street, trying to be heard over the wailing of the wind, desperately clinging to their hats. Unlike the other figures in the storm, they could not simply hold their hats in their hands. These were Jews, mindful not to walk even one step bareheaded.

The two figures were well known within the Jewish ghetto, as well as in the Old Town where they were now walking. There were no two men so different as these in all of Prague; in all of Prague, too, there were no two men who complemented each other so well.

*Time Bomb* / 85

One was Eliezer Tischler, treasurer of the Jewish *Kehillah*. He was a handsome man with an impressive look, tall and slender, radiating an aura of power and strength. His florid face sported a long gray beard. His forehead was high and his eyes blue as the sea. He had cherry-red lips and a nose so refined it looked as if it had been created by the careful hand of an expert sculptor. Leizer Tischler was now in his 50's, and his life was proceeding smoothly and serenely. When he was younger, though, he had bravely set himself against the seductions and temptations of Prague's Christian establishment. The reputation of the fine young man had spread throughout the city, and many priests saw him as destined to join the clergy and make his way up the Church ranks. They saw him as the embodiment of human potential and were certain that he had been sent to this world to reach the greatest heights — the papacy, perhaps? Wealthy Christian men and titled nobility desired him as a son-in-law, husband to their beloved daughters.

But all were sent away, disappointed. Leizer Tischler was a proud young Jewish man. He loathed the Christian religion from the depths of his heart and was prepared to leap into the fire should they attempt to force him to change his beliefs.

Much water had flowed beneath the bridge since that time, more than the Vltava surging beneath the Charles Bridge. Leizer Tischler had married Yona Pessil, daughter of the wealthy goldsmith Naftali Schmidt. He was happy with his lot and never harbored a regretful thought on the assured place that he could have attained among either the nobility or the Church hierarchy, which he had relinquished because of his Jewish obstinacy. "This world passes; today here, tomorrow the tomb," he would tell his friends. "Seventy or eighty years allotted us pass like shadows. Then the body rots in the earth. The skeleton of the most beautiful man looks just like that of someone deemed ugly. But the soul is eternal. If a man has sinned during his lifetime — and how much more so if he has abandoned his heritage and married a non-Jew — he will not leave the flames of *Gehinnom* until he has been purified. Will he remember, in the depths of the netherworld, the temporary pleasure that this world has given him?"

Truth to tell, his friends did not understand what he was talking about, when he spoke of wealth and honor as things that he had lost. "What's he missing?" they would ask themselves. Tischler was one of the richest and most respected men in all of Prague, a man whose position was solid as a rock. In his capacity as treasurer of the *Kehillah* he was a financial power, which he used as a lever to influence the life of the Jewish community of Prague. It was an open secret that Leizer Tischler had his eye on the position of community head.

Leizer's sweet dream, though, would never came to fruition — as any schoolchild in the ghetto could tell you — because to be head of the community, and particularly a difficult community such as Prague, one needed a "head."

Leizer Tischler was perfect in outer appearance, but less so in intelligence. He was not a great wise man, nor was he a small fool. Firmness, diligence, faithfulness, and sacrifice were the most noticeable characteristics in his personality, but shrewdness and quick wit were never his strong points.

The absolute opposite, though, was Getzel Fernbach. Fernbach, the rich banker, was decidedly different from his closest friend. First of all in appearance: Getzel was short and paunchy, with thick legs. Prague wits called him the earth crawler. Getzel's face, too, was not one of Prague's more attractive sights. He had a thick, rounded nose and a pimply red face. He looked out at the world through two beady eyes and he had the thin gray beard of a goat.

"Don't look at the container, but rather at what it contains," Prague citizens would quote the famous *Chazal* when they discussed the affairs of Getzel Fernbach. Those beady eyes were the wisest and shrewdest in all of Prague. Whatever his Creator had deprived him of physically had been paid back — and more — in his mental acuity. A wise man among wise men, shrewder than ten foxes, and quick thinking. A brain such as Getzel's one could not find in all the community. People in the know related that he knew the complete accounts of the Bank Fernbach by heart and had no need for ledgers. He was a mathematical genius, able to add and subtract long columns of numbers in seconds. Without ever having studied the subject, he could have bested any learned economist in a debate. He lived and breathed finance and spoke of it often. He was familiar with all aspects of the flow of money in Europe and always knew where to invest, when to withdraw money at the right time — moments before this or that bank went bankrupt or a particular country went to war, destabilizing its currency.

Surprisingly, Getzel was not just a dry financier to whom one could not speak of anything but numbers. He was a spellbinding conversationalist with wide general knowledge and wisdom on a host of subjects. Because of his sharpness many men came to take counsel with him and listen to his advice on whatever issue had come up. Thus Getzel Fernbach knew almost all the secrets of the Prague community: who was shortly going to be engaged, who was on the verge of divorce, who was sick, who had some well-concealed defect. Bank Fernbach had lying in its vaults not only money; it was a veritable collection house of knowledge. And none knew better than Getzel how to make use of it for his own interests. Because of his brilliant financial abilities and the sixth sense that kept him away from failing businesses, there was always a long line of men — gentiles and Jews alike — at the entrance to the Bank Fernbach, men who not only sought Getzel's monetary advice, but who had chosen, also, to deposit their monies with him, knowing that the head of the bank would increase their capital gains.

Getzel had never disappointed his investors, neither Jew nor gentile. Depositors received their money in return, principal and interest — and sometimes the interest was greater than the principal. Bank Fernbach had huge reserves of hundreds of thousands of reichsthaler and was considered one of the wealthiest banks in all of Bohemia.

An incredible friendship existed between Leizer Tischler and Getzel Fernbach, two opposites who complemented each other at every turn. In Prague they were called "David and Jonathan." They represented true friendship and amity without any ulterior motive and when someone wanted to bring an example of men bound in heart and soul, two people who could not exist without each other, they immediately mentioned the names of Getzel and Leizer.

Getzel and Leizer particularly complemented each other in the business world. Here they were truly a pot and its cover. Leizer, treasurer of the community, was responsible for the community funds, but because of his weak abilities he did not exactly know what to do with the money and with the responsibility allotted him. He needed the professional advice of his talented friend just as he needed air to breathe. Getzel provided detailed advice and showed him to whom he should lend money, who needed help before a holiday, who honestly needed assistance in marrying off a child, and who was just pretending. During quiet times when the community funds were not urgently needed for charitable purposes Leizer would invest the money in the Bank Fernbach, knowing that faithful Getzel would return it on the very day he would ask for it back.

Getzel occasionally had need of Leizer's funds for his private business dealings that were outside his bank responsibilities, and he knew that whenever he had a sudden need for a large and immediate infusion of cash, Leizer was the right address. Leizer Tischler had never lent Getzel a penny of community funds; he used, instead, his own personal inherited wealth that had ultimately tripled in value, thanks to Getzel's wise advice. He would lend Getzel huge amounts at low interest for unlimited amounts of time, using a *"heter iska"* written by the rabbi of the community. There was only one condition that Getzel had never broken: to return the money on the day it was requested; the same condition pertained to the community funds deposited in Bank Fernbach.

For these thirty years Leizer and Getzel had been the closest of friends, neither stirring without his comrade. Wherever one appeared, every Prague child knew that in another minute the other would turn up.

They were like Siamese twins — and only a surgeon's scalpel could separate them.

※

The two friends approached the ghetto gate.

The large gate was locked, as usual. The heavy metal doors had not proved adequate during the last pogrom, when the seething, inflamed Christian horde had burst into the ghetto and mercilessly massacred the Jews of Prague. Men, women, and children had been slaughtered, in homes and streets, dying all manner of cruel and brutal deaths, for having been born Jewish. Since then the Jews of the Prague ghetto went about like frightened rabbits, their ears carefully attuned to any unusual noises. The doors, strengthened measurably, were kept locked and anyone wishing to enter the ghetto underwent careful scrutiny.

They grabbed the heavy rusted door knocker and banged it firmly. The lone gatekeeper gazed at them from a thin peephole. "Oh, good news. The two notables have returned from the city."

The envy in his voice was ill concealed. Getzel and Leizer were the chosen ones, two of a group of nine Jews who were permitted to walk through all the quarters of Prague without fear of harm. It was a veritable treasure, this status. The others who shared it were the rabbi of the city, respected by dint of his position; three judges; and the Jewish doctor whose skill had saved many critically ill patients. Two women, also, shared this honor: the venerable Rebbetzin Tzeitel Cohen, who had forged good relationships with the nobility of Prague, and Rivka Flinker, a woman wreathed in mystery of whom eyewitnesses were willing to swear that she had been seen in three or four places at once. The truth was more prosaic: Rivka Flinker raced from place to place with extraordinary swiftness due to her fleet carriage and speedy pair of horses. No one knew exactly how to label Rivka, who was a behind-the-scenes activist, a public relations expert in an era when the term had not yet been coined. But it was clear to all that, thanks to her, a certain measure of tolerance for the Jews of the ghetto could be found among the Christian population of Prague.

The squeak of hinges heralded the opening of the gates. Lipa, the gatekeeper, welcomed them warmly, giving them a fawning and obsequious look. Leizer thrust a coin into his hand. Lipa's watchman's wages were never enough to cover the expenses of his large family, and since the murder of his wife, Perel, during the last pogrom, by the inflamed Christian mob, the task of raising his youngsters had grown that much more difficult.

The two friends now walked through the byways of the ghetto. The howling of the wind grew even greater and freezing air mercilessly whipped against their faces.

"Next week I'm traveling to Hamburg," Getzel shouted, his hands hanging onto his hat.

"Hamburg? What's the matter?" Leizer screamed back, trying to outshout the shrieking wind.

"I need a large loan," Getzel answered, circling around a big puddle that had drawn a group of youngsters, who were happily splashing in it, sending up a spray all around them. Getzel lovingly grabbed one of the children by his hand. "Little boy, where's your mother? Why are you wandering around in such cold?"

"I have no mother," the child replied impatiently, looking longingly at the muddy mess.

"What's your name?"

"Elyakim Schissel."

Smiling, Getzel tapped the small palm, reddened with cold. "We are equals! My name is also Elyakim; my full name is Elyakim Getzel."

"How interesting," the little one shouted over his shoulder, as he leaped with one bound over to the other side of the large puddle, missed and instead fell, with a happy scream, right into the mud. Brackish water flew to all sides, to the sound of the revelry of the youngster's friends, who immediately tried the same game. The ragged and torn clothing that they wore was soaking wet; mud covered their bare feet.

"Oh, orphans, Prague you are orphaned," Getzel sighed, continuing to walk through the rain with Leizer. "Since the last pogrom we've been enriched with 200 more orphans."

"Getzel, don't change the subject. I don't understand why you have to travel to Hamburg," Leizer said, still shocked. "If it's for a loan, don't you have me?"

Getzel was silent, and his head was cast down. Had Leizer caught a glimpse of his eyes he would not have missed the sly look that flashed through them for a millisecond.

"Leave it alone, Leizer, we're talking about a sum that you wouldn't be able to manage."

"How much do you need?" Leizer was very sensitive about such matters; any hint that he had financial limitations upset him.

Getzel ran a finger over his elegant blue velvet collar, cleaning off the mud that had landed on it from the puddle. "Leizer, I'm telling you, it's not for you. I need 50,000 reichsthaler."

"Fifty thousand?" Leizer shuddered and stared down anxiously at his mud-covered boots. He should live and be well, but what in the world had possessed Getzel to hang around those children with their runny noses and filthy clothes? Yona Pessil, his faithful wife, she should live long, wouldn't even let him come into the house with these dirty boots, lest he soil her shining and elegant new floors. Just two weeks ago they had been covered with a layer of wood imported especially from China.

"What are you planning to do, Getzel, to buy the Seasonal Clock or Kralovsky Palace?"

Getzel smiled. "Leizer, Leizer, you've never left Prague; the world you know is bounded by the Vltava River and the Altneushul. You're a narrow citizen of Prague. The Seasonal Clock is a lovely work but at this moment it doesn't interest me. The Kinsky Palace may be considered one of the most beautiful buildings in the city, but I wouldn't buy it — unless it floats. I've gone into the merchant marine business, import and export. I want to buy two commercial ships."

"Your appetite is like a bottomless pit," Leizer declared. "The bank is not enough for you, so you bought the glass factory, 'Crystal Zhizhkov.' Now that, too, is not sufficient, you need ships too? What for? 'He who increases his possessions increases his worries.' You don't have enough to worry about?"

The wind died down a little. They stood in their usual spot beneath the tree in Leizer Tischler's courtyard. Getzel lived two houses away. Each of them had beautiful, large homes, unequaled in the ghetto. But while Leizer's home was merely in keeping with his position, Getzel's house was breathtaking, filled with a vast assortment of luxurious items, most of which seemed singularly useless. Persian rugs in a variety of patterns were spread in every room; there were wooden cedar chests from Turkey, pipes from Egypt, ivory-handled flatware that he had brought back with him from one of his trips to India, and on and on.

Getzel looked quizzically at Leizer, as if trying to gauge what impact his words would have on him. "Leizer, you're unbelievably naive. The money in the bank doesn't belong to me. The crystal factory hasn't brought me even a small profit yet and I'm stuck now without cash flow. I've figured it out; I will only be able to make serious profit if I go into the import-export business. I've negotiated for the purchase of two ships, and as I told you, their price is 50,000 reichsthaler."

Leizer fell deep into thought. "Getzel," he finally said, "you know that I've never said no to you. On the other hand, you never asked for such a gigantic sum before. Give me a day or two to consider it."

"You don't have to think about it at all," Getzel objected. "I've already told you, I'm going to Hamburg in a few days. My two ships are already anchored in the Hamburg port, on the Elbe River, and I'm hoping to get the loan on easy terms in the local bank. Have a good day, Leizer; I'll see you tomorrow."

Getzel left his friend and walked quickly back to his house. He did not have to turn around to know that Leizer Tischler was standing, open mouthed, staring at his receding back. Getzel was no *tzaddik* and Leizer no animal, but the verse, "The *tzaddik* knows his animal," was appropriate here. Getzel knew his friend well, knew that his words would pierce through Leizer's brain all night, allowing him no rest. The treasurer of the Prague community was a man who thought much of himself, and he could not bear the thought that there might be doubts about the extent of his wealth, his talents, his personality, or anything that belonged to him. Getzel's refusal to ask him for a loan wounded his self-esteem and he would do anything he could to get the money in order to ensure that he, Leizer, loaned the money to Getzel, and not some bank in Hamburg.

Getzel's ships would ultimately sail the high seas, thanks to the money provided by the community treasurer.

# 9

Leizer pushed the courtyard door and walked into the small but beautiful garden that encircled his home. The Jews of Prague lived in frighteningly crowded conditions, with the ghetto houses leaning one upon the other, but Leizer's house was relatively spacious. With his wealth he bought two adjoining homes, knocked one down and on the site planted fragrant bushes and ornamental and fruit-bearing trees surrounded by ditches for irrigation. The second house, too, had been gutted to its foundations, and a new building, his pride and joy, was built on the site. The architect Hans Gruta, who planned several wondrous buildings in Prague, had been appointed to lead the project. Leizer had lived in the house for ten years and yet he still stopped in his tracks each time he entered, in order to contemplate its beauty and thank Hashem for granting him an abode that refreshed a man's spirit so well.

Yet now Leizer saw nothing. The wind blew at his back and he walked despondently toward the door. Getzel's words burned with their implicit humiliation. He had never before let his friend Getzel Fernbach go away empty-handed. That was what made the knowledge that Getzel had ignored him and planned on going directly to a bank in Hamburg even more painful.

Abish Kessler, his faithful valet, was standing by the door, quick and helpful as always. He swiftly removed the fur coat from his master, pulled off his boots and offered him slippers. With a face radiating dedication he led him to the warm foyer, seated him on an upholstered armchair facing the well-lit fireplace, and placed a footstool beside him. With rapid, light steps he then went to the kitchen and poured a hot cup of tea from a lovely ceramic jug, souvenir of Getzel's last trip to China. It was one of only three handcrafted by a Chinese artist. One stood upon the table of the emperor of China; the other two Getzel had bought, one for himself and one as a gift for Leizer.

The Tischler family called it "the Chinese jug" and used it only on special occasions. Today, indeed, was a special occasion in the house. An important visitor to the Prague community was dining with the Tischlers — the *dayan* and *rav*, R' Kasriel Kahane of Pressburg, who had come to inspect the situation in the ghetto after the terrible pogrom and to strengthen it in its time of need. Leizer was extending him royal hospitality throughout his visit.

The sight of the jug disturbed Leizer, reminding him of the conversation he had just had. Getzel was not relying on him. Why hadn't he even asked him, Leizer, for the loan? Perhaps he hadn't wanted to pressure him? That was just like Getzel, that faithful friend. Friendship, actually, was not an adequate word to describe even a portion of the deep love and amity which flourished between them.

Later, after the *dayan* had left the house, Leizer would sit and make his calculations. If he would be able to lay his hands on 50,000 reichsthaler, Getzel would get his loan.

***

The *dayan* left the house late that evening, after having eaten a sumptuous meal and going with Leizer to *Minchah* and *Ma'ariv*. The community welcomed their illustrious guest with great warmth, but in a low-key fashion. The Prague community was not what it had once been. In the days of the Maharal and R' Yechezkel Landau, the "Noda B'Yehudah," it had been a beacon of light to all of Europe, but then the winds of the Enlightenment had blown in and almost extinguished the flame. At this time it was Pressburg, under the unyielding leadership of the Chasam Sofer, that was one of the most fortified cities in its Jewish practice. Compared to Pressburg, Prague was almost on the border between Orthodoxy and Reform. At the beginning of this year, 5598 (1838), R' Shmuel Landau, son of the Noda B'Yehudah and *rav* of Prague, had died. He had served as *av beis din* in the city from the time of his father's death in 5553 (1793). The city was in a transitional era, between the leadership of R' Landau, who had loathed Reform, and the upcoming leadership of R' Shlomo Yehudah Leib Rappaport, who had already been snared by the Enlightenment and who would begin to serve as *av beis din* in Prague in 5600 (1840). At that time a strong core of observant Prague Jews remained in the ghetto, flanked by the synagogue, "Yeshivas Maharal of Prague," and traditional community organizations that persevered in keeping the flames glowing. But around them, in the alleyways far from the center, the winds of Reform were blowing.

The religious community of Prague numbered about two thousand, Jews who fought tooth and nail against the Enlightenment phenomenon on one side and the Christian world on the other. The Prague ghetto was an isolated island in a hostile sea threatening to engulf it, just waiting for the right moment. The last pogrom had greatly damaged the struggling community and terrified its members. "The only thing that will strengthen us now is unity," R' Todros Miller had beseeched his flock. "If there is controversy among us, it will be the end."

Leizer remembered the rabbi's plea as he escorted Dayan Kahane to his carriage. He was lost in thought, and did not hear the *rav's* question until it was repeated three times.

"What will you do with them?"

Leizer awoke from his reverie. "With whom?" he asked, trying to sound interested, so that the *dayan* would not realize he had woken him from a dream.

R' Kahane gave him a melancholy glance. "You have eighty orphans, girls and boys, who have reached maturity. You will have to marry them off soon. What will you do with them? Who will take care of them? Won't they ever reach the *chuppah?*"

Leizer almost jumped. The question had shot straight to the mark. "R' Kahane must know," he said, "that this is the problem that has not given me a moment's rest since the pogrom. I've already spoken with the venerable rabbi, R' Todros Miller, he should live and be well, and we decided that when the time comes, the community will marry off these orphans using the communal funds. As treasurer of the *Kehillah* I am responsible for the matter."

"That's why I brought it up to you," the *dayan* said, giving a deep and satisfied breath. "The tears of the orphans of Prague have turned into a mighty river, that reached all the way to Pressburg. We don't have strength for more troubles. At least you've reassured me on this one point."

The conversation that Leizer had with the *dayan* vanished from his memory the moment the horses rode away on the narrow street. He happily turned his thoughts back to the matter that he had been brooding over earlier. The rabbi had spoken of unity and peace, on avoiding controversy and giving in to another.

Unity! What a lofty idea. How did one achieve it? By giving to others in need. *Which means I should take my account book, do a detailed reckoning, and see if the balance allows me to give Getzel a larger loan than I've ever given him before. Fifty thousand reichsthaler!*

※※※

Getzel looked almost disappointed when Leizer knocked on his door the next morning, right after prayers, his face radiant with the joy of self-sacrifice.

"Getzel, I didn't sleep all night because of you, but the main thing is that the money is there," he almost danced on the threshold, as he fervently kissed the mezuzah. "I've got 50,000 for you. What do you say to that?"

Getzel's face grew scarlet. "Leizer, you didn't have to; you don't owe me anything. I told you yesterday I'm going to Hamburg in any case, to buy the ships."

"*Macht zich nisht narish*, Don't be a fool, Getzel. We know each other for a long time," Leizer said earnestly. "You need the money and I will lend it to you, naturally under our usual terms: you will return it to me when I ask for it."

Getzel hastily capitulated. He brought Leizer into his house and poured him a snifter of brandy with a magnificent bouquet. "Let's drink to your health, Leizer, and to our eternal friendship," he announced dramatically, downing it in one gulp. Leizer's happiness was boundless: Getzel had agreed to take the loan!

From his side Getzel constantly had to look at his fingernails in an effort to keep from bursting out laughing. He had cunningly managed to get Leizer to think that he, Getzel, was doing Leizer a favor by graciously agreeing to take the huge loan. Leizer's terms were considerably better than any Hamburg bank's. Leizer was a G-d-fearing Jew who would never dream of taking more than the 4 percent interest that the rabbi had worked out in the "*heter iska*"; the bank in Hamburg took a full 9 percent a year.

The two now walked to the synagogue for *Shacharis*, their hearts light. Leizer glowed like a new bridegroom, full of enthusiasm and joy, his hands waving merrily in the air. His head was often turned toward Getzel, who walked with a more somber countenance, occasionally gesturing in response to Leizer's words. His eyes seemed riveted to the ground, staring at the cobblestones as if searching for something lost.

Klonymous Bendele, the clerk, met them, and favored the two with a piercing look. "'The ox lows when it sees feed, but the lion roars when it sees meat.' You look pleased with yourself, Getzeleh," he hissed quietly in Getzel's ear, and immediately disappeared, departing with his long, loping stride.

Klonymous Bendele looked as if he had stepped out of a painting by an artist who specialized in caricatures. He was called "Bendele," shoelace, and he did, indeed, resemble a long string. He was tall and gangly, with an Adam's apple that protruded and seemed to jump up and down in his throat. His bulging eyes flitted from side to side, desperately trying not to miss a thing. Klonymous had the fine-tuned instincts of a detective and he put them to good use. He could sniff out unarticulated thoughts, guess words that had never been said.

Klonymous was married to a difficult woman. They had been childless for many years. She had grown embittered, and she heaped her sorrow upon his head. Klonymous fled from his home as often as he could, using every available opportunity to escape the lash of her tongue. In the community he was known as a chronic mischief-maker, a lover of intrigue, a man who sowed seeds of controversy and rifts even between fast friends. If three men were meeting, it was more than likely that Klonymous would be there, passing along the latest tidbit of juicy gossip. He enjoyed uncovering people's weaknesses; when he was fortunate enough to do so, he would fly to the person and with studied politeness, whisper into the ear of the latest victim news of the revelation. "Your beard is dirty." "I can see your right toe; there's a hole in your shoe." "It's not nice to peek into your neighbor's private property." "The way you led the prayer service today wasn't really good, but it's a lot better than last year. Do you think, like everyone else does, that you've lost your voice?"

The rabbi of the synagogue, R' Isaac Posen, did not call him Bendele, because of the prohibition against nicknames, but occasionally he would put his arm around his shoulder and sigh, "*Oy*, Klonymous, your name is appropriate: you reveal the *kalon*, the shame, of others. But maybe you should try to use the other half of your name — *nymous* — that means good manners!"

Klonymous's unbearable personality was balanced by his occasional spurts of kindness. At times, perhaps when he felt he had overstepped the limits, Klonymous would dedicate himself to the sick and suffering. There were those who contended that though Klonymous could not overcome his scandal-seeking personality, his deeds actually revealed his true inner self, his good heart. Others judged him less favorably: he was a reincarnation of Rivka Imeinu, with two factions struggling within him — Yaakov and Esav, with Yaakov occasionally atoning for his brother's sins. Be that as it may, the religious community of Prague sometimes suffered from Klonymous's schemes and sharp tongue, and other times benefited from his generous benevolence.

One thing, though, was not subject to debate: Klonymous was universally acknowledged as an important personage by dint of his job as clerk. He had a particularly lovely handwriting and men enjoyed receiving letters that he had written, regardless of their content, just because of the beauty of the letters and the style. He was fluent in his country's language and other tongues as well, and anyone who had to compose a letter to the government and its official institutions needed the services of Klonymous, who demanded a hefty sum in exchange. Klonymous possessed a literary flair and often wrote letters for others: rabbis writing to their students, students writing to their rabbis. He wrote on behalf of a loving son communicating with his parents, for a worried mother who had not seen her child for a year. With the passing of time Klonymous actually organized his craft into a book of letters for all occasions. He sold it at an exorbitant price, but many of the Jews simply copied out of it. A joke that went through the streets of Prague was about the man who wrote to his friend, sending him a poetic letter, replete with a flowery literary style, that he had copied word for word from the book, "*Letters for all Occasions,*" by Klonymous Bendele. The friend answered shortly: "I have received your letter. I was very moved by its contents, and you can read my reply in '*Letters for all Occasions,*' on the very page after yours."

Klonymous Bendele had long had his eye on the two close friends, Getzel and Leizer, and more than once had attempted to drive a wedge between them. But the two knew him well, and looked out for each other, never believing a word that Bendele said, even if he would bring all of heaven and earth as his witness.

Getzel's sly tactics had not escaped Bendele's sharp eye; in his cleverness he realized that Getzel molded Leizer like a potter formed his wares, but he had never been able to prove it. He would often ask himself how two such opposites clung together like iron to a magnet. Leizer was the most scrupulous man in the universe. He could find millions of reichsthaler or marks in his grasp, but if they did not belong to him, they did not belong to him and that was that: he would not touch even a single coin. The man was as straight as a surveyor's rod. That was the reason he had been appointed community treasurer. Getzel, on the other hand, was a snake, all sly schemes and plots. Getzel and integrity were two parallel paths that would never meet.

How to drive a wedge between two such different entities? Wait for the right moment.

And so he waited for the right moment.

Leizer Tischler's three oldest sons were his pride and joy. From their father they had inherited their good looks, from their mother their good nature. Yona Pessil Tischler resembled the bird, *yonah*, dove, for which she had been named: quiet and good, gentle and obedient, pure and innocent. She was no cleverer than her naive husband. The Tischler household was a bit of heaven on a stormy earth: no one raised a voice, and anger, tension, and hurting words never made an appearance within its portals. The good wife managed her home with cheerfulness and, usually, with a smile that testified to her inner contentment.

The fourth son was another story. Yoel Tischler seemed to have been sent to the Tischler family by mistake. He bore little resemblance to his three older brothers. He was hot tempered and quick to anger, suspicious of others and, strangest of all in this house, a clever and sly young man, reminding one more of Getzel Fernbach than of his own father.

The "David and Jonathan" friendship of the fathers was passed along to their families. Yona Tischler and Genendel Fernbach were friends almost as close as their husbands. The children, too, felt as if they belonged to one large family and in their youth frequently played together.

Yoel Tischler was the ugly duckling of this extended family. He had negative feelings about the friendship between his father and Getzel and unknowingly shared Klonymous Bendele's impression that Getzel was taking advantage of Leizer and doing as he pleased with him. Having been educated with values such as politeness and respect, Yoel dared not say a word that might cast doubts upon his father's talents and wisdom.

The three older brothers had already married and made their homes close by. Yoel, 17, lived at home with his parents, and he kept his eyes open, always.

Yoel Tischler, like Klonymous Bendele, waited for the right moment.

---

Getzel was short and stout. His wife, Genendel, was over a head taller than he was and unusually thin. When the two walked through the narrow ghetto streets, the contrast was very noticeable and soon led to the nickname "*Lulav* and *Esrog.*"

The Fernbachs had three children: a daughter and two sons. Baila was the eldest, followed by Avraham Abba and Zekil.

Getzel Fernbach's children were children of privilege. At a time when the Prague ghetto teemed with dozens of barefoot orphans who went to bed hungry, the Fernbachs drank coconut milk and ate dried fruits their father had brought back with him from the Far East. The children of the ghetto raced through muddy and infested puddles while Baila, Abbaleh, and Zekil Fernbach donned the attire of princes, their cheeks rosy and glowing with good health. Their mother, Genendel Fernbach, like Getzel, was not native to Prague, and the sufferings of her fellows did not keep her awake at night. She had been born and raised in Amsterdam, where she married Getzel. Getzel himself had been born in Poland to a "mixed marriage": his father was German and his mother Galician. From his father he inherited his keen financial ability, from his mother his outstanding cleverness. One year after Getzel and Genendel married, the couple came to Prague as part of Getzel's business travels. The place appealed to both of them and they successfully settled there. In the thirty years he had been there, Getzel had become one of the most prominent of its citizens. No one recalled any hazy memories or tales from the distant past.

Baila Fernbach, Getzel's only daughter, did not marry one of Leizer Tischler's sons, contrary to what all expected. She married Yuda Shmugler of Warsaw and soon afterwards moved with him to Poland and disappeared from the scene. Avraham Abba was a quiet boy, very smart, who loved to write during every spare moment and who served as his father's adviser. After his marriage he moved one block from Getzel. Only Zekil remained in his father's house. Like his father he, too, was clever and brilliant. He, too, was not enthralled by the friendship between Getzel and Leizer. Since the days when he had jumped up and down on the Tischlers' sofa with the other children many reischsthaler had flowed from the Bank Fernbach. Oddly enough, this youth felt that it was his father who was being taken advantage of by Leizer Tischler, giving him business advice gratis for which he could have charged a fortune. In Zekil's opinion Leizer saw Getzel as always owing him something, and in the depths of his love saw Getzel as another possession among his many treasures. Had it been possible, Zekil would have happily destroyed the rare friendship, but one could not even push a pin between the two men.

And so Zekil Fernbach, like Klonymous Bendele, like Yoel Tischler, awaited the right moment.

# 10

Getzel returned the large sum of money in five monthly installments beginning one month after taking the loan; within half a year it was completely repaid. Leizer was pleasantly surprised. In his innermost heart he had been plagued by doubts whether Getzel would be able to meet the payment obligations. Even in Leizer's rosiest dreams he had never imagined such swift repayment. When he asked Getzel how he had managed the feat, Getzel just gave a mysterious smile and patted him on the shoulder, as if to say, "You don't have to know everything."

Had Leizer known the truth he would have fainted from the shock. Getzel had done absolutely nothing with the money! He changed the bills in his bank so that Leizer would have no suspicions, and placed it all securely in a bundle in his personal vault. He bought the two ships from the proceeds of a loan that he had raised in a Hamburg bank, at a yearly interest rate of 9 percent.

There could be two explanations for his behavior. First, Getzel was afraid that the mercantile business would not prove profitable, and did not want to involve Leizer in the possibility of failure. The second, completely opposite in nature, was that Getzel had never intended to use the money, but rather wanted to increase his friend's faith in him in preparation for the next loan, which would be much, much larger.

Leizer was full of compliments to Getzel for the speedy repayment. Truth to tell, Leizer had lost some sleep over the fate of his money. How wonderful that his worries had proved to be groundless!

His gratitude had still another reason: on the very day that Getzel had repaid the last reichsthaler Leizer had had a visit from R' Todros Miller, rabbi of the Meisel Synagogue, in whose environs the core of Prague's religious Jewry had united.

R' Miller, a known and respected figure in Prague, had been appointed rabbi of the synagogue after the passing of R' Elazer Flekles, the author of the *Sefer Teshuvah M'Ahavah*.

R' Todros's visit left Leizer terribly shaken up.

"Leizer Tischler," the venerable rabbi began without ceremony, his eyes giving off sparks, "you will have to answer for this when your time comes, and I don't envy you the judgment that the Heavenly Court will give to you. You know, of course, that that Court cannot be tricked, and excuses are of no avail in Heaven. The shame that you will feel will burn you from within. That is *Gehinnom* I'm referring to, if I haven't made myself clear."

Leizer paled. In his own home, in his spacious and lovely salon, near the large window that overlooked the spectacular Prague landscape, in front of his own valet, Abish Kessler, stood this rabbi (he had refused to sit down) and threatened him with a hell of shame. In the Name of Hashem, what was he talking about?

For a moment he thought that Abish had curled his fingers into fists. Imagination, surely: Abish was absolutely faithful to him, body and soul, but he was also a G-d-fearing man who, even if he heard the rabbi threatening his master, would never take such a step.

An interesting man was this Abish Kessler. As tall as his master, with a slender and reedy build, yet physically unusually strong. Beneath his yarmulka was a bald head, with only wispy *peyos* at the sides. He had ocean-blue eyes, a long and hooked nose, and two deep wrinkles that gave him the look of a perpetual smile. His short, skimpy beard did not cover his determined chin. Abish was Leizer Tischler's right hand. He was a man of about 50 who had despaired of married life after two failed attempts, and his master's home was his entire world. His appearance had occasionally deceived some of the thugs who had planned on attacking the wealthy Jew Tischler when he walked in the Christian quarter; it never occurred to them that his emaciated escort could throw a punch with fists of steel that would send them to their beds for weeks at a time.

"What's wrong?" The words came out of Leizer's mouth with a great effort.

R' Todros continued to stare at him with threatening eyes. "You don't know what I'm talking about?"

Leizer envisioned the events of the past few years. The great pogrom, perhaps?

"Is the *rav* speaking of something connected to the pogrom?"

"Absolutely. I'm speaking about the outcome of the pogrom. You promised me that you would give me all your help in marrying off the orphans, and you've done nothing. Eighty boys and girls must be married; the community must establish forty households. Next week two orphans are getting married. The *chasan* has no father or mother, the *kallah* has only a father."

Leizer calmed down. If so, the threat of *Gehinnom* had dissipated. "The rabbi need not worry," he promised ceremoniously. "I made a promise and I will honor it, with G-d's help. The first ten couples will be married with my money; all expenses are on me. For the next thirty couples I will co-sign on a loan that the community will borrow from the bank."

The clouds miraculously disappeared from the radiant face of R' Todros. His eyes cleared and shone once again. He sat down carefully upon a chair. "Is that what you say, Reb Leizer?" he said exultantly. "If so, praised are you and praised is your lot. To marry off a *kallah* is a great mitzvah, a great mitzvah."

R' Todros did not leave the house until he had drunk to the health of Reb Leizer and blessed him with great things. Even Abish Kessler got warm blessings from the aged rabbi before he left the house.

One week later, in the middle of a normal weekday, the Prague ghetto wore its holiday best. This was the first wedding since the terrible tragedy that had overtaken the community during the last pogrom and the entire congregation was moved and excited. The food for the event had been prepared by neighbors, who delegated all the tasks. Two women took care of the fish, two others dealt with the meat, three volunteered to bake the challahs for the wedding meal. It was Leizer Tischler, of course, who provided the funds for all the foodstuffs, as well as the other wedding necessities, including new clothing for the bride and groom, a few pieces of furniture, jewelry for the bride, rent for the first two years, and money to live on for the first six months, until the groom could become self-supporting.

Before the *chuppah*, a poignant and tear-filled moment took place, when the *chasan* and *kallah* went on the traditional visit to "invite" their parents, killed in the pogrom, to the wedding. The groom, Yechiel Beitel, accompanied by his friends, a group of yeshivah students, most of whom were orphans like him, went to the new cemetery in the Zhizhkov quarter, some distance from the city. There, adjacent to the Mahler Gardens, the martyrs had been buried.

The *chasan*, a young man with a long and ascetic face and melancholy eyes, stood dressed in his wedding clothing near the tombs of his father and mother, his face hidden in his hands. The fur of his *shtreimel* blew softly in the chilly wind. "Father, Mother," he said brokenly, "today you should have been bringing me to the *chuppah*, but the axes of the Christian murderers ended your lives and you went up to an elevated place beneath the Holy Throne."

Yechiel was a top student in the Prague yeshivah, and his friends had vast respect for him. They stood in a circle around him and listened thirstily to his every word. Quiet sobbing could be heard all around.

"I've come to ask you to come down from *Gan Eden* and take part in my *chuppah*." Yechiel's voice trembled. "Dear Father, beloved Mother, come stand by my side when I say to your daughter-in-law — whom you have never met — the words '*Harei at mekudeshes li.*' Come, Father and Mother, to my wedding and pray for me before the Holy Throne that we should know better days, that the *goyim* should no longer murder us, and that I should build a home for all eternity."

*Time Bomb* / 107

There was not a dry eye among the group. But what was happening not far away, next to the gravesite of the bride's mother, almost threatened to stop the entire event.

The group accompanying the *kallah*, Mindel Fenig, was startled by the cries of the bride on her mother's grave, and joined her in bitter wails that came from a heart left torn and bleeding. The bride's face was buried in a *Tehillim* and her entire body trembled with uncontrollable weeping. "My dear mother," she sobbed, "I was a tiny piece of flesh when I came to the world. You raised me, you took care of me. You gave me your days and your nights. You taught me everything. You gave me understanding, feelings, an eye to see with. You showed me how to look at the beauty of a budding flower, to hear the chirping of a tiny bird in its nest, to pat a newborn calf on the grass in the courtyard. I loved you, Mother. I've loved you from the time I was an infant. In one moment the hammer fell upon you and ended your life. From all my love there was left nothing but a mound of earth. Why did they kill you? You never did anything bad to anyone in your whole life!"

Mindel's aunt, a sister of the murdered woman, stood by her side and rocked back and forth, her green headscarf swaying in rhythm. She murmured to herself, "Holy Rechel, you were a pure *tzaddekes*, ready to give your last piece of bread for an unknown, impoverished guest."

The bride's sobbing grew stronger. Without warning her eyes suddenly closed shut and she collapsed onto her mother's grave.

The women were stricken with panic; their frightened cries echoed through the silence of the cemetery. It was then that the aunt proved herself a wise woman. She had foreseen that the *kallah*, a sensitive girl, might be overcome by emotion, and had equipped herself for the possibility. She took out a small bag of smelling salts and a bottle of alcohol from a bundle. She rubbed the bride's temples with the alcohol for some minutes, while other women held the smelling salts beneath her nose and fanned her face with fresh air. After some tense minutes the bride opened her eyes.

The first *chuppah* was an extension of those emotional moments. All of Prague wept, sobbing that had not found an outlet for the past six months. R' Todros Miller, his voice trembling, recited the first two blessings. After the reading of the *kesubah* by Leizer Tischler, the *rav* of Klausen *Shul*, R' Isaac Posen, was honored with reading the seven blessings. The first ones were said without incident, but when he reached the words "let the barren woman rejoice," the tears choked him and it became difficult for him to continue. With great effort he controlled himself and stared with misty eyes at the two lanterns that gave off an orange glow beneath the *chuppah*. He continued and ended the blessing: "Who brings rejoicing to Zion through her children."

Before the next blessing he took a deep breath of fresh air and tried to speak calmly. "Gladden the beloved friends."

The meaning of the words proved stronger than R' Isaac's powers; the sobs erupted against his will. All the long-held sorrow, the agony and despair, came through in those tears. Someone handed him a cup of water to help calm him. R' Isaac pushed it away with his left hand and continued to recite the blessings while still crying uncontrollably. "Who created rejoicing and gladness... mirth, glad song, pleasure, delight... Let there soon be heard, Hashem our G-d, in the cities of Yehudah and the streets of Yerushalayim, the sound of joy and the sound of gladness..."

Then his voice dwindled, and died down. The atmosphere was strained and tense. An ocean of tears stood ready to burst its dam, looking only for the first tiny crack, and here it was —

The bride said but one word: "Mama!" The wails began. First it was her sisters. Then the defensive walls of the men were breached, as surging emotions and anguish demanded the outlet so long denied them.

Men and women, old and young, modest girls and pious boys; an entire community stood and poured out its tears, crying for its tragedy into handkerchiefs and open hands, into sleeves and coats. Only the legions of orphans standing at the side of the street, wearing their ragged, shabby holiday garb, did not take part in the wailing. Some of them had no tears left, having already cried themselves out; others barely knew how. Dry eyed they stared at the sobbing crowd waiting with rumbling stomachs for the sumptuous meal that would take place in Leizer Tischler's home, a meal whose aroma had already wafted into the air and quickened their appetites. Would that every day there would be a wedding in Prague, with a proper meal at the end instead of a dry piece of bread with a warm cup of murky water flavored with herbs, which adults stubbornly insisted on calling soup.

***

If the first part of the wedding was all despair and sobbing, the second part came to prove that the Jews of Prague had not forgotten that a wedding was actually a joyous occasion, and the Torah has a special commandment to gladden the groom and bride. With the end of the meal, the *klezmorim* took the conductor's baton into their hands. Drums and pipes, harps and trumpets, accompanied by the great cymbals, accomplished their job, and the large crowd joined in stormy dancing that banished melancholy and sadness completely. The faces of the *chasan* and *kallah* glowed with happiness as the men in the large courtyard and the women in the crowded living room surrounded them with circles of rhythmic dancers.

No one went home after *Birkas Hamazon*. Everyone sat down once again upon benches and waited impatiently to hear the witty poems of Itche the *Badchan*.

Itche Guatah was one of the most interesting men in the city. He was a unique and fascinating character and the Prague community could boast of only one like him. His father had been R' Tzion Guatah, one of the Sefardic *chachamim* of Jerusalem, who had gone on a fund-raising mission for the impoverished Jews of his city. When he came to Prague he was still single. One of the rabbis of the city, enraptured by his capabilities and vast Torah learning, suggested that he marry his daughter. Thus was born Itche Guatah, a product of east and west who inherited the traits and talents of both sides. He was equally fluent in Yiddish and Arabic, was thoroughly conversant with medicine and with astrology, knowing as he did all the works of the Rambam by heart. Though a learned scholar, he was a man with a ready smile who enjoyed making people laugh. His happiness was contagious and he could tell joke after joke with his quick wit.

His appearance at a wedding was impressive. He wore his father's traditional garb, a purple tarboosh on his head and a brown cloak on his body. To bring more laughter to the group he would tie to his large stomach a pillow that swelled him to outlandish proportions.

When Itche jumped onto the table, his face shining like the full moon, everyone immediately began to smile. The excitement climbed to fever pitch, and sudden outbursts of laughter accompanied the witty poems of the *badchan*. Itche joked and proved to the community that even within a sea of tragedies there was a droplet of laughter and comfort.

It was only late at night that the crowd dispersed to their homes, gladdened and joyful.

Prague had begun to smile.

⁂

After the first wedding came a second, then a third. The entire Prague ghetto was flooded with happiness. People longed to rejoice after all the sorrow. The dead had already died; the living wanted to live. The first wedding, it is true, looked more like a house of mourning than one of mirth, but the weddings that followed were as joyous as all weddings should be.

On one side of the market hired workers built a large wooden building that served as the ghetto's wedding hall. Leizer had been forced to renovate his home after that first wedding, and he had no desire to see it decimated once or twice a week. The building provided ample space, and Leizer covered all the expenses.

After ten weddings Leizer went to the Royal Bank and obtained a hefty loan which he signed as representative of the Jews of Prague. In addition, he put his name down as guarantor, in the event the community was unable to repay the loan.

Two days later, he and Getzel walked home together after the wedding of yet another pair of orphans. Leizer noticed a cloud on his friend's face.

"Getzel, has something happened?"

Getzel sighed but gave no reply. In the distance they could hear the singing of the community still celebrating the wedding. The windows of the building were open and the light of the torches cast the dancers' shadows upon the wooden walls. Getzel stared with interest at the sight, and burst into sudden laughter. "Just look at that shadow," he pointed to a long, thin black figure that leaped up and down in a strange motion. "He hasn't even learned to dance, that Klonymous."

"What do you care about Klonymous?" Leizer retorted. "I asked you what's wrong. Don't change the subject."

Getzel began to walk rapidly, as if trying to get away. His heavy round figure bounced upon short legs; he looked like a walking mushroom. Leizer, with his long legs, caught up in a few strides. "Getzel, don't run away from me. 'If a man has a worry in his heart, let him discuss it.' Tell me what's bothering you. Have you had a fight with someone? Is your Zekil causing problems? I've heard that he doesn't want to go to yeshivah. Is that true?"

At the mention of Zekil's name, Getzel gave a deep sigh. "Leizer, if you love me don't mention Zekil's name right now; don't pour salt on my wounds. If Zekil's desire to learn had gone into a cat, it would cry all night in Aramaic. But leave it alone. I'll manage with Zekil. The problem is another one: I'm drowning in a sea of debt. I made a bad mistake: when I needed liquid funds I took capital from various lenders. Now, if five of my wealthiest customers all withdraw funds at the same time, my bank will go under. Only a loan of 150,000 reichsthaler will save me from bankruptcy."

Leizer stopped short and stared, his eyes protruding. "Getzel, you're not kidding?"

Getzel glumly shook his head. "Leizer, do I look like someone making a joke?" His eyes grew moist.

Leizer stood, dumbfounded. Finally he spoke. "Getzel, that's more than all my assets put together. How can I give such a loan?"

Getzel put his hand upon Leizer's. "Did you hear me ask for a loan? Don't I know that you don't even have 100,000 reichsthaler? One hundred? Not even 70! Last time you barely managed to scrape together 50,000. I would ask for 150,000 reichsthaler from you?"

"Don't insult me!" Leizer protested vehemently. "I have 100,000, and even 130, but it's not all in liquid funds. Some of it is invested in land, some in homes. You know."

"I know everything," Getzel sighed again. "So it seems that next week I'm going to have to declare bankruptcy. Who needs the Bank Fernbach? It's just been a hole in the head for me, that bank. I'll be rid of all my creditors and *shalom al Yisrael*."

"You're talking like someone who has given up, Getzel," Leizer blazed at him. "Don't be so quick to despair, when you have a friend as faithful as Leizer. I don't know if I can give you everything, but a loan of 70,000, maybe 90,000 reichsthaler I can promise you. The money is already yours!"

A broad smile split Getzel's melancholy face. He gave Leizer a warm hug. Over Leizer's shoulders, Getzel's eyes sparkled with a devilish gleam.

# 11

**G**etzel descended to the cellar the next morning to bring a bottle of fine wine to celebrate his victory. Bank Fernbach faced bankruptcy no longer. To be more exact, the bank was, and had always been, in outstanding financial shape. Getzel needed 100,000 reichsthaler in order to expand his fleet with four more ships. His request for a loan had been made to increase his own profits. Nothing would incur Leizer's friendship and support like a sob story about the impending crash of Bank Fernbach. Leizer had fallen into the trap, as usual, and his sense of responsibility had led him to rescue his friend, even at the risk of losing his entire fortune. The cash would flow into Getzel's pocket and when his investment flourished he would return the money with thanks. Certainly a good reason to down a glass of Tokay wine vintage 1805.

Getzel had not entrusted the keys to the wine cellar to anyone, not even his faithful retainer, old Feitel. Feitel was half blind and could set fire to the basement and the house together if he forgot his candle in the wrong place.

The barrel of wine that he wanted was nowhere to be seen. Getzel angrily kicked away a piece of junk in his way and, his fury increasing, checked barrel after barrel.

From upstairs he could hear the heavy footsteps of Feitel coming down the cellar stairs. The door opened, letting the light of day sneak inside.

"You miserable old man!" Getzel roared angrily. "I've told you a thousand times not to bother me when I'm in the cellar!"

The old man apologized. "Your friend is waiting for you upstairs."

"Who is my friend?" Getzel approached his servant, his candle in hand, looking as if he were about to hit him. "When I drink I have no friends."

Feitel timidly retreated toward the door. "Leizer Tischler, your best friend, is waiting for you upstairs in your private room. He says it's urgent."

Getzel's face lit up. "Why didn't you say so? Leizer Tischler is another story entirely. He's probably brought the money, or the notes, or the bonds, or whatever it will be." His voice softened. "By the way, Feitel, did I tell you perhaps where I put the barrel of 1805 wine, you know, the wonderful Tokay wine that I bought?"

"Certainly. You told me that you hid the barrel in the first row, near the opening on the other side, so that you wouldn't have to look for it."

"That's right," Getzel said warmly. "How did I forget? *Nu*, and they say that you're the one who's senile. Look, you remember better than I do."

The treasure was immediately uncovered. Feitel helped Getzel open the barrel and held the small funnel in the neck of the elegant bottle while Getzel removed the wine from the barrel.

He breathed deeply. The wonderful bouquet attested to the superiority of the dark, praiseworthy liquor.

They went upstairs, the elderly retainer holding the candle while Getzel carefully transported the wine. If Feitel's shaky legs gave out, it would be the candle that was broken, not the precious bottle.

Getzel burst into his chamber, the bottle in one hand and two crystal glasses in the other. "Leizer, come and have a drink."

Leizer looked at him, hollow eyed. "Getzel, I've just come to tell you —"

"It can wait, it can wait," Getzel interrupted. "The only one we want to hear from now is the rabbi from Tokay. Leizer, you absolutely must try this wine. There's nothing like it."

Leizer looked harrassed. "Getzel, I have to tell you something. It's about the —"

Getzel wouldn't let his friend finish. "Leizer, why are you so talkative this morning? First we drink, then we talk. You know what it says: 'Wine goes in, secrets come out.'"

Leizer gave up. When Getzel decided something, a wild bull could not move him.

Getzel downed three cups, one after the other. "Good wine," he said, licking his lips with pleasure and capturing two drops that had dripped down onto his thick lips. "Every little bit counts."

Leizer made do with one cup. He was uncharacteristically reserved and restrained.

"And now that we've enjoyed our drinks," Getzel announced merrily, "let's hear what you want to tell me."

Leizer's face drooped. "Look, Getzel, I don't know how to tell you this. But I made a mistake. My reckoning was completely wrong."

Getzel, busily pouring out a fourth cup, hardly heard his friend's words. His hand held the bottle up and poured the liquid out. "Leizer, I'm telling you," he murmured cheerfully, "I haven't drunk wine like this in ages. I bought four barrels from the Hungarian wineseller, and I'm sorry I didn't buy more. They were expensive, but worth every penny."

Leizer waited politely for the enthusiasm to die down. "Did you understand me, Getzel? I made a mistake when I told you I could give you the loan. I can't!"

The cup making its way to Getzel's mouth hung in midair; Getzel's eyes opened wide. "What are you talking about, Herr Tischler?"

"Herr Tischler" was the designation reserved for moments of intense anger.

Leizer shrank into the large armchair. "Getzel, with all my good will, I can't give you the loan."

"You said that already." Getzel place the brimming cup carefully onto the desk. "What happened?"

Leizer tried to clarify his words. "Getzel, you remember the loan that the community took from the Royal Bank in order to marry off the orphans."

"What business is that of mine?" His voice was that of a stranger.

"It is your business. Because of it I can't give you the loan you're asking for."

"What is the connection? If the community has more money, why should you have less?"

Leizer glanced around at his friend's private room. If another person would have entered, Getzel would have flown into a rage, but Leizer had special privileges, among them the opportunity to frequent Getzel's inner sanctum. The room was elegantly and tastefully furnished, containing, in addition to the heavy cedarwood desk, a wide bed, for those times when Getzel's eyes began to close over long rows of figures. A small laquered chest held Getzel's most confidential papers; on the wall, paneled in rich dark wood, hung oil portraits of Getzel's father and mother. The paintings were lifelike and expressive, the work of a talented portrait painter, giving the impression to the viewer that live people were gazing out of the frames. Getzel closely resembled his father, but the deceased man in the portrait had eyes larger than the dark slits of the son. Leizer was suddenly terribly afraid of those dark slits, but he had to say the words:

"I signed as a guarantor for the community of Prague. My money is tied up to the bank in the event that the community cannot repay the loan."

Getzel stood up on his chunky legs. "Leizer, are you mad?" His scarlet face grew red as a ripe beet. "Because of some scribbles on a paper, you can't lend me the money?"

Leizer waited for the ground to swallow him up. Getzel seemed like a volcano on the brink of explosion. "Guaranteeing a loan is not a 'scribble,' as you call it. If the community can't return the money, the bank will turn to me. And if I don't pay up, I go to jail, or they sell everything I own."

Getzel walked over to Leizer and grabbed him by his dark suit. "What is this nonsense? It's never happened that the community couldn't repay debts it undertook. You're just looking for an excuse. Nice to know: after thirty years of friendship, I'm seeing your new face. I never saw you like this before."

Leizer tried to placate him. "Getzel, why are you so angry? You know I'm your faithful friend, but I'm also straight as the railroad tracks. Is it for nothing that in Prague they call me 'Leizer, the straight one'? The moment I signed on a loan for 90,000 reichsthaler, the money no longer belonged to me. That is, it's in my possession, but I can't touch it until the community has repaid the loan. On the day it does so, the money is yours."

Getzel's rosy cheeks turned purple; his voice was hoarse. "But I need it now! You're talking about another year or two. Leizer, you're plain crazy! You have the money and you won't use it? If you put the money into my bank you could be making nice interest." The narrow slits opened somewhat and pierced through Leizer. "If a person only walks straight, he winds up walking into a wall. Leizer, you know that even railroad tracks have to curve when the train has to go around a mountain —"

Leizer stood up. "Getzel, not with me!"

Getzel raced after him to the door. "Leizer, do you want me to speak with the head of the community, Shraga Shwartzer? He'll calm you down and assure you that the community can repay the loan, and then you can do what you want with your money."

Leizer then sprang more bad news on Getzel: "I forgot to tell you. Half an hour before I left my house Shraga's son came to me and told me, crying, that his father had a stroke last night. He's dead, Getzel. The funeral is today."

Getzel froze. *"Baruch dayan emes,"* he said, thunderstruck.

His shrewd brain immediately analyzed the new situation. "Leizer, you know that in the list of the seven city notables, I am first, after Shraga Shwartzer." (The seven city notables were the political and economic leaders of every European community, with limited law-making authority, who represented the people.) He took a deep breath. "Immediately after the *shivah* I will be appointed the head of the community of Prague."

"Mazal tov," Leizer pumped his hand. "I wish you all the best in your new position."

Getzel grabbed the bottle again and poured another cup of wine for Leizer. "Let's drink a *l'chayim.*" He gave Leizer a sly glance. "Leizer

Tischler, let me inform you that I have now consulted with the new head of the Prague community, Getzel Fernbach, and he assured me faithfully that the community will repay the debt to the bank, up to the very last reichsthaler." His voice rang with victory. "What do you say to that, Leizer, straightest of men?"

Leizer stared at him, shocked. "It seems to me that you're being a little hasty in dealing with the loss of our friend. Let me inform you, then, that in my conversation with the heir to the post of community leader, who has not yet been appointed, I gave my answer, and it was negative. As long as that debt is not repaid, my money sits idle, to guarantee the loan!"

The cup that was making its way towards Getzel's mouth once again stopped in midair. The banker banged the crystal glass on his desk in a fury. The glass shattered and a thin stream of purplish liquid dripped onto the fine wood. "Leizer, you're making me very angry today."

Leizer's lips trembled. This kind of quarrel went totally against his nature; he was a man who always liked peace.

Getzel gave one last try. "Tell me, Leizer, if I bring you the signature of our great rabbi, R' Todros Miller, allowing you to lend me the money, will you change your mind?"

Leizer thought and slowly nodded. "I don't believe that R' Todros will sign such a thing."

"And if he does?"

Leizer again thought deeply, and this time nodded his assent. "If the *rav* allows it, that's entirely different."

"*Gevaldig*!" Getzel laughed happily. "Give me a few days and everything will be fine."

The two parted in perfect amity. Only the drops of spilled wine and shards of shattered crystal attested to "David and Jonathan's" first quarrel.

~ ~ ~

That afternoon Prague escorted their deceased leader, R' Shraga Shwartzer, dead at 55, to his final resting place. The large crowd walked slowly behind the carriage that held the black-draped coffin. The religious citizens of Prague chafed beneath the custom that had been forced upon them by the rulers. They wanted to carry the coffin themselves, as was traditional, but they could not ignore the decree, since municipal policemen were stationed at every funeral to ensure that the directive was strictly adhered to.

In the front of the line, directly behind the wagon, walked the venerable rabbi, R' Todros Miller, his flowing beard white against his black fur coat. His legs trembled and he came close to falling several times, kept upright only by the firm hands of his escorts. By his side, not surprisingly, walked the heir to the post of community head, Getzel Fernbach. The dumpy banker whispered earnestly in the old rabbi's ear, making certain that Leizer Tischler, walking beside him, could not hear a word. Leizer, figuring out what was under discussion, made no particular effort to listen.

The funeral procession went out of the ghetto gate and passed through the city streets on its way to the new cemetery. After a few minutes Getzel left the venerable rabbi, who, too weak to continue, had stopped in order to return to the ghetto and his home. Getzel turned to Leizer with a victorious smile. "What did I tell you? The rabbi said that you can give me the money without any problem."

Leizer was surprised. "That's what the rabbi said? I've always learned that if you sign for a loan you're responsible for the money. I don't understand the rabbi."

Getzel's voice was colder than the body of the deceased community head. "That's what the rabbi said." The narrow glaring slits of his eyes were as cold as icicles.

The community treasurer fell deep into thought as he walked reflectively in the wake of the carriage. "You know what?" he turned to Getzel. "If the rabbi gives me the instructions in writing, I'll be glad to give you the loan. 90,000 reichsthaler."

Getzel looked pleased. "Wonderful!" he said clapping his hands in open glee. "I'll get you the confirmation in the rabbi's own writing in two or three days. What will you say then?"

Leizer felt his burden ease. The fear of losing Getzel's friendship had disturbed his tranquility. "The money is yours," he said with a smile.

"'And the nation, do what you will with them,'" Getzel finished the verse from *Megillas Esther* and broke out into happy laughter.

"Quiet, you two rogues," Klonymous Bendele's face suddenly appeared next to them. "Have you no shame? You're bringing the dead to his resting place and you don't stop laughing and chatting right next to the coffin. A shame! Getzel, you look very happy. The post of community head fell into your lap like an overripe fruit."

He spoke and disappeared, before Getzel's open palm could smack him.

"Did you hear that insolence!" Getzel fumed. "Just wait and see what I'll do to him when I'm appointed head of the community. I'll persecute him; I'll forbid the public from using his services. I'll bring in ten competitors."

"Leave him alone, Getzel," Leizer advised. "Bendele is an unfortunate creature. He has nothing in the world: a wife more bitter than death, no children. His only pleasure is to get people angry or make them argue. Let him have some joy too."

"Maybe you believe in that, to let a wicked man enjoy himself at your expense," Getzel sniffed, his eyes following the figure of Klonymous as it disappeared behind a nearby building. "I'm not so smart. I'll destroy him as one destroys a flea." He balled his fists. Leizer stared at him, shocked. This was a new face of Getzel, a face he had never seen before.

## Israel, 5761 (2000)

The intifada of 5761 (2000), known as the Al Aksa Intifada, destroyed some firmly held beliefs within Israeli society. For the first time in the nation's history, an entire country stood, its hands tied, facing gangs of barbaric murderers that diligently made use of various means of murder. What began with stone-throwing and Molotov cocktails soon escalated into sniper fire that killed soldiers and civilians alike.

The IDF did not respond. The soldiers were given clear instructions to maintain a low profile, both from their worried mothers and from their commanding officers, who themselves had been appointed by a left-wing government. The left-leaning officers, with their defeatist attitude, were quick to follow the political establishment, even if their orders endangered Jews — particularly "settlers."

Cars were routinely ambushed. A mortar was shot at a bulletproof bus bringing children to school; two adults were killed and three children from one family lost limbs. The IDF response that night was to bomb fourteen empty buildings in Gaza: the terrorist organizations had been given advance notice to evacuate.

From day to day the situation worsened. One of the ministers in the government, who was considered the father of the ideology of diplomacy, and thought by many to be responsible for all the bloodshed, spoke unashamedly of the necessity of giving the Palestinians a day without funerals; this, during a time when not a day passed without Jewish dead being buried. The left, which had lost much of its confidence during the first days of the intifada, recovered swiftly and soon decided who was responsible for the deteriorating security situation: not Arafat and his murderous gangs of terrorists, but the settlers. Even when a public bus in Hadera became a target, the left-wingers didn't discuss "evacuating" Hadera; it was "evacuate the settlements."

The Israeli public asked, How much more? Who is responsible for this endless failure, when an elected government fails to supply the minimum of security to its citizens, leaving the country's population to the "mercies" of merciless killers?

In private forums still another question was heard: What legitimacy does the government have to legislate for and to judge its citizens, when it has failed to provide the "freedom from fear" which is one of the four basic freedoms leaders must provide?

Max Landau had many interesting meetings during those days. He and his cronies were sent to fruitful conferences, full of the anticipation of creating a lasting peace. He would meet Arafat, who had ceased to be a "partner in peace" at 10:30, had become a partner again at 10:31, and by 10:33 had decided to leave the process. At 10:35, however, he was quite ready to cooperate completely.

Men began to wonder if unstable people were at the helm of government, people who needed immediate psychiatric attention. But Max Landau was satisfied. He seemed oblivious to the suffering of his people;

as long as they were shooting only at Gilo and the Karni-Netzarim Road in Gaza, and not at his own home, things were okay. When asked what he thought of the catastrophic sitution, he answered that the situation was fine. He was pleased to know that he was one of the elite of the State of Israel.

And the deteriorating situation gave him an excellent reason to be pleased.

## 12

*Prague, 5598 (1838)*

On the wide table in the *Kehillah* offices lay piles of yellowish-brown cards. A large inkwell filled with black ink rested in the middle of the table. Hershel, the young and energetic secretary of the community, sat next to Leizer, a metal-tipped quill in his hand. Occasionally he dipped it into the glass inkwell. The nib of the pen drew in a few drops, enough to write one or two lines across the card.

Leizer dictated from a long piece of paper that he held in his hand. "Hershel, write: The *chasan's* name is Yaakov ben R' Meir HaLevi and Gela, may Hashem avenge their blood. The bride is Rivkah Chanah bas R' Hillel Stern, may Hashem avenge his blood, and Tema Perel, may she live long. General wedding expenses, 760 reichsthaler. Paid on account, 400 reichsthaler. Did you get that, Hershel?"

"Yes." The pen raced over the card; the black letters filled the lines with details of the wedding expenses incurred in marrying off Prague's orphans in one column, and repayment of the debt in a second. Leizer breathed a sigh of relief: It looked like things would work out. It seemed that the community would be able to carry the expenses and repay the debt to the bank on that very day. Getzel was right, as usual, and the 90,000 reichsthaler could be taken from the safe and transferred to the account of his beloved friend.

Getzel did not bother knocking on the door before entering. His face glowed as he waved a piece of paper in his hand. "The rabbi signed! The rabbi signed!"

The paper was placed on the table for Leizer's perusal.

"To my friend, the esteemed R' Leizer Tischler, faithful treasurer of our community: In response to the request of my friend R' Getzel Fernbach, head of the Prague *Kehillah*, this is to inform you that I have studied the sides of the question and after deep and probing thought, it seems that there is no reason for you to withhold the loan from him, even though you have agreed to be a guarantor for our lofty community, because he faithfully promised me to return the loan within three months, and I know him as a trustworthy man. Therefore I have no fear, since the day the loan must be repaid to the Royal Bank is after that three-month period. The mitzvah of lovingkindness is a great one and in its merit Hashem will guard our community, which has known days of suffering and pain. From now on let there only be peace and tranquility in our borders. Signed, R' Todros Miller."

Leizer read the letter intently, checking every word. Nothing could have been clearer. Getzel had arrived at the right time, too; just when it was obvious that the coffers were sufficiently full for their needs.

"The money is yours." His eyes seemed to laugh as he recited the words of *Megillas Esther* in the traditional Purim melody.

"And the people to do with what you would like,'" Getzel finished the verse, breaking out into laughter. "Leizer, now I see who is a true friend. You've earned your World to Come in this hour! And in the future listen to me: Don't sign as guarantor for the community. You don't owe a thing to anyone."

Leizer Tischler was not blessed with great insight, but he was not a complete fool either. Before taking out a huge sum from his savings he wanted to be 100 percent certain he would not be left holding the bag. Leizer knew the rabbi for a very long time. R' Todros Miller was careful and straightlaced. Why was he suddenly extending himself for the benefit of Getzel, who had never been close to R' Miller, and who was not among those who frequented R' Miller's shul or the classes he gave there daily? Leizer himself never missed a day in shul and knew that when the time came for him to face the Heavenly Court, after 120 years, and he was asked, "Did you set aside time for Torah study?" he would be able to give a definite reply of "Yes." Getzel, though, hardly ever attended lectures, not on Shabbos, not during the week. Leizer decided to visit the rabbi and hear an unambivalent promise that the community would repay the loan on time. Or at least, to clarify how he could give an unequivocal promise that Getzel would repay the enormous loan to him within three months.

That night, when the ghetto streets were bathed in darkness, Leizer went to Rabbi Miller's home. He wanted to be certain that no one saw him. Getzel was a sly one, and would certainly figure out what he was going for. *Only I'm Leizer the fool,* he thought moodily, *the one who understands nothing, the one at whom everyone laughs behind my back.*

He was well aware of his lack of sharpness, and he remembered the words of Rashi: "One who isn't sly is called simple." Whenever they told jokes he would be the last to understand them, occasionally only after someone took the trouble of explaining the punch line. Usually he made peace with his shortcomings, just as he recognized his strengths.

And Leizer's primary strength was his integrity.

Before one withdrew 90,000 reichsthaler intended as a huge loan, even to a bosom friend such as Getzel, one had to examine every aspect to scrupulously ensure that it would not lead to troubles.

The rabbi's house was wreathed in darkness, as were most of the habitations in the ghetto. But it was certain that one who loved Torah study as much as Rabbi Todros Miller would not waste these night hours. Leizer bypassed the house and walked through the dark courtyard, treading carefully to avoid stepping on some rusted piece of iron or the tail of a drowsing cat.

Leizer's surmise proved to be correct: the dim light of a small oil lamp could be seen in the rabbi's study. The rabbi's sweet voice sang a quiet, lovely tune. On the wall Leizer could see a giant shadow moving slowly back and forth. Leizer's imagination supplied the details: the venerable rabbi was undoubtedly sitting and swaying in a chair whose upholstery had grown ragged with the years.

Leizer knocked lightly upon the window. The chanting ceased. Rabbi Todros was approaching his 90th year, but his senses were sharp. He pulled himself toward the window. "Who is there?"

"It's me, Leizer Tischler." The whisper was loud enough to be heard in the street. But he had no choice; the rabbi could not hear a quiet whisper through the closed window.

The window opened and the rabbi peered out.

"Leizer, why are you coming like this? Why don't you use the front door?"

"And awaken the *rebbetzin*?"

The rabbi nodded. "You're right. She hasn't been feeling very well, and has been having trouble getting to sleep these past few nights. If you awaken her, she'll be tossing and turning until dawn. So what do you want?"

From behind the gate came a shuffling sound. Leizer, startled, turned around, but in the blackness saw nothing suspicious. "I wanted to consult with the *rav* on a subject that's been disturbing me greatly."

"Which is?"

Leizer pulled himself closer to the window frame. If it was decreed that he must reveal his secrets, at least let them not echo near and far. "It's about the loan that the rabbi has authorized me to give to Getzel."

The old rabbi's brow wrinkled. "What are you talking about?"

"The authorization that the rabbi gave to Getzel, allowing me to lend him 90,000 reichsthaler even though I've signed as a guarantor for almost that same amount on behalf of the community. It was the *rav* who came to my house and pushed me when I didn't put enough effort into marrying off the orphans," he added, seeing the quizzical and puzzled look on the rabbi's face.

Leizer did not understand. Just a minute before he had felt a stab of joy seeing the ancient rabbi behaving like a young man and yet now, before his eyes, R' Miller's hands began to shake, as if at last they were finally in harmony with his advanced age. The light in the room was dim and wavery, but it was bright enough to show the rabbi's face growing red and white in turn.

"Doesn't the *rav* feel well?" Leizer asked, concerned. "I apologize that I came to disturb the *rav* at such a late hour. Perhaps the *rav* shouldn't have opened the window at night. The cold, the wind. But I wanted badly to get some advice from the *rav*, under what terms I should make the loan. We're talking about 90,000! I rely on Getzel not to make problems, but still, I'm uneasy —"

R' Todros could not open his mouth. His hands were shaking violently. He tried several times to frame a sentence, but each time his mouth seemed to be paralyzed.

Finally, he recovered a little of his composure. "I have to think about it. It's a serious topic. Let me think."

The window was slammed shut. The rabbi, known for his perfect manners, had not even bothered wishing him a good night.

If he had been concerned on his way there, the treasurer was even more disturbed — almost in a panic — on the return journey. The rabbi's reaction had been strange, to say the least. Leizer walked awkwardly through the darkness of the courtyard, tripping twice on large rocks, getting pricked by thornbushes, and almost falling headfirst onto the muddy ground.

When he had finally exited, with some difficulty, from the courtyard, he walked heavily through the streets, not noticing anything around him. Slowly, though, he became more aware of his surroundings. He turned his head from side to side. Something did not feel right here.

But what?

When his shadow had turned a corner, a head popped out from behind the gate. Protuberant eyes scanned the area. Everything was quiet; he could come out now.

The figure of Klonymous Bendele was revealed. His hand rubbed his chest, trying to calm the wild beating of his heart. It had been a good many years since he had sunk his teeth into such a fat and juicy piece.

True, it was not so nice to listen in on private nocturnal conversations. But what could he do? Was it his fault that his wife had chosen this particular night to be in such a dreadful mood? The argument between them had grown more inflamed and louder and her voice had woken the neighbors. He had fled the house and wandered the streets with a bitter heart. It had been heaven that had sent him here to overhear Leizer's whisperings.

The treasurer of the community did not understand what was going on under his very nose, but Klonymous Bendele understood; oh, he understood well. From the beginning, when rumors of the loan had come to his ears, Klonymous had figured out all that sly Getzel was planning, and he understood that Getzel had managed to fool Leizer, whom he was leading to ruin. The secret conversation between Leizer and the rabbi had only reinforced Klonymous's suspicion of Getzel.

Klonymous knew well what to do with the fatty bone that had fallen into his mouth this evening. Prague would be engulfed in flames as it had not been for many years.

༺❦༻

Leizer waited for the rabbi to call and give him an answer. But the next morning in shul R' Todros avoided his eyes, both before and after prayers. Leizer assumed that the respected rabbi had not yet managed to examine all the sides of the issue as thoroughly as neccessary if he were to give a wise response. Leizer did not dare turn to the rabbi again, and decided to wait until the next morning.

When Getzel had finished his prayers and was folding his *tallis,* he found a small piece of paper underneath his *tallis* bag:

"You will certainly be happy to know that late last night your 'good friend' Leizerke Tischler visited our rabbi, Todros Miller, and spoke to him through the window. They did not talk about the weather."

Getzel quickly folded the note and looked fearfully toward the rabbi. His face, usually florid, lost its ruddy tinge and turned pale. He found it difficult to breathe and sat heavily down on a stool to recover. "May your name be blotted out, Leizer Tischler," he muttered between clenched teeth. "I'll bring you to a black end yet."

*Who had written the note?* he wondered, his eyes racing back and forth like rats in a trap, examining the congregants. They fell upon the tall form of Klonymous Bendele, who was winding his *tefillin* straps, his lips muttering piously.

A mystery.

But it did not really matter. Whoever had written that note knew what was going on. Only someone well aware of the affair could have penned it.

He hoped that no one had noticed him, but from behind a bookshelf a pair of eyes kept him under strict scrutiny. Klonymous was now busily placing the *sefarim* back onto the shelves. An act of kindness! Help for Feivel, the aging caretaker. Occasionally Klonymous would help Feivel in replacing the heavy books into the closet. Like today, for instance, when it was worth his while to stand and tranquilly watch the miraculous reaction that his note evoked. Writers of broadsides and posters would give a fortune to see their arrows reach the target so neatly, right into the heart of the unfortunate victim. Truly there was no joy like the joy of covertly hitting one's friend.

By the blood draining from Getzel's face, Klonymous knew that his arrow had been tipped in deadly poison. He longed to stand and endlessly enjoy the suffering of the proud man of wealth but he suddenly grew afraid that Getzel's gaze would meet his own eyes. Getzel, man of razor-sharp wits, would understand in a millisecond. Getzel was not Leizer Tischler.

Klonymous turned his back toward the benches and grabbed a heavy volume of *Midrash Rabbah* from the shaking hands of the weary caretaker. "What's wrong with you?" he said in a friendly growl to Feivel. "You could fall together with the *sefer*, desecrate the Torah within it, and hurt yourself!"

"Thanks, Klonymous, you're a real *tzaddik*," Feivel said. "You're the only one of the people in the congregation who remembers to help an old *shamash*. A great *tzaddik*, a true *ba'al chesed*."

Klonymous was embarrassed by such compliments and muttered, "There's no reason for thanks, Reb Feivel; I'm just doing my duty."

Feivel did not agree. "If it's the duty of every member of the congregation, why are you the only one who comes to help me? No, it's a sign that you are a hidden *tzaddik*."

Klonymous felt a sudden choking blush. He hastily put the *sefarim* in their places and turned to leave the *beis midrash*. He wondered where the arrows that he had shot off this morning would land.

※

Leizer was preoccupied that day. Four times he had to rip up the pages that he worked on in the community office, because the rows of figures that he had set down were completely in error. Such a thing had never happened. Mathematics had always been his strong point. But today it seemed as if his head were detached from the rest of his body. His thoughts constantly strayed to the events of the previous night, and to the rabbi's strange reaction. What did it all mean? Unthinkable to believe that the holy rabbi, he should live long, the glory of the congregation, could have ganged up with Getzel against him.

Leizer reached the community offices from the opposite direction today. He studiously avoided passing Getzel's house. As long as he was not certain how the loan would be guaranteed he would not remove even a single reichsthaler from his safe, and he preferred not to speak with him at this juncture. What would he tell Getzel if he asked him about the loan? "I haven't been able to count out 90,000; it takes some time"?

Getzel, too, had carefully planned his moves on this day. At 9 o'clock in the morning he peeked out from the curtains toward the street. This was the time when Leizer should be walking to work, stopping for a moment by the courtyard and waiting for Getzel. The two would normally walk together, Getzel to the Bank Fernbach and Leizer to the *Kehillah* office not far away.

Leizer did not pass by at 9 o'clock.

Getzel waited, hidden behind the curtains, until 10 o'clock. No Leizer.

Getzel cursed under his breath, his mouth spewing forth profanities that would have embarrassed even the members of Prague's Christian underworld. Now he was certain that trouble was brewing. The writer of that note (*who was he?*) had based it on solid information. What else could explain the unusual phenomenon? It had been the first time in years that Leizer had failed to pass his, Getzel's, home. Leizer was obviously avoiding him, and it seemed that there was a good reason for him to do so.

※

That evening Leizer Tischler's patience ran out. He had to decide what to do. He could not go through another day like this one. To work without working, to eat without eating. He had been nervous and annoyed with his wife and children, not to mention that he had been compelled to detour around Getzel's home. He must put an end to this insane situation. He just had to find a way to get the funding to Getzel and rebuild their friendship.

This time he came to the rabbi's home in the early hours of the evening.

The aged *rebbetzin*, Sarah Blima Miller, met him at the door, her wrinkled face lighting up at the sight of her unexpected guest, the treasurer of the community.

"R' Leizer, what an honor. What brings you to our home?"

Her voice wafted out through the open door, making its way through the quiet air until it reached the sharp ears of Klonymous Bendele.

Klonymous had guessed that this evening, too, it would be worthwhile to stand near the rabbi's home, and it appeared he had not been mistaken. Half an hour after the rabbi's son, R' Yuspe Miller, entered the rabbi's home, Leizer Tischler had arrived.

From the *rebbetzin's* question Leizer understood that the rabbi had not broken his faith by discussing the matter with her. Clearly she knew nothing of what had happened the night before at the window.

"I have something very important to discuss with the *rav*," he said shortly.

The *rebbetzin* would not let him go so readily. "How is your wife, Yona Pessil?" she asked courteously.

"She's feeling well," he answered, nervously drumming his fingers.

132 / *Time Bomb*

Sarah Blima was tempted to put him in his place: a little respect for a *rebbetzin*, after all. However it was obvious from his demeanor that he was in a state of great tension. She turned and walked toward the rabbi's study.

After a moment she returned. "The *rav* is deeply immersed in a difficult *sugya* with his *chavrusah*. He wants to know if you can come back tomorrow."

If he had entertained any doubts about whether something had occurred, now everything was clear. The *rav* was certainly entitled to be involved in a difficult *sugya*, but Leizer had never heard of him refusing a visitor because of it. At the most, he could have asked him to wait for half an hour.

"It's a question of life and death for me," he said in a voice that was almost a sob.

Rebbetzin Sarah Blima was horrified. She had never seen Leizer Tischler in such a state. Once again she hurried to the rabbi's study on her swollen legs and was back with a swiftness more appropriate for someone half her age. "The *rav* said you should come in."

The *rav's* study looked like a miniature library. Bookshelves and more bookshelves, from the floor to the ceiling. Thick volumes bound in leather were jammed on all the shelves. Except for the library in the Strahov Monastery, *l'havdil,* there was no room in all of Prague that contained such a quantity of books. Those in the know claimed that in his youth R' Miller had been a wealthy man and he had chosen to relinquish ownership of a large concern and had used his money to buy *sefarim,* which he pored over most of his waking hours.

The *rav* was, indeed, sitting over a large *sefer* that looked like a Gemara. He was not alone; his *chavrusah* was sitting nearby. This was his oldest son, R' Yuspe, a dedicated activist in his middle years who had joined Leizer in the ambitious project of marrying off the eighty orphans.

Father and son rose respectfully when Leizer walked in and they warmly shook his hand. Leizer's brow furrowed in dissatisfaction: he had hoped to see the rabbi alone.

The *rav* offered him a simple wooden chair on the other side of the table. "R' Leizer, I see that you are uneasy."

"That's true; I'm all out of ideas," Leizer confessed, blushing. "I desperately need the *Rav's* advice."

R' Todros spoke calmly. "Let's hear what we're talking about. Tell me everything, from the beginning, one thing at a time. Don't leave out any detail."

Leizer glanced at R' Yuspe. R' Todros gave a faint smile. "You can trust him. My Yuspe can keep a secret. His lips are sealed."

Leizer began to recount the past events. He told everything: the previous loan, repaid before it came due, the request for another loan, his reason for refusing.

R' Todros's eyes remained shut during most of the recital. His son, R' Yuspe, did not take his piercing eyes off Leizer. Leizer, looking at the rabbi, grew silent, wondering if he had fallen asleep. "*Nu*, go on, I hear every word," the rabbi assured him.

When he had finished, the room was still. The *rav* was silent, lost in thought. Occasionally he would open his eyes and favor Leizer with a clear and intense stare.

The silence lasted for quite some time. Only the ticking of a wall clock in the hallway disturbed the hush.

"And so," R' Todros finally began, breaking the stillness, "I assumed you would be coming here this evening. That's why I called Yuspe. He has something to tell you."

Leizer, surprised, stared at the father and the son.

R' Yuspe wasted no time. "Before I speak I have one condition. I must ask you for a clear and unequivocal promise not to tell another soul what you will hear from me."

"I promise," Leizer said, his voice trembling.

# 13

**R'** Yuspe seemed in the throes of an internal debate. It was clear that the words he was about to say were terribly disturbing; indeed, he would have been much happier not to say them at all.

"Regarding the signed authorization that my father purportedly gave to Getzel: It is all lies and falsehood; my father never signed any such document."

Leizer almost collapsed. "What are you saying?" he whispered incredulously. "The handwriting was your father's."

"Where is the paper? Can I see it?" R' Todros asked gently.

Leizer fished through his pockets but found nothing. "That's right, now I remember," he said, hitting his forehaed. "Getzel took it back with him."

"Thereby taking away all evidence of forgery," the rabbi finished the sentence. "If I had the paper I could prove that Getzel had forged my handwriting. There's nothing to say; he's a talented man. And this isn't his first forgery."

Leizer stood silent, paralyzed and suffering. He could see the scene of the previous day playing before his eyes: the funeral of Shraga Shwartzer, deceased head of the *Kehillah*, Getzel speaking confidentially to R' Miller during the procession.

"Getzel was discussing something with the rabbi during the funeral; I assumed that it was regarding the loan," Leizer murmured.

"Getzel's a sly one: he carefully set the scene." Wrinkles of ironic laughter appeared on the venerable rabbi's pale face. "I'm very sorry to have to say this, but Getzel is a rogue and a trickster."

"How can the rabbi say that?" Leizer burst out, from the depths of thirty years of close friendship.

"I stand by every word," the rabbi said emphatically. "During the funeral he told me what he was planning to do as the head of the Prague *Kehillah*. I didn't understand what was so confidential about these things, that he had to whisper them to me in my ear. Now we understand how he was trying to trick us. But what happened?" the rabbi said in the singsong tone usually reserved for learning, as he stroked his white beard. "Getzel thought he had you in his pocket and you wouldn't check my signature with me, and that's where he was wrong." His weary glance rested upon his ancient, beloved books, as if whispering to them a secret promise to return to them soon. "I suggest you stay as far away from Getzel as possible. He's a dangerous man."

What could have come over the rabbi, normally such a patient and reserved man, so careful with every word? Why was he ascribing every evil to Getzel?

Leizer's thoughts were transparent, clear from the look of skepticism and shock on his face.

"Bank Fernbach is one big mirage; he's building castles in the air," the son, R' Yuspe, said bluntly. "A spider's web held together with a little saliva. It has no solid economic foundation; it exists on lies and falsehood."

Leizer could not have been more shocked if they had hit him on the head with a blacksmith's anvil. "I have to disagree with your words. I know Getzel's business from without and within. The bank is built on firm credit lines that Getzel received from the Royal Bank in Munich."

And Getzel had used that money in illegal ways — Leizer knew that too, though he did not mention it, lest he destroy the last vestiges of Getzel's credibility in the eyes of the rabbi and his son. That is, if there was any credibility left.

None at all. It seemed that the rabbi and his son had never believed in Getzel's honesty. "Do you know how Getzel received the funds from the Royal Bank in Munich?"

Leizer thought for a moment. "No, actually I don't."

"And you never wondered how a person, and that person a Jew, was given such an enormous line of credit?" R' Yuspe asked.

"I — I assumed that Getzel knew what to say and when. He's not a fool like me."

The rabbi broke his silence with a deep sigh. "*Oy*, Leizer, Leizer, why are you so low in your own eyes? Your 'foolishness' is a synonym for honesty, for faithfulness, and Getzel's talent and wit is a synonym for lies and swindles. You are a man of integrity and he is a bundle of falsehood and deceit."

"I'm a fool and he's a wise man." Tears coursed down Leizer's gray beard.

R' Todros's heart melted with pity. This afternoon he had seen Getzel standing in the courtyard of the synagogue surrounded by a group of idlers, venting all his venom onto the head of Leizer Tischler. He did not delineate just what had made him so angry, but he hinted broadly that Leizer was sitting on his money, hoarding it like a rat guarding its cheese, instead of using it to help others. The first word he used to describe him was "fool"; the second, "miser"; the third, "thief." Leizer himself did not know about it yet. He had preferred to *daven* in the Pinkus shul that day, and had stayed away from the Meisel Synagogue in order to avoid meeting Getzel. R' Todros was the last person who would stoop to gossip and tell Leizer what Getzel had said of him.

"'They are wise to do evil'," the rabbi quoted, "'and know not to do good.' Getzel's wisdom is used only for negative things. He has been fooling you for many years, just as he has fooled the bank in Munich, just as he has fooled his own banking clients, with many varied schemes. For Getzel wisdom means trickery and you, Leizer, are no fool. Your foolishness means you are honest, that's all."

"The rabbi keeps referring to Getzel's lies. How did he actually fool the bank in Munich?" Leizer's curiosity overcame him. R' Todros did not speak lightly; he must have meant something specific.

The rabbi sighed once again and gave Leizer a searching glance. "I must have you vow not to reveal this to anyone."

"I promise," Leizer said, listening attentively.

"Yuspe, tell him."

R' Yuspe spoke.

---

*Nuremberg, Germany 5579 (1819)*

That day was a holiday in Nuremberg. The streets were filled with flags, emblazoned with their triangles of red and white. The Royal Bank of Bavaria, headquartered in Munich, was opening a branch in Nuremberg.

The bank's new building was a large and impressive one with the Corinthian columns fronting it carved by a skilled artisan. Blue-uniformed guards with white shirts decorated with pink sashes wandered here and there, full of their own self-importance, keeping the throngs of curious children away from the area.

The marble floor of the new bank gleamed like a mirror, reflecting the daylight onto the beige-white walls. Large framed oil paintings offered scenes of tranquil country settings, breathtaking sunsets upon the sea, red poppies in a blue vase, and a herd of cows peacefully grazing in a picture so realistic it made the viewer certain that in a moment one of the cows would move her head and he would hear the sound of the little bronze bell hanging around her neck ringing its melodic chimes through the corridor of the bank.

Otto Brauner, bank manager, strolled through the building in an impeccably tailored cutaway, striped trousers, and black bowtie. His fleshy face smiled in every direction and his small brown mustache quivered with pleasure and anticipation. He held a small glass in his hand that he repeatedly filled with liquor. Otto drank with all the many honored guests invited that day, anticipating that a large portion of them would become regular clients. One could open a new bank branch with quite a reasonable infrastructure just from the swollen purses of some of them.

One of the guests, particularly, drew his attention. A Jew, obviously, identifiable by his hat and beard. The man was almost a midget, with a florid face and half-closed eyes. Beneath his jacket he wore a tailored shirt whose buttons seemed almost ready to burst open over his pot-bellied stomach. But he walked with great self-confidence, the kind of bearing that only a man in a responsible position boasts.

He must exchange a few words with the strange figure. First, a handshake.

"Are you Herr Klaus Schmidt, by any chance?"

The guest nodded his head. "You're talking about Klaus, from the beer factory in Baden-Baden? I resemble him, but I am not he. I am Ludwig Schlesinger. The well-known shipping company Nacht Aber Mahl belongs to me."

He was a Jew, but his accent was heavily Germanic. Otto was embarrassed to admit that he had never heard of the shipping company; he had trouble even pronouncing the name. A grin appeared on his face. "Of course, how could I have mistaken you! Ludwig Schlesinger! How are you, Ludwig?"

"Excellent," the scarlet-faced man replied. "Business is excellent; this past year we have doubled our profits, and according to my financial advisers in the first quarter of the coming year, 1820, we should see them double again. Nacht Aber Mahl Company is facing a brilliant financial future."

The future sounded lovely, according to this little man, who spoke like some kind of financial wizard.

"Are you considering doing business with us, Mr. Schlesinger?"

"Perhaps," the man answered cautiously. "The Royal Bank is certainly a firm worth working with. The question is what financial advantages will I derive from it."

Otto took a deep breath. Now he was standing on familiar ground. The home office had given him an enormous line of credit for this opening in order to solidly establish the Nuremberg branch. "Herr Ludwig, it's worth your while to come to my office in the next few days. The bank is prepared to give serious clients such as you preferred interest rates, better than all other banks. But don't quote me on that," he said, lowering his voice until his words were almost lost in the surrounding cacophony of laughter and clinking glasses. He pulled the short, heavy man to a quieter corner. "I have a free hand to offer what I please," he whispered, his eyes darting from side to side. "If you come into my office between the hours of 9 a.m. and 2 p.m. we can talk more freely. You won't lose by it."

Ludwig Schlesinger pulled out a visiting card from the pocket of his elegant coat. "I am staying at the Blue Lagoon Hotel. If you need me urgently, I will be there within the half-hour."

Otto watched him as he left the crowded building. Ludwig Schlesinger knew quite well that a bank manager does not go to someone's hotel to do business there. This was simply a tactic used to show off his status. The Blue Lagoon Hotel, new and extraordinarily luxurious, was frequented by only the wealthiest men.

❦

Two days later Ludwig Schlesinger entered the bank and walked directly to the manager's office. Otto Brauner was happy to greet him. "*Gut morgen*, Herr Schlesinger. I see that you're interested in our bank."

Ludwig grinned from ear to ear. "I've come to deposit 70,000 reichsthaler. On the condition that the news you give me is pleasing."

Otto nearly fainted. Seventy thousand in one fell swoop! He jumped forward and gestured to Ludwig to sit down on the other side of the desk. "We certainly have matters to discuss."

After half an hour Ludwig left the bank, his smile that of the cat that swallowed the canary. The manager had swallowed it all, hook, line, and sinker, and offered him unprecedented terms.

That day Ludwig visited the home of Anton Friedberg, a simple Nuremberg Jew who toiled just to earn his daily bread. He offered him a deal that began with the words, "Do you want to earn 5,000 reichsthaler without any effort?"

The next day Anton Friedberg came to the bank, in spanking new clothing that Ludwig had procured for him from some unnamed tailor, and asked for a loan of 500,000 reichsthaler.

That request caused Otto Brauner to raise his eyebrows. Such an amount was available only in the main branch in Munich. "I don't know you at all; I can't lend you even one reichsthaler."

The man introduced himself, handing the banker an elegant business card, "Shimon Frankfurter. I own entire streets in Nuremberg's Jewish quarter. I can give you collateral of three or four homes."

Otto took a long pull on his thick cigar while suspiciously eyeing this new client. "Listen, that's not enough," he murmured, blowing a cloud of smoke at the man. "Herr Frankfurter, you're proceeding too quickly. For me to lend you such a sum, I need references."

The man did not hesitate. "Rabbiner Levi Itzkowitz, rabbi of the Jewish community. He knows me well and will be glad to recommend me."

Otto breathed in a ring of smoke and coughed contemptuously. "The name means nothing to me. Give me someone whom I know, a man who has the wherewithal to guarantee the loan in the event that you can't repay it."

"My homes will be my collateral," the Jew protested, but the bank manager was insistent: he wanted someone's name.

"Okay, if you insist," the man finally said. "I have someone with whom I occasionally do business. Ludwig Schlesinger."

Otto's eyes opened more. "The head of the shipping firm Nacht Mit Fisch knows you?"

"Nacht Aber Mahl," the man corrected him. "That's right. We're good friends."

Otto's lack of experience, coupled with his burning desire to get to the top quickly, led him to make the dreadful mistake. "Ludwig Schlesinger is acceptable to me. If he provides a clear letter of recommendation I'll get you half a million reichsthaler."

The fraud continued to grow. "Shimon Frankfurter" brought Ludwig Schlesinger's letter of recommendation and within two weeks he received the princely sum in large bills.

*Time Bomb* / 141

Ludwig Schlesinger traveled from Nuremberg to Hamburg, where he deposited the bills in another account, this one opened under the name Fritz Borman. After two weeks he withdrew the sum, placing the bills — different ones than those he had deposited — in a safe in his room in the Blue Lagoon. The next month "Shimon Frankfurter" made his first payment on the loan: 20,000 reichsthaler.

A few days later Ludwig Schlesinger entered the bank, warmly hugged the manager, who had become a close friend, and handed him another 20,000 reichsthaler to deposit with the initial 70,000. Otto glowed with happiness. The financial reports he was sending to the major branches in Munich and Berlin were proving his worth to the bank and looked wonderful. The small Nuremberg branch was doing big business! Hefty deposits, loans on a scale almost unknown.

The next month Shimon Frankfurter missed his payment.

In a panic-stricken letter sent via messenger, Otto Brauner nervously demanded that the debtor appear before him in his office the very next day.

Frankfurter arrived, full of apologies, but still radiating self-confidence. "I'm having some cash flow problems this month, but next month you'll get 40,000 all at once, together with interest for this month."

Next month Frankfurter did not pay even a single reichsthaler. Again, he brought the excuse of cash flow problems. He promised 60,000 reichsthaler next month.

Otto Brauner was in a complete state of panic. That was all he needed: to be forced to start selling real estate and houses. There would be articles in the newspapers about the bank's difficulties.

That afternoon Otto took a carriage to the Blue Lagoon Hotel, hoping desperately that Ludwig Schlesinger was not in cahoots with his friend.

Ludwig was in his room, immersed in financial calculations. He warmly welcomed his guest and asked him to take a seat on the couch. Otto, though, stood, fingering Ludwig's visiting card. "When you gave me this I didn't think I'd need it."

"What's the matter? You look upset."

"Naturally," Otto flared out angrily. "You've led me into big trouble. Your Frankfurter won't give the money back!"

Ludwig's jaw dropped open. "Impossible. Frankfurter is a very honest man. Maybe he's just having temporary problems."

"That's what he says," Otto shouted. "He keeps talking about 'cash flow' and 'liquidity troubles' and promising to pay more and more the next month. But in reality he's only made one payment out of three."

"I'm very sorry," Ludwig nodded his head and stroked his thin beard. "Let me speak with him. I'll get back to you in a few days."

Otto felt better as he left the hotel. Ludwig Schlesinger radiated strength and confidence that lent him an air of integrity.

Two terrifying days passed. Otto could not sleep those nights. Would Ludwig come?

On the third day Ludwig appeared in the bank. In his hands he carried a brown leather bag. He asked Otto to lock the door to his office and in front of his astounded eyes he counted out 480,000 reichsthaler in large bills.

"I — I don't understand," Otto stuttered. "What's this?"

Ludwig stood, stone faced and cold. "My name, Herr Brauner, means more to me than half a million reichsthaler. I spoke with Shimon Frankfurter and understand from him that he has recently come into certain financial difficulties. It is possible that next month some assets will become available and he will be able to return even 80,000 reichsthaler at once, but I can't allow you to experience difficulties because of me. Because I am the man who recommended him, I stand behind my word. Though I didn't sign as a guarantor, only gave my reference, here is the money."

Otto almost cried, he was so moved. He gave Ludwig a long embrace and covered his bearded cheeks with kisses. "You are a good man," he said, his voice breaking. "I would never have believed that such honest men existed in the world."

"I am a simple man," Ludwig said modestly. "I just fulfill my obligations."

"What's the matter with you?" Otto shouted. "It wasn't your obligation. At the worst I would have sold some of Frankfurter's houses."

Empty words, really. Otto knew well that only in the worst case scenario would he have sold the possessions of a debtor, and there were the newspapers standing and waiting for him to fail.

*Time Bomb* / 143

They parted the best of friends. Otto felt deeply grateful to Ludwig, who had gotten him out of this mess.

When Ludwig came the next month asking the manager for an emergency loan — for one month only — of 300,000 reichsthaler, in order to expand his shipping firm, Otto did his utmost to get him the money as quickly as possible. A man who was prepared to lose half a million reichsthaler just to keep his good name intact deserved the closest relationship and the highest respect.

---

### Prague, 5598 (1838)

"Ludwig Schlesinger took the money and the next day the little bird flew out of the Blue Lagoon and totally disappeared from Nuremberg streets," R' Yuspe Miller gave a melancholy smile and shook his head in distress. "Anton Friedberg, too, who had been acting the part of 'Shimon Frankfurter,' vanished. With the 5,000 reichsthaler that he had made out of the huge extortion scheme of Ludwig Schlesinger — who is none other than your friend Getzel Fernbach — he bought himself a house in a distant city and began a new life."

"And what happened to the bank?" Leizer asked from between thin lips.

"What could happen?" R' Yuspe laughed. "The Nuremberg branch closed within a short time and its manager, Otto Brauner, died not long afterwards of a broken heart. The police are still searching for Ludwig Schlesinger, but no one would ever connect the rogue from Nuremberg with the respected owner of the Bank Fernbach in Prague. Now do you understand where Getzel got his capital to open a bank?"

Leizer found it difficult to breathe. "I can't believe what I'm hearing," he said, speaking slowly, his eyes glazed. "May I ask who told you the story?"

"Anton Friedberg is my cousin," interrupted the elderly rabbi, answering in place of his son. "If not for my fear of desecrating Hashem's Name, and also because I am afraid it will cause even more problems to the Jewish people, I would turn Getzel over to the police without hesitation."

Leizer Tischler rubbed his forehead. "It looks as if he wanted to pull a similar scheme now. He asked for a large loan of 50,000 reichsthaler and returned it quickly. Obviously that was preparation for the 90,000 reichsthaler —"

He lapsed into thought, his face growing scarlet, his entire body shaking. "Getzel has a double standard. With me he says that guaranteeing a loan does not obligate a person at all, but there he returns a loan only because he gave a reference for a friend."

Against his will R' Yuspe broke out into laughter. A fool remains a fool; there was nothing to be done. "Are you going to fall into the same trap as Otto Brauner?" he asked, slapping Leizer on the back. "What do you think? Don't you realize the entire loan was just a tactic to win the bank manager's confidence and swindle 300,000 reichsthaler from the National Bank?"

"And what will be now?" Leizer was suddenly gripped by a strong feeling of panic.

The venerable rabbi rubbed his hands together. "I don't know. I just hope that Prague won't be destroyed by the controversy. Our city is well schooled in bitter conflict; only with difficulty have we gotten out of them. There's always something new. Once it was the Shabsai Tzvi affair, with the city full of his followers; once the fight between R' Yonasan Eybeschutz and R' Yaakov Emden over the writing of amulets. Even in the days of the Noda B'Yehudah the city seethed many times, and it didn't settle down in the time of his son, R' Shmuel. Now a new wave is coming.

"Certain men in the *Kehillah* are trying to carve a wedge between you and Getzel. Prague will burn; we can only hope it doesn't go up in flames!"

Leizer began to tremble. The rabbi's eyes glowed; he looked like an image of a prophet in a Rembrandt painting. Could he see the future?

Time would tell.

# 14

*Jerusalem, 5561 (2000)*

"So when I saw those brutal soldiers," Nufar Talmi said, "standing ready to shoot rubber bullets at small children who had done nothing worse than throw rocks and Molotov cocktails, I decided not to keep silent. I took a sweet Palestinian boy of 6 with me and came within a meter of the soldiers standing ready with guns cocked toward the child's head. I pulled out my camera and threatened that the next day the photos would be seen all over the world, just like the famous picture from the Warsaw ghetto: of a little boy holding his hands up and surrendering to ten Nazi soldiers. They gave in immediately, and quietly submitted to the rocks, the spit, and the curses. It doesn't matter that later on one of the boys took a huge cement block and threw it at a soldier's head. Believe me, they deserve it, and I feel fine about it."

"But you created an artificial situation," her mother Ariella Talmi-Sturm said thoughtfully, her hand on her forehead. "The Nazis weren't just setting scenes. They really did kill small children. Has the Israeli army murdered a million and a half young Palestinians? You just set a scene. Your behavior just doesn't meet ethical standards."

"It makes no difference," protested Nufar. "Two children or a million and a half, the principle is the same. Anyway, in this case the end justifies the means. We must help the Palestinians gain independence and eject the occupying army. Right, Abba?"

"Absolutely right," Dori Talmi drew deeply on his pipe and looked with pleasure at his daughter. She dared to do what he could just think about in his ivory tower of academia.

That night the lights in Judge Talmi's house stayed on until well after 3 a.m. Dori and Ariella sat comfortably in recliners in their living room enjoying the stories with which their daughter, home for a visit, regaled them.

Not many Israelis enjoyed the judge's daughter's tales. "Nufar Talmi" was a name that gnashed the teeth of a great many of the state's citizenry, every time they read one of her articles or heard her speak. Nufar Talmi was a journalist, a columnist for a well-known Israeli periodical, living in Gaza and reporting from there. If Professor Talmi was a leftist, his daughter was a fanatical leftist, one who loathed her people and her nation and served their worst enemies. The things she wrote in Hebrew looked like faithful translations of the propaganda doled out by the Palestinian Authority. Nufar, with all her fervor and enthusiasm, had been inducted into the service of the Palestinians, suffering as they were beneath the heavy tread of Israeli occupation. Even the lynching in Ramallah did not concern Nufar Talmi. "It's horrifying," she said, quickly adding in the same breath, "but don't forget that Israelis have also lynched Palestinians."

She was referring to an incident that took place in Beit She'an twenty-six years earlier, when the body of a terrorist was filmed being thrown out of a window by Israeli citizens. There was a major difference between the lynching in Ramallah in 5761 (2000) and the event in Beit She'an in 5734 (1974). There an armed terrorist had sneaked into a house, killed all those inside, and was eventually killed himself by security forces. His body was flung out the window by terrified citizens. But these minor details did not concern Nufar. She assumed, always, that justice lay with the Palestinians. The bloody crisis of 5761 (2000) wasa result, in her opinion, of seven years of trickery and lying by the State of Israel vis-a-vis the Palestinians.

Nufar Talmi compared the struggle to the internal conflict that took place in South Africa for many years, ending in May 1994. The Jews were the whites. The Israeli government was the government of apartheid. The Arabs were the blacks and she was the white heroine who had come to assist them. She was trying to persuade her readership that all the trouble that existed between Jews and Palestinians was a result of a lack of respect for human rights and age-old discrimination. Nufar often described with great enthusiasm the demonstrations supporting the Palestinian cause that took place in other Arab states — demonstrations that routinely called for the slaughter of Jews, wherever they may be, and, if possible, the Americans as well.

The average Israeli who read this kind of thing was horrified to his very core, cursing the Jewish writer who allied herself with the murderers of her people. He assumed that her problem was that she was living in a fantasy world, cut off completely from reality. It was as if she had never studied the history of her country during the past century. But in truth Nufar Talmi did not suffer any doubts. She had simply been raised in an atmosphere of liberalism, humanism, and leftism, handed to her by her father, Judge Dori Talmi.

Dori Talmi had a very good reason for embracing this worldview, and it did not have very much to do with hatred of the right.

---

*Prague, 5598 (1838)*

The next day found Klonymous Bendele extremely busy. He orchestrated a careful drama in three acts.

In the morning Getzel Fernbach again discovered a small piece of paper on his *shtender* in the synagogue. The handwriting was identical to that of the day before; Bendele had gone to great pains to change the writing from his own elegant calligraphic script. "Last night, too, Leizer

Tischler visited R' Todros Miller's home, and had a long talk with the rabbi and his son, R' Yuspe."

The mention of Yuspe Miller's name stung Getzel like a sharp crack of a whip. He had not spoken with Yuspe for seven years, since the time that Yuspe had sent him regards from one "Shimon Frankfurter." Getzel had acted the puzzled innocent, not understanding what Yuspe was talking about. From that time on he wondered over and over again: What did the father, R' Todros Miller, know of his fraud? Would he speak of it — and to whom? In any case, Yuspe himself had been marked as a dangerous man, one who could turn into a stool pigeon one day and start singing in a local police station.

Now Getzel knew for certain that Leizer must be aware of his extortion scheme in Nuremberg. The veneer of honesty and integrity that he had been so careful to preserve was shattered beyond repair. He needed a new idea: how to keep Leizer quiet. He swiftly went over the facts. There was no fear of a police investigation; almost twenty years had passed since the affair. The one who would have served as the key witness, Otto Brauner, had long since died, and there was no one else to testify against him, with the exception of Anton Friedberg, who no doubt would not want to incriminate himself. He, Getzel, could always deny everything and claim it never happened.

Leizer had left his usual place of prayer in Meisel Synagogue two days before and had gone to the Klausen *Shul*, in order to avoid meeting Getzel. He still hoped that they could iron out their differences, and that peace would once again reign between them. R' Isaac Posen shook his hand warmly and asked what had brought the treasurer of the *Kehillah* to the *Shul* and honor it with his presence. Leizer stammered out some flimsy excuse.

Immediately after prayers Bendele came to the *Shul* to set the stage for Act One. His skinny body twitched with excitement. He walked directly to Leizer's seat and whispered something in his ear.

Leizer grew pale as death. He tried to speak, opened his mouth, but only gasps came out; he slumped down in a faint.

"Water! Water!" came the cry from all sides.

In the foyer of the synagogue stood a bucket full of water. Each of the congregants would take a little water in a metal cup and wash his

*Time Bomb* / 149

hands into a large, uncovered wooden barrel in a corner. Itzik Shpitz, the synagogue's caretaker, raced to the bucket, filled a cup with water, and jumped over the benches on his way to the unconscious man. His ungainly figure jumping through the air, water spraying in all directions, filled Klonymous with the uncontrolled desire to laugh hysterically. He turned his scarlet face to the side and forcibly held back the laughter. He was filled with a wondrous pleasure: his ability to use words afforded him an exquisite feeling of power. What had he said to Leizer? Just a few words: "Getzel told everyone that you are a thief, and has hired a few thugs from Prague's underworld to break your bones."

It was true; Getzel had actually said it. After prayers he had gathered a group of young men in the synagogue courtyard and had told them that had he known what a crook Leizer was, he would never have been friends with him.

"Crook?" The young men raised their eyebrows. "Leizer is the most ethical man in the *Kehillah*."

Getzel burst out laughing. "You are like a flock of sheep! Leizer is a real criminal. For many years he's been putting away community funds under the hat of the 'most ethical man in Prague.'"

The young people shrugged. "You're just slandering him," they argued heatedly.

Getzel lowered his voice to a shrill whisper. "As manager of the bank of Prague I know — and you don't — how much of the community funds Leizer deposited with me. He earned a fortune on your money and didn't share even a single coin of the profits with the community. It bothered me, but I thought, let him be well, it's not really theft, just a little swindling. But yesterday I sat and inspected the books of the treasury." He hit his forehead with his hands, to make a stronger impression, and shouted, "Hashem have mercy! This man has quietly put thousands of reichsthaler into his pocket without anyone being the wiser. I promise you I will give him into the hands of the police or hire some thugs to break his bones. I'll teach him a lesson: that the money belonging to the people isn't free to all. People save money that should buy them bread in order to marry off unfortunate orphans and he shamelessly pockets it."

His florid face grew even more scarlet. The serious accusations, along with the self-righteous expression on his face, were enough to persuade some of the more gullible among them, and they ran after him as he walked, head bent, homeward, begging him to give them further details of Leizer's deceptions.

Klonymous Bendele left the scene and raced off to the Klausen *Shul*. He knew Leizer Tischler well, and knew how the shock would paralyze him. Leizer was a coward through and through, and when faced with the possibility of being struck he would tremble with fright and flee like a frightened child.

Klonymous showed great diligence in his care for the faint man, displaying more concern than any of the others, and only when he saw Leizer's eyes open and the color returning to his face did he prepare to leave.

As he passed the brown wooden doors, a firm hand clutched his arm. R' Isaac Posen gestured to him to join him outside.

"Tell me, please," the rabbi demanded, "what did you whisper in his ear that caused him to faint? Why has he come here to *daven*? What in Heaven's name is going on?"

Klonymous waved his hands in a gesture of surprise. "The *rav* doesn't know? The *Kehillah* is burning with terrible controversy. The two bosom friends, Leizer and Getzel, have turned into mortal enemies. None of the congregation comes to Leizer's defense when Getzel heaps blood libels upon him, as if Leizer had been stealing community funds for the past ten years. That's why Leizer left the Meisel Synagogue and came to you."

R' Posen was shocked. While he was trying to recover his composure Klonymous pulled away his arm, until then still held in the iron grip of the rabbi. He nodded his head and declared, "Hashem should help Prague to be saved from the conflict. We must close Getzel's mouth before his words reach the police."

R' Posen watched him leave, his eyes troubled.

*Time Bomb* / 151

Klonymous raced from the Klausen *Shul* to Leizer's home, for Act Two. He banged firmly on the door. When Yoel Tischler came to answer, Klonymous was hard put to conceal his delight. Bendele had long since observed that Yoel did not look fondly at the friendship between Getzel and his father. Yoel was the right man at the right time!

"Yoel, come quickly! Don't ask what happened to your father!" The news came as a blow.

"What's happened to Father?" the boy screamed fearfully.

Klonymous took a deep breath. "Your father is lying half dead on the floor of the Kluasen *Shul*. He found out that Getzel Fernbach hired thugs from Prague's underworld to kill him, and he lost consciousness."

Yoel himself was saved from fainting solely due to his healthy physique and his youth, but still he grew pale as snow and began to tremble. "I don't understand. What's this about Getzel? What are you talking about?"

Klonymous urged him to make haste. "Come, already, stop wasting time. Hasn't your father told you that Getzel is persecuting him, and is slandering him?"

Yoel donned his coat and ran quickly from the house. Fortunately, Yona Tischler was not at home. She was at the market buying fish for Shabbos, and thus they were saved the panic attack that would undoubtedly have ensued.

"Tell me what happened," Yoel begged Bendele as they strode rapidly towards the synagogue.

Klonymous almost danced with inward glee but his face remained somber. "I don't know what happened to Getzel. I always thought he was your father's friend. Suddenly he opened his mouth against him and is accusing your father of being a thief and embezzler."

Yoel could hardly take it all in. "My father a thief? My father an embezzler? There isn't anyone more honest than he is in the entire world! Getzel himself is an out-and-out swindler. I don't know what my father ever saw in him; you can see just by looking at his eyes that he's a no-good rogue."

"Getzel also accused your father of being a police informer." Bendele maliciously voiced the lie. This bone was so juicy that it was impossible not to suck out the marrow to the very last drop. "Are you aware that your father visits the government offices in order to tell them exactly what's going on among us?"

Yoel stopped short in the middle of the street. His iron fists grabbed Bendele's thin neck. "Say those words again and I'll crush your throat right here and now."

Klonymous gave a thin croak and waved his arms and legs. Yoel released his hold on him and Bendele collapsed onto the ground like a rag. Passersby stared at them in shock; one of them offered to help make peace between them. Yoel politely refused, explaining that this was simply a friendly dispute.

Klonymous recovered quickly. "I'm not the one who said it. I was telling you what Getzel had said about your father," he defended himself.

Yoel relented, though his fury remained fierce within him. "If I get hold of Getzel I'll — I'll —" He almost trembled with rage. "What does he want from my father?"

"I don't know," Bendele declared. "Honestly I don't know what happened. Just me? All of Prague is asking what happened. Those two were the best of friends."

"Everyone knows and I'm the last to hear the news," Yoel complained.

Even before they entered the shul courtyard Yoel could see the tumult. He ran inside, breathing heavily.

Klonymous took advantage of the opportunity and quickly left the scene.

―――

Act Three took place in Getzel's house.

Klonymous got there while Getzel, his wife Genendel, and their son Zekil were eating breakfast.

The Fernbach dining room could compare to the most ornate royal establishment. The whole house was exquisite but the dining room was Getzel's particular temple: after all, he loved to eat. It was beautifully designed, its walls paneled with light wood inlaid with graceful designs of fruits and vegetables. A buffet on the southern wall displayed a spice cabinet whose glass jars were filled with a variety of spices in many hues, brought from the Far East. A crystal chandelier hung from the ceiling, with dozens of candles illuminating the room even by day.

Getzel placed great importance on all the gastronomic aspects of his life. His routine revolved around one meal and the next. He had been stuffing himself for many years; the folds of fatty flesh on him had not been created out of nothing.

Getzel, his wife Genendel, and their son Zekil, wrapped in flowered aprons, were busy consuming mounds of vegetables, eggs, and spicy cheeses. Zekil had successfully combined his parents' features: From his father he had inherited sharp wits and a vast appetite; from his mother he got his stature. The result was a mountain of a man who bore the name Zekil Fernbach.

Getzel's jaws moved like a swollen grinder, diligently crushing a fresh loaf of bread spread with homemade butter, together with a soft-boiled egg seasoned with garlic and olive oil, the whole thing coated liberally with salt. On the right side of the master of the house stood a generous cup containing fragrant tea; Getzel would occasionally take a huge sip from it, in order to wash down the pile of food and prepare for the next wave.

Feitel, the aging valet, stood ready to be of service. Every few minutes Getzel or Zekil would send him to the kitchen to replenish what was missing: cheese balls giving off a sourish scent; cups of fresh milk brought daily from the herds around Prague; pickled cucumbers from the large barrel in the yard; a pinch of peppercorns or a bottle of wine from his cellar.

In the kitchen Zissel the cook toiled near the small brick oven, a chef's hat on her head and a snowy-white apron tied around her waist. In a pan filled with hot oil she fried blintzes stuffed with sweet cheese and raisins. Feitel raced between the kitchen and the dining room, bringing the blintzes to the table, where they went straight into the maws of Getzel and Zekil, disappearing in one gulp.

"Would you like more blintzes, *tzaddikim?*" Zissel called out from the kitchen in a honeyed voice.

Zekil turned around. "Why not?"

And Feitel ran once again to the kitchen to bring some fresh fare.

Right before *Birkas Hamazon* the Fernbach family were interrupted. Feitel brought the unexpected guest right into the dining room. Getzel almost choked in his fury. "Don't you know that we are not to be disturbed while we're eating!" he growled at the elderly servant.

"He says it's very urgent," Feitel defended himself, then disappeared into the kitchen.

"What do you want?" Getzel demanded ungraciously. "Keep it short."

Klonymous's bulging eyes almost fell out of their sockets as he looked at an abundance he had never seen in his entire life. "I'll start with a little parable for the dear Fernbach family," he said, a sarcastic smile on his face. "A fat man once came to a doctor with his request. 'I want to get rid of my belly.' The doctor wrote out his prescription: Breakfast, four eggs, two pieces of cheese, and thirteen blintzes. Lunch, shoulder of beef. Dinner, roast duck and custard. The man was astonished. 'That's how you get rid of your belly?' 'Absolutely,' said the doctor. 'That's how you get rid of it, right into the ground!'"

"Very funny," mumbled Getzel, his face stony. "Why are you here?"

"I've come as an emissary from our holy community, to bring peace."

Getzel's jaws stopped their motion. His eyes pierced through Bendele. "What are you talking about, you pious hypocrite?"

"I forgive you the insult," Bendele said pacifically, his voice smarmy with flattery. "Honored Getzel, as head of the Prague community, it is not fit for you to quarrel with Leizer. Even if he called you a gangster and threatened to turn you over to the police, I think that you should make —"

The cup of tea missed Bendele's face by a hairsbreadth and crashed with a terrible bang on the white marble floor embedded with red tiles. Getzel was suddenly standing on his short legs. "You tell Leizer that I'll be the one who gives him up to the police. I'll make him a quick and black end! Get out of my house!" His piercing scream seemed to shake the entire room; the thin glass of the spice cabinet shattered onto the buffet.

Bendele pranced out, his hands jammed into his swollen pockets to protect the cheese he managed to snatch from the table with one quick

*Time Bomb* / 155

sweep. After all, were the fruits of this world only reserved for Getzel Fernbach and no one else?

He was afraid of the wealthy man. Getzel was really angry. That yell of his could have stopped a lion about to eat its prey.

Getzel's head throbbed. Klonymous was not speaking idly. It seemed that Leizer had begun a rebellion against him within the community. He had to blacken his name quickly, before Leizer could bury him.

His swift brain came up with a plan within minutes.

The flames of discord took hold in Prague.

## 15

*Chechnya, 5760 (2000)*

In the cave at the bottom of the valley between the mountains, a small fire served for both illumination and warmth. A cloud of steam rose from an old tin coffepot that stood upon it. The fragrance of perking coffee spread through the cave, tantalizing the taste buds. Dozens of young men in the cave looked longingly at the coffeepot. "Patience, comrades," the dark-skinned young man with the curly hair and the burning eyes encouraged them. "Another minute and the coffee will be ready."

And precisely one minute later the coffee did, indeed, come to a boil, bringing its brown froth up to the lid of the pot. Selim Yagudayev hastily pulled it off the fire, seconds before it would boil over.

The dozens of Chechen fighters downed the hot coffee and listened silently to the words of their leader.

"We've promised the world revenge for the capture of the Gray Fox, Salamon Radeyv, and we've fulfilled just a portion of our promise," Selim began. "We've burned down the communications tower in Moscow, we've bombed a few houses. We've killed dozens of Russians. But we haven't

*Time Bomb* / 157

achieved our goal. I don't have to remind you that Russian forces are systematically wiping Chechnya off the map, slaughtering our citizens, with no one to stop them. If this situation is allowed to continue, with no reaction from our side, in another two years the world will forget that there ever was a country called Chechnya. Men will ask, 'What is Chechnya? A cut of beef, or an American firm that manufactures diapers?'"

The faces of the underground fighters wore grim masks of fury. Yagudayev had deliberately toyed with the patriotic fervor of his men.

"What can we do that we haven't already done?" one of the fighters asked, expressing the question many felt.

Yagudayev flared up. "We've done nothing!"

The cave echoed with sounds of surprise.

Their young, charismatic leader explained. "Comrades, we must get Chechnya back into our hands and in order to do this we must bring Putin and all of Russia to its knees, so that they beg us to take Chechnya back from them."

The atmosphere grew electric. "How do we do it?"

Yagudayev's voice grew hushed. "I've thought of many things. The plan I've been considering most strongly this past month was to punish the Russians and Americans, and also the entire hypocritical world, by putting a car bomb beneath the U.N. building in New York next month, when the General Assembly begins its deliberations. The entire world is cooperating, at least passively, in the obliteration of Chechnya from the face of the earth. Imagine, then, what would happen if, in the middle of the deliberations, they'll hear a gigantic explosion, sending the U.N. off into destruction — together with the Americans, Russians, and everyone else."

The young men's eyes gave off sparks of hatred and reflected their thoughts of sweet revenge. "So let's do it!" they cried.

"If you're so excited, it shows you haven't really grown up yet," Yagudayev laughed quietly, sipping the coffee that had grown cold as he'd spoken. "What will we get from that? Sweet revenge? Will that get Chechnya back into our hands? No! The entire world will be against us, even more so than before."

Yagudayev's deputy, Kareem Nisadov, refilled the cups with the fragrant brew.

Selim peered out of the narrow entrance into the dark. On the summit of some of the hills nearby were searchlights set up by the Russian army to trap the last of the Chechen guerrilla fighters. If Anatoly Ivanov, commander of the Russian brigade in the area, had known where his hated enemies were hiding, he would have collapsed in dismay. The guerilla warriors left and entered the cave through a hidden, narrow path that only the most hardened and courageous of mountain climbers dared to scale.

Yagudayev scanned the faces of his men, trying to decide if they were able to carry out the daring mission he had devised during the many sleepless nights, when hatred seemed to take over every cell of his body until he was ready to suffocate. These men, it seemed, were made without fear. With a little help from his direct superiors, Chatav and Dudayev, he would be able to execute his plan. The president of the Republic, Aslan Maschaduv, would undoubtedly give it his blessing.

He lit a cheap cigarette with slow, deliberate motions. The smoke was foul smelling, but this was all the fighters, on the run, were able to procure. Yagudayev was not from the regular Chechen military; he had joined only two years earlier. The intensity of his patriotism and commitment could match anyone within the nation. His fighters had accepted his authority without a murmur.

"Listen carefully," he finally said. "I have a plan, a carefully prepared plan. I won't detail it now, because the time has not yet come, but I'll give you the main idea.

"We need an impetus that will return our occupied homeland to us, an effective impetus that will force Russia to leave Chechnya and eventually whip the face of the hypocritical world that lets this holocaust happen without stopping it. I recognize only one person in the world who, if we kidnap him and threaten his life — and I mean a real threat — not 'make-believe' and not a joke — Russia will have to give in and retreat from our land within days. We will free him only when the last of the soldiers have returned to Russia.

"This man has hundreds of millions of believers throughout the world, men who will seethe with rage and murder without discrimination if even a hair on his head or a fingernail of his is damaged."

The fighters stared at him, shocked. No one said a word.

Yagudayev again took a deep lungful of smoke. He was enjoying every moment of this. He carefully enunciated each word.

"Yes — that's right. I mean — the pope."

---

## Prague, 5598 (1838)

R' Isaac Posen, rabbi of the Klausen *Shul*, was a man who did not know the meaning of the word laziness. After morning prayers he would give a Gemara *shiur* in the synagogue. At the end of the *shiur* he would hurry home and eat something quickly in order to stave off his hunger until noon. His wife, the *rebbetzin* Devorah, would prepare a simple sandwich and a cup of hot milk. Five minutes later he would already be hurrying to the "new" *beis midrash* on Parziska Street, where he would learn with a *chavrusah* for five solid hours. At noon he would return home for a light meal. He would rest for a few minutes and quickly return to the *Shul* for learning, *Minchah* and *Ma'ariv* prayers, and classes in Mishnah and Halachah. After his busy day he would return home tired and hungry, but whoever thought R' Isaac would now enjoy a long and satisfying meal was mistaken. A dry cracker baked by the *rebbetzin* and another cup of milk and R' Isaac was immediately flying back to his Gemara. Devorah would often wake up in the morning and find his bedding unwrinkled and unused: he had not slept on them for even a moment.

When she first noticed the phenomenon after their marriage she watched him surreptitiously and discovered that he was sitting and learning until the early hours of the morning. When fatigue overtook him he would lay his head on the desk and nap for less than an hour, waking up and returning to his studies with fervor.

Devorah tried to battle his ascetic life but soon surrendered, seeing that she was confronting a stone wall. When R' Isaac spoke of hunger, the *rebbetzin* knew he was referring to his hunger for learning.

"But how can you exist without food?" she would occasionally implore him. Her husband would answer her, in all seriousness, "My studies satisfy me."

Two days after the Prague community had become a flaming cauldron of burning conflict and hostilities without end, R' Isaac — the man who never left his learning, not even for a minute — closed his Gemara and went out into the fray, driven to action until peace reigned once again.

He was assisted by the students of the Yeshivas Maharal of Prague, who were disturbed to the very core of their being by the wild, irresponsible behavior of so many, who were running back and forth to spread fresh gossip and new slanders: "Getzel has revealed that Leizer stole 2,000 reichsthaler last year from the community." "Leizer Tischler claims that Bank Fernbach is defrauding the government." "Genendel Fernbach has complained that her husband's life has been threatened." "Shmuel Tischler, Leizer's eldest son, disclosed that Getzel got his place as first among the city's notables through fraudulent schemes. That is, he bought the position." "Zekil Fernbach was caught tonight trying to burn down Leizer Tischler's house." "Yoel Tischler organized twenty youths, who stood beneath Getzel Fernbach's window and screamed, 'Thief, get out of Prague,' for three solid hours!"

Klonymous Bendele worked overtime. "I will restore quiet," he yelled at every street-corner gathering. "I am leaving everything and I am going to make peace." Indeed, he raced like a madman from here to there, from there to here, trying with all his being to "bring peace." However, his efforts bore no fruit, with matters becoming more and more entangled and the fires of controversy burning more brightly after his visit to this side or that one.

The situation was intolerable. The tranquil community was drowning in filthy water and no one knew how to pull it to safety — except for R' Isaac and a few students of the Yeshivas Maharal.

Immediately, R' Isaac recognized Bendele for what he was and understood that which only few comprehended, that in truth he was the man behind all the fighting and arguing. Though Klonymous pretended to be a man of peace he was instigating conflict the likes of which had never been seen.

R' Isaac decided to grab the bull by the horns. He went to Getzel's home and spoke there for many long hours. The yeshivah students spoke, at the same time, to Leizer and his son Yoel. Then they switched places:

R' Isaac visited the Tischlers, and the dedicated students used all their persuasive powers on the Fernbachs.

After a day of intensive "peace talks" it appeared that things were taking a turn for the better. Getzel promised that if Leizer would not speak about him or slander him for a period of seven days, he would make peace. Leizer declared that he had never wanted to fight with Getzel and if Getzel so desired, there was no reason to wait even seven minutes. Getzel replied that he would shorten the waiting time to one day.

On Tuesday night R' Isaac summarized the agreement: On Thursday morning the two would pray together in the Meisel Synagogue and after *davening* they would share a *l'chayim* in the presence of R' Todros Miller — and the conflict would be at an end.

It was late at night when R' Isaac finally returned home, allowing himself to eat and drink something after a day of fasting. "The controversy is behind us," he told the *rebbetzin*, taking a deep, relieved breath.

❦

It was on Wednesday morning that the police entered the Prague ghetto.

The surprise was absolute. Not a person knew the police force's intention beforehand.

The policemen went from house to house looking for signs of illegal businesses, financial crimes, and unlicensed manufacturers. It seemed an orderly, house-to-house search, but the more sharp-eyed noticed that the policemen gave a cursory look at most of the houses and paid serious attention only to a specific few. After several hours in which the ghetto was virtually under siege, and even prayer services were not held, the policemen came out with their booty: two illegal currency traders, two smugglers who had arrived just days earlier and were apprehended with their merchandise intact, and the icing on the cake, Reuven Fischgold, bootlegger. Beneath the floor of Reuven's home was a full-fledged homemade distillery for making liquor. Reuven had inherited it from his father, Shmuel Fischgold, who had invested a fortune in its construction.

Naturally Reuven, like his father before him, had not paid any taxes to the government on his illegal income which was considerable. In truth, the liquor factory was an open secret in the ghetto, but every Jewish child from the age of 3 knew it was not something one discussed with or in the presence of strangers.

Pale and downcast Reuven was dragged into the policemen's black carriage. His wife, Chana Fischgold, burst into heartrending sobs and flung herself down in hysterics before the horses' pounding hoofs, screaming, "Don't take my husband from me!"

The policemen ignored her, as they had ignored the families of their other prisoners. The panic was widespread: men shrieked and shouted at the oblivious men in uniform, begging them to have mercy on the unfortunates.

The policemen tore the suspects forcibly from the arms of their loved ones, led them with blows toward the carriage, turned the horses to the side in order not to run over Mrs. Fischgold, lying semiconscious in the street, and left the place. The metallic sound of hoofbeats on cobblestones echoed long after they had departed; no one moved.

Something dreadful had befallen the ghetto of Prague. Something had been shattered. An unspoken trust of many generations' standing had been destroyed.

Someone had informed. A foul-smelling, ugly thing, this informing, with harsh ramifications that would be felt by five families for many years to come. The government of Bohemia, in the throes of difficult economic conditions, looked upon financial crimes with the most deadly seriousness, and the punishment of the five, particularly Reuven Fischgold, could be, at best, thirty years' imprisonment and, at worst, the gallows.

In the minds of the community leaders, one question begged for an answer: Who was this contemptible informer who had handed over his brethren, his flesh and blood, into the merciless hands of the Bohemian justice system?

The Prague ghetto seethed all that day. No one did any work. Men, women, even young children, wandered about, confused and melancholy, their hands thrown up in despair. They gathered on every street like chickens clucking together in sorrow. The topic of conversation everywhere was the same: Who was the informer?

In the afternoon the dire news spread. The informer's identity had been revealed. A group of activists had bribed one of the officers in the Prague police force and he had divulged the name of the informer.

Eliezer Tischler!

———

"But why did he do it?" Bendele, as always first to hear the news, screamed.

The rumormonger did not bother answering the question and disappeared.

Actually, the question of why was no longer relevant. The Jews of Prague felt they could bear no more. Getzel's accusations against Leizer's honesty had not been accepted by these people, who knew Leizer from the day he was born in Prague, and knew that it simply could not be. Leizer was incapable of taking money that did not belong to him. He epitomized the commandment, "Do not steal." But informing was another story entirely. Perhaps he had some personal grudge against the accused; perhaps, because of his own fanatical integrity, he believed that a citizen's first obligation was to give evildoers up to the government and rid the vineyard of its weeds.

That evening a spontaneous demonstration took place next to Leizer Tischler's home. Spontaneous, but huge: hundreds of men stood yelling, "Leizer is an informer!"

Leizer had not yet heard the rumor that linked his name with the betrayal, and did not understand what was occurring near his house. He walked over to the window and looked down. His astonishment was complete. "What? Leizer, an informer?" he screamed. "Yona, what's happened to them?"

A tearful woman jumped out from the rows of people, which had, until now, kept relatively calm, and began to shriek toward the window, "Leizer! You cruel murderer! You've killed my husband!"

It was, of course, Chana Fischgold, and her echoing shouts were the sign that hostilities were about to commence.

The first stone shattered the window and miraculously missed Leizer's head. The second stone hit him squarely in the face. A stream of blood flowed from his nose and he raced inside with a terrified cry.

Faithful Abish Kessler wandered through the house like a caged lion. He begged to be allowed to go out and break the heads of some of the thugs, but Leizer forcibly restrained him, explaining that to go out and face an inflamed mob was an act of suicide.

The chaos grew. "Death to Leizer Tischler!" came the first cry. In the general pandemonium no one heard Klonymous Bendele's voice, but it was he who was responsible for the wildest, most inciteful words.

"Why are we sitting here quietly, we've got to do something! Destroy his house!" The call came from somewhere, and immediately reached its mark. Inflamed young men armed with rocks and sticks broke into the landscaped garden and vented their wrath on the lovely shrubs and blossoming trees. After five minutes of frenzy it was impossible to recognize in the ruins what had once been a luxuriant, fragrant place of beauty.

From the garden the rioters ran to the door of the house. Here they were met with disappointment. The door was a massive one and all their blows and kicks did not budge it. Red-faced youngsters went around the back and began breaking the windows, one after the other.

"Stop that! Now!"

The shout froze all of them.

R' Isaac Posen approached the seething mob. His radiant face stopped even the most brazen of them, who might have considered including him in their wide-swept destruction.

"In the name of Heaven, what is going on here?" he demanded.

A chorus of cries filled the street. "He's an informer, he's a scoundrel!"

"Who?"

Dozens of accusing fingers pointed toward the silent house whose occupants were trembling beneath their beds.

"How do you know?" R' Isaac asked calmly.

Again there was an outburst, which made no impression on the rabbi. "'Two voices cannot be heard,'" he quoted. "If one person speaks, I'll be able to hear."

*Time Bomb* / 165

Klonymous Bendele volunteered. "Like the rabbi, I, too, feel the crowd has been hasty and hasn't heard the other side, but the terrible rumor is that Leizer Tischler informed to the Prague police in exchange for a large sum of money."

No one had yet heard about the matter of this large sum of money, but that was Klonymous's strong point, the ability to merge what had happened with what might have happened in one breath, always managing to stay on the side of piety.

But not before the sharp wits of a scholar such as R' Isaac, who had honed his power of discernment to an astonishing degree.

"Who says so?" he shouted at Klonymous.

"Says what?" asked Bendele, confused.

"That Leizer informed for the sake of money."

Bendele's confidence was shaken. His eyes darted back and forth in all directions. Now he was in trouble: he would have to confess that much of what he had said had originated from his own mind. "He probably did it for the money. Is there another explanation?"

What came next stunned everyone.

The hand of the rabbi and *tzaddik,* which had never been lifted against a fellow Jew, flew through the air and smacked Klonymous squarely and heavily in the face. The loud slap was followed by another, and another.

"You villain!" the rabbi shouted, his face contorted in fierce anger. "Wealthy Leizer needs a few vile pennies that the government gives informers?"

Klonymous was in shock. R' Isaac's heavy black brows arched; his gaze seemed to pierce into Bendele. "If I had the authority I would put you in the stocks that are in the courtyard of the synagogue, I would bind your hands and feet and leave you there for three days, with the congregants spitting on you as they come and go. Do you have anything else to say? You are the worst scandalmonger I have ever seen. Running everywhere, spreading your slander from Reuven to Shimon, from Shimon to Reuven, and having the gall to pretend you are a *tzaddik*. For shame! Who knows how many 'probablies' like this you've spread in your wickedness, and who knows how much of this horrendous scene that I see before me has occurred on your account."

Klonymous shuddered; his Adam's apple twitched uncontrollably. This was the first time that someone was setting the truth before him in such a sharp manner, unmercifully tearing the mask of piety from his face.

He broke out in sobs. "*Yidden,* have mercy! Don't you have mercy on me? You let the rabbi hit me one, two, three times? From the moment I was born I never had a good day in my life. My parents were bitterly poor; I went hungry for days at a time. They married me off to a hard and wicked woman so that every day is cursed. I have no children. I live the life of a dog; I have nothing and no one. When I die there won't even be someone to say *Kaddish* for me."

The best show in town was to be found beneath Leizer's window. The mob was confused and angry. Klonymous's sobs and his confession captured their imagination and their hearts and swiftly weighted the scales in his favor.

R' Isaac Posen himself was not terribly impressed by the wails of Klonymous, who continued to sob quietly. "Perhaps because you are a scandalmonger, G-d has punished you by not giving you children?"

He turned to the agitated crowd with a wave of his hands. "Gentlemen, I ask you to go home. Leave this place. Tomorrow we shall seat a *beis din* of three judges and we will take testimony in order to clarify whose hands were in this and who has done this dreadful thing. Until we've investigated and gotten to the bottom of this, I forbid anyone from calling Leizer any derogatory name."

R' Isaac continued to plead with the crowd for a long while until they finally dispersed. But the damage had been done. Leizer Tischler's name was blackened. Men promised each other through clenched teeth that when Leizer dared show his face in public he would be torn apart like the prey of a wild beast.

But no one tore Leizer apart. There was no need to.

Leizer's heart could not bear the humiliation. The next morning the ghetto was startled by the unexpected and bitter news: Leizer Tischler had died of a stroke at midnight.

*Time Bomb* / 167

# 16

The consternation and shock in the Prague ghetto were enormous. The events had happened so fast; the changes had been so dramatic. It was as if a huge hand had thrown the entire community into a barrel and sent it rolling down a steep mountain. Someone had to stop it before it fell into the abyss.

It had been only a short time since the death of the *Kehillah* head, Shraga Schwartzer, and now the community faced a second tragedy, the passing of Leizer Tischler, also cut off suddenly and at a relatively young age. But what a difference between the two! Shraga had died suddenly, but he had died peacefully. Leizer Tischler had been all but murdered.

The Prague police force actually received an anonymous complaint regarding his death. (Bendele did not always seek to be identified.) Upper echelon officials came to investigate the matter, delaying the funeral procession for some hours until they could assess if there was any truth to the complaint.

As the community waited, the people beat their collective breast, for the sin of persecuting Leizer and causing his untimely death.

Messengers were sent by R' Todros Miller to go from house to house and bring the entire community to the city square for a *teshuvah* gathering. These messengers were the students in the Yeshivas Maharal of Prague. Generally these men were not seen in the streets; they spent the long day devoting themselves to Torah, leaving the *beis midrash* only to eat and sleep. The community regarded them highly: sensitive and fine young men who had learned to curb their desires and lose themselves completely within the labyrinthine intricacies of learning. These young men were "snatched up" when it came time for making a match. The yeshivah trained its students for a variety of tasks in the Torah world and their fame spread throughout all of Europe.

Because of this accustomed admiration, and particularly because of the unusual circumstances, each young man was received like a king, and his words fell upon receptive ears.

In the morning hours, while awaiting the police force's declaration that Leizer's death had, indeed, been of natural causes, the community joined in the mass meeting, taking place in the large square in front of the Altneushul.

The atmosphere was frenzied. Everyone denied his involvement in the violent demonstration that had taken place near Leizer's window. But R' Isaac's eagle eye supplied accurate information. Even in the middle of yesterday's tumultuous events the rabbi had not lost his composure, and he had carefully and swiftly gazed at the faces of all the participants. The next day, when the community members wandered about like shadows, R' Isaac prepared a detailed list of the names of those who had taken part. The results did not surprise him; it was clear, as he had thought, that with the exception of a few spineless men who had been pulled along by the tide, almost all of the participants came from the outcasts of the community, the loafers and idlers. Serious yeshivah students were not there, nor the respected householders. None of them had set foot in the courtyard of the Tischler home on that ill-fated day.

R' Isaac considered publicizing his blacklist by displaying it throughout the ghetto streets, but he was afraid of fanning the flames. The tension was high enough without it. The atmosphere was heavy with incendiary materials, and all it would take was one spark to set it

*Time Bomb* / 169

off and possibly incinerate the entire ghetto, putting an end to its centuries-old glory.

R' Todros Miller, wrapped in a *tallis,* ascended the large wooden platform that some of the yeshivah students had built. Tears dropped onto his grizzled beard.

"*Ashamnu,*" he said, his voice choked with sobs. "We are guilty. The blood of our brothers is on our hands."

"*Ashamnu,*" came the voice of the crowd, a voice like rolling thunder, one great voice that issued forth from thousands of individual mouths.

"*Bagadnu.* We have betrayed." The masses beat their breasts. But the one most responsible for the betrayal was nowhere to be seen: Getzel Fernbach was spending the day hidden in his home.

"*Gazalnu.*" The wind carried the voice of the elderly rabbi upon it. "We have stolen the life of an innocent man."

"*Gazalnu,*" the people answered, conscience stricken.

"*Dibarnu dofi.*" R' Miller's sigh grew into a poignant scream. "We have spoken *lashon hara.*"

Before the others could repeat what he had said, the yeshivah students gestured for them to wait.

"We have spoken *lashon hara,*" said R' Miller, changing the traditional words of the *vidui.* His voice was now a terrible roar. "Now do you understand just what *lashon hara* is? Our Sages, may their memory be blessed, have told us that *lashon hara* kills three. Now Leizer Tischler's dead body lies chilled in his home. Who killed him?"

"Who killed him?" Thousands echoed the question.

"*Lashon hara* killed him!" the rabbi cried. "One man gave an evil report, and someone else volunteered to carry it further. How could you not have thought of what you were doing with your tongues to an honest man, one of the most outstanding individuals in our community?"

And so the confession continued, until it had been completed.

It was an enormous outpouring of repentance: an entire community standing and honestly regretting the sin that had sent Leizer Tischler to the world of truth.

But there are always a few who must destroy the hour of goodwill. When the crowd had dispersed, some men stood about wondering aloud if it was proper to make such a prayer gathering, when there was still no proof that Leizer Tischler was not the informer.

"How can you say that?" their friends attacked them. "You saw what happened; he died."

"Maybe he died because he knew his shame had been discovered," the men reasoned. "Maybe not because he was innocent."

The seed of doubt had been sown.

***

The first order of business was to find an answer to the day's burning question: Had he or hadn't he? Was it Leizer Tischler who had informed, or someone else?

R' Isaac Posen convened a special *beis din* to investigate the matter. He himself served as head of the rabbinic court, which also included the *Rosh Yeshivah* of Yeshivas Maharal of Prague, the brilliant R' Dovid Katzman, and the pious kabbalist R' Asher Lemel Fromme.

The people placed great faith in the composition of the *beis din*. R' Dovid Katzman was one of the best loved figures in the community, a scholar of great stature, possessor of a razor-sharp mind, a firm man who bowed to no one and who spoke the truth no matter how unpleasant, directly and without hesitation. The kabbalist R' Asher Lemel was one of the *tzaddikim* of the *Kehillah*, an image of holiness who spent his days in prayer and mystical pursuits not discussed openly. And the *av beis din* himself was beyond reproach; only a man such as R' Isaac could have appointed himself to the *beis din* without inviting devastating criticism.

During the first session of the *beis din*, which met the very next morning, even before the funeral procession, the question was raised: How shall we find out the truth? R' Asher Lemel suggested a solution brilliant in its simplicity. "Let us send the activist Rivka Flinker to the police station in order to ascertain what really happened."

*Time Bomb* / 171

"Just to hear that idea," R' Isaac said excitedly, "it was worth calling together this special court."

Before the curious of Prague could get a whiff of what was happening, R' Isaac sent his wife, Devorah, to Rivka Flinker's house, to entrust her with this special task.

The mysterious activist had returned exactly five minutes earlier from a journey. Her two horses still stood, snorting in front of her home. A cloud of steam rose from their noses, as they impatiently neighed, awaiting their water and feedbags. Devorah Posen met Rivka as she stood, loosening the reins on the animals and preparing to send them to their stable. Flinker's eyes lit up as Devorah told her the tale: missions such as these were the breath of life to her.

"You'll get double portions later," Rivka assured the horses as she slapped their hindquarters. "We're in a hurry now."

The carriage raced out of the confines of the ghetto just minutes after it had returned there. Lipa the watchman closed the ghetto gate behind her, his head nodding in admiration. Rivka Flinker was even more mysterious than most people realized. She had just returned from the gentile side and here she was, off again. "May she be successful in her mission," his lips whispered in prayer as he gazed at the swiftly flying carriage. "Bring peace and tranquility to the Prague ghetto."

He had no idea that this time her success would bring just the opposite.

⁂

The police investigation did not come up with a firm cause of death for Leizer. "It appears he died of stroke," wrote the doctor on the death certificate.

In the midst of the funeral procession, with thousands walking behind the coffin of the community treasurer, their feelings mixed, and with the sound of the wife and four children's wails in the background, Rivka's carriage returned, speeding wildly. Foam licked the lips of the exhausted horses, who had borne the wagoner's merciless whip. They stopped suddenly at a bend in the road not far from the approaching procession.

Rivka peered out from behind a curtained window. She identified the figure of R' Isaac Posen, walking in front, his head bent.

A child, one of the orphans of the pogrom, passed nearby.

"Child, do you want to do me a favor?"

The youngster lifted his eyes. Rivka handed him a sealed envelope. "Can you give this to R' Posen?"

"My pleasure," the boy answered, skipping away. To help the mysterious activist? He would be the envy of all his friends!

R' Isaac withdrew from the procession for a moment and, his heart thumping, opened the envelope. She should live and be well, when had she found the time to write this letter and seal it with wax? Never mind; what was important was what was within — and his heart told him that it would have fateful consequences.

> "To the honored rabbi,
>
> The chief officer of the Prague police, Yerzei Kaprova, has been good enough to reveal to me the name of the true informer, who gave the policemen details of those breaking the law:
>
> 'The head of the community, the banker Getzel Fernbach.'
>
> These were the exact words told to me by the police chief.
>
> Yerzei added that Getzel Fernbach bribed several police officers to say that it was Leizer Tischler who informed.
>
> I hope my mission has achieved its purpose."

The rabbi's heart beat wildly. The paper shook in his trembling hands. It was now clear: Getzel was truly a low creature, one who did not shy away from the worst acts of treachery. What to do? To reveal or not to reveal the secret? If he would reveal it, expose Getzel's true colors, it would restore Leizer Tischler's lost honor. Though nothing could bring Leizer back to life, his family would be able to hold their heads up once again. On the other hand, Getzel was now uncovered as a dangerous man, a rogue capable of destroying the lives of innocent Jews, of covertly stabbing his best friend in the back. Who knows what else he was capable of doing?

"I have to think about this and discuss it with the members of the *beis din*," he murmured to himself, his eyes looking upon but hardly seeing the crowd of people walking not far away, following the body.

*Time Bomb* / 173

He had not noticed the pair of sharp eyes belonging to a tall quiet figure standing behind his shoulder, hastily reading the activist's letter.

Bendele left the place as he had come, with the silent footsteps of a cat edging toward his prey. In a moment he was lost among the crowd. He fought a brief battle with his bruised conscience, but he could not resist the temptation. This was the greatest scoop that he had ever uncovered! Within a minute the circle around him knew all about the letter that R' Isaac had just received, and the amazing revelation of the identity of the informer. Two minutes later ten additional men had managed to hear the news. The process was now unstoppable. R' Isaac suddenly noticed that all eyes were upon him, the same questioning, fiercely angry look within all of them. Before he could start to wonder why everyone was so furious with him several men approached.

"*Rabbeinu*, we've heard that you received a letter from Rivka Flinker."

R' Isaac maintained his composure. He knew that many eyes had seen the young orphan hand him the envelope. "And what of it?" he asked tranquilly.

Yankele the butcher seemed to roar. "And what of it? He's a rogue, a villain!"

"Who?" Perhaps, somehow, they did not know all.

"Getzel Fernbach!" The infuriated butcher balled his fists as he walked to the front of the crowd. He screamed again. "That foul fiend! He is the informer that gave our brothers into the hands of the government and who slandered poor Leizer and caused his death!"

More and more shouts joined the butcher's. Within minutes the quiet and mournful funeral had turned into a storm of vengeance. Everyone searched for Getzel Fernbach, eager to pay him his due. But the shrewd banker had not shown up at the funeral of the man who, not long before, had been considered his best friend.

R' Isaac deeply regretted the fact that he had not withdrawn further from the funeral when he opened the envelope, thus revealing the secret not meant for curious eyes. But there was nothing to be done; the genie was out of the bottle.

While R' Isaac sat with the other judges and discussed what should be done to Getzel Fernbach, Bendele came to the Tischler home to pay a *shivah* call. He pulled Yoel into a quiet room and told him what Rivka Flinker had written.

"That's what I thought," Yoel nodded, but he said no more. The shock and agonizing emotion had numbed his feelings. The desire for vengeance had not yet taken hold. Bendele tried to get something stronger out of him, but failed. Oddly enough, it was Yoel's older brother Binyamin, a quiet and sensitive man, who reacted. When he saw Klonymous returning to the room with Yoel, he asked his brother what the secret had been. When told what the clerk had revealed, his face burned and he made a choking sound.

"Bendele," he told him bluntly, "listen to me. Take the keys to the community office. Father had important documents there concerning the installation of the seven city notables. I saw them a month ago. My father, may Hashem avenge his blood, kept quiet, but we will not. Go and look for them," he said, handing over a set of brass keys.

Bendele needed nothing more. Keys in hand, he went quickly toward the community office. He worked, as always, swiftly and covertly.

❦

The office was dark. Bendele took a wax candle in his hands and edged his way carefully through the large room. His forehead was covered with cold sweat. If someone in the street would see the light of the candle flickering in the blackness and would be curious enough to investigate, he would be in deep trouble.

The drawers in Leizer Tischler's desk were sealed with a heavy lock, one uncommon in such an insignificant piece of furniture. Leizer had carefully guarded the *Kehillah's* secrets, but Binyamin had equipped Klonymous well.

The drawer held two thick bound ledgers. How to know which contained the treasure? He skimmed one hastily by the yellowish glow of the candle. It was eliminated immediately: long rows of accounts and numbers. There were no sensational revelations about the seven notables here. He moved to the second volume.

"Community of Prague. Community journal. Listing of Jews born and circumcised, girls and boys. Brides and grooms. Dead people, including the engravings on their monuments. Rabbinical matters. Community head. Seven notables…"

He slammed the book shut. The great hunt had begun. This very night he would go through the book, page by page, secret after secret, until he would uncover the lies. No one had exactly said there were lies, but Bendele never waited for people to say such things.

---

The next day, when the mourning brothers were eating breakfast, they heard urgent knocking on the door. Abish Kessler rushed to answer. Bendele was shocked by the appearance of the faithful attendant. It looked as if Abish had been spending all his time weeping; his eyes were red and swollen. In his devastated world nothing remained, not a straw to lean upon, unless one of the sons would have mercy upon him and ask him to remain and take care of the house.

Bendele was clutching the *Kehillah* journal as a diamond merchant would hold a sixty-karat gem. His look of triumph and satisfaction lent him the air of a bridegroom on his wedding day.

"You were right!" he turned merrily to Binyamin, who was holding a piece of bread in his hand. He had not been able to swallow a single bite; mourning had stolen his appetite. "Getzel Fernbach was not supposed to have become head of the community. It was Tuvia Rottenberg. But Getzel coerced both Tuvia and the one who came after him, Shimon Helefant, to give up their places in his favor. Who knows with what that monster threatened them," he added, before Binyamin had managed to digest the import of his words.

The journal went from hand to hand. It was clear that the deceased treasurer had been afraid to open his mouth and reveal what had been going on, but instead had decided to attest to the injustice in the *Kehillah* records. Someone quickly copied Leizer's lists and distributed them throughout the ghetto. After a few hours every bird in the ghetto of Prague knew that Getzel Fernbach's appointment as head of the community was a fiction, a ruse, and that he had bought his position by fraud and strong-arm tactics. Sharp-tongued individuals designated him "leader without followers."

The next step was inevitable: Getzel was shorn of his position through community pressure. Next came a spontaneous action, as the vast majority of the Bank Fernbach clients withdrew their funds as a means of protest. The bank had collapsed even before the Tischlers rose from their week of mourning.

A ban of excommunication was pronounced upon Getzel Fernbach. He was shunned, a pariah. No one would exchange a word with him. The area around his seat in the shul was left vacant. If nine men were waiting, he was not asked to join and form a minyan; they awaited someone else's arrival. Humiliation followed humiliation, each time scorching him anew. He longed for a drop of human contact, and would have been grateful to the poor urchins had they spit in his direction or thrown stones as he passed on the street. But the community treated him as if he did not exist, as if he were nothing but a gust of wind. Only the children stared at him as he passed. Other than that, there was virtually no reaction to him at all.

Getzel believed that the furor would die down. But as time went by, he cracked, realizing that the game was up. There were days when he tried to speak with rabbis, community leaders, anyone who might defend him, but even Klonymous Bendele would not glance in his direction. He had fallen from the summit to the deepest depths.

It was then that he came to the decision to betray his people and convert to Christianity.

In the middle of one dark night he visited the home of Cardinal Matthias Bilcav, the man who, in addition to holding the keys of twenty Prague churches, wielded almost unlimited power.

## 17

*Prague, 5761 (2000)*

Dawn settled upon Prague.

The tale was cut off at the climax of the drama. No further word was told of what had happened afterwards, of what the Cardinal and Getzel Fernbach had discussed, of what had been the final destiny of Prague's Jews.

Shmuel Bilad and Zerach Britman finished reading the journal. A soft blue light crept through the window into the hotel room, bringing tears to their weary eyes.

"What did I tell you? A piece of history," Zerach said in wonderment. "An extraordinary story." He yawned loudly and glanced at his watch. "It's already 5 o'clock in the morning. Do you think you'll get a little sleep?"

Shmuel was disappointed. "A great story that limps out at the end, like one who has his foot cut off. Who is this author, this Avraham Abba Schriftgiss? Why didn't he finish it?"

"A Jew from old Prague, may he rest in peace," Zerach suppressed another yawn. "I'm dying of exhaustion."

"We'll get to bed soon," Shmuel assured him. "Tell me, doesn't it seem strange to you?"

"Why strange?"

"Your brain doesn't seem to function this early in the morning," Shmuel teased. "First of all, it's as if the person who wrote up the tale, didn't exist during these stormy events in Prague. He has no part in the action, doesn't participate at all. Didn't he have any impact on what was going on? Look closely: his descriptions are absolutely realistic, as if he was there during the entire episode. Next, in the story there are many details that one could have learned only from Getzel Fernbach himself. And that brings me to my second question, the trust that a sneaky individual like Getzel put into some anonymous scribe. Doesn't that seem odd? Third, what happened with the matter of the seven city notables? I'm beginning to suspect that Leizer Tischler was a partner in Getzel's scheme of putting together the list in a way that Getzel would be in first place, right after Shraga Schwartzer."

"Many difficulties that R' Akiva Eiger addresses end with the words '*tzarich iyun*,' this warrants investigation. What's the difference? Won't you enjoy breakfast if you don't know the answers?" Zerach fell onto his bed. "I'm half dead from exhaustion. Let me go to bed."

"*Mazal tov*. Before you were completely dead, now you're only half. Looks like you'll be a new man very soon. Then, maybe we'll explore this mystery further."

No answer came from Zerach Britman; he was fast asleep, still wearing his clothing.

Not Shmuel. Silently he slipped out of the room. From there he walked through the lobby and into the street. The mysterious events in Jewish Prague's past disturbed him. He hoped the cool morning air would revitalize his musty brain. If he could only get his hands on a cup of hot coffee! But the hotel dining room would not be open for another two hours.

The morning proved better than any cup of coffee. A ten-minute walk, along with several deep gulps of the clear air, effectively cleared his weary brain.

Avraham Abba — wasn't that the name of Getzel Fernbach's oldest son? The quiet one, who liked to stand on the side and write. There, the first veil was removed. It was possible that this author "Avraham Abba" was no less than Getzel Fernbach's son; hence, his knowledge of everything that went on behind the scenes. "Schriftgiss." *Schrift* meant writing; *giss*, to pour. The root of this family name which Getzel's son adopted as his pen name was obviously the profession of typesetter in a print shop, the man who took molten lead and poured it, casting it into typeset letters. Perhaps Avraham Abba was nicknaming himself: he poured the letters into his writings. At the same time he had suppressed his own part in the stirring events that had rocked Prague's small community one hundred and sixty years earlier.

Shmuel felt a sudden wave of dizziness pass over him. A picture of abandoned children flew through his memory: a Katamon street, a building that no longer existed. In the courtyard grew a large fig tree that provided succulent fruits every summer. The children of the neighborhood loved to congregate beneath that tree. To treat their calloused hands they would break off a young branch near the blossoming fruit and squeeze the white sap onto them; the youngsters claimed it helped. The family did not particularly appreciate the milling crowd and the noise in their yard, beneath the house's windows, and on Shabbos afternoons they would yell at the revelers.

The family's name was Fernbach.

---

Could there be some kind of link between the legendary Fernbach of Avraham Abba's tale, and the Fernbach family living in the Katamon neighborhood of Jerusalem forty years ago? The family, he recalled, was not well liked in the area. But perhaps that was just the memory of a young boy which recalled only the shouting and fights.

Why had he, Avraham Abba, decided to end the tale at this point, at the climax of the tension?

The ancient tome was in Shmuel's hand and he stared at it again.

Actually, it was not really a book at all. A bundle of papers, handwritten, in unusual Rashi-script letters, bound together in aged leather.

Perhaps a page or two was missing; perhaps something had been lost. Impossible that someone capable of writing such a fascinating story would chop off the ending, just as it neared the climax, without any explanation. It was absurd, silly. It was as if someone had taken the book and clumsily cut parts away with a pair of dull scissors.

Perhaps that was exactly what had happened.

Here in the middle of the street, sitting on a bench beneath a tree, the cars of the early risers whizzing past him, he could not properly examine the book. He returned to his room and placed it beneath a powerful reading lamp.

He burst out laughing. No need for the bright halogen bulb; a simple fluorescent would suffice. It was primitive, almost brutal. Someone had crudely ripped out the book's last pages, not even bothering to keep his actions hidden. The threads binding it together had been cut and the last pages torn out. Afterwards someone had tied the threads back together with a shaky hand, the knots unprofessional. He and Zerach Britman had missed it only because of their fatigue and half-closed eyes.

So where was the ending?

---

Zerach Britman took hold of himself and after a short nap somehow, wondrously, managed to wake up. Not exactly refreshed and not exactly energetic, but awake, and ready to travel to the mikveh of the Ba'al Shem Tov, in the mountains near Pilsen. This was the city known for the breweries that manufactured the famed Pilsen beer, as well as the Skoda car factory. The mikveh was not far from the city proper; it was a narrow and deep hole in the ground, built over a spring.

The water was very cold. The watchman offered to warm up the water in honor of the tour group, and he lowered a heating element that looked like a huge electric fork into it. After the instant heating an interesting phenomenon occurred. The top layer of the water was heated to boiling, the bottom remained freezing.

"That reminds me of the student's answer to the question of what is average," Zerach laughed. "He answered: 'When your head is in an oven and your feet in ice, the stomach is the average.' But the main thing is that we've immersed in the Besht's mikveh," he comforted himself as they walked toward the bus that would take them back to Prague. "It is known that there are special healing powers connected with this mikveh, for children and all manner of salvations."

Shmuel was impatiently awaiting his arrival at the hotel. He all but fell upon him in the lobby. "Zerach, we've got to get going."

"I have been going," Zerach said, flopping into a comfortable armchair. "What's new?"

Shmuel scanned the lobby. The other tourists who had returned with Zerach had hastened to the dining room to eat something after the long trip. The area was quiet and empty. He quickly told Zerach about the missing pages.

"This is getting exciting," Zerach said. "Where do you think the ending is?"

"My question exactly," Shmuel said.

Zerach's eyes lit upon a loud drunken group of tourists who were passing by. He shuddered in distaste, and focused his look and attention back to Shmuel. "When Calev ben Yefuneh went to spy out the land, he prayed at the graves of his ancestors in Hebron. This teaches us that when you are in need of guidance, you pray at ancestral tombs. We've been here in Prague for several days already and haven't yet gone to the ancient cemetery, to pray at the gravesite of the Maharal of Prague and the other *tzaddikim* buried there. Let's start there."

---

Stary zidovsky hrbitov, the ancient Jewish cemetery of Prague, is the oldest cemetery in all of Europe, preserved more than two centuries after it was no longer in active use. Twelve thousand headstones in varying degrees of decrepitude stand side by side. Beneath them lie over 100,000 graves, buried in layers due to space constraints. Many of the headstones bear engravings and symbols which indicated the deceased's position: a bunch of grapes, a jug of oil, a fish or a dove holding an olive branch in its beak can be found, symbolizing, apparently, the profession that the deceased followed in his lifetime. *Kohanim* have hands on their stones, their fingers outstretched in blessing; a man named Tzvi might have the engraving of a deer, a mighty lion appears on the stone of a person named Aryeh, and a ferocious bear reminds one of the dear departed Dov.

The most ancient headstone of all, today replaced by a faithful copy, is that of R' Avigdor Kara, rabbi of Prague and court poet to King Vaclav IV, the man who saw Prague's despair and the massacre of its Jews during the brutal pogroms that took place more than 600 years ago. It was R' Avigdor who composed the lament, *"Es Kol Ha'tilaeh"* — "All the tribulations," which was customarily recited in Prague during the *Mussaf* prayers of Yom Kippur.

Shmuel and Zerach stood in fervent prayer next to the tomb of the Maharal of Prague: a wide headstone was topped by a large knob upon which were inscribed small circles and the famed image of a lion, together with the praises which the Jews of Prague offered to their beloved rabbi.

The two Israeli tourists were not alone. Groups of people from all over the world come to this place, considered one of the main tourist sites of the Czech Republic. The gentiles, too, esteem this giant of the spirit, but only the Jews understand his erudition, which encompasses the entire world of man. Shmuel and Zerach pondered profound thoughts culled from the Maharal's writings, feeling like students who have come to their teacher's grave.

From there they turned to the burial site of R' Shlomo Efraim of Lenchitz, author of the *"Kli Yakar."* Zerach felt deeply moved. "I learn his work every Friday night; I never believed I would stand by his resting place."

He lost himself in prayer. Praying at a great man's burial site affords a person a special feeling, particularly when one feels a deep spiritual connection with the *gadol* buried nearby; it is almost as if one is bonding and uniting with someone close.

In an unobtrusive corner they noticed a neglected headstone that silently proclaimed that here lay an evil man, an apostate, buried on the fringes of the cemetery. They could not make out the name, but it reminded them of the manuscript they had just read. Shmuel felt a burning desire to uncover exactly what had happened to Getzel Fernbach after his visit to Cardinal Matthias Bilcav. And then it came to him: the Cardinal would be their key to uncovering the truth.

They spent half a day burrowing through the Prague city archives with the help of a round-faced municipal employee by the name of Sizhur Bayzhka, who spoke a passable English. They found no mention of the name Matthias Bilcav among the lists of prominent clergymen, which was odd: a man of that position would not have been an anonymous figure. One got the definite impression that someone was not proud of Bilcav and had managed to expunge any reference of him from the records.

Only after a strenuous search did they find a single reference; one "Matthias Yohann Bilcav" was mentioned in a list of citizens. Next to his name was the single dry description, Archbishop — as if he were a baker or dairyman. At least they now knew his place of residence; adjacent to Prague's old city hall.

"Let's go there now," Shmuel said, excited. "That's where the dog lies buried. Someone has tried to sweep Prague's head priest under a rug. I assume he had a good reason."

Sizhur Bayzhka, the municipal clerk, offered his services as translator and guide. They jumped at the proposal.

Evening had already fallen upon Prague when they arrived at the Old Town. In the heart of the tourist-filled area still stood some inhabited homes. They walked through the teeming streets following Bayzhka.

A brass railing on the sidewalk marked the meridian that cut through Prague. "In this spot," Sizhur pointed to it, "stood a 17th-century monument marking the Hapsburg dynasty's victory in the Thirty Years War. The shadow of the monument fell across the railing at exactly noon every day."

Shmuel and Zerach concealed their smiles. Their tour guide was certainly trying to justify his existence. They only hoped he would be as helpful when it came to uncovering Matthias Bilcav's past.

They reached a large, neglected courtyard. Even the statues inside had all but disintegrated to dust. A dirty path led them to a house which had been mercilessly stricken by the ravages of time. A child's flattened nose and dull eyes looked out at them from behind the dusty window set in a rusted iron door.

An old man in a much-patched purple sweater opened the door. His bleary, moist eyes brightened immediately when he noticed the $20 bill that Zerach was clutching.

Sizhur murmured something in Czech.

The old man affirmed that he was aware that a famous person, the cardinal of the holy church, had once dwelled there. "But there is nothing left from that era," their translator passed on the man's disappointing news.

Shmuel felt a pang of bitterness. Once again they had lost the trail.

He suddenly had an idea. "Maybe there's a storage area here, or an attic?" he asked the translator.

Sizhur again muttered some words from beneath his mustache. In place of an answer the old man's greedy gaze fixed firmly upon Zerach's hand.

"He wants something for the information that he will provide," Sizhur said excitedly. "It's worth it."

Another green bill, this time worth $10, exchanged hands. The old man gestured to them to enter the house, leading them on shaky legs. His last remaining gray hairs stood out on the side of his head, making a kind of crown around his bald pate.

A spiral staircase in a corner of a guest room led to a dusty attic.

Shmuel and Zerach climbed up. "If my wife had told me before I left that I would be going up to explore some *'boidem'* belonging to a mysterious priest I would have thought she'd gone mad," Zerach breathed as he reached the top of the stairs. "Look what you're dragging me into," he added, with just a touch of irony.

"Zerach, with all your complaints, one would guess you weren't enjoying yourself."

At the top they found an old library, its books covered with dust and spider webs laden with the remains of dead flies. The old man brought them a kerosene lamp that seemed just as ancient as the rest of the place. They perused the books for more than an hour, Sizhur helping them in their search of some evidence, some discovery, but they came up with nothing. The shelves were laden with Christian works and dusty, valueless volumes.

As they were on the verge of giving up, Sizhur's eyes spotted the top shelf. "Don't despair," he consoled them. "We haven't checked here yet."

He gave a shout of surprise and pointed to one of the books. "I have this book in my home as well. 'Studying with Students.' It's a Latin manual dating about two centuries ago, for beginning teachers. My father inherited it from my grandfather, who was a well-known teacher. I wonder if it's the same one."

There was no ladder in the ancient library, and the sole chair in the room had seen better days. They were certain it would disintegrate into a pile of firewood the moment one of them attempted to stand on it. Shmuel and Zerach offered to make their hands into a ladder and boost the diligent translator.

Sizhur pulled down the book and skimmed through it. In the middle he blinked, as he stared at an unexpected discovery.

"These pages don't belong here," he whispered in carefully controlled excitement. "They're handwritten, and not in Latin."

Zerach stared at the papers and gave a shout of surprise.

"Here they are, the missing pages. These are Hebrew letters, in ancient Yiddish-German, just like the others that we found." He picked up the book. "Look, they were crudely sewn in. Anyone could see it."

"What do they say?" Shmuel demanded. "Read them quick, before I explode!"

Zerach looked at Sizhur. "Do you have the patience?"

"Whatever it takes," the translator said courteously.

Zerach Britman began to read.

# 18

*Prague, 5698 (1838)*

Cardinal Matthias Bilcav looked searchingly at Getzel Fernbach. "As a Christian, your contribution to Christianity will be questionable. But as a Jew, you can be very helpful."

Getzel's slyness was no less than that of Matthias, but now he looked at the Cardinal, dumbfounded.

"Are you saying that I should stay a Jew, here in this quarter of Prague, put on *tefillin* and keep Shabbos and *kashrus?* Impossible."

Matthias's thick lips widened into a crafty smile that gave an unpleasant cast to his face. "Rabbi Fernbach," he said mockingly. "Maybe you will first hear me out and then ask your questions."

Getzel subsided, defeated. His renowned stubborn rigidity, which he had used so effectively against his fellow Jews, melted like wax before this man of the Church. He wore a look of obsequiousness and flattery.

"I'm all ears, Cardinal."

Bilcav's eyes glittered like hot coals. "You return to the ghetto now as if nothing has happened. As far as I am concerned, you can put on *tefillin* morning and night and keep your Shabbos on Friday too. Or you can eat pork six times a day and make the sign of the cross every hour. It's all the same to me. Whatever you decide: If you do what I'm asking you, you will have earned your place in Paradise."

He suddenly walked over to the windows and pulled the heavy drapes shut.

"Now we're safe from curious eyes," he told Getzel. "The house of a Cardinal such as myself is often the focal point for people who are bored or obsessed. There is no lack of madmen in Prague, as you certainly know."

Getzel burned with curiosity; he had no patience for this. He coughed politely.

"I'm getting to the point," Matthias understood the hint. "As head of the Prague community you know many of the Jewish secrets, true?"

Getzel nodded. "True."

"You know all the community's weak points. For example, the men of weak personality who would, for monetary gain, agree to convert. Orphans, for instance —" He gave the bankrupt financier a look fraught with meaning. "I believe that there are a large number of orphans wandering around the Prague ghetto."

Getzel felt a sudden stab of conscience. "Have you murdered and also inherited?" he wanted to ask the Cardinal. "You killed their parents and now you will lure their children into your religion?" But no: After all the suffering and humiliation that he had undergone, not even a shred of identification with or mercy for his people remained. He heard himself say weakly, ashamed of his words, "I have a detailed list of every boy and girl in the ghetto."

"Excellent," Matthias jumped up in delight. "You give me that list, and a few others. All the impoverished, the unfortunates, etcetera"—

Getzel, too, rose from his chair. Matthias's steely gaze seemed to push him back down into his place. "Don't get up; I'm not finished. Simultaneously with your handing me the lists, you will sow controversy and conflict in the ghetto. As head of the community you know who is fighting with whom, who hates the other. In short, you ignite the ghetto like a huge bonfire; whoever doesn't make for the secure haven of Christianity will find himself sunk in the seas of strife."

The Cardinal walked out of the room and returned a few minutes later, a small metal box in his hand. "There's a tidy sum here: 5,000 reichsthaler. That will help you get back on your feet financially. You won't be humbled again. In the next few days 100,000 reichsthaler will be deposited into your bank, to restore your financial credibility. The Church is not lacking in funds. But the money is given on a condition, you understand: If the cow doesn't give the milk, the cash is withdrawn immediately."

"The cow wants very much to give the milk," Getzel all but shouted. "But there's one problem. The plan is brilliant but it won't work."

"Why not?"

"I've been excommunicated. No one will speak with me." He gave a bitter laugh. "Furnishing you lists? Easy. But to sow discord and conflict — it can't be done."

Matthias sank deep in thought. He paced up and down the room. *Everyone has their own way of concentrating,* Getzel thought with a flash of irony. *Now me, I like to eat something tasty in order to think.*

"Tell me," Matthias's voice broke the silence. "Isn't there someone in your community who's always complaining? Someone who likes a good fight, a gossip who carries tales between one person and the next, lighting fires between them? There's no society that doesn't have a few characters like that."

Getzel again jumped out of his seat. "Of course," he said excitedly. "We have Bendele."

Bilcav's stern glare followed him. "What kind of name is that?"

Getzel laughed. "I'm so used to calling him that, that I almost forgot it was a nickname. 'Bendele' means a shoelace. That's what we call Klonymous the clerk, a poor Jew, thin as a shoelace. The description of who you're seeking fits him like a glove. But Bendele is my sworn enemy; he played a large role in my downfall. And they say he has repented since Leizer Tischler's death."

"If Bendele is the right man you'll have to make up with him so that you can work together." The Cardinal was firm. "I'll give you another

*Time Bomb* / 189

1,000 reichsthaler to bribe him. Don't tell him who you're working for. Let him think that you want to sow a bit of discord, here and there, in order to avenge yourself on two or three cronies who betrayed you. He must not know your ultimate goal."

Getzel returned to the ghetto before dawn by the same route he had used earlier, careful to avoid the gate. Lipa the watchman did not have to know of his nocturnal comings and goings. Getzel knew secret paths that led from the courtyard of an abandoned building out of the ghetto walls. When he lay down on his bed in the early morning hours he slept a sweet, satisfied sleep. Bank Fernbach would recover, Getzel Fernbach would recover, and the community would go up in flames. No promptings of conscience disturbed his slumber, which lasted well past the time for the morning *Krias Shema* and prayers.

※

Klonymous the clerk was not fundamentally a wicked man. The opposite was true: If a poor man asked for charity, for example, Klonymous's compassion would be aroused and he would immediately hand him several coins. Was there a contradiction between that and the fact that he often commented publicly on the pauper's crooked teeth, his runny nose, his inarticulate speech? He poured coins into the unfortunate's hand while at the same time making faces at him behind his back, mocking him openly before others standing nearby.

This was the man; this was his nature. Klonymous was certain that this trait, too, brought blessing to the *Kehillah*; after all, was it a small thing to make people happy? True, today the people were happy laughing at Reuven courtesy of Bendele the mimic, while tomorrow the people — Reuven among them — would be laughing at Shimon.

In the last few weeks, since Bendele had unveiled his incomparable scoop, revealing the identity of the unknown informer and exploding the story publicly, the entire community had undergone an internal purification. Leizer was buried, Getzel excommunicated, his bank undergoing financial tribulations, but soon life went on. The community was at peace with itself.

But not Bendele.

The temptation to act as prankster and destroyer which was deeply engrained within him now knew hard times. He felt like someone whose life no longer had meaning. Everything was a bore. Everyone loved everyone else, everyone was pious and pleasant and conciliatory — and dull to the point of nausea. Sweetness and light was everywhere; it could make you throw up. Who was there to show men their true faces, to watch for corruption and reveal it to all? R' Isaac Posen's public rebuke — and the slaps on the face that accompanied it — had, according to Bendele, been off the mark. Bendele was convinced that every community needed two or three men like himself. He was the public watchdog, the man who held a mirror up to society's hideous face and told it: this is you! He was the man who would not allow people to wallow in the mire of self-satisfaction. He absolutely believed that he was like one of the prophets of yore, bent on carrying out their task.

In the climate of sanctity and atonement that overcame the community, when normal days took on the cast of Yom Kippur, Bendele was forced to assume the role of an obedient and praiseworthy son in the huge family of penitents that was Prague. But his eyes still darted back and forth as they always had, looking for the unusual, the potential target. His finely honed hunter's sense lay perpetually in wait, searching for human weakness, both small and large — particularly large. He longed for a good fight, for a controversy that would wake up the ghetto and take it out of this repugnantly mundane daily routine.

Nothing happened. Bendele, as always, scrupulously watched all that went on, anything slightly unusual or strange; he noted the absurd, the eccentric, the grotesque, storing each detail clearly in his powerful memory. But everyone was pious, holy, pure; when he asked, with a small smile, if the entire community of Prague had, like Eliyahu, gone up alive to heaven, he was answered with angry looks and thin-lipped replies. Bendele was certain that, like him, everyone was putting on an act, waiting for some change in the situation, for the tension to ease, but no one dared break through the suffocating siege of piety. *Tzaddikim,* all of Prague!

He would have to wait for a miracle.

The miracle happened.

For a few uncomfortable days Getzel wrestled with a difficult dilemma. In the home of the top church official had behaved like a frightened lamb; he had arrived waving the white flag of surrender. And he had not done too badly: that suggestion of Matthias's was, to be honest, fairly good and the main thing was — the money!

From his youth Getzel had longed for money. He knew its power, knew what could be done with it. In these long weeks when he had experienced what it was like to be without it, he had almost given up on living. Getzel knew that without money — a lot of money — there was no life.

But when his fury and desire for vengeance had abated somewhat and with a level head he assessed Bilcav's suggestion, his dormant hatred for that accursed Klonymous was roused. He was the one most responsible for what had happened. After all that the fool had done to him, he, Getzel, was to call him to his home, be polite to him, give him money?

Several days passed like shadows. Finally, he came to a conclusion: He must bring Genendel and Zekil into the picture, let them know all that had happened.

In the midst of a dinner replete with meat roasted in fragrant sauces and baked with potatoes, served with bowls of tempting hot soup, Getzel shared with them the content of his discussion with Matthias Bilcav, emphasizing, particularly, the financial aspects of the affair.

The two had identical reactions. "Excellent, very good." Their faces shone.

Getzel knew that the roots of faith of both his wife and son were not very solid, but he had not suspected just how weak they were. More than anything they were driven by a consuming hatred for the Prague community that had cast them out. Just as Getzel did, Genendel and Zekil wanted to see the entire *Kehillah* drowning in the waters of the Vltava River.

Zekil crowed with triumph. "The bank is saved!" His dreams of inheritance, that seemed to be vanishing, would not be lost. Bank Fernbach would proudly continue, even after his father's demise. Zekil Fernbach had inherited his father's acute financial sense together with his quick wits. "You'll go far, Zekeleh," Getzel used to tell him.

"But I have a problem," Getzel continued through a mouth full of chicken. "The Cardinal suggests — suggests, no, he demands — that I take Klonymous Bendele as partner. I loathe the man. I tell you, if Bendele had not opened his mouth, R' Isaac Posen would never have publicized that letter of Rivka Flinker's; he's too afraid of me. I know him. He would have called together his *beis din*, discussed the situation, and they would have unanimously voted to hush up the affair and bury the information. If that hag Flinker hadn't stuck her nose in the business, we wouldn't be in this mess at all."

"Feitel, bring the wine!" Zekil roared. He licked off the last vestiges of fat from his lips. "Father, the situation isn't so bad. I have a great idea, how we can kill two birds with one stone — to pull Klonymous in for our own purposes, in order to turn the community's life into complete disarray, and, at the same time, to avenge ourselves against Klonymous."

"How?" The black slits lit up.

Between loud gulps of fine wine Zekil outlined his plan. His father listened intently.

The color returned to Getzel's cheeks.

⁂

Half an hour later an unexpected visitor turned up at Bendele's house.

"Zekil Fernbach?" Bendele called out, shocked. "I don't believe it."

Zekil pointed a finger at him. "Quiet, make sure the neighbors don't hear you."

"Come in," Klonymous said courteously. Zekil refused, explaining that his father wanted to meet with Bendele with the utmost urgency, on a matter that would be of great benefit to the clerk.

"You're not setting a trap for me?" Bendele asked, his suspicions aroused. "Your father isn't numbered among my many fans. To tell the truth, he has no reason to be."

"My father is above all that," Zekil explained. "Klonymous, you won't lose out."

Klonymous thought for a short moment and came to a decision: He would go to the banker's house.

Getzel received him with obvious joy. "Klonymous, my friend," he hugged him, the shoelace folding into the fat pillow half his height. "You can't imagine how much I've missed you."

"You missed me?" Bendele cautiously untwined himself from the embrace and laughed, not bothering to hide his scorn.

Getzel gave the patient smile of a man who had risen above human frailty. "I know exactly what you did to me during Leizer Tischler's funeral, but I've forgiven you. I've thought about you quite a bit these past few days, when I was hardly able to step out of my house. Don't you think that our honored community is mired in a black swamp?"

"My thoughts exactly, Getzel," Bendele said, his eyes still suspicious. "Since Leizer's death the people have stopped smiling. One would imagine that all of them had conspired to kill him. There's a limit to self-mortification; enough of all this piety."

"*Nu*, so don't you think we should put a little life into the community?" Getzel chortled. "Make merry, put a smile on people's faces?"

"How?" Bendele demanded.

Getzel laughed. "You're a good actor, Bendele, and suddenly you don't know how to make people laugh? You have to teach the rooster to crow? You know better than anyone in Prague how to make people happy. Besides," he said, pulling out some bills, "I want to make your life a little easier."

Bendele looked at him, wide eyed. Always he had faced rebuke and lengthy harangues because of his behavior. This was the first time that someone was actually offering to pay him to give in to his nasty and low instincts.

"What's this?" he demanded.

Getzel tried to soften the hard edges of bribery. "In my eyes you are an artist. If you had grown up among the gentiles you would have been an actor and the world would have recognized your artistry and rare talent. To your misfortune you were born in the benighted Prague ghetto, among men of small vision. You should be remunerated for your talents."

Klonymous's long-buried conscience tried valiantly to surface and remind him who these benighted men were, men prepared to take off their last garment to hand it to a pauper; to think of those enlightened gentiles in the Christian quarters of Prague and how they dealt with the poor and sick. He had, with his own eyes, seen gentile youths kick a crippled beggar while mocking his infirmity. These were the theatergoers, those civilized ones not born beneath the dark ghetto skies.

Again, as always, living temptation overpowered an almost-dead conscience; his fingers hungrily grabbed the bills from Getzel's hand.

"What do you want me to do?"

"Make things a bit merrier." Getzel preferred to avoid explanations; this way, no one could blame him for anything.

"You want the full menu?"

"Whatever you think best." Getzel yawned. He was not interested in the professional tactics of the full-time slanderer. "The main thing is that Prague should smile again."

---

Prague smiled again. The smile was so wide it tore its face apart.

Fattened with 500 reichsthaler, Bendele set off to work.

He did not rush; he weighed each step with the calm cunning of a snake. He had always known people's weak points, their anger, their ancient enmities. He knew who wanted revenge upon whom, who was brooding over another's slights. Who had been offended and who had carried out the insult, who was embarrassed and who had humiliated him. Now was the time to tap this enormous reservoir of knowledge. In an almost indiscernible way he began to incite, to sow arguments, to strike covertly with the assistance of his most beloved weapon, the anonymous flyer.

Knowing he was under suspicion he scrupulously took care that his actions were not observed, so that no one could point a finger of guilt at him.

In addition to the controversies that seemed to crop up in every corner, the Prague ghetto suffered several stunning blows. Three of the pogrom orphans suddenly disappeared. After several anxious days the news surfaced: They had converted to Christianity in a lavish ceremony in the St. Vitus church in the Prague Castle. A dreadful fear fell upon the community, but because of the infighting and hostility they could not unite against the outside enemy. The Church struck again and again, without mercy. Within a year ten children had converted. No one knew how it could happen but four entire families, from the unfortunates of Prague Jewry, also quietly took the Christian vows. They left the ghetto, converted, and were whisked away to some unknown place.

The causes, like the vanished Jews, remained cloaked in terrifying mystery. The Jews of Prague walked about horrified in the face of this enemy that struck so quietly.

Cardinal Bilcav, Getzel, and Bendele were serene. Bendele sowed conflict without knowing a thing of what the Cardinal and Getzel were up to. Getzel supplied the lists, and church officials brought their poison on moonless nights to the homes of the poor and weak.

Unfortunately, just at that time R' Isaac Posen left Prague for an extended stay in Poland and that other pillar of the community, the venerable R' Todros Miller, died of a broken heart, leaving his flock without a shepherd.

Cardinal Bilcav laughed as he had never laughed before. He had Getzel by the throat and, through Getzel, Bendele too. Occasionally he would send them a bit of money, rationed in small portions. Too much money, he knew, would free the two from the chains that bound them.

Within two years the Prague ghetto was on the verge of collapse. Outside enemies and a fifth column within had joined together to destroy their lives and had succeeded almost completely. In the year 1840, two years after Cardinal Bilcav's venomous teeth had sunk into the ghetto, the strong core was all but shattered. The Jews of Prague began to emigrate to western Europe and America and the ghetto remained almost deserted.

---

Getzel Fernbach's vengeance was almost complete. His son Zekil had received his "spiritual legacy," whose content was concise and clear: Destroy the Jews from within. Never go out, work always as a fifth column. Zekil knew that he would pass on this legacy to his own children, for one simple reason: The Church saw to it that it kept the rope in its hands, slipping him money in carefully controlled portions. Bank Fernbach must survive, for Zekil in his time and his children after him. They would inherit the bank, they would inherit, too, the shadow of their big brother. In order to ensure that the Church would not pull out its deposits — thus destroying the bank — the Fernbach family must follow the orders of Cardinal Bilcav and his fellow priests. That included marriage to a non-Jew: Zekil Fernbach was one of the first to assimilate in Prague, and his children no longer were halachically Jewish. But still they remained, always, "insiders." After all, the one who has the money is the one whose voice is heard. His wife seemed strange, and rumors claimed that she was a gentile, but no one really knew.

But the banker's vengeance was not yet perfect. Bendele still went unpunished.

---

Klonymous the clerk merited a second chance at life. His conscience, dead and buried for so many years, awoke from the depths of the grave and began to stir. Until now he had never known the agony of an uneasy conscience as he did now, looking at the outcome of his unruly behavior. In front of his eyes families were destroyed, men held their swords in each other's throats — and in every conflict you could find his meddling hands.

When he finally understood what he had wrought, it was too late. Flames licked the ghetto, flames of hatred and slander, of anger and enmity. He longed to turn the wheels back but the carriage was out of control. To enrage him further, Zekil Fernbach now revealed the truth: "You were working for the Church. Cardinal Matthias Bilcav is grateful to you for your assistance." The knowledge almost destroyed him.

Prague was left with small groups of besieged Jews who somehow managed under the worst conditions.

And one day as Bendele walked on the narrow street, his eyes weary with pain and regret, he did not notice a heavily laden cart drawn by two large Belgian horses approaching him. The horses started when confronted with the thin figure; they rose up on their powerful legs and came down upon him with their heavy hooves. Bendele tried to jump away but he was already trapped in the kicking legs. The horses stamped down upon him with the weight of their thousands of pounds. Panic stricken, they raced around in circles, while the heavy load in the carriage began to fall out, burying Bendele alive. Christian passersby pulled him out, his body crushed and broken. No one could understand how he had not died on the spot.

For two days Bendele hovered between life and death in a large Christian hospital in the city, far from the ghetto which he had helped destroy. In the rare moments when he was not screaming like a madman from the pain he managed to confess within the depths of his heart: "It was G-d's Hand that has struck me. G-d is righteous and I have rebelled. May my death be my atonement."

Two huge golden crosses looked down upon his bed. On the wall across from him hung a sculpture of one being crucified, placed there by a merciful nurse for the benefit of the unfortunate Jew's immortal soul. As he stared at the images Bendele cried in despair: "Hashem, You have punished me measure for measure. I betrayed my people and helped their enemies so it was decreed that I die in this place."

And indeed his soul departed in the shadow of those two huge crosses, without the comfort of a single Jew. No *Krias Shema*, none of the verses said at such a time.

Again it was that mysterious woman, Rivka Flinker, who somehow learned of Bendele's death and used all her connections to see to it that he was not buried in the Christian cemetery with a cross inscribed on his headstone. After great effort she managed to get his mangled body to the *chevrah kaddisha* of Prague. Once again the Jews of Prague showed their nobility of soul: They swallowed their anger against the slanderer and gave him a decent burial, though many had suffered from his tongue. His death served as a searing reminder and lesson to the embattled population: This is the punishment of one who always carries tales.

Getzel continued to wear his crafty smile. Those Belgian horses had not just happened to be in the area where Bendele was walking. His vengeance was now complete. He had another reason to smile as well:

His descendants would continue his work of revenge years after his bones had turned to dust.

*How can I, the author, know who was behind Getzel, who planned and who executed the evil scheme?*

*Getzel himself told me.*

*And did you think that to his good friend, Avraham Abba Schriftgiss, he wouldn't tell?*

# 19

*Prague, 5761 (2000)*

"So that's it: Getzel Fernbach sold his soul to the devil and volunteered to be a fifth columnist," Shmuel said, tight lipped.

"'Your destroyers shall come from out of you'," Zerach finished. "Look, there's another paper here."

This last page had been folded by some unknown hand. As he opened it Zerach could not keep back a cry of shock. The folded paper was almost completely covered with a stain. A brown stain, ominous: blood. There was one big blot and several small splashes. The page seemed to be screaming of some horrifying violent act that had taken place in its vicinity.

Zerach read the few lines: "I, Avraham Abba Fernbach, who calls himself by the name Schriftgiss, testify with my own signature that all that I have written on the previous pages, all is absolutely true. I know that my father, Getzel Fernbach, does not approve of my actions and has called me several times a 'traitor to your father,' but I cannot be false to myself. After he went to Cardinal Bilcav to convert I sat *shivah* for him; he is no longer my father and I am no longer his son. I hate him with a deep and abiding hatred, as stated in the verse, 'Those who hate You, Hashem, I hate.' From my youth I loathed his greed and was more interested in the wisdom hidden in our Torah and the words of our Sages. I wrote an entire work entitled *'Shem Nirdaf'* — *'Synonyms,'* in which I worked very hard to clarify the synonyms used in Tanach. If you read it you will understand, for instance, why the lion is called by several names: *aryeh, layish, shachal,* and *k'fir*; or what is the difference between the words *sason, simchah, gilah, rinah, ditzah,* and *chedvah,* all meaning joy; or why there are so many words denoting fear: *pachad, eimah, charadah, magor, morah, yir'ah*. Many of my explanations are based on the writings of our great teacher, R' Loewe of Prague. I can explain almost all of the synonyms. But now the word 'hatred' has, in my life, a new synonym: my brother Zekil.

"My brother Zekil loves money just as I love the pen. It was my brother Zekil who signed on a paper obligating himself to spy on our community on behalf of the Church and Cardinal Matthias Bilcav. I saw his signature and I wept. Zekil is prepared to sell his nation to its worst enemies, those who seek to devour us alive, in exchange for money. When I cried and begged him not to do this terrible thing he assured me that he would teach his children, too, to be like him: Jews outwardly, apostates in secret. 'I will have two worlds,' he mocked. 'The Church will take care of my finances all my life and after my death the Cardinal will see to it that I have entry into Paradise. You will not have even one world: a pauper all your days, and after death you will go to Hell for not having been smart enough to join the religion of love.'

"In the near future I will go to R' Isaac Posen and tell him everything about my father and my brother Zek —"

The final word was unfinished. Someone, apparently, had surprised Avraham Abba as he was deeply immersed in his writing and stabbed him. A few drops of blood punctuated that last sentence.

The mysterious attacker had apparently taken the incriminating document and hidden it in a secure place.

Large tears dropped onto Shmuel's cheeks. A tragedy from the distant past that had been lost for so many years had now burst forth from its hiding place and stood lifelike, before him. His heart melted with pity over the bitter fate of the unlucky author, Avraham Abba Fernbach, who may have paid with his life for his faithfulness to his nation. Some unknown murderer — His brother Zekil? A lackey of Bilcav's? — knew of his intention to inform on his father and brother and reveal their satanic deeds, and had killed him.

Sizhur Bayzhka flipped through the pages of the book and gave a shout of joy. "There are more pages hidden here! They're written in Hungarian, which is my mother tongue. Do they interest you?"

"Everything connected with Cardinal Bilcav interests us," Zerach answered. Shmuel's enthusiasm had infected him; gone was his apathy and disinterest.

The translator cleared his throat ceremoniously, settled his glasses firmly on his nose, and began to read:

"Today, the 24th of December 1838, was a holiday in the St. Vitus Church. How lovely. In honor of the holiday we baptized five Jewish children from the Prague ghetto. None of this would have been possible if not for the greedy Jew, Gezil Fernbach."

"Getzel," Shmuel corrected him.

The translator looked at him from above his glasses. "Do I read Hungarian or do you? It says here 'Gezil'."

"Go on," Zerach urged him, avoiding an argument.

Sizhur continued to read.

"Gezil Fernbach is the goose that lays the golden eggs. The lists he supplied me with helped me to open a world that had always been closed to us. Gezil received 50 reichsthaler from me for every Jewish head. I, Matthias Bilcav, didn't do badly either: Gezil didn't know that I was receiving 200 reichsthaler for each child from the Papal Nuncio of Bohemia, and I declared 70 children. Gezil received 2,000 reichsthaler from me, while I pocketed 12,000. I told the secretary to the Nuncio that the other children were on the way and that Gezil was working hard to get them. I hope that Patrus II will turn a blind eye to my little sin, since what is

12,000 reichsthaler compared to forty innocent Jewish children baptized to Christianity, proving our religion's superiority. Christianity, after all, has never been as interested in converting others as it has been in converting the Jews — believers in the religion from whence Christianity sprang, from whence it derived many of its important fundamentals, whose existence is a slap in the face to all true believers. The Jews in essence deny our religion and therefore we want them more than others. Every Jew who is baptized a Christian validates us in the name of the Old Testament. When the last Jew converts to Christianity we will know that we have succeeded in our great battle!"

"Please don't be angry with me," the translator — a Christian — said, stuttering a little as he spoke, when he saw the increasing fury of his Jewish listeners. "I didn't write this, I'm just reading what he wrote. Even if, as a Christian, I can't help but feel that what he says may be valid —"

"We're not here for theological debates," Shmuel interrupted him coldly. "Go on."

"It's not so easy," Sizhur apologized. "You're angry, and the language is archaic. I don't understand every word; occasionally I add something to make it clear."

"Fine."

"The date changes. Now there's a long paragraph dated the 6th of February 1840. 'Like a fool Gezil Fernbach put himself into my hands. I gave him a few cups of wine to loosen his tongue, and he revealed to me how twenty years earlier he had swindled the Royal Bank in Nuremberg with a shrewdness that eclipses even my own notable schemes. When I pushed him further he told me, with obvious enjoyment, how he had threatened his two colleagues from the "seven notables of the city." "Those rogues," Gezil said, "by the names Tuvia Rottenberg and Shimon Helefant, had broken the laws of the land. Rottenberg routinely hid smuggled goods in his house and Shimon Helefant speculated in real estate. I threatened them," he said. "I told them that I would hand them over to the government if they didn't place me first on the list. Then I consulted with an expert pharmacist who prepared for me a special white powder, one without taste or smell. At a *bris* celebration that we all attended I sent the head of the community, Shraga Schwartzer, to speak with R' Todros Miller, who hadn't called him and who had no idea why he was there. In the two minutes that Shraga was gone I poured the powder into his cup of wine; six hours after he had drunk it, Shraga Schwartzer was dead. I became the head of the community and Leizer Tischler agreed to give me a loan. When Leizer went back on his promise I used an effective weapon against him: I informed on several Jews who were involved in criminal activities, and spread the rumor that it was Leizer who was behind it. Leizer was absolutely broken and died that very night. Those fools of Prague thought that his heart could not bear it. They did not know that his heart was strong and healthy as an ox. The solution to the mystery was — Abish Kessler!

"'Abish Kessler, the faithful valet, was an agent that I had placed long before in Leizer's home. For many years he spied for me. Leizer was certain that Abish was more loyal to him than any of his own sons. From Abish I learned what was happening in Leizer's house, what his financial situation was. For that alone he justified the salary I paid him each month. On the day the people demonstrated in front of Leizer's home I sent a letter to Abish wrapped around a rock. It contained three words: It is time. I had one of the demonstrators throw the rock into a window; it actually hit Leizer in the forehead, and he ran like a sheep to hide under the bed. Abish picked up the rock. I had given him the poison some days before, and told him I would give him my instructions. He read the message and then worked hard to calm Leizer down. He handed him a large cup of wine to help steady him — and the wine contained a double dose of the powder, enough to kill an elephant. Thus I had my revenge on Leizer for refusing me the loan. Truth to tell, Abish was supposed to covertly transfer Leizer's fortunes to me, but that rogue pretended to mourn his master's death and after the *shivah* he fled to Hungary with whatever he could lay his hands upon, and there he vanished."

"'That was Gezil's confession to me and I, Cardinal Matthias Bilcav, brought two priests with excellent memories to stand by and hear every word. When he had sobered up the two repeated everything to him — word for word. Gezil turned whiter than snow; he realized that from this day on he was in my hands, for good or for bad. Obviously, I decreased the monies that I was giving him.'"

Zerach and Shmuel had silently heard the translator's words. Now, deeply moved, they spoke. "All the mysteries are solved," Shmuel whispered. "We suspected Leizer wrongly; he was a man of integrity until the end. The affair of the seven notables is just another indication of Getzel's manipulative personality. He was a man who used all means, everything was permitted, even murder of innocents, if they happened to stand in his path. Leizer Tischler must have suspected something was wrong, seeing that they had given up their positions so suddenly, but he couldn't have realized what was going on."

"Do you want to hear more?" The translator seemed amused.

"Of course," both answered eagerly.

"So, I continue: 'I then noticed that Gezil Fernbach's oldest son, Pupa...'"

"He means Avraham Abba," Shmuel whispered to Zerach.

"'...Gezil Fernbach's oldest son, Pupa,'" Sizhur repeated, in the tone of a patient teacher facing his unruly charges, "'was a dangerous man with an independent streak, much closer to his Jewish people than the rest of his family. I told his brother Zekil to keep an eye on him, promising him a reward for his efforts. Zekil understood what I meant and kept his brother under close scrutiny. When he discovered that his brother intended on handing his father over to R' Isaac Posen he sneaked up on him, as Pupa was writing out his incriminating document, a sharp knife in his hand. Pupa was only lightly wounded, and he succeeded in overpowering his brother and fleeing the house, but in the struggle Zekil managed to pull the last pages from his hands. He handed them to me, in order to cover our tracks. I paid him 1,000 reichsthaler for his work. Pupa disappeared; apparently, he fled Prague. We have heard nothing further of him. I suspect that he is terrified of the long arm of the Church, and thus he is not revealing what he knows of his family's betrayal of their people. Zekil is my hope: he and his sons after him will take my orders and fulfill them faithfully. But even toward him I heed the principle that I learned from Gezil Fernbach himself: Respect him and suspect him. He claims that he was ready to stab Pupa in the heart but Pupa sensed him and swung around, so that the knife only cut his arm. But I suspect that this was done purposely, that he had mercy on his brother. I have decided to cut the money that the Church gives him. But I won't stop it completely, I want to keep him a faithful Christian.'"

*Time Bomb* / 205

Sizhur wrinkled his brow and continued after a short pause.

"'4 July 1840. Just to myself I ask: Is this the reward of a faithful servant of the Church? After all I've done for the benefit of the Church they've thrown me out like a dog, taken away my high position. And for what? Because Gezil was a little bit smarter than I had thought. To avenge himself for my having cut his funding he informed on me to the Church, telling them that I'd defrauded them of their money when I told them that thirty more children had converted. I assumed that Patrus II would forgive me my slight transgression, but instead I was cast out like a common thief from my position as Cardinal of St. Vitus Church. But I, Matthias Yohann Bilcav, was not the only one with my hand in the till: I reported Gezil Fernbach to the Bavarian police, telling them all regarding his fraud in Nuremberg. Gezil was arrested and will spend the rest of his days behind bars. That is the end of his career as a thief and an informer.'"

---

The diary came to an end. The Cardinal's confession had reached its tragic conclusion. Old questions had been answered; new ones had arisen. One question — how had the diary come into the museum's possession? — had a probable explanation: The property of the Fernbach family had been appropriated by the Nazis, together with all the other Jewish possessions.

"Are you satisfied?" Sizhur asked politely. Shmuel understood the intent of the query and pushed two bills of 1,000 koronen into the eager translator's hand. Bayzhka's face grew angry. "Are you making fun of me?" he objected. "Our koronen are garbage. For a full day's work you're offering me $70?"

Zerach quickly appeased his anger with another $50. The translator still seemed dissatisfied, but calmed down when Zerach explained that he himself did not earn $120 a day, nor even half of that.

Shmuel and Zerach said goodbye and left the house. The owner's eyes followed them from the window until they had disapppeared among the many tourists crowding the street.

Sizhur Bayzhka stayed in the old man's home. "I've got a deal for you, Mr. — "

"Paltiro Bilcav," the man said, taking the outstretched hand.

"Are you related to the Cardinal?" Sizhur asked, curious.

"My grandfather was his nephew," the old man explained.

"Then, Mr. Paltiro Bilcav, do you want to make some money?"

※※※

Cardinal Frantis Shkarta, head of the Maria of the Snows Church, was a childhood friend of Sizhur Bayzhka's, and thus it was only natural that Sizhur, a loyal Christian, should show him the journal that had been uncovered in Matthias Bilcav's attic, which Sizhur had just purchased from his grandnephew.

Frantis, a member of the bishopric of the Czech Republic, gave the aged pages a quick glance. "It doesn't seem very interesting to me," he told his disappointed friend. "But if you promised the old man money take $100 and give the old man $50. Believe me, it's not worth even that."

Sizhur was already at the door when Frantis called him back. "Maybe you should give me the names of those two Jews, just in case."

"I don't know their names, but I know what hotel they're staying in," Sizhur said.

The Cardinal wrote down the name of the hotel.

As soon as the translator had taken his leave, the Cardinal hastened to phone the Papal Nuncio of the Bohemia region. "Don't ask what's happened," he said, his voice quivering with panic.

The Pope's representative was ready to reproach the Cardinal for interrupting him, but when he heard what he had to say, he was shocked. "It can't be," he cried out.

"It can be. And it is."

"At least do you have the pages?"

"Yes, but the secret is out."

*Time Bomb* / 207

"This is terrible," the Papal Nuncio shouted. "This can open up a Pandora's box that will destroy us all."

A short silence followed.

"How many men know of the journal?" he inquired, recovering some of his composure.

"Four," Shkarta shot back. "Two Jews, Sizhur Bayzhka the translator, and the old man, Paltiro Bilcav, who lives in his great-uncle's house."

"You want to be promoted?" the Nuncio barked. "See to it that by tomorrow evening not one of them is alive. And that includes your friend, Bayzhka."

---

"Prague has three Jewish cemeteries. The most ancient of them is where the great R' Loewe is buried," the taxi driver explained. "The second is the one near Zhizhikov Hill, in Mahler Gardens, by the edge of the television tower. The third is the new Jewish cemetery, where the famed author Franz Kafka is buried. That was opened in 1890. Where would you like to go?"

Shmuel and Zerach did a quick reckoning. Getzel Fernbach was still alive in 1840. Even if he had lived for many years after his imprisonment it was unlikely that he had seen the sunrise of 1890. Most probably he was buried in the cemetery in Mahler Gardens.

The driver took them there, all the while complaining of the giant television tower that they had built, with an observation tower that stood at a height of 650 feet. Because of the height and distance, he grumbled, it was impossible to make anything out on the ground. It was an eyesore among the beautiful buildings of Prague. And, he added, during its construction in the 1970's, they had destroyed many Jewish tombs.

Shmuel was apprehensive. If that was true, perhaps this trip was a complete waste of time. Getzel Fernbach's grave might have been one of those that had disappeared to make room for the ugly tower.

"Why are you so intent about finding the grave of that apostate?" Zerach wondered.

Shmuel spoke as if he were explaining some difficult concept in Gemara. "In order to know what is happening in the present, one must first clearly understand the past."

"What's bothering you about the present?" Zerach was even more surprised. "Getzel Fernbach is dead, and his bones have rotted away."

"Getzel Fernbach is dead, but his descendants may still be alive, and they are following their grandfather's heritage," Shmuel said in a singsong voice. "You read the writings of Avraham Abba Fernbach. His brother had signed a contract to continue his destructive actions in the guise of a faithful Jew. Maybe at this very minute some of Getzel's grandchildren are shooting poison into the veins of the Jewish nation. Perhaps Getzel's grave will give us a little more information about his family."

He had a startling theory, actually, but until he had made certain there was a connection between the Fernbach family in Katamon and the conversion of the Levins, he did not want to be more specific.

The taxi reached the cemetery. They paid the driver and got out.

Disappointingly, Mahler Gardens was not full of greenery as its name implied. A few trees grew in the area, but mainly it was covered by large tombstones, some of them taller than a man. The area was not included in tourists' maps of the city because it did not bring in fees, and so it had a neglected, abandoned look, with weeds poking out of the headstones. For two hours they wandered among the graves, carefully scanning each stone, pushing away the uncut grass lest a grave be hidden behind it.

It was easy to identify the gravesite of R' Yechezkel Landau, the Noda B'Yehudah; a pile of stones was carefully placed upon it, just as it was at the Maharal's. The area where he and his family were interred was surrounded by a metal fence, and had been cared for by his descendants. Next to R' Yechezkel lay his son, R' Shmuel. As they had done at the grave of the Maharal the two prayed fervently, feeling a strong sense of connection with the *Shechinah*. The two of them had studied the works of the rabbi of Prague, both his famed responsa, "*Noda B'Yehudah*," and his *chiddushim* on Talmud, known as the *Tzlach*. His holy body was buried here; his great spirit lived in the hearts and minds of Torah scholars.

*Time Bomb* / 209

The sun was beginning to set. The two knew, though, that here in Prague twilight would last for more than an hour and a half. Still, they immediately *davened Minchah;* after all, you never knew what might happen.

Next they passed by a pathway near a fence that was mostly destroyed. Shmuel spent most of the time searching in this area.

Again, it was Zerach who found it first.

"Shmuel, it's here," he said excitedly.

The headstone was in ruins, but the name "Fernbach" could be clearly discerned.

They crouched next to the mute stone and cleaned it as best they could from the generations of dirt and dust that had settled upon it. The engraved letters had grown dim, but could still be made out.

> Here lies
>
> a good man, good to all,
>
> who gave of his bread to the poor,
>
> and helped raise up those who had fallen,
>
> R' Elyakim Getzel
>
> son of Avraham Abba Fernbach z"l
>
> who died with a good name
>
> 25 Av 5608

They silently read the inscription, each lost in his own thoughts. Those long-ago, faraway events felt as real, as solid as the stone standing before them. The identification was absolute. The evidence of both the name and the date made it obvious that the hero — villain — of the tale was buried here.

"The headstone contradicts the entire story," Zerach broke the silence. "'A good man, good to all...helped raise up those who had fallen...' Only the honorific 'the *tzaddik* of the generation' is missing here."

Shmuel grinned ruefully. "It looks like that other apostate, in the ancient cemetery near the Maharal, didn't have the good fortune of having a son like Zekil."

"What do you mean?" Zerach demanded.

"Very simple," Shmuel laughed. "A son like Zekil, with all his connections and the money that he has backing him, could see to it that his father's headstone — his father, remember, was also his spiritual mentor — bore the appropriate words. A perfect example of 'honor thy father'... Zekil turned his father into a *tallis* that was completely made out of *techeiles*: Getzel the thief died a felon's death in some forgotten cell, and look what it says here."

Zerach suddenly looked behind him nervously at a wide-trunked tree at the other end of the garden.

"What's the matter?" Shmuel asked. "What's there?"

"I thought I saw someone watching us. As soon as he saw that I noticed him, he vanished."

"Nonsense," Shmuel grinned. "The atmosphere of mystery and drama is beginning to get to you."

"I hope that's it." Zerach sounded skeptical.

They heard the thunder of the gunshot. The bullet zoomed straight toward them.

# 20

Though neither had any training in how to cope in such situations, their basic survival instincts sent them both plunging headlong to the ground, seeking shelter among the marble stones. Zerach's hat flew to the floor; he saw, horrified, that its brim had been pierced twice.

"The bullet went in through one side and out the other," Zerach whispered to Shmuel, pointing at the black felt. "I felt something whiz by me. It's a miracle I was saved."

"Quiet," Shmuel hissed, pulling him forcibly lower. "It's not over yet." He peeked out from the headstone and immediately heard another shrill whistle. Behind them, shards of shattered stone flew in all directions.

Someone was trying to kill them.

"How can it be?" Shmuel murmured, his beard touching the cold earth and his lips full of dirt. "What do they want from us?"

"Maybe it has nothing to do with us. Maybe we've gotten involved in some kind of feud. You know, gang wars, things like that."

"We'll know pretty soon."

"How?"

"If our attacker comes toward us in order to get a better shot," Shmuel said drily, trying desperately to keep calm despite his paralyzing fear.

Before the shooting had begun they had noticed several other visitors to the cemetery; suddenly, though, everyone had disappeared. Just when they needed help, someone to rescue them, there was no one about.

Half an hour crawled by as they lay beneath the headstones, terrified, their ears listening acutely for any sound. Finally, night fell. Under the security of darkness they dared to lift their heads.

"Should we go out?" Zerach wondered doubtfully. "Maybe they're waiting to trap us in the blackness?"

"Do you want to stay here until dawn?"

"No, but I'm afraid."

"So say *Krias Shema*."

"At least we *davened Minchah* earlier."

"That's true."

They continued to whisper for another few seconds, breaking the tension with a few macabre jokes. Several minutes passed without any suspicious sounds and they finally crawled toward the exit, crouching all the while.

No shots were fired; all remained still.

They walked swiftly along the main road, trying to put as much distance as they could between themselves and the cemetery. Finally they flagged down a passing taxi and rode the rest of the way to the hotel. They got there during dinner and joined the few people eating; most of the group had left for a two-day trip to Munich and Salzburg, where they planned on visiting the "Eagle's Nest," the famed castle located on a spectacular mountaintop where Hitler (may his name be blotted out) had planned his strategies during the Second World War.

When Shmuel finally got to his room he realized immediately that something was wrong. His bed was disheveled and upon it his briefcase lay open, with its papers dumped all over.

He broke out in a cold sweat and shivered. Someone had been searching here, and had not even bothered covering his tracks. He first checked his briefcase. In it he had hidden his money and his ticket to Venezuela in a small wallet.

The money was there, intact; so was the ticket. He breathed deeply. At least this anonymous intruder had not robbed him.

But what did he want? And who was he?

It was not difficult to conclude that some kind of thread — a thick rope, actually — connected the incident in the cemetery in Mahler Gardens with this search among his belongings. The unknown arm that had shot between the gravestones had sent its long fingers, too, into his personal luggage.

He paled: Someone wanted to know where he was heading.

He remembered the letter he had received from Caracas to his home in Jerusalem, the letter that threatened that if he went to Venezuela he would return to Israel in a coffin. Was that, too, linked to this business?

He walked to the telephone, an ancient instrument from neolithic times. He dialed.

"Reception, good evening," came the voice, in English.

"I'd like to make a call to Israel."

They cleared a line for him and Shmuel dialed his home number. When his wife answered, he asked her for another number, avoiding any anxious questions, and then dialed once again. This time, it was the office of Yad L'Achim, the organization which had declared war on missionaries and cults. He asked to speak to the director.

He introduced himself, hoping (fruitlessly, as it turned out) that they would know who he was, and told the voice on the other end from where he was speaking.

"It's difficult to give you an immediate answer. First, we would have to know more about you, before furnishing that information. Second, we are talking about an old story that took place about forty years ago. Those are the days when we were known as 'P'eylim.' Once we have checked you out, we can look in our archives, but that will take hours, maybe days."

"I'll call you in a few days."

His request had been quite precise, if unusual. He wanted official validation that the Fernbach family of Katamon had been working on behalf of missionaries. Furthermore, he wanted many details, particularly concerning the red-haired man who had made himself so at home in the Levin household before they left the country.

---

"Are you coming with me?"

"Not only am I not going, but I'm not letting you go either. It's a matter of life and death."

"Come with me."

"No!"

Shmuel felt a flash of anger. "Zerach, I don't understand you."

The two were sitting in a public garden on a quiet street not far from the hotel. Zerach, fearing "walls with ears," had refused to hear Shmuel's confidences within the confines of his room. But even here in the street one could detect traces of nervousness, souvenirs of yesterday's nightmare encounter in the cemetery.

Shmuel gave Zerach a brief account of the threatening letter that had come from Caracas, and asked him to join him on his trip to Venezuela. The answer was an unequivocal no.

"But I'll pay you back for all your expenses," Shmuel promised. "The time you lose from work, patches on hat brims that have gunshot holes — even duty-free gifts for the kids on the way back home. What else do you want?"

"On the way back home?" Zerach repeated sarcastically. "I'll tell you the truth, my dear Rabbi Bilad, when I read Schriftgiss's old manuscript I wasn't too excited. A nice story from the past, I thought. How much impact could it have on my life? Yesterday, when they shot at us, I didn't get it; I thought we'd simply stumbled into some gang war. But last night I did a careful calculation and began to realize that there is a direct link between our visit to the Cardinal's house and the attempt on our lives. It seems we've awoken some bears from their hibernation."

"We've walked into a nest of cobras," Shmuel added a zoological metaphor of his own.

"Exactly. I suspect that our pleasant translator is not as innocent as he seems. I'm prepared to swear by Getzel Fernbach's goat's beard that Sizhur bought those scandalous papers from the old man for a few coins and went directly to the Church to sell his discovery for a tidy sum. It seems that the information in those pages is worth its weight in gold; but unlike gold, it's explosive. Someone in the Prague Church, maybe in St. Vitus Church, knows something that we don't know. Maybe he is very friendly with Getzel Fernbach's grandsons. Maybe they're still working for the Church. Someone is afraid that we'll uncover information that will undermine the entire Church structure. Or maybe it will reveal that some Jews are actually spies sent by the Church to infiltrate the community."

"I've been thinking the very same thing," Shmuel answered. Then, suddenly, he asked, "So why won't you go with me to Caracas?"

Zerach gave him a long stare. "I want to live — *ani chafetz chaim*."

"Oh, the new Chafetz Chaim of the generation." Despite the smile on his face, Shmuel did not sound amused.

Zerach did not care. "Yes, I want to live. I'm not embarrassed to say it. This trip is sure suicide. You have no idea who you've started up with here. Do you know what it's like when the Catholic Church is persecuting you? Seventy-seven ghosts following you around like shadows. Maybe at this very moment some sniper is pinpointing us in the hairs of his telescopic lens from one of the rooftops across from here."

"What a thought," Shmuel said, smiling again. "You see the leaves on that tree? Maybe they're not just green leaves; every leaf might have some kind of listening device and optical sensor that focuses on your mustache and can, with the help of ultraviolet rays, follow the movement of your lips. That red car parked nearby is carrying a small neutron bomb. The broom in the hands of the street cleaner is a rifle that shoots off rubber bullets made of bubble gum — peppermint flavored — and the flies hovering near the garbage can are being maneuvered via remote control held in villains' hands."

"So laugh," Zerach said angrily, standing up. "I'm trying to talk to you about serious things and you're telling me jokes. Shmuel, I beg of you, don't go to Venezuela. It's dangerous."

"I'm going." Shmuel ended the discussion.

"So go by yourself." Zerach was equally determined. "I'm not getting involved."

Shmuel's eyes suddenly were riveted on a car that had burst onto the street and was approaching them at great speed. "Get down!" he screamed, as he jumped onto Zerach and ducked.

The car's window opened as it neared the two men lying prone on the sidewalk. The car suddenly slowed down. A hand holding a gun emerged from it.

The revolver jerked forward twice, making a noise reminiscent of a cork popping out of a bottle of champagne. The bullets whistled toward them. The hand disappeared back into the car, the tinted glass window closed, and the car vanished around the corner with the shriek of burning tires.

They lay on the ground for a full five minutes, not daring to stand up. The street cleaner approached them, broom in hand, and spoke excitedly. They did not understand a word of his frenzied Czech, but his gestures were universal: Get up, get out of here. They heard the word "Mafia" repeated several times. They raced in the direction of the hotel.

"That's the second time we've been miraculously saved," Zerach said, wide eyed. "I've already lost my hat, now I almost lost my head. You saved me."

"You said you're not involved," Shmuel reminded him as they raced along, breathing heavily.

"Involved up to my ears, it seems," Zerach conceded. "Rabbi Bilad, do you think someone is gently hinting that our presence in Prague is bothering him?"

They reached the hotel courtyard and slowed down. They inhaled deeply and felt slightly calmer.

"Rabbi Bilad, you haven't answered me."

Shmuel patted his suit pocket, making certain his passport had not fallen out during their mad dash. He felt the plastic-encased cover. "The danger is much greater than we supposed. We must have touched a raw nerve. It's no sleeping cobra we've awoken, it's a seven-headed dragon. That was not the Prague Mafia, as that street cleaner thought, they were the messengers of the Church. They used a rifle in the cemetery, here they used a revolver with a silencer. Next time — may Hashem have mercy."

Zerach was adamant. "This only strengthens my resolve to go back to Israel. In another two hours the group is leaving for the airport." His voice took on a beseeching tone. "Shmuel, come with us. Don't fly to Venezuela. Leave this business and go back home, to your blessed daily routine. You don't need dangerous adventures; you're not a 15-year-old youth."

Shmuel looked at him seriously. "Zerach, I envy you. You are a fortunate man. You're not burdened with feelings of guilt; you're unencumbered by horrible memories. Since my bar mitzvah I've been beset by terrible feelings of guilt that don't leave me, not by day, not by night. I caused someone's death by my negligence. I enjoyed a thriller in a warm library and left my good friend Dudy Levin to freeze to death in the storm."

His voice broke on a choked sob as his body shuddered. "Do you have any idea what it is like to carry such a burden of guilt, the burden of an entire family that converted to Christianity because of you? It's worse to cause someone to sin than to kill him; I did both. I killed Dudy Levin; his twin brothers, Moishy and Ahrele, and his mother, Hadassah, I brought to sin. I know, I didn't actually kill him and I didn't actually cause the terrible sin. But I fervently believe my actions will be held against me in *Shamayim*. Now I received a letter from Caracas, from someone who wants to meet with me. I want to go; I have to go. Okay, I got another letter threatening my life if I come. But I must! I will go to Venezuela and perhaps Hashem will help me to return from there with a less troubled conscience. It's worth the try."

---

The KLM flight from Prague to Caracas, via Amsterdam, was set to take off at 10:30 p.m. Shmuel prepared himself for the lengthy journey. His companions from the tour group had left the hotel earlier, at about 4 p.m.

Shmuel would have a few leisurely hours after bidding his new friend, Zerach, farewell.

Zerach was terrified for Shmuel and did not bother to conceal his feelings when they said goodbye. "I won't say, 'Take care of yourself,' the way people do at such times, because we've seen how twice we've been saved through miracles. Instead, I'll give you the blessing that Hashem should watch over you. I'll *daven* the entire way back, and in Israel too, that nothing should happen to you."

"In the battle between holiness and dark forces, the more the negative side seems to overpower the good, the more it means that goodness is close to victory," Shmuel answered. "When you see impurity standing tall, that's the sign that holiness is about to win. 'The man wrestled with him,' it says of Yaakov, because that's the final stage before daybreak."

"Be very careful," Zerach beseeched him. "Impurity is capable of hitting pretty hard before it's defeated."

"Did you buy any souvenirs?" Shmuel said, trying to break the gloomy atmosphere.

Zerach patted his large suitcase. "Two wine bottles and three vases, all made of crystal — one for my mother, one for my mother-in-law, and one for my wife. What else? Some wood and straw toys for the little ones, some ceramics for the house. An incredible alarm clock for my father-in-law, who gets up every morning for prayers at sunrise, and a stereo system that I bought for pennies in the Tesco department store. Think it's enough?"

"When did you manage to buy it all?"

Zerach sighed. "In the time that I wasn't being persecuted by messengers of the Church."

Shmuel returned to his room to pack. In the bustle of the tour group's departure, he managed to quietly leave his suitcase and backpack with the porter. Then he helped an old woman burdened with two large suitcases, insisting that he take one onto the bus for her. With the elderly woman's thanks ringing in his ears, he got on the bus and sat down next to Zerach. The two winked at each other. The diversionary tactics had begun.

*Time Bomb* / 219

"Prague Ruzyne," the Czech Republic's only international airport, is located in the western portion of the city. The closer one gets to it, the less one sees of the decorative, colorful houses of old Prague, and the more one is surrounded by simple buildings of modern design.

A Mercedes automobile with tinted windows began to follow the bus. Zerach noticed it and gently tapped Shmuel on the arm. They were being followed.

The bus drove past Prague's Old Town and sped toward the modern city. The road grew broader. On each side, green fields flew by.

They reached the airport, pulled their luggage to the terminal, and waited in a snail-like queue. Shmuel's eyes darted back and forth, watching all sides. No one seemed to be following him. He felt a moment's hope. Perhaps they would leave him alone, thinking he was departing.

He walked toward the passenger lounge, waited for a moment until the electronic eye opened the wide glass doors, and left the building. A taxi driver was leaning, bored, on his steering wheel. "You want to go to the city?" he asked, hailing his passenger joyfully. Shmuel returned quietly to the hotel and shut himself in his room until evening.

One minute after Shmuel's cab had roared off, a young man wearing sunglasses walked into the terminal. He approached Yekutiel Sharabi, of the Israeli tour group, and asked him in accented English where he could find Rabbi Samuel Bilad.

"Rabbi Samuel Bilad?" Kuty repeated, puzzled. "Oh, you mean Shmuel."

"Yes."

"Rabbi Britman," Kuty called out, "someone is looking for Rabbi Bilad."

Zerach paled. Now he knew that the diversionary tactics had not been mere foolishness. The surveillance surrounding them was as strong as ever. The man in the sunglasses walked closer. Zerach swiftly turned, left the long line, and went off to look for the public bathrooms. The man in the sunglasses shrugged; he would not waste his time with this one, his job was to locate Bilad.

Zerach cautiously stuck his face out of the bathroom door. His pursuer was nowhere to be seen. Cautiously Zerach walked toward the large waiting room.

His luggage was still there, not yet checked in. He blessed the incredible slowness of the airport, left the terminal, and raced to find a cab.

<hr />

Shmuel returned to the airport that evening, this time for real. He had settled on a price with the driver when he ordered the car. The hotel reception clerk had warned him that not only were most cabbies in Prague inveterate overchargers, but a significant number were members of the local Mafia. "Keep a sharp eye out before you get in," he emphasized. "If it seems dangerous don't hesitate to cancel your trip, and don't get in."

The driver seemed fine, certainly not "dangerous." The luggage was stowed in the trunk and Shmuel settled down in the back seat.

The blow, when it came, was completely unexpected and shocked both the driver and his passenger equally. The black Mercedes pulled alongside them on the left and tried to run them off the road.

Shmuel felt his confidence draining with each passing second. His strategy had failed; they would not give him a moment's peace. He assessed the situation in a millisecond. It seemed they were trying to get him out of the car in order to shoot him.

"Step on the gas!" he shouted in English.

The cabbie answered in the same language. "What's going on?"

"I don't know. But please, drive as quickly as you can."

The Mercedes bumped into them again, pushing them onto the shoulder.

The cab driver expertly pulled his car back onto the road, hissing Czech curses all the while. "I know these thugs. They're from the Mafia. I have nothing to do with them. It seems they know you."

"Absolutely not," Shmuel hotly denied the charge. "I am a law-abiding citizen; I have nothing to do with criminals."

"They want your money," the driver said. "These Mercedes that push cars to the side are interested in robbing the occupants."

"I don't have a lot of money," Shmuel groaned, fearfully watching as the black automobile approached them a third time.

*Time Bomb* / 221

"If you don't, I'm slowing down," the driver declared, looking at his passenger in the rearview mirror.

Shmuel understood the hint. "Don't worry, you'll get paid."

"How much?"

"In dollars."

"How much?" The driver hit the gas pedal.

"One hundred dollars."

The car slowed down.

"Two hundred."

"Excellent." The car flashed ahead, putting some distance between it and the Mercedes. The cabbie wove through traffic, passing most cars, trying to shake off the luxury automobile.

As they approached the airport, the Mercedes took off. But the chase — the second in a few hours — was enough to sap Shmuel's courage completely and fill him with a fear he had never experienced before. As he walked through the security inspection in the airport he looked around him like some kind of wild animal being pursued by panting dogs. He did not bother with the duty-free shop; he concentrated solely on the moment when the airplane's wheels would retract and he would safely depart this dreadful place.

He could not even be sure that the cab driver had not been in league with the Mercedes, in order to extort money out of him. But this had not been the first attempt to kill him.

One thing was sure: Someone was after Shmuel Bilad.

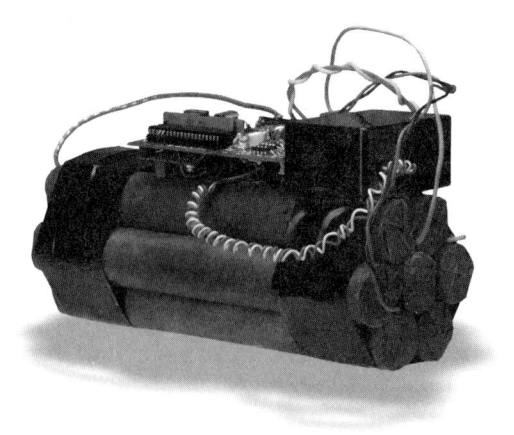

# 21

## "T *Israel, 5761 (2000)*

he Arab village of Tantura was surrounded by the Alexandroni brigade. The Arab soldiers, members of Abad al-Kadhr al-Husseini's organization, were no longer there. Some of them had fled, terrified of the cruel Jewish fighters, while others had been killed in battle. The village stood helpless as a day-old kitten before the armored brigade. Loudspeakers warned the residents, innocent Arab citizens, tillers of soil and herders of sheep, to leave their homes and gather in an open area near the well. The confused villagers were promised that nothing would happen to them. They believed the promises and so their fate was sealed. Hundreds of villagers, men, women, and children who had done nothing wrong — their only sin having been born Arabs — were herded together. The Alexandroni fighters went from house to house making sure no one was concealed there. When the search ended, the slaughter began, the Jewish soldiers shooting with pleasure at close range. Within five minutes the place became a giant slaughterhouse. Not one of the Arabs was left alive.

"After many years, the sleeping conscience of some of the murderous soldiers began to awaken and they took part in a public soul-searching at a reunion of the brigade members. But compared to the few who expressed regret at the brutal murder, most of their comrades declared that the affair was justified. The State of Israel had to come into being in areas such as Tantura and there was no choice but to 'evacuate' them. Even today, forty years later, by their own testimony, they feel no trace of conscience or regret for the barbaric killing that they perpetrated upon defenseless men."

Dr. Ofir Gal concluded his report and turned off his computer with every indication of satisfaction. He knew the article would create a storm of protest when it was published, and he was not fearful. Perhaps veterans of the Alexandroni would have him up on libel charges; however the ensuing publicity would only enhance sales of his new book. The graphics artist had already designed the cover: The title, "The Original Sin," was in bright red, with a three-dimensional effect, and the subtitle underneath it — "The War of Independence, Lies and Myths." The background showed a fictional Palmach soldier gazing arrogantly in front of him, a lock of hair blowing in the wind, his feet planted on the corpse of an Arab child. There had been no such picture, but the Arab graphics designer had not had a problem; a simple process had changed the German SS soldier into a Jewish one, the slain Jewish youngster into an Arab. The transformation had not troubled him in the least; indeed, he was quite proud of his creation. Not to mention that Dr. Gal had paid him well, in cash.

Dr. Ofir Gal, the German-born historian, was a man of few notable physical characteristics: a thin body, short of stature. One looking at him noticed only the eyes, large and feverish.

Dr. Gal enjoyed destroying myths. He was not alone. In the last decade an entire unit of historians and researchers in Israel had come into being, men and women who burrowed through archives and records, triumphantly pulling out obscure documents and using the information they found buried there to diligently deny all that had been accepted in Israel for five decades regarding the battles and wars with the Arabs, particularly the War of Independence.

These myth-wrecking historians painted the following picture: It was not the Jews who were forced to defend themselves against seven Arab armies that had come upon the tiny fledgling Jewish state that had just declared nationhood. The opposite was true: The Palmach brigades, armored battalions with well-supplied troops, soldiers with large biceps and small consciences, had fallen brutally upon the innocent Arab population. With unmerciful determination they slaughtered them in an effort to get them to flee the country and then looted their abandoned lands in order to build villages, *kibbutzim*, and cities in the new Jewish State.

Veterans of 1948 watched with failing eyesight as these new historians came on the scene and with inexplicable glee exploded all the familiar beliefs. These reinventors of history did not stop at boldfaced lies and terrible slanders when describing the horrific massacres and carefully planned mass deportations. The simple truth — that the problem of Arab refugees was created at the behest of the Arab leadership, which called upon the populace to leave their homes and villages and flee for safety to Arab countries with the assurance that they would soon return — had no impact on them. Jewish researchers, graduates of Zionist educational institutions, happily slandered their own people. They cooked up a stew of falsehoods and threw their brothers and fathers into the boiling cauldron. Their hands stayed steady as they wrote their villainous research papers, their goal to undermine any and all justification of the Jewish State in Israel. Their work was joyously received by the Arabs, particularly the anti-Semitic Palestinian apparatus that watched its onerous task being done by others; not merely others, but by Jews who had pulled themselves away from their own people and were serving the interests of those who wished them ill.

At the head of these researchers, wallowing happily in the mire of self-hate, stood Dr. Ofir Gal. The publication of his work, "The Original Sin," was the apex of his career of destruction, the culmination of years of weekly columns and "scientific research" whose sole purpose was to reveal the cruelty of the Zionist entity and of the Jewish State toward the Arabs.

These hostile researchers, colleagues of Ofir, were by and large following their fathers' examples. It was their parents who had rebelled against their Torah-observant families, mocking the magnificent history and tradition of countless generations, raising children cut off from all ties to their Jewish heritage.

Ofir himself had yet another motive in heading this small group of men who did everything in their power to undermine the Jews in Israel. He would not cringe before any step that might help them reach their goal: to bring about the absolute destruction of the State of Israel, to cast it into the hands of its Arab enemies.

Lately he had good reason to feel satisfaction.

### Caracas, 5761 (2000)

Simon Bolivar Airport near Caracas, capital of Venezuela, overwhelmed Shmuel Bilad as he walked, weak kneed, from the KLM plane. His head was spinning: from the sleep deprivation which had already begun to overpower him in Prague; from the thousands of deeply hued pictures that flashed through his brain like a demented kaleidoscope; from the cacophony that struck him so suddenly in the airport. How many times had he regretted his hasty decision to fly to Venezuela, a land so far away, at the end of the earth itself. A day before his departure from Prague he had phoned home and told his wife, Shoshana, that he had decided to extend his stay abroad. She applauded his decision. "This is what I wanted: that you should air yourself out a little, renew your energies."

She knew herself well enough to realize that the reason she had been so quick to approve of her husband's absence was her well-grounded fear that he was slipping into a deep depression.

Quite a personality was Shoshana Bilad. Her unique therapy method was based on strengthening the spiritual energies of her patients. She believed fervently in the system of Dr. Bach, declaring that the vast majority of bodily ailments and physiological disturbances and pains were rooted in spiritual or emotional disorders that had caused them to be formed.

"You must understand," she would tell her husband, "that spiritual and emotional problems such as depression, fear, or anxiety are in essence blockages that keep the potential energy locked in the soul from coming to fruition. Negative thoughts can turn into chronic illness, while an optimistic outlook opens the energy passages in the body and helps bring on radiant good health."

In the many classes that Shoshana had taken in Dr. Bach's methodology she had learned that these blockages of energy did not possess clear physical characteristics. Being that these passages were not physical in form, they had to be treated in the realm of spirit and emotion.

Shoshana treated her patients, many of whom quickly became her "chassidim," with the Bach flower remedies. "The essence of these flowers fills the body with a physical element, the energies of the herb or plant," she explained to every patient during the first visit. "Currently there are 38 essences that are known, with each one having its own energy frequency, each of which can open, in a natural and gentle manner, specific areas of blocked energies, allowing the potential locked within to flow freely. In other words, to restore the body's correct balance."

They came to the Bilad home: parents of youngsters with learning or concentration problems, hyperactive children, children who suffered from fears or hot tempers. Adults came too, with an even wider variety of difficulties, characteristic of our stressful modern lives. There was tension, as well as nerves, depression, despair, addictions, poor self-esteem, lack of direction. And, of course, there were feelings of guilt.

It was with this particular challenge, with one particular patient, that Shoshana threw up her hands in hopeless despair. Her husband, a noted and respected rabbi, was consumed by feelings of guilt, and she had no solution to offer him. She knew that his problem stemmed from an emotional disturbance in his own brain; for this reason she encouraged him to take an extended trip, in order to clear his thinking and rid himself of those negative emotions that were pulling him down.

Now her husband was standing at the exit of the Simon Bolivar Airport, his goal to meet with an anonymous letter writer who might, just might, help shed some light upon the dark fate of the Levin family — and to avoid meeting the other anonymous letter writer who had threatened his life.

He was out of ideas. The spoken language in this country was Spanish, but English is an international language and hand gestures are likewise understood by all. Someone directed him to the taxi stand; there he was told that the price of a trip should be about $11. Armed with this information he went out to the street and hailed a cab, which stopped immediately.

Upon his arrival he had changed some money into the local currency; he received 500 bolivars for every dollar. But he did not need much; he realized that here, as in Prague — everywhere, really — his dollars would be most welcome.

Luckily the taxi driver spoke a passable English and was a sympathetic and pleasant person. He offered Shmuel a free, brief lesson on Venezuela in general and Caracas in particular. During the course of the trip, that passed through a coastal mountain range via three tunnels, he managed to tell Shmuel about the nation that had once been impoverished and debt ridden until, in 1914, huge stores of oil had been discovered beneath its soil. This discovery triggered an economic boom that had swiftly pulled the nation out of poverty. Venezuela had become one of the richest nations in South America and for many years was the world's largest oil-producing country, until the Arab countries took its place in 1970. Caracas, the nation's capital, was a huge metropolis with more then five million residents.

"Is it a friendly city?"

"Absolutely not." The cabbie burst that particular bubble. "It's a cold place, where everyone's life is separate. Because of the high crime rate in the city, most of the residents spend their nights at home. It's only in the city center, in the Sabana Grande area, that you'll find the city active and alive until late at night."

"There's a lot of crime in the city?" Shmuel asked, concerned.

The cabbie laughed. "All of Venezuela is crime ridden, but the capital city of Caracas, that's the most dangerous in the entire country!"

Shmuel grew silent, feeling his heart sink. He felt a sudden powerful urge to ask the driver to make a U-turn at the next intersection and return to the airport.

"The city now is suffering from poverty and unemployment," the driver continued. "That makes the crime rate escalate, obviously. I would suggest that you don't walk by yourself through residential neighborhoods at night, and certainly not in the outlying areas. But don't only see the negative: Caracas is one of the most modern and developed cities in Latin America. We've gone through an incredible surge of development; we've built skyscrapers, paved wide, fast roads, built cultural and educational institutions."

"Who is 'we'? You and your wife?"

The driver grinned. "'We' are the residents of Caracas. I'm only a cab driver, after all, but I'm proud to live here. We have an extraordinary nation, in spite of the crime."

"Anything else encouraging to tell me?"

"Certainly. First of all, let me give you a little tip. As you might have noticed, you've bumped into the name 'Bolivar' more than once. You'll be hearing it dozens of times. Simon Bolivar is considered Venezuela's saint. We call him 'El Liberatador.' His memory is perpetuated on every site and important building, in every square and park. He was our great fighter for independence. If you sit in the Plaza Bolivar and put your feet on a bench, or even just drag large packages through it, you'll have to deal with the police. It's considered a desecration of a national holy place."

"Practical advice. Anything else?"

"Sure," the driver said graciously. "On Avenida Los Asias in the Sabana Grande you'll find a concentration of inexpensive hotels. Have you reserved something yet?"

"No. Is that all right?"

"What's with you?" the driver said. "Where do you think you've come to? In most hotels you have to make a reservation even before you buy your plane ticket. An expensive hotel will leave you bankrupt. Sleep in the street? If you wake up alive, you should be glad they left you with your clothing. Really, where are you going?"

"I don't know," Shmuel confessed.

The cabbie glanced amusedly in his rearview mirror. "You're kidding me. This is the first time I've ever met a tourist who didn't know where he was heading. Why have you come here?"

"Private matters."

*Time Bomb* / 229

"You haven't thought this out at all," the driver told him with brutal honesty. "You've made rather a mess of it."

The picture the cabbie had drawn was not very promising. Shmuel suddenly realized he had not the faintest idea of what he would be doing in the next hours. Now he had to make some decisions. He sank into a reverie for a few minutes, concentrating on thoughts of Hashem, ignoring the scenery rushing by and the cabbie's affable chatter and explanations.

Finally he spoke; he had just had an idea. "Take me to Caracas's Jewish quarter."

"That's an idea. I was thinking of something else for you. The national tourist office in Park Centrale could give you valuable information. But maybe you'd prefer the San Bernardino synagogue on Avenida Francisco Austritz."

"Exellent, take me there." Shmuel leaned back on his seat with a vast feeling of relief. Even though this synagogue's name sounded suspiciously Christian, one never knew in these Latin American countries. Under the circumstances this seemed to be the best solution.

---

## Israel, 5761 (2000)

After two months of nonstop guerrilla warfare, Israel's security forces felt themselves seriously undermined. Terror attacks had become a way of life — more accurately, a way of death — for a discernible segment of the populace: the 200,000 Jewish citizens who had chosen to live beyond the Green Line. News of attacks were relegated to the second and third tier of headlines, and were sometimes ignored entirely by the media, determined not to stir up nationalistic sentiment among the people.

In less than two months, the Al-Aksa Intifada claimed forty lives while hundreds were seriously wounded. There were thousands of shooting incidents and rocks and Molotov cocktails were hurled regularly. The roads of Judea and Samaria became battlefields, with only one side fighting. The Palestinians shot at settlers' homes and the army hardly reacted, or did not respond at all. The army did assassinate several terrorist leaders, but that immediately produced a hail of protests against the illegal killings by members of the left wing.

Deputy Prime Minister Max Landau was seen by the public as the man most responsible for the difficult situation. After two and a half months of failure, the polls showed that the previous prime minister was the man most sought after by the public to take the reins of power and act more resolutely against the Arabs who were celebrating over spilled Jewish blood.

Max Landau understood that the public had had enough of him. Mention of his name was sufficient to elevate one's blood pressure, even among those who had supported him and brought him to power. He had moments of weakness when he considered resigning his position but he quickly recovered his well-known determination and launched a new and brilliant maneuver, one that would destroy his former political opponent and stabilize his, Landau's, increasingly shaky position. He would reach a peace agreement with Yasser Arafat. It would be a short-lived agreement between him and that aging murderer whose hands were steeped in blood. It did not matter if this peace treaty were signed amidst the sound of explosions and shooting and the screams of dying Jews; the main thing was that there would be an agreement.

A discernible segment of the population began to feel that there were those who were pleased that they were being killed, shot at, and that their lives had become unbearable. The images of daily funerals might encourage the settlers to flee their homes. Max knew that the peace agreement was not worth the paper it was written upon — the deadly attacks would not stop for even a minute. It would only whet the Arab appetite, Israeli security would be irretrievably damaged, and the demise of the State would just be a matter of time.

In his mad dash he rushed into the waiting arms of Assad, the ruler of Syria, offering the Golan Heights without even blinking. With the same determination he was ready to give up a good portion of the Jordan Valley and a total of 98 percent of Judea and Samaria, as if they were radio active. He offered, too, to give sovereignty of the Temple Mount to the Palestinians, including the Armenian Quarter. What's more, with elections approaching he began a series of talks with the Palestinians, who were pleased to accept all that Israel was offering — East Jerusalem, including placing the Western Wall under international auspices, and other generous suggestions.

Those who did not know Max well were shocked. Why was he doing this to his people? Was his job as leader to protect his nation or to close his eyes as they were being readied for slaughter?

But those few who knew Max's past were not at all surprised. It seemed that the man would not shed a single tear if, as a result of his policies, the nation would be lost. On the question of why he was doing this to his people they would have answered with still another question: And are these, indeed, his people?

The public fury grew and reached the boiling point. People did not believe the brainwashing of the media. They waited impatiently for the first opportunity to rid themselves of a government that had thrust the Oslo process upon them. This was the Oslo Accord that had brought Palestinian murderers almost to their doorsteps. In the seven years that had passed since it had been signed, 77 people had been killed, on average, every year, with a total of 544 dead — compared to 16 people a year in the fifteen years prior to the insane agreement. In response to those educated professors, men and women with pleasant voices who had soothing explanations for everything, who sought to anesthesize the nation on its way to the abyss and to whisper in its ears the hypnotic mantra of peace, a terrible fury began to awaken. Not everyone was as inclined to commit suicide as they were. The healthy will of the people overpowered the madness of "Peace at Any Price" that the Oslo gang had tried to inflict on their brains. The public waited impatiently for the moment it would get to the polling station and, by means of a small piece of yellow paper, be able to kick the ruling government down the steps and out the door. They wanted only to exchange it for a new government, a sane government that would not run indiscriminately into the hands of the first Palestinian murderer to sign a "peace agreement." Men in this wounded land truly desired peace — to live in peace, not to rest in peace.

But the leftist government did not understand this — and it was to pay a high price for its denseness, in the middle of the month of Shevat 5761 (2001).

## 22

*Prague, 5761 (2000)*

Before leaving the airport Zerach Britman extricated his luggage from the pile of baggage awaiting check-in for the Israel-bound plane and placed it into a locker. He would be back here tonight; hopefully, the luggage would be waiting for him, untouched. Then he drove to the hotel, planning to go to Shmuel's room (he was certain that Shmuel was there; where else, after all, did he have to go?) and tell him of the change of plans. He, Zerach, would not be returning to Israel; he would be going with Shmuel to Caracas. The chase and pursuit had given him a new perspective. It seemed as if some sort of blood bond existed between him, the chassid who taught in a renowned *cheder* in Bnei Brak, and the Lithuanian yeshivah lecturer. He knew that one needed an entry visa for Venezuela, but Zerach had been born in London and carried a European passport which should afford him entry.

As he approached the hotel he felt himself growing tense. He looked suspiciously at the plaza in front of the hotel. His heart skipped a beat when he recognized a face. Zerach was observant, and in the split second before they had been shot at in the cemetery he had seen the face of the man now standing before him. The same frozen features, the same gray jacket, the same wrestler's shoulders. *One step forward, two steps back*, he murmured to himself as he turned around quickly in the other direction. *Did he see me, or did he not?*

He had.

Zerach, much to his open consternation, saw how the man left the courtyard of the hotel and quickly stepped toward him. *We're both in their sights*, he thought. *Not just Shmuel Bilad; they want me too.*

For the next few minutes he walked as quickly as he could, hoping to lose the man, but a quick peek over his shoulder informed him that his pursuer was swifter than he was, and the gap between them was narrowing.

*Okay, I'll change the rules of the game. You want to pull me into some dark alley and get rid of me quietly. Not quite.*

He stopped short and stood on the sidewalk surrounded by passersby walking back and forth. He pivoted around and saw his pursuer stop about 50 yards away, an expression of surprise on his face. Zerach hesitated for just a moment and then determinedly walked toward the man.

*I've got a surprise for you. An idea straight from the Sages. Did you ever hear of "the gnat that frightens the lion"? The gnat is a small creature with a strong, shrill cry. When the hungry lion tries to put its paws upon it, the gnat gives off such shrieks that it scares off the lion.*

Zerach waited until the man was about six feet away. He was taking a calculated risk; the man's hand was placed firmly in his jacket, and there was a suspicious bulge within. A revolver, equipped with a silencer, no doubt. Suddenly Zerach roared thunderously, "Help! This man wants to kill me! He's got a gun in his pocket!"

The man was dumbfounded; he had never expected such an outburst. Zerach had the advantage of surprise. The man saw people beginning to gather around Zerach, who was pointing toward him with bulging eyes: "Look at the gun! Look at the gun!"

The man gazed at Zerach with the eyes of an experienced hunter. To shoot him now would be arrant foolishness. The bullets might hit some of the others and miss their mark completely. And far too many people had seen his face. He raced away.

No one dared follow him; the word "gun" had frightened them all.

"Where are the police?" Zerach demanded. His words aroused bitter laughter. "If you're waiting for our police," an English-speaking youth volunteered, "wait in a restaurant. Until they show up in the street you can die of hunger."

Or of bullets.

The crowd dispersed. Zerach walked aimlessly through the crowded streets, his alert eyes scanning the vicinity. He was careful to avoid side streets. Every unexpected movement caused his heart to beat wildly; he was in a cold sweat. Whether this was the long arm of the Church or some other organization it was clear that they were dealing with a swift and efficient establishment whose agents were in close contact with each other. The man waiting for him at the hotel was not the same one who had pursued them in the airport.

Zerach spent the time wandering about; when night fell upon Prague at about 9:30 his fear increased geometrically. Hunger gnawed at his vitals; his mouth was dry with fear and thirst. He had eaten at noon, before leaving to the airport, and had not touched a morsel since. He should have been landing in Israel just about now. Lucky that he had thought of that. He pulled out his cell phone and called home to tell his wife about the delay.

"What happened?" she asked, shocked and upset.

"I have to stay abroad because of a unique circumstance," Zerach said, avoiding a clear answer. "I'll tell you an extremely interesting story when I get back."

"You don't sound right. Has anything happened?"

"I have to hang up. I'll talk to you later. Bye."

For the next two hours he walked in circles like a rocket in some kind of erratic orbit. His head was bursting with feverish thoughts, fear was making him tired, and worry about Shmuel added to the tension. He felt an extraordinary weakness, completely drained. He glanced at his watch and felt a stab of panic. Almost midnight! KLM's night flight to Amsterdam took off at 12:15. He hailed a cab and raced back to the airport. When he got to the terminal he heard the ominous roar of a jet engine being revved up for takeoff. Maybe a miracle would happen and there would be a delay?

His luggage was waiting in the locker where he had left it. The bags were heavy with crystal and toys; at least he would have something to give his family.

As he picked up the bags he heard the roar of a jet rising. If he would meet Shmuel again it would only be in Caracas. The next plane out was a Munich-bound Lufthansa flight, due to leave in about an hour. Without hesitation he bought a ticket and swiftly boarded. Once in his seat he felt more secure. Only one hour before the end of the nightmare called Prague.

At 1:15 a.m. the jet took off into the night.

### Caracas, 5761 (2000)

The San Bernardino synagogue in the heart of Caracas was deserted at this noon hour. Shmuel stood with his suitcase in the couryard, feeling alone and foolish. He ought to have made careful plans before arriving here. He lacked travel expertise; he was no man of the world.

The street itself was full of traffic. Cars streamed along like a rushing river. Pedestrians busy with their daily affairs passed by hastily, not sparing him a glance. The driver had been right This was indeed a strange and uncaring city. It was hot outside and the humidity hung heavily upon him as he stood entangled in his luggage and packages. Next to his seat on the plane he had found a colored pamphlet which gave some basic statistics and information about Venezuela. It told him that the climate was temperate, averaging in the 70's. Maybe the flyer was full of lies, or maybe it was just his bad luck, or perhaps the global warming everyone was talking about had begun to affect this particular country; whatever it was, before they landed the captain announced that the temperature was 85 degrees.

The next day he was slated to meet the anonymous letter writer in the

B'nai Brith building. With no choice, he would sleep in the synagogue tonight. Certainly it would be open by this evening, for *Minchah* and *Ma'ariv*. If he grew thirsty he would drink water from the tap. Hunger? So, he would fast a little —

"*Shalom aleichem, Reb Yid.*"

The sudden greeting, in a pronounced South American accent, pulled him out of the tangled skein of fruitless thoughts. A pleasant-looking man stopped short in front of him and grabbed his hand to shake it. His clothing was well cut and clean, and a stylish hat sat on his head. He had a well-combed gray beard and a pair of smiling blue eyes. "Where are you from?"

"Israel," Shmuel answered briefly.

"From Israel! What an important guest!" the man said, again warmly shaking Shmuel's hand. Shmuel felt encouraged — a ray of light in the darkness.

The man, it turned out, had arrived for a regularly scheduled class in Gemara organized by a group of workingmen who enjoyed their *"shtickel"* Gemara with *Tosafos*. The class would begin in another quarter of an hour, and this man had come early in order to turn on the air-conditioning and make the place comfortable. The Jew was sympathetic and pleasant and gave Shmuel a good feeling. He introduced himself as Arthur Taubman ("In shul they call me Azriel, but the name I use is Arthur"). He was a senior employee in an accounting firm, and he learned Torah twice a day. When he went out for lunch he headed toward the shul and at 10 o'clock in the evening he studied Gemara in depth with a *chavrusah* in his home.

That day Arthur did not return to his office after the class. Instead, he took Shmuel to his home. It was a lovely two-story villa in a Jewish residential neighborhood. "Be my guest for as long as you wish," he emphasized again and again. He settled Shmuel into a well-furnished, light and airy private room that included air-conditioning. His wife, Sylvia, a woman who radiated warmth and whose face was as pleasant and open as her husband's, served him a hot and satisfying meal, watching over him like a worried mother as he ate until he assured her he could not touch another bite. After the meal Arthur made sure that his guest grabbed a nap.

After a refreshing nap, Shmuel felt rejuvenated and renewed. Arthur then took him for a trip around the city, to show him both old and new Caracas. "You must see our city," he told him, as he drove his comfortable automobile, "in order to understand the great revolution it has undergone. Until fifty, sixty years ago we were a poor and weak country; suddenly, in one giant leap we raced forward. In the mad race for modernity, most of the old buildings were destroyed, those dating back to our colonial days. You know, beautiful homes, stylish buildings, all replaced by 20th-century architecture. It's a modern mix, an eclectic combination, from plain buildings lacking all character to skyscrapers that are nothing more than colored glass cubes."

Their first stop was — inevitably — the Plaza Bolivar in old Caracas. The business center of the city had moved from here to the newer sections, but in the eyes of many of its residents this was the heart of the metropolis. "A beautiful area, that has a lot for the tourist to see," Arthur sounded patriotic and proud, like a mother showing off her bright youngster's excellent report card.

They parked nearby and strolled contentedly through the lovely, multihued gardens. Elegant trees cast their shade upon the gigantic statue of El Liberatador, Simon Bolivar; the freedom fighter was mounted upon an equally huge horse.

"This bronze statue was cast 130 years ago, in Europe," Arthur said. "They brought it to Venezuela in pieces and put it together here."

"They told me it's illegal to put your feet on a bench here," Shmuel repeated the taxi driver's admonition.

Arthur gave an uncomfortable laugh. "That's quite true. The Venezuelan nation is very proud of Simon Bolivar. Not far from here, on the eastern side of the plaza, there's a large monument dedicated to the man and his family, but I won't take you there, since it's located in a cathedral."

"Are there many churches here?" Shmuel shuddered at the memory of cross-filled Prague.

"Absolutely," Arthur answered. "Caracas, like all of Venezuela, possesses a very Catholic character. In the course of a year there are dozens of festivals and holidays, all reckoned by the Church calendar. The greatest of all, the Carnival, you've probably heard of from its Brazilian counterpart. We get the day off on all these festivals but I stay at home and avoid going outside."

A Catholic city — Shmuel grew lost in thought. *All these years I believed that Yehoshua Cohen brought the Levin family to Caracas because it was on the other side of the world. Now I've learned another reason. Yes, and I still have to check with Yad L'Achim to learn more about that despicable kidnapper.*

"You're looking thoughtful," Arthur smiled.

"Yes," Shmuel nodded. Perhaps it would be a good idea to ask this fine Jew for some help. "I'm supposed to be meeting someone tomorrow at the B'nai Brith building, and I haven't a clue how to get there."

They sat down on a bench. "Legs on the ground only," Arthur commanded, smiling. "For one who's come to Caracas from Israel without any itinerary at all, it doesn't seem logical that such a small thing should bother you. I think that something much greater is disturbing you."

Shmuel was silent for a few seconds, his fingers rubbing his furrowed brow. *I would like to tell him everything, unload the burden that is sitting upon my heart, but it's hard for me to speak about it. But maybe if he talks to me, I'll be able to open up.*

It was as if Arthur had read his mind. "May I ask why you've come to Caracas?" he said, his tone carefully polite. "Do you have to marry off a son or a daughter? If you'd like I'll go with you from home to home to collect. I have many wealthy friends. You've heard, most likely, that Caracas is a city of contradictions: incredibly poor people living in barrios near wealthy residents who make as much in a week as the average worker does in a year. My friends and I are, thank G-d, among those."

Shmuel laughed. "No, I haven't come here to raise funds; that's not my problem, even though I have gotten involved in some huge, unexpected expenditures. Something completely different is bothering me, weighing me down every step of the way."

Arthur sat quietly. A clergyman clad in a brown cloak passed by, casting a hostile glance upon them. Shmuel blinked nervously. Had his pursuers come here too? No, false alarm: the man in the cloak kept going, evincing no further interest.

"Do you really want to hear?" he asked hoarsely, his throat dry. He had never thought that the very sight of a priest would almost paralyze him like this.

"If you want to tell me, please," Arthur said pleasantly.

Shmuel revealed everything, beginning with his childhood in Katamon, that bleak and tragic day when his friend had contracted the fatal illness, and continuing through the frenzied chase on the way to the airport in Prague. He did not omit a thing.

Arthur sat quietly all through the exciting tale. Occasionally, his mouth would open and he would be ready to interrupt, but each time he thought the better of it and awaited the end of the story.

Silence fell. Evening shadows began to darken the garden paths. "We have to go to the synagogue for *Minchah* and *Ma'ariv*," Arthur said.

They left Plaza Bolivar. As they were sitting in the car Arthur spoke. "I don't know if you want to call this *hashgachah pratis*, or a miracle. In our office we have a secretary, a non-Jew, who once told me something about neighbors of hers who had come from Israel as Jews and converted here."

"What?" The word came out as a scream.

"Don't get so excited yet," Arthur put a damper on his excitement. "The missionaries are very diligent, and undoubtedly have sent more than one group of Jews to Venezuela. The city is full of churches, and many of them include former Jews, apostates who have been brainwashed or who were seduced by the missionaries. Tomorrow I'll ask that secretary to refresh my memory and tell me the name of the family and some details."

"You think the family I'm searching for kept the name Levin? It sounds way too Jewish!"

"That's true," Arthur agreed, stopping at a red light. "But we can try. Maybe we'll find some thread."

"Do you think I should go to that meeting tomorrow?" Shmuel gave him a beseeching look that almost said the words: *Would you go with me?*

Arthur had been graced with an understanding mind and a caring heart. "I think it's worth a try. That's why you've come, after all. On the other hand, you've obviously gotten involved with a dangerous element. If the Church suspects that you're about to open the Pandora's box and let the scandals emerge, it will do all it can to get its hands on you. Remember, in Rome, the Mafia and the Church are neighbors, and, it seems, good neighbors."

Shmuel shuddered at the threat in his voice.

"I think," Arthur said, noticing his guest's obvious fear, "that I will go to the B'nai Brith building with you. But not openly. I'll stand from afar and watch what is going on. I know the place; there's an excellent lookout point on the roof of the very next building. If this is some kind of trap, I'll know it immediately. The police here are not the fastest, but if I tell them that someone is scribbling graffiti on one of the Bolivar memorials, they'll get there quickly."

"And in any case," Arthur added thoughtfully, after a moment's lapse, "I won't rely solely on the police. After all, I wouldn't be surprised to learn that the Church's dark connections extend into the police force. What was your friend's name, did you say? Zerach Britman?"

"That's right. But what can he do? He went back to Israel."

"I'm thinking about bringing him back here. Three are better than two." Arthur turned the wheel and pulled into the shul's parking lot.

Shmuel remembered that before they had parted Zerach had given him a business card which included his cell phone number. It was worth a try.

He handed the card to Arthur. "If you're looking for him, here's where you can find him. This includes his home number in B'nai Brak and his cell phone number."

"Excellent." Arthur shut the engine. "Now, let's go to *Minchah*."

"*Minchah, Ma'ariv,* and a *shiur* in between," Shmuel agreed happily. He felt an almost physical hunger for Torah learning.

"Gemara, with *Rishonim;* everything you'd like," Arthur laughed. "Thank G-d, you haven't fallen among ignorant people. Would you like to learn *b'chavrusah*?"

"What a question!"

They disappeared into the building.

The commercial vehicle that was standing nearby glided smoothly and silently away. The man sitting next to the driver lowered the binoculars from his eyes. "Look at that, Julio, how the Jews find friends so quickly. But they are so innocent and vulnerable," he said with great satisfaction to the driver, a fellow with the look of a mestizo, half Indian, half European.

"I've been following him from the moment he got off the plane, and he hasn't turned around once to look."

"Tomorrow he'll turn around, Don Juan," Julio grinned.

The man who answered to the name Don Juan said coldly, "I don't care if he turns around or not. Better for him to look straight up at the sky."

## 23

"**Y***Chechnya, 5761 (2000)*

ou don't mean that seriously!"

"And how I do."

"To kidnap the pope?"

"Absolutely," Selim Yagudayev nodded before his officers' obvious consternation.

"But it can't be, it's absolute madness!" one of them declared. "You might as well suggest that we dig a hole from one side of the globe to the other with a shovel. It's impossible to get within five miles of the man. He's surrounded by bodyguards on all sides twenty-four hours a day."

Selim Yagudayev was unimpressed. "I said it and I meant it. I've been working on this plan for months. We have top intelligence. I know everything about the pope there is to know; I have an inside source in the Vatican who gives me real-time information. Next week the pope is leaving on a trip to Africa, to visit his followers in the third world. He will take off from Rome in a leased Alitalia plane and land in Zaire. From there he goes to Cameroon and then Nigeria, then Chad, where he will

*Time Bomb* / 243

address thousands. This majestic visit will culminate in the Ivory Coast and Guyana, with a quick stop in Senegal. I've got an exact itinerary, from the moment he leaves Rome to the day of his return. That covers all take-offs and landings, start to finish, including all refueling stops. I opened a special file on it — code name: Popemobile — that includes everything: the names of his staffers, including bodyguards, assistants, the head of his office, spokespeople, personal physician, his cook and his secretary, who doesn't leave his side for a moment."

"Congratulations on your impressive data," his deputy, Kareem Nisadov, said, his voice edged with mockery. "But if he's surrounded by a human wall like that, how do you think we'll manage to get close to him? And you haven't even mentioned the security that each country is going to provide."

"I have a plan," Yagudayev's eyes burned; he ran his hands over the brown earth of the cavern floor. He slowly threw one clod after another up into the air.

"And what is this plan, if one may ask?"

The question came from Sayid Mashtatov, one of the top fighters of the indomitable guerrilla band.

Selim looked at him through fiery eyes kept partially closed, as if he were afraid he would scorch him with them fully open.

"When I say I have a plan, I have a plan. And believe me, I am providing you a generous share in a heroic deed that men will read about in history books."

Sayid grew silent. Selim was blessed with a powerfully charismatic personality and sweeping leadership abilities. He knew how to wipe out even a flicker of opposition well before it could begin to grow. His influence on men was immense, and when he spoke of the Chechen destiny, the prize that was coming closer and closer, he could take the spark of love for their homeland that burned in the breasts of the persecuted warriors and fan it into a great flame. There was electricity in the air whenever he was present, and the underground fighters shared the absolute conviction that one day he would return Chechnya to the Chechens and take his place as their leader. The veiled look he gave to Sayid was sufficient to convince all, including his deputy Kareem

Nisadov, who in the depths of his heart nursed a feeling of resentful envy at the man who had turned up so suddenly two years earlier and had so rapidly risen to greatness, unsurping his own place like a storm.

"So what are we going to do?" Kareem asked. His obedience seemed absolute; only the wagging tail was missing.

Selim looked carefully at his men. Face after face came under his x-ray scrutiny, his steely personality searching for the tiniest crack of weakness or, worse, an absence of total dedication — a betrayer.

The test ended successfully. No signs of betrayal here, not even a trace of doubt. This was a group of tough, inflexible patriots, forged without mercy, ready for anything even at the price of their own lives. Ten men who would follow him through fire and water, follow him anywhere. Behind them were hundreds of Chechen fighters, courageous and strong, but these were the fine edge of the blade.

He crouched before the smoldering fire. The charcoal cast a reddish glow upon him, giving him a mystical appearance. Blue-white lightning bolts seemed to dance deep in his eyes. Carefully planned leadership tactics or spontaneous, natural behavior — it did not matter; the man was a born leader.

"The operation is called 'Steel Fist' and will take place in exactly nine days. We will divide the time into hours; every hour will be critical to success. We have 216 hours. We will work on an exact schedule. Everyone will be given specific tasks, with each detail worked out. Tonight we will be leaving here and going to the Sheep-Shearer's Cave near the fields in the swamps of Torbakov, that stubborn stretch that neither Russian tanks nor soldiers have managed to uproot. There we will practice every point, every period and comma of 'Steel Fist.' A mock-up of the airplane is already waiting for us there. We'll rehearse dozens of times. The plan is completely worked out in my mind; tomorrow I'll finish polishing it and then give you the details."

The fighters looked at him with unconcealed admiration. Only Kareem, as usual, dared to ask a question.

"How are we going to manage to get on the plane? After all, if I understand correctly, this is no regularly scheduled flight. The plane is chartered by the Holy See and his staff. Why will they open the door for us?"

"A good question," Selim praised him — one had to throw an occasional positive word to this rebel who had never forgiven him his takeover of the leadership. "The answer is simple. During one of the stops — you will be given details later — we will approach the plane and someone inside will open it for us —"

A dozen mouths opened at once. "What?"

A mischievous glint danced in Yagudayev's eyes. He stared at Kareem for an extended time, until the deputy lowered his eyes in submission.

"You will be the one," he said confidently. "You will open the door for us."

❦

*Prague, 5761 (2000)*

"You have failed."

He hung his head and made no reply.

"You will have to reach your own conclusions; that is, you and your revolver." The voice whipped him in its steeliness. "I thought you were Prague's top hired gun, and do you see what you've done? Those two bearded Jews have gotten away without a scratch. You were a big hero with that 85-year-old man, Paltiro Bilcav. That really did look like a case of theft and homicide. By the way," the tone suddenly became pacifying, "what about the city translator, Sizhur Bayzhka?"

"Tonight he has a dentist appointment." The dark eyes showed no trace of emotion. "I will be taking over as assistant. Anesthesia, you know."

"As a religious man I have no desire to hear anything about it," the man in the brown cloak cut him off. "I am relying on you to deal with the unfortunate translator. May the Lord have mercy upon his sinning soul and take it beneath his wings this evening. But why did you leave the two Jews in the cemetery? They were in your hands!"

"They were not in my hands," the voice of the man with the wrestler's shoulders was adamant. "A tourist bus suddenly stopped right by the cemetery entrance. Is it my fault? The minute they turned up the rules of the games were changed — to make a successful hit, one needs a clean area."

"And what about afterwards?"

"They're as quick to react as monkeys," the assassin complained. "But don't worry; my friends in Caracas will take the job. Julio Rodriguez and Big Don Juan are professional killers who have no competition — the best in Venezuela. As far as I'm concerned, those two Jews are already dead. They haven't a chance of escaping Don Juan's rifle, or the knife of Julio Rodriguez. Or maybe it will be — it doesn't matter, I don't have to make that decision. They've got a variety of means, and a considerable army. They're each hand picked. You can relax."

### Caracas, 5761 (2000)

Shmuel passed the night in the home of Arthur, his indefatigable host. In his honor Arthur had forgone studying with his regular *chavrusah*, and instead learned with Shmuel a difficult *sugya*, one on which Shmuel had given several *shiurim* in the past. Arthur was in awe at the many brilliant explanations which, in their time, had made quite a stir in the yeshivah world. *Which yeshivah*, he wondered aloud, *was lucky enough to have a scholar of Shmuel's caliber in its ranks*?

A cloud seemed to settle upon Shmuel's face; his eyes begged his host to change the subject. Arthur realized that he had unwittingly stepped on some aching toes and quickly and suavely redirected the conversation. Instead, he showed him the lovely silver items he had purchased in honor of Pesach which sparkled behind the glass of a well-stocked breakfront in the beautifully furnished living room.

*He's a modest and humble man,* Shmuel thought, *even when he's showing off his wealth, he only shows things used for mitzvos.* There were many more beautiful objects in the room, fine art hanging on the walls, but he ignored these. Shmuel thought, wryly, of a saying he had once heard: "A rich man who shows me his wealth is like a beggar who shows me his poverty; one is seeking the gift of my pity, the other the gift of my jealousy."

But Arthur was not seeking the gift of jealousy. He was not trying to show off, he was simply displaying his Jewish pride that he had merited to honor the holidays with cherished vessels.

When Shmuel walked upstairs to his bedroom late that night he had considerable food for thought. The reading lamp near the bedside table caught his attention for a moment. Its soft light fell on a lovely ornament of artificial pink roses. Points of light gleamed like stars on the edges of the flowers' stems — optical fibers that reflected the light from the base — casting a magical, peaceful glow upon the environment.

Sleep pulled him into some distant place the moment he had finished saying *Shema* and lay his head on the pillow.

---

It was precisely a quarter to 10 when Arthur drove him to the B'nai Brith building. Shmuel actually got out a few blocks away and made his way there on foot. It was a large, impressive building, with the words "B'nai Brith" displayed on it in both Spanish and Hebrew. Shmuel's throat was tight with nervousness. Was his anonymous correspondent indeed waiting inside as he had promised?

There was a small flow of traffic in the courtyard. Two secretaries — a stream of musical Spanish issuing from their lips — were walking with brown cardboard boxes. They spoke quickly, swallowing their words. A gardener wielding a large pair of pruning shears was clearing the undergrowth near a carefully designed hedge. A yarmulke-wearing clerk carrying a bottle of spring water passed by, occasionally putting the bottle to his lips and drinking thirstily. Nothing seemed unusual or strange.

There was no one waiting for him.

Disappointment struck him with full force. Had he come all this way — this long, arduous way — for nothing?

He glanced at his watch. 10:15 a.m. The mysterious writer had told him to be here at 10 o'clock. Could he be late?

He suddenly noticed that the courtyard extended further. An extremely narrow path led between the hedges, turning past the back of the building itself. The lovely garden seemed to continue there. Worth a look.

He walked the length of the path.

In the middle of the garden he saw a white plastic table and two plastic chairs. A cheerful umbrella was opened in the center of the table, shielding it from the sun.

An elderly woman was sitting on one of the chairs. She wore a large-brimmed brown hat and stared at him with sharp, curious eyes.

He gazed at her questionioningly.

The woman stood up. "Are you Rabbi Shmuel Bilad?"

He nodded, feeling unable to speak. He thought her voice was familiar, but wanted to hear one or two more sentences.

"You can stop wondering," the woman said with a smile. "I am Sabrina Lombardo, but you remember me as Hadassah Levin, your neighbor in Katamon."

Shmuel felt faint. Now he recognized the voice. A little hoarser, perhaps, but it was the same voice. She had been younger than 40 years old when he had known her; now she must be close to 80. But the eyes were her eyes; full of expression, full of interest. Deep in the pupils one could discern wellsprings of bitterness and sorrow.

"I am happy to see you, Shmuel Bilad," the old woman said, still smiling. "If I had passed you on the street I would never have recognized you. When I left Katamon you were a 13-year-old boy without a trace of a beard, without glasses. Now I see before me an aging, graying man."

"Thanks for the compliment," he said sarcastically.

"Nothing in this world remains the same," she laughed. "Look at me; I was in the prime of life when I left Israel. Now I'm an old woman."

"To be perfectly honest, I'm stunned," he said. "I didn't know who was going to meet me. I thought maybe it was one of your sons, Moishy or Ahrele."

The elderly woman sighed. "I didn't want to identify myself. I was afraid of how you'd react; I was worried about who would read the letter. I am full of fears and suspicions, always."

"Why?"

The woman pointed to the blue skies above her. "You're lucky. You've arrived in Caracas when the weather is fine. Usually we have summer rains and you can't sit outside like this. If it had been raining, I would have taken you to a more convenient place."

"You'd rather be outside?"

"Absolutely. Walls have ears, you know. I am often followed. My life has been hell," she added, her face growing sober.

"Where are the twins?" he asked eagerly.

She took a deep breath and sighed once again. "You've remained a good Jew. You have a long beard, you look like a truly respected rabbi. My sons never had that chance. They are not Jewish."

A few persistent tears streaked down her cheeks. With difficulty she tried to keep her composure.

"Where do they live? Can I see them?" He was both curious and pained at the same time.

Mrs. Levin shook her head firmly back and forth. She pulled out a handkerchief and touched the corners of her eyes. "I would advise you not to meet them. You remember two sweet Jewish boys. What you will see today are two grown men, full of bitterness and despair, men who have destroyed their own lives. They are angry at the entire world — and you are no exception."

A few yards from them, around the bend and hidden from their eyes, the gardener stood, his giant shears in his hand. He listened to the Hebrew conversation intently; it appeared that he understood every word. He kept a firm grasp on the clippers — a broad-bladed affair that could easily be transformed into a first-rate weapon.

Shmuel tried to understand. "Why are they angry at the whole world?"

The old woman burst out in bitter laughter. Unshed tears sparkled in her eyes. "What a stupid question," she said fervently, following with an immediate apology. "I'm sorry. I have been in pain for so many years. You don't have to be my sacrifice. Do you know what happened to my boys? They were two talented, bright children, weren't they?"

Shmuel nodded his assent.

"They are garbagemen!" the wounded woman blurted out, like one revealing a deeply held family secret. She lapsed into silence.

"Garbagemen? What do you mean?"

"What's so hard to understand?" she said, her voice frigid. "They empty trash cans into the municipal garbage trucks. They work different shifts, but at the same job. Do you understand why they had to convert? So they could become trash collectors in Caracas. It may be different elsewhere, but in this society, there is no more degrading punishment, nothing crueler, than to force a person into this type of employment. The Church punishes my sons every day, every hour."

"But why punish them? Hadn't they become good Christians?"

The steel shears lay firmly grasped in the gardener's hands. He listened intently to every word that Sabrina was saying.

"It's a long story. I can't tell it all at once."

Green leaves once again started falling to the ground.

"Why have you called me here?"

"To awaken your sleeping conscience," Sabrina hissed. "Is there no justice in the world? I checked before I sent that letter; I learned that you've become a Torah scholar, you've established a proper Jewish home. Why didn't my boys deserve that? Why do they have to pick up garbage in Caracas while you sit and enjoy Torah learning in Yerushalayim? I want you to suffer a little with them!"

She glanced all around her and furtively pressed a piece of paper into Shmuel's hand.

Shmuel read the few lines:

"I am afraid of eavesdroppers and that's why I have to talk to you like this. Don't be insulted. Play the game. I have called you for an entirely different reason. I'll tell you about it in my home."

"My conscience is not asleep." Shmuel was, indeed, playing the game. "Believe me, I've suffered over this until today. I have no rest because of my part in what happened to your son, my dear friend Dudy Levin."

"Gonzales and Santos have used up all my tears. I have nothing left for Dudy," the old woman sighed.

"Who are they?" he asked, immediately realizing what her answer would be.

"Gonzales is Moishy, and Santos is Ahrele," she said dully. "At their *bris* we named them for Moshe and Aharon. My husband, Shalom, may he rest in peace, and I were certain that they would be the new Moshe and Aharon. Look where they wound up instead!"

*Time Bomb* / 251

Her pain tore at his heart. He felt a surge of compassion and a burning desire to help her.

"What can I do for you, Mrs. Levin — excuse me, Mrs. Lombardo?"

The old woman stood up heavily. "Right now, do nothing for me. I just wanted to put a few cracks in your image. When you gaze at yourself in a mirror, your reflection won't look so perfect anymore."

She winked and stared at the rolled-up piece of paper that lay on the plastic table. He grabbed the wad.

"Call me at home. I have a lot to say to you. I'll answer any time, even at 3 o'clock in the morning."

On the edge of the note she had scribbled an address and phone number.

"I appreciate the opportunity to explain myself," Shmuel said. "It's very important to me." He quickly jotted down the name and address of his host and the phone number, and put the paper down next to her. She grabbed it with one swift motion.

He turned to go.

The gardener whispered into his palm, "He's leaving," and immediately turned to the weeds.

The car parked next to the building roared to life. Its driver stooped down and whispered into his hand, "Got it."

Shmuel passed the gardener, lost in thought. The old woman stayed in her place, her eyes gazing at the note he had passed her. If only the connection would continue. If only evil hands would not destroy the wonderful idea that she had had.

Shmuel passed the building's entrance and looked up at the windows of the nearby office building. Arthur Taubman was standing behind one of them peering down at him through small binoculars. Shmuel could just make out his figure. Arthur waved his hand in front of him. That was the pre-arranged signal that meant "You are being followed."

Shmuel waited tensely for Arthur to join him.

A commercial Mazda van pulled up next to him. The driver opened the window. "Senor, can you help me?" he asked in English.

Shmuel wheeled around toward him.

"I am a tourist here and I'm lost. Maybe you can help?"

He opened a city map and spread it on his knees.

A trap!

"I am also a tourist," Shmuel said hastily, looking worriedly at his watch. Where was Arthur? Why was it taking him so long to get here?

"But maybe you can still help?" the driver pleaded. "I don't even understand the street names. What's right and what's left? I'm completely confused."

He sounded absolutely innocent. Shmuel walked cautiously toward him. A battle raged in his usually soft-hearted breast. To refuse help went absolutely against his nature. But his experience in Prague had shown him that he was facing a strong and merciless enemy.

He slowed down, stopping about a yard from the car. The driver gave him another beseeching look, as if willing him to approach.

In the doorway of the office building the image of Arthur suddenly appeared. "Run, it's a trap!"

The van's door flew open. From beneath the road map a lasso flew out, landing firmly around his throat.

"Help! They're strangling me!" Shmuel wanted to scream. But no sound issued from his mouth. He was dragged to the ground and two powerful arms pulled him into the vehicle.

The van swiftly lurched away.

Arthur did not waste a second. He jumped into his car, revved his engine, and raced after the van, all the while honking in order to attract attention.

The pursuit continued onto the next street, but the distance between them grew greater and greater. Arthur was afraid he would lose the van completely. He grabbed his cell phone and called the police.

"I want to report a kidnapping," he said dramatically. "The victim is in a Mazda van, and I'm on its trail."

"Where are you located?"

"Not far from Plaza Diego Ibara, on Route 67. We're traveling north to south."

"Keep us posted," the policeman said. Arthur did not hang up; he wanted to hear the reaction in the station. To his disappointment, he could not discern any unusual activity. The police were taking their time.

Two more streets and the distance between them had grown even greater. The driver of the fleeing vehicle knew his business; he took every opportunity to increase his lead, and soon had moved out of Arthur's sight.

*Just like in the movies. There's nothing for me to do but wait for the police,* he fumed to himself. *How did I allow him to go?*

He began to tremble. As an old resident of the city he knew well how the "organization" worked, and he realized that the chances of seeing his scholarly guest again were close to zero.

# 24

"The chances are just about zero."

Zerach Britman arrived in Caracas on a Lufthansa flight exactly twenty-four hours after Shmuel. Like Shmuel he, too, felt lost and friendless in a strange and distant land, but even more he was burdened by the possibility that this entire journey was for nothing, since the chances of his running into Shmuel were close to nil.

Like Shmuel a day earlier, he, too, decided to travel to Caracas's Jewish neighborhood.

As he was driving from the airport to the city his mobile phone rang.

"Am I speaking with Zerach Britman?" an unknown voice asked, speaking Hebrew with a pronounced South American accent.

"Who is this?" he asked cautiously.

"My name is Azriel Taubman," the man identified himself. "I live in Caracas. Shmuel Bilad told me about you and gave me your number. I need your help urgently."

"Where are you?" Zerach was miserly about imparting information. Let the other man tell him the facts, then he would decide how much to reveal.

"I'm in my home in Caracas. Shmuel was my guest and he told me we could rely on you. It's urgent that you drop everything and come to Caracas."

"How do I know if that's a good idea?" Zerach was still suspicious.

The line was silent for a moment. "You are afraid of a trap?" he laughed. "Okay, I'll give you a proper password — a *'vort'* that I heard from Shmuel yesterday. Here it is..." The words of the brilliant halachic explanation poured out.

The introduction melted away the last vestiges of suspicion. "Where do you live?" Zerach interrupted him. What he had heard was sufficient.

Arthur gave him his address. Zerach hung up without revealing anything. The man sounded very upset; obviously, something important had happened.

In a half-hour Zerach's cab was parked before Arthur's door. Zerach pulled his heavy baggage out from the trunk and paid the driver $11. "Now it's my turn to surprise him," he thought with a grin as he rang the doorbell. The man of the house would not believe that he was standing there in front of him just half an hour after they had spoken. Surely he thought that he had been calling Zerach to come from Israel or Prague and it would be days before he could arrive.

Indeed Arthur was shocked by the prank that Zerach, a broad smile on his face, had played on him.

Five minutes later the smile was wiped off his face.

"He's been kidnapped?"

Arthur stood next to him in the foyer, helping him bring in his luggage. He gave a melancholy nod of assent. "I didn't want to tell you on the phone. You never know who is listening."

"What's happening now?"

"We're waiting."

Arthur sat down next to him at a table laden with food and urged Zerach to eat. If someone had told Arthur the week before that he would be hosting two Israelis, and that one would be kidnapped in front of him, he would have enjoyed a good laugh.

"So what do we do?" Zerach asked dejectedly.

"There's nothing to do. We have to wait for the police to begin their investigation. I haven't any idea where he's been taken."

The terrible thought weighed heavily on Arthur's heart. Caracas's criminal element was not known for delay in carrying out its operations. He was afraid that Shmuel was no longer living.

The phone shrilled. Sylvia Taubman picked up the receiver and handed it to her husband. "Arthur, it's for you."

"This is Sabrina Lombardo of Caracas," a weary voice said. "I believe I am speaking to Shmuel Bilad's host."

"That's correct." Arthur's eyes fell upon Zerach, sitting across from him, stony faced. He had barely tasted the soup that had been set before him; news of his friend's disappearance had sent him into a depression.

Sabrina's next words came as a surprise. "I know that he's been kidnapped," she said flatly. "I met him yesterday in the garden of the B'nai Brith building. I left right after him, and managed to see how they grabbed him. My G-d, it was terrible!"

*She must have been the old woman in the brown hat that I saw through my binoculars,* Arthur thought. *The woman who invited Shmuel here.*

"Did you have something specific to tell me?"

"Yes."

Arthur was not surprised at the loud background noise. Evidently she was speaking from a public phone in the middle of the street. She was clearly accustomed to the fact that her home phone was tapped, and it had probably been years since she had made a private call from there, using, instead, a different public phone each time. This time she had chosen one on Avenida Bolivar, Caracas's main street, near the Park Centrale. Here, no one could eavesdrop on her words.

"What is it you want to say?" The old woman had been silent for too long. Had something happened to her? Maybe she had forgotten; maybe she had Alzheimer's. Who knew?

*Time Bomb* / 257

But Sabrina Lombardo had not forgotten. "I think I know where they've taken him. I know how the Mafia works here. They take their victims to building sites and tie them to great steel beams that are due to have concrete poured on them. Their men are building contractors, and they keep an eye out on the area, making sure no one is watching as the concrete is poured. The next day half a meter of cement covers the unfortunate one. He's buried there forever, and no one ever finds a trace of him."

"So tell me, where did they take him? Quickly!" Arthur felt a stab of panic.

"I'm not sure, but I suspect it was to the Los Fantakos building site, where they're building a new high-tech development. Do you know it?"

"Vaguely." Occasionally Arthur would pass the new industrial area, and he had seen the signs proclaiming the high-tech center being constructed there.

"I'm guessing that he's been taken there," the old woman continued. "But if you wait too long the chances of his being alive grow smaller and smaller."

"How do you know all this?"

The phone clicked off.

"We've got to go right now," Arthur cried. "We've got a lead at last."

---

Shmuel looked around him, at what little he could see. He felt a throb of despair, and his lips murmured the words of *vidui* for perhaps the tenth time.

His throat was still hoarse and aching from the suffocating rope that had snared him like an untamed bronco in the America's Wild West. He had never seen such a thing before. The seemingly innocent driver had thrown something out with lightning swiftness and before he could understand what was going on he had been pulled into the van with a mighty tug.

Once in the vehicle someone had fallen upon him and covered his face with a black blindfold. He could see nothing; even breathing was difficult. No one said a word. He had been taken to this deserted building; the frame of a building, to be more exact. His arms and legs had been bound with a merciless, cutting rope, the black scarf had been removed, revealing more blackness around him. Then they had disappeared.

He did not know exactly what to expect, but from the look of the beams around him he suspected that concrete was going to be poured on the area shortly. The air was thick with the smell of newly poured cement.

He lay between piles of steel beams. It seemed that the next construction job would turn him into a piece of a wall in an unknown building in a land so far away, a land he had never dreamed he would visit.

"Prepare to meet your G-d, Israel"; the words of the verse repeated themselves in his consciousness over and over. You are about to meet your Creator. It is the end, the circle is closed. Your actions brought the Levin family here; it was decreed that you come after them to see what your negligence caused. For your sins, you will pay with your life.

There is justice in the world. You destroyed an entire family. You took two shining youngsters and transformed them into Venezuelan trash collectors, apostates, their lives empty and without meaning. For this reason you were brought to die in their city. There is no other way to repay your debt. No other way.

The terrible misfortune was that his own family would have no gravesite to visit. Actually, they would never know what had happened to him. His wife would be an *agunah* forever. No one would be able to attest to his death. In the morning he would hear the sound of cement pouring down on his head; he would hear nothing else.

"Your eyes saw my unfinished form..." The words of the verse in *Tehillim* suddenly flashed through his brain. When I was a fetus in my mother's womb, *HaKadosh Baruch Hu* saw my unfinished body, the raw material that had not yet been formed into arms and legs. I was in His Hands like the material in the hands of the craftsman, like glass in the hands of the glassblower — with His Will he forms it and with His Will He melts it — just like the words of the Yom Kippur prayer. If He so wills, the Craftsman pours the material into a form; if He wills, He throws it into the oven and melts it down to form something new.

Already then I was in Your Hands, *Ribbono Shel Olam*. I could have been stillborn, never have seen the light of the sun. The Creator judged me, decided to let me live. Perhaps now, too, He will have mercy on me?

The gates of repentance are never shut. I will repent completely, from the depths of my heart. If my repentance will be accepted and my sins atoned, perhaps I shall be saved. If not, let my death be my atonement.

Hot tears poured down his cheeks. He had never cried like this, never in his entire life.

Now he knew. Everything was being judged, being weighed and measured. There was no way for him to get out of here. Only a miracle could save him. Would there be a miracle?

He remembered the words of the Gemara: "One makes a vow in a time of distress." *Ribbono Shel Olam, if my life is saved I will sanctify it only for You, merciful Father. I will have no other goal in my life than to bring others back to You.*

*I've been looking for work in order to feed my ego, so that no one should call me a retired and useless pensioner. I've forgotten that so many Jewish souls are searching for a ray of light in their dark lives, for someone to bring them back to their Creator. I vow this: I will devote myself entirely to them.*

Something changed. Suddenly he did not feel the bonds cutting through his flesh.

He hoped for the best.

❦

Darkness fell on the city at 10 p.m. Arthur and Zerach silently left the house. A few hours earlier Arthur had parked his car two blocks away. Now they sneaked out, separately making their way to the vehicle. Arthur got in; then Zerach sat down and the car drove off.

The city flew by them. They passed the center, with its busy flow of traffic. Merry lights and the sound of revelry surrounded them in the busy streets and pedestrian malls, a surge of effervescent vitality that grew dimmer as they grew more distant. Now they were passing the night's shadows, their headlights the only rays in the dimness. Caracas had tucked itself in for the night. The poorer the neighborhood, the deeper the blackness.

In the distance they could make out the mysterious skeletons of half-built buildings in Caracas's new industrial area. "This is what she meant," Arthur whispered, a glint of fear in his eyes.

"It's like a jungle," Zerach said, also in a whisper, though there was no one to hear them speak. "A jungle of towers. Who can find someone here? Do you really believe we'll find Shmuel? And there must be watchmen here; we might be faced with an army of them. If every building has one —" His voice died out.

"That's what they say: 'A question finds an answer with a *chavrusah.*'" Arthur said with a grim smile.

"What question? What answer?"

"You'll understand soon," Arthur said, his smile coming more naturally. "Zerach, you've lit up the night. You're worth your weight in gold."

"What did I say?" Zerach blushed in the darkness. It was nice to be complimented, even if he had no idea why.

"You asked how we would find him. The watchmen themselves will do it."

They left the car and walked toward the construction site. Large metal fences concealed huge pits slashed into the earth. Arthur looked for watchmen, but the place seemed deserted.

They passed by a partially built multistoried building, taking care not to trip over beams and heaps of sand or gravel. They detoured around lathes and cranes with outstretched steel arms.

A chorus of harsh barks greeted them. "While we're looking for the watchman, he's come and found us," Zerach grinned.

The smile froze on his face. From the deep blackness came the figure of two murderous mastiffs, circling him with wild barks.

"Help!" Zerach shrieked. "Get away from me; I haven't done anything to you!"

His heart pounded like an African tom-tom. Another moment and the dog's sharp teeth would be sinking into his throat.

"'And to all the Children of Israel no dog shall whet its tongue,'" he quoted in desperation.

Perhaps the charm worked, or maybe it was the appearance of their owner. The watchman appeared from the dimness, a large flashlight in his hand. "*Basta*! Enough!" he shouted at the two enormous dogs. They hung their tails and slunk away.

The flashlight played upon the two frightened men as the watchman gazed at them suspiciously.

"Who are you? What are you doing here this time of night?"

Arthur answered with a few quick sentences. The watchman showed particular interest in his outstretched hand, and the crackling sound of crumpled bills being fingered within it. His angry countenance took on a wholly different cast. "Yes, two men came here at noon. One of them looked like you, Jewish. They went to the Los Fantakos building site. I suggest you check over there. I'm the only watchman in the area."

"We'll need your flashlight for the next twenty minutes."

"I don't leave my flashlight for one second at night. I could break my neck here," the watchman said firmly.

Another crackle of bills.

"How long did you say? Twenty minutes?" The watchman changed his mind with amazing swiftness. "I can do without a flashlight for twenty minutes."

They were indeed fortunate to have the light with them. They passed numerous obstacles and pitfalls and several times almost fell into gaping holes. The construction area was larger than they had imagined and they managed to get quite lost until they finally stumbled onto the Pantcom building frame.

This was going to be a gigantic building with a base of more than 1,200 square meters. Four levels of the building seemed ready for the pouring of concrete. Where should they look?

Zerach again proved the readiness of his wit. "I'm trying to get into their criminal shoes. If I wanted to bury someone in concrete I would take him to the deepest place. Two reasons: First, so he would not be found before the concrete is poured. Second, if there's a problem with the cement, there's a smaller chance of the body being found. Let's go look in the cellar."

Arthur had learned not to ignore the advice of this chassid from Bnei Brak. "Fine."

They carefully made their way through the darkness, the beam from the flashlight only partially illuminating their path. They descended two stories and began wandering, slowly and cautiously, through the massive room.

"Shmuel!" Zerach shouted his name. "Shmuel, can you hear me? It's me, Zerach Britman!"

Heavy silence.

They strained their ears, trying to hear any unusual noise, some stifled groan, perhaps, or a distant echo. But the silence was absolute, as unbroken as the darkness. Only from some far-off corner came the sound of water dripping from a leaky faucet into a metal pan.

"There's no one here," Arthur said despondently. "That old lady, Mrs. Lombardo, needs more updated sources."

"I think she knows what she's talking about," Zerach answered obstinately. "Maybe he's already been killed, or maybe they've gagged him. Let's take a look through the entire basement."

"Are you crazy? You know how big it is?"

"Let's try."

With unsteady legs they walked through, stumbling with each step over discarded items: electrical cables, plastic sewage pipes, large barrels half-filled with cement that had hardened into stone.

The newest obstacle suddenly appeared beneath their weary legs — a huge latticelike pile of metal beams crisscrossing each other.

Zerach breathed deeply. "Arthur," he said, his voice trembling, his teeth chattering. "This area is ready to have the concrete poured."

Arthur played the light over the metal.

Suddenly they gasped and shrieked involuntarily.

The beam of light shone on a dark bundle almost lost in the site.

The flashlight fell from Arthur's numb fingers. An unbroken blackness fell.

Sabrina Lombardo returned from shopping at the neighborhood grocery, two heavy bags in her hands. The ravages of age were not visible here: at 81 she looked good, her legs carried her well, without the need of a cane or other support. Deep in her heart she believed that G-d was repaying her for the lack of pleasure or satisfaction in her life by awarding her a relatively healthy old age. Her senses and thoughts were all still sharp, her heart "strong as a tractor's motor," as she liked to tell her doctor during her annual checkup. "I hope I'll look as good as you do when I'm in my 80's," he would always remember to tell her. "If one has to grow old, it should be as you have, Mrs. Lombardo."

She rode the elevator to the third floor and stepped vigorously towards her apartment. Standing next to the door her sharp eye saw that something was wrong. The door had been opened in her absence. The tiny toothpick she had placed so carefully on the threshhold before she had left to shop had disappeared.

Someone was waiting for her in her home. It might be Gonzales or Santos.

Or an uninvited guest.

Quietly, ever so quietly, she returned to the elevator, the heavy bags still in her hands.

Her decision had been the right one.

As she stood in the elevator the door of her apartment flew open and a young man peered out. In his hand he held a menacing-looking revolver. He had been waiting in ambush for her and had come out to look for her when she had not come in.

The gun was equipped with a silencer. The young man aimed directly at her and pulled the trigger. The mirror in the elevator shattered into a thousand pieces.

Sabrina jammed her finger on a button and the door slammed shut. The elevator started its slow descent.

She guessed his next step. He would run down the stairs and wait for her in the lobby, his gun in hand.

Coolly she pushed the button for the second floor. When she reached it she took one bag of groceries with her; the other she left propped up against the elevator wall.

The young man had, indeed, been waiting for her. When the elevator came down to the first-floor lobby and the door opened he sprayed the interior with gunfire, and followed the hail of bullets with a flow of curses. The bag leaning on the elevator wall had exploded; he had wasted his bullets on cans of vegetables and fruits, staining the lobby and elevator with puddles of sweetened prune juice — Sabrina's favorite.

Without wasting another moment he raced up the stairs. He realized that the old woman had fooled him, exiting the elevator on one of the other floors. Now she will see the superiority of youth over age.

She was waiting for him behind a turn in the stairwell and let him have a huge can of olives full in the face.

The gun flew out of his hand as the heavy can shattered his nose. His face flowed with blood. He gave a shriek of pain and clutched his face.

Sabrina raced by, stopping only to throw two or three more cans at him, and a tube of toothpaste. She disappeared outside and hailed a passing cab.

"I hope they haven't gotten to Santos's place; he's only living there two weeks," she murmured to herself. To the driver she said crisply, "Avenida Dalmido del Casol, near the Kodra de Bolivar Theater, as fast as you can."

## 25

"Where's the flashlight?"

Zerach simply wanted to ask the question, but it came out as a shriek that echoed throughout the cellar.

From one corner, the spot which they had illuminated just moments before, came a groan.

"Shmuel, is that you?" Zerach cried in a voice not his own.

The groan grew louder. The two bent down and carefully felt the ground beneath them.

"I found it," Arthur said exultantly. "I've got the flashlight here."

Another moment and the beam of clear light flooded the dark cellar. Arthur aimed the light into the corner once again.

The black bundle could be seen more clearly.

Their hearts beating heavily, they approached slowly and gingerly, inch after inch. Was this Shmuel Bilad, or was this some new kind of trap?

Zerach burst into tears. He had seen harrowing sights in his life, but never something like this.

Shmuel was curled up in a ball, each hand bound to a foot, like a calf before slaughter. A filthy rag was stuffed into his mouth. He was covered by a black blanket; only his silvery-black beard stuck out. A large funnel was suspended over his head.

"Only the Nazis could have done such a brutal thing," Zerach breathed, tears running down his cheeks.

"Do you understand?" Arthur whispered, his eyes staring at the huge mouth of the funnel. "In the morning they would have sent tons of concrete through the funnel. If we hadn't hurried —"

Shmuel was fully conscious, though on the verge of collapse.

Zerach hastily pulled the rag out of his mouth. "Shmuel, are you all right? The nightmare is over. We've come to rescue you."

Shmuel tried to speak, but his strength failed him. He moaned weakly in pain as Zerach and Arthur, with superhuman efforts, opened the bonds that had held him fast.

"Water," he managed to whisper through cracked lips.

"Soon," Zerach soothed him. "We don't have any here."

They tried supporting him on both sides, but Shmuel could not walk. "My legs and arms are broken," he groaned.

"I think it's just pain from being tied up for so long," Arthur calmed him. "The blood hasn't been circulating for some time. Soon you'll feel much better."

Shmuel limped slowly, leaning heavily on the two men. They approached the door, Arthur illuminating the way with his flashlight.

The watchman was waiting for them outside, impatient to retrieve his flashlight. His eyes opened wide when he saw Shmuel. Like a man seeing a ghost, Arthur thought; this was the first time the watchman was seeing a dead man walking. In the list of Mafia victims in the construction site he was the first man who had not been turned into concrete.

"What now?"

The three were sitting in Arthur's foyer. Shmuel, to be more accurate, was lying down, slowly sipping hot tea. He still found it difficult to speak. One could clearly see the effects of his harrowing ordeal on his face, and particularly in his eyes, which betrayed confusion and fear.

"So what do you think, Zerach? What do we do now?"

Zerach spoke slowly. "I think Shmuel and I should get out of here as fast as we can."

"Meaning?" Arthur demanded. "You're not comfortable with me? It's too crowded here? You want me to repaint the walls? Just say so."

Zerach smiled. Arthur was a man after his own heart, a Jew with a sense of humor. With the help of his infectious grin Zerach had in the past managed to lift the spirits of terminal patients in the most dire conditions, infusing them with a spark of hope. As a member of the volunteer organization, *Berachah u'Refuah,*" he had seen almost daily gratifying and surprising responses to a smile among terminally ill patients.

"It's really quite simple," Zerach answered. "Shmuel came here in response to a letter that played on his emotions, his feelings of guilt, feelings that were already well developed. He's already met the respected grandmother, and the bad guy as well, and what came out of it? They tied him up under a steel beam and were on the verge of turning him into a permanent part of modern Caracas's industrial zone. What do we have to find here? I don't know how, but we've hit the Church of Prague in the gut and it's about to hit back. Someone put a contract out on us from Prague to Caracas; we've got to get out of this mess."

Shmuel raised a feeble arm in protest. "Don't put words in my mouth. I disagree. The Church and its underworld allies don't scare me."

"Big hero," Zerach said. "You've managed to forget how you looked two hours ago. Or are you having a hard time giving up the idea of a cement shower?"

"I haven't forgotten anything," Shmuel said. "My arms and legs are still burning like *Havdalah* candles. But I came to Caracas with a certain goal, and I haven't done anything to achieve that goal. I have to meet again with Sabrina Lombardo — Hadassah Levin, as I knew her — and hear what she wants to tell me. I think she desperately needs my help. Don't forget that if not for her information I would have been —"

"And where does an old lady get such detailed information on the assassination methods of the underworld?" Zerach interrupted him angrily. "Shmuel, this isn't right. You walked into the lion's den with your eyes open. Will you do it a second time? The woman is an actress. I don't believe a word she says. She's a plant of the Church."

"Zerach, you're a smart man, but not a scholar," Shmuel said in a yeshivah singsong. "I received the first letter from her before I ever dreamed of visiting Prague. I ask you, did Sabrina Lombardo know that I was planning a trip to Prague, did she ever think that I would stumble upon the journal of Avraham Abba Fernbach — Schriftsgiss? That was when the Church began to follow us. I suspect the messengers of the Church will try to attack her as they did me. She's in terrible danger!"

"Why do you think so?" Arthur broke in tensely.

"Because she wanted to give me some information," Shmuel explained. "I think the information is dangerous to the Church, and it will try every means it can to prevent her from communicating with me. We've got to find her before they do!"

Zerach tried to salvage the shards of broken pride. "Shmuel, you just told me I'm not a scholar. Let an unlettered fool like me ask you something, like a student to his teacher: If the Church has been after us only since we uncovered a secret in Prague, and if they weren't on your tail when Sabrina wrote to you, why do you believe that the Church is trying to keep her from giving you dangerous information, and for that reason they are trying to kill you?"

"It's confusing," Shmuel admitted, his eyes lighting up. "But I think I have the answer. Let me go through this point by point.

"Point one: When Sabrina Lombardo wrote to me, no one knew about it.

"Point two: Then someone, a mysterious person, found out, and therefore I received an anonymous letter threatening my life if I came here. But that person would have been satisfied with preventing our meeting.

"Point three: In Prague we angered the local church, or perhaps the international church — that depends on just how important the Fernbach affair is. Therefore, someone set their sights on us.

"Point four: Everything has gotten completely confused, a true Gordian knot. Somehow the Prague journal is connected to the Levin family. My own suspicions are that the Fernbach family of Katamon had something to do with their conversion.

"Point five: In light of all this, there's no reason to leave now and go back to Israel. Zerach, we're deep into this. There's nowhere to run. We've got to grab the bull by the horns and deal with this until we've gotten to the bottom of the mystery."

Arthur had been listening, entranced, by Shmuel's step-by-step account. "To think they wanted to turn you into an integral part of a building," he murmured. "They have to build a yeshivah around you, not a high-tech skyscraper."

"My students say I'm a man with a good foundation," Shmuel gave a weak laugh. "The thugs of Caracas decided to see if they were right."

Arthur's wife, Sylvia, entered with cups of coffee for the council of war. "It'll refresh you, wake you up. I suspect you need every ounce of instant energy," she explained, with a shy and pleasant smile, as she set the table with all manner of delicacies.

Zerach waited for his host to drink and then helped himself to a cup of piping hot coffee. "This is really good," he said, sipping the steaming brew gingerly. "You can tell you are near Colombia." He turned to his friend. "Shmuel, in light of the '*shiur*' you just gave us, what are you planning to do?"

Shmuel rubbed his bruised wrists and looked thoughtfully at the bandages Arthur had placed on his deep wounds. "I think I'd better get a tetanus shot, or I might get blood poisoning."

"I've already called my doctor," Arthur said, stretching into the deep couch. "He'll be here in half an hour and will give you whatever treatment you need. On the house, of course."

"*Gracias*," Shmuel said.

"You've learned something," Arthur laughed.

Zerach would not be distracted. "Shmuel, what's your next move?"

"First, I'm going to call the Yad L'Achim office in Yerushalayim. One of the clerks there is waiting with an answer for me, I hope, regarding the Fernbach family."

His hand moved toward the phone, but Arthur held him back. "Don't use this; call on Zerach's cell."

"A new member of the miser's union?" Zerach said, puzzled but certain his hospitable host was not showing an unexpected display of frugality.

Arthur glanced at him. "My telephone is bugged, or my name isn't Arthur."

"You're right," Zerach apologized. "Whoever was following Shmuel surely saw you as well. Woe to the evil man, woe to his neighbor. You've gotten mixed up in a conflict that has nothing to do with you."

"There's no such thing; everything comes through *hashgachah pratis*, Divine Providence," Arthur said firmly.

Shmuel dialed the Yad L'Achim office. Two rings, three. Someone picked up.

"Hello, this is Shmuel Bilad."

"Hello Rabbi Bilad." The voice on the other end sounded pleased. "You're very lucky that I'm often here at all kinds of odd hours. I apologize for my caution during our last call. I didn't know who you were; now I do, and I'm honored. My name is Betzalel Schmidt. My brother, Pinchas, learned in Yeshivas Meoros Elimelech in 5754 (1994). He remembers you very fondly."

"I'm glad to hear it." Shmuel rejoiced in this return to more tranquil times, even if only for a fleeting moment. "I remember Pinchas Schmidt too. He was a student with a head on his shoulders. And now, what about the affair I asked you to check into?"

"We've done a thorough investigation," Schmidt said with ill-concealed satisfaction. "We had to really delve into the archives for you, but we managed to unearth papers that are more than forty years old."

"And what have you found?"

"The Fernbach family in Katamon were, indeed, diligent workers on behalf of the missionaries in those days. You won't believe this, but we also found material about the Levin family. Information about the bereaved family, easy prey for missionary claws, was given to the Good News Church in Nazareth by the Fernbachs of Katamon."

*Time Bomb* / 271

"Why did they go all the way to Nazareth?" Shmuel wondered. "There are no missionaries in Jerusalem?"

"True, under normal circumstances; unfortunately, they have workers everywhere," Schmidt explained. "But this affair was different. The Fernbach family had decided to include a relative of theirs in this case. The various branches of the family are very close and they thus chose a missionary based in Nazareth, who was related to them, in order to get him credit in the eyes of the Church."

The activist added, "The Fernbach family destroyed many people before they disappeared from the horizon. They are presumably Jewish, but secretly they are sinking the boat that we all share."

"Who was the missionary in this instance?"

"A man by the name of Yehoshua Cohen, one of the most dangerous men among the missionaries in Israel. The messiah, in the eyes of the Fernbachs of Katamon. He was one step ahead of them and converted."

"He's still alive?"

"According to the information we have, he is alive and active, despite his advanced years. He must be over 70."

Shmuel felt a throb of excitement. "Where does he live?"

"He wanders all over the world, enjoys the best of health, but his headquarters are in —"

"Let me guess," Shmuel cut him off. "Is it Caracas, Venezuela?"

"That's right. How did you know?" Betzalel Schmidt asked, surprised.

"I have my own sources," Shmuel closed the conversation with a touch of the "end" button.

He looked triumphantly at Arthur and Zerach. "What do you say to that? It's the merciless apostate, Yehoshua Cohen, who convinced Hadassah Levin to come to Caracas to get treatment for her ailing children. That was the lure and it worked, getting them to his sanctuary. By the way, am I wrong, or is this city full of churches?"

"No, you're not wrong at all," Arthur agreed. "I told you that this is a faithful Catholic city. I couldn't compare the number of churches in Prague and Caracas; both of them have dozens."

"When I was a youngster in Katamon," Shmuel said, "everyone knew that the red-headed missionary had fed the Levin family nonkosher food without their knowledge, thus beginning the process of dulling their Jewish senses. He began the brainwashing process in Yerushalayim and then, it seems, pulled them straight into the arms of the Catholic Church in Caracas."

He lapsed into thought for a short while, then roused himself. "Arthur, Mrs. Lombardo's phone number is written on a piece of paper in my jacket pocket. It's hard for me to look for it, with these injured hands. Would you mind?"

"What a question!" Arthur began to rummage through the jacket, that was filthy and wrinkled after its encounter with the building site. "Here it is. She lives at Los Mongatos Street 17, telephone 515-4921. I'll call her right now."

He quickly pressed the numbers into the phone, prepared with an apology for the lateness of the hour, but the phone rang more than twenty times and went unanswered.

"She evidently unplugs the phone at night," he said, disappointed.

"What are you saying?" Shmuel retorted. "Don't you see what she wrote: 'Even at 3 o'clock in the morning.' I'm afraid that she's dead."

"'One assumes a person is alive,'" Zerach broke in, reminding Shmuel of one of the basic concepts in Gemara. "If you saw someone healthy and well within the past twenty-four hours, one should act as though he is alive unless you've heard that something happened. I think, if we continue with your analysis of the matter, that she's afraid to return home since she met you, because she suspects that a Church official is waiting in ambush for her."

"Bravo," Arthur shouted.

"That reminds me," Shmuel turned to him. "Have you spoken with the clerk in your office? The one who told you about neighbors who had come from Yerushalayim and converted here?"

"No," Arthur admitted. "I didn't have the head for it."

"Maybe you can do it now," Shmuel said, with a quick gesture toward the mobile phone.

*Time Bomb* / 273

"Now, at 1 o'clock in the morning?"

"It's an emergency," Shmuel said, nodding. "A person's life is more important than one clerk's beauty sleep."

Arthur picked up the phone. He seemed put out, but Shmuel was adamant. "I don't even remember her number," Arthur muttered, as he checked screens on his Palm Pilot. "Oh, here it is: Gloria Granada."

He put the phone to his ear. "Hello, Gloria."

"This is her husband," a sleepy voice said. "Who is this?"

"Arthur Taubman, from the office."

"You work so late?" the voice yawned. "Gloria sleeps at night."

"I know," Arthur stammered an apology. "I need her urgently, in a matter not related to work."

"It can't wait until morning?"

"Absolutely not."

The receiver was placed on a table in the Granada household. Moments later they heard Gloria's voice, bright and alert, as if she had not yet gone to sleep. "Yes?"

"This is Arthur Taubman. I apologize a thousand times for the lateness of the hour."

In short sentences he stated his request.

A moment's silence was followed by her voice. "That's right, I remember. You must mean our neighbors." She lowered her voice. "The Lombardo family. His name is Santos Lombardo, but he once told me he was born in Israel, where his name was Levin."

"What does he do now?"

Gloria hesitated. "It's not the most pleasant profession. He's a garbageman."

Arthur hoped to finish up, but Shmuel was acting like a tough boss, forcing the interrogation to go on.

"Where does he live?"

"In an old ruin near the Carabobo Park. I was there in the house once; they're terribly poor."

"Do you know his phone number?"

"No, but you'll find him in the phone directory. He lives on Avenida Mexico. I don't remember the exact address."

"I don't know how to thank you, and again, I am sorry for the bother."

"It's okay. In any case I would have been getting up soon; my little one needs to be fed."

As if to confirm her words a baby's wails sounded in the background.

Arthur gave Shmuel a furious look. "You're lucky we're talking about a fine woman, otherwise I'd have been fired tomorrow morning. Do you think you're in Meah Shearim?"

Shmuel moved uneasily. "Don't tell me you're really angry."

"Yes I am. We don't do this kind of thing over here." Arthur was truly upset; it was hard to recognize the affable host in this indignant person. "We're made differently. We don't have these crazy ways."

"I really do apologize," Shmuel said sincerely. "But these 'crazy ways' of mine are necessary, given the facts. But this time I'll save you the discomfort — I'll call Santos Lombardo myself."

Arthur looked up the number in the directory. Shmuel dialed.

"No answer," he said after the tenth ring. "I'm the world champion in losing leads. We don't have a single one that will lead us to Mrs. Lombardo."

The ringing of the doorbell echoed throughout the house. It was the soft musical notes of a guitar playing a popular chassidic tune.

Sylvia Taubman walked to the door. "It's Dr. Steingold."

The doctor gave Shmuel a thorough physical examination. His arms and legs were bruised and bloody and still showed signs of the ropes that had bound him at the construction site. Arthur stammered a short explanation; the doctor did not ask too many questions. He gave Shmuel a tetanus shot, bandaged his wounds, and left him a pile of prescriptions for various drugs.

"And now it's time for all of us to get some sleep," Arthur announced, stifling a yawn, after having paid the doctor twice his usual fee because of the late hour. "We've all had a long hard day and you, Shmuel, have another long day before you tomorrow."

"You won't believe it, but I'm actually afraid of the dark," Shmuel said, trembling slightly. "I'm afraid I'll see before me a pipe full of cement, and imagine it slowly dripping on me, cold and wet. I still can't believe that I'll wake up tomorrow safe in a bed."

"Keep the lamp on next to your bed," Arthur suggested.

Zerach had other words of comfort. "Think how upset the criminals would be if they knew you weren't sleeping in cement," he grinned.

# 26

*Rome, 5761 (2000)*

The Alitalia night flight from Paris landed in the Leonardo Da Vinci airport in Rome at 1:30 a.m. Fifty-eight passengers left the plane on their way to the arrivals terminal. After getting their passports stamped, each went his own way.

A young man sporting a mustache, wearing a light checked jacket, stood before the clerk at passport control. The customs agent was unusually methodical, and checked the man's face carefully against the photo in the passport.

"Antoine D'moré. How long are you going to be staying in Rome?"

"Two weeks."

"You have family here?"

"Cousins."

The agent once again scanned the photo. Something was disturbing him. The French passport was fine, the picture was that of the tourist standing before him. If, that is, he really was a tourist.

*Time Bomb* / 277

The young man answering to the name Antoine D'moré felt a trickle of cold sweat pour down his back. If this functionary would investigate all his statistics too closely, the project might fail before it even began, even though his supplier claimed that there wasn't a chance in a million that the forgery would be noticed. He, of course, would keep his mouth shut if there was a police investigation, but under torture he was not so sure of himself.

"Okay, you can go," the agent handed him the passport.

"Antoine D'moré" gave a sigh of relief and left the terminal, his small carry-on bag in his hand. He had hardly brought anything with him; he planned on buying whatever he needed in one of the department stores in Rome. What kind of sixth sense did these airport officials possess? What alerts them when they see certain passports? Had a little bird whispered in his ear that Antoine D'moré was a Chechen freedom fighter born Kareem Nisadov?

Actually, the thought that the traveler could be a terrorist had not occurred to the customs agent. The man's behavior reflected Italy's policy toward the flood of illegal immigrants that had washed into Italy, and specifically into Rome, over the last few years. There were immigrants from the Philippines, Somalia, Ethiopia, North Africa, and Eastern Europe being swallowed up among the native-born citizenry and if they would not be stopped one of these days they would become the majority. Luckily for him Kareem's Far-Eastern features were not too pronounced, and his declaration that he was here for only a short time placated the immigration official.

Kareem Nisadov planned on spending the next seven days in a moderately priced hotel. He would wander through the small Vatican state, learning everything he could about it. He had a carefully designed working plan that he had received from Selim Yudayev. "It's a plan that cannot fail," Selim had assured him. "It's constructed with scientific accuracy, piece by piece. You have a detailed itinerary and if you don't veer from your instructions by even one iota you'll be on the pope's plane when it takes off from Rome, and you'll be the one who will open the door of the 'Holy Father's' plane to us — and open the eyes of the entire world."

Kareem Nisadov longed with every fiber of his being for the scheme's success. If it worked, Chechnya would be freed from the tyranny of Russian domination, and Selim would rise to the top of the Chechen political hierarchy. When that happened, he, Kareem Nisadov, would be there. Of course, he had no chance against Selim; the man had too much charisma. But Kareem would cling to Selim on his way up the summit. And when Selim had paved the uphill road, then he, Kareem, would consider how to rid himself of him, and Chechnya would fall into Kareem's waiting hands like a ripe fruit.

Kareem had no idea that Selim had given his handwriting a thorough analysis. Selim had learned graphology from a world-renowned expert in France and knew everything there was to know about the intricacies of handwriting and how one could discern personality through it. Selim had given him several documents to complete and had then carefully scrutinized the writing. So it was that he had guessed Kareem's secret ambitions, as obvious to him as if they had been carved on the man's forehead. His nature, given to betrayal, as well as his overweening ambition, were clearly inscribed in the letters he formed.

No problem, Selim had laughed, sending Kareem on the hardest mission of his life. "Work hard, sweat as you join me on the road to success — and when it happens, you won't be there. Your name will be inscribed in the golden book of history as someone who gave his life for his homeland."

*Caracas, 5761 (2000)*

"You're an imbecile with a diploma, Diego. Explain to me how an 80-year-old woman managed to escape, and to break your nose in the bargain!"

Diego, a young man with a lean, pliant body and a catlike look, was suffering. Every breath hurt. But the humiliation he was enduring from his boss, Julio Rodriguez, wounded him even more. They were standing in a neglected apartment in one of Caracas's poorer neighborhoods; Diego had fled there after Sabrina Lombardo had escaped.

"How was I supposed to know that she was so smart and would realize I was hiding in her house?" he asked Julio. "You told me to wait for her there, and that's what I did. If you had told me to shoot her in the elevator, for example, she would already be lying in the morgue refrigerator awaiting identification."

"You've just done something unspeakable," Julio hissed venomously. "You dared to argue with your superior and doubt his actions."

The thin body tensed, its wounds forgotten. The green, feline eyes stared fearfully at Julio.

"I'm sorry," he stuttered.

Julio relented. "You don't have to apologize, you have to think. I've told you a thousand times: Use your brain, think. You have golden hands and you're one of our best men but look what happens because you don't think — an 80-year-old woman made a fool of you. See how I operate. This morning I kidnapped the Jew. You should have seen me place the lasso around his neck, how precise it was. What expertise! And then a quiet, neat assassination, without a body to be found. I brought him to the usual site and left him, alive and breathing, under the cement pipe. In a few hours he'll be part of the new building. Don Juan was very pleased," he added with a broad smile.

"So what do I do now?"

"Use that lazy brain of yours," Julio said wickedly. "Don Juan was not happy to hear about this. The old lady is dangerous and we have to close her mouth. That's top priority."

"My nose is broken!" Diego said with a sob.

Julio rammed him viciously in the ribs. "She has two sons in the city. Twins, Santos and Gonzales Lombardo. She's certainly staying with one of them. Find her quickly and silence her forever. Otherwise your nose won't hurt anymore. I'll cure you of all your pains — permanently!"

<hr />

They rose early and *davened* with the San Bernardino synagogue's sunrise minyan, despite their fatigue and the lack of sleep. "There's no other minyan in this area," Arthur apologized to Zerach, who had grumbled due to the lack of a mikveh in which to immerse.

"I can give up my morning cup of coffee," Zerach said, explaining his priorities as Arthur sped along on the quiet streets on his way to shul, "even though I'm addicted to it. But I can't give up my daily immersion in the mikveh."

"I have an idea," Shmuel grinned.

"Which is — "

"Immersion in a coffee cup."

"That's what's called 'freeze-dried,'" Arthur finished.

The three were tired and fairly frightened, and the light banter broke some of their tension and served as a catharsis. After *davening* they would have to continue their search for the missing old woman and find her before the Mafia's hired guns did — if they hadn't already.

It was 6:30 when they were done. Arthur suggested that they drive directly to Santos Lombardo's home. "What we can't do by phone we can do in a face-to-face meeting."

The sagging building near Carabobo Park was indeed a ruin, as Gloria Granada had said. It was located in the heart of a neighborhood that was slated for destruction and rebuilding, on the intersection of Avenida Mexico and Los Lahusos Street. It was a three-story building, whose cement walls seemed too weary to battle the neglect. A nerve-wracking chorus of howls from a pack of dogs greeted the intruders. Weeds poked their way through the cracks in the sidewalk, and bundles of old newspapers balanced precariously on garbage cans.

"What a disgrace," Zerach said, pointing at the foul piles of trash and holding his nose. "When they say the cobbler's children go barefoot, believe it. Where do you find the most garbage? Next to the garbageman's house!"

They checked the broken mailboxes and found the name Lombardo written in a marker on one of them. However, next to it hung a small sign: "New tenant: Mario Paluta."

"Well, here's the reason why the fellow didn't answer his phone last night," Arthur sighed. "He's moved. Everything seems to be working against us."

"We're going upstairs," Shmuel declared assertively.

"Why?" Arthur asked, surprised.

"Because," Shmuel snapped. "We have to start somewhere."

"So go yourself," Arthur patted him on the back. "Do you have any idea who lives here? The lowest of the low: criminals, drug addicts, people who murder in their leisure hours."

"Let's go," Shmuel said, unimpressed. "Take a risk. The worst that could happen is that he'll throw a shoe at you for waking him up at 7 o'clock in the morning."

Arthur and Shmuel warily made their way up to the new tenant's apartment, while Zerach waited in the car. Too many people might arouse suspicions.

Arthur knocked gently on the door.

Silence.

"Even the mice won't hear you," Shmuel protested. "Knock louder or ring the bell."

"I'm afraid to get him angry," Arthur stammered.

"It's our last chance. We've got no choice."

Shmuel gave the bell a tentative ring. He immediately regretted the action. The chime sounded eerily like an alarm or a call to war, unusually shrill and dreadfully loud.

After a few seconds, the door opened. Much to their surprise an old man, short of stature and pleasant faced, stood before them. He was dressed in shorts, and his shirt had obviously just been flung on. He apologized for the unpleasant surroundings and explained that the previous tenant, Santos Lombardo, had moved to Avenida Dalmido del Casol 39, near the new Kodra de Bolivar Theater, about three miles from here.

Arthur thanked him heartily and turned to go. "I've got the address!" he announced ceremoniously. Shmuel stopped him short. "One minute, not so fast," he said, whispering something in his ear.

"You're right." Arthur turned to the old man again. "Don Paluta, would you like to earn 1000 bolivars?"

The man's eyes lit up. "Of course."

"Arthur handed him five bills of 100 bolivars each. "You'll get five more like these if you don't tell anyone besides us where Santos Lombardo is now living."

"But he asked me to tell people who were looking for him. No one knows his new address," Paluta said, astounded.

"But now everything is different," Arthur said shortly. "This information could be fatal to Santos. Someone wants to kill him and is looking for him."

"*Mama mia!*" the old man's eyes rolled in fright. "Okay, I won't tell a soul."

"Do you think we can rely on him?" Arthur asked Shmuel in Hebrew.

"I'm not sure," Shmuel replied. "He looks like a coward. One threatening gesture and the information will pour out of him like water from a broken faucet. Give him Zerach's cell phone number and ask that at the very least he let us know if someone suspicious comes here."

Arthur followed the instructions and the two returned to the car. Zerach listened to the outcome of the meeting. He shared Shmuel's concerns. "We're only one step ahead of the killers. Time is short."

"Let's get to Avenida Dalmido del Casol," Shmuel said, rubbing his hands together impatiently. "Arthur, step on the gas."

"We won't get there any faster if we have an accident on the way," Arthur answered calmly. "And if we hit someone, we'll never beat the Mafia."

※

Compared to his apartment in the poor neighborhood, this new dwelling of Santos seemed like a palace. It was a two-story villa in the heart of a newly built neighborhood that boasted its upper-class lifestyle, lovely gardens, and a large playground. The proximity to many cultural institutions was also a plus. "Where did he get the money for this?" Zerach wondered.

"There's a lot of work here, a lot of garbage," Shmuel mused.

Again Shmuel and Arthur approached the house while Zerach remained behind in the car. They stood in the verdant courtyard, rang the bell, and waited.

The door was opened by a balding man of about 50, with a stocky build and a squarish, ill-tempered face. Shmuel tried to find — without success — some trace in this angry man of the sweet Jewish boy in Katamon. This was a complete gentile, a heavyset man who scrutinized them suspiciously. "What do you want here so early?"

"We have to speak to your mother." Arthur shot the words out without warning.

"Who are you?" he said, backing up, prepared to slam the door in their faces.

"My name is Shmuel Bilad!" Shmuel put out a friendly hand. "I believe that you are Ahrele Levin."

The door slammed shut. They could just make out the words. "Get out of here!" the man screamed from behind it. "Get out of here before I call the police. What kind of business is this, coming and waking me up this early!"

Even as they walked away they could still hear him, fuming and cursing. They stood outside and looked around.

"He has a lovely garden," Shmuel said, impressed. "A pergola, glider, blossoming bushes. When he opened the door I could see the patio; it's even more beautiful, with its tiled floor and glass brick walls. He's found some money, this lad. Maybe he won the lottery."

"'Do not covet,'" Arthur grinned, shaking a warning finger.

"I'm just commenting," Shmuel smiled back. "And wondering what happened to this guy to change his life so much. But one thing is clear. He's not very hospitable. Maybe my direct approach scared him off."

"Should we leave?" Arthur asked.

"No," Shmuel answered firmly. "If she's not here she must be at Gonzales's house. We'll ask him to at least give us his twin brother's address."

They heard a terrible din coming from behind the closed door. Arthur listened closely. "He's saying that he refuses to open up. Wait a minute — " he put his ear to the door. "I can hear an old woman shouting back that he should open the door at once."

Patience pays. After a minute the door was flung open. Sabrina Lombardo stood inside, wrapped in a long blue robe and a matching scarf. A broad smile played on her face at the sight of Shmuel, but a look of suspicion settled on her features as she noticed the stranger standing next to him. "Who's that?" she asked curtly, pointing toward Arthur.

"He's one of us," Shmuel assured her. "My host, the one you spoke with on the phone."

"Come in," she said, gesturing toward the large patio. "I feel much better seeing you. I was afraid for you, and thank G-d that you've been saved from the thugs."

"That's right. And I will be making a *seudas hoda'ah,* a thanksgiving meal, for my salvation," he answered. "But Mrs. Lombardo," he added urgently, "we're very pressed for time right now. These 'thugs' of yours are coming back. A gang of Mafia assassins is after all of us. I've been in their sights for quite a while and I have reason to believe that they are looking for you as well."

Sabrina guffawed. "Look who's talking. What came first, the chicken or the egg?" She gestured toward the door. "Come in. Don't worry, I'll be brief."

Shmuel longed to see Ahrele Levin once again, though he did not verbalize his desire. For Shmuel he had remained little Ahrele, and not some ill-tempered heavyset gentile. He hoped that the son would join the mother once they were inside the house.

They sat on the patio on a wide bench upholstered in leather. Mrs. Lombardo served them fruit and mineral water. "In my home I am as kosher as you are," she declared. "But here, I don't know. In any case the fruits aren't coated with anything, and the water comes straight from a well."

"Thank you," Shmuel's heart sank as he heard the woman's apologies. What a tortured soul, coping all by herself with the hellish existence, spending so many years in a strange city, lonely and unloved, subtly opposing the brutal Church that had stolen her children from her — and still she felt the need to prove that she had maintained her standards of kashrus.

She sipped water from a disposable cup, but first said the *Shehakol* blessing with great intensity.

"Look," she began suddenly in a fluent Yiddish, "I know the situation is very tricky. My son hasn't shown much sympathy or friendship. You can understand him. He works very hard for his sustenance. His life is garbage, literally."

*Time Bomb /* 285

"May I ask you something?" Shmuel drew himself up. "This house doesn't exactly look like a pile of trash."

"You sound like a tax auditor," Sabrina flared. "That's what I wanted to speak with you about. You're right, this beautiful house — and you haven't seen even a small portion of it — this house attests to a high standard of living. So —"

A heavy silence fell. Shmuel finally broke it, speaking in almost a whisper. "You wanted to tell me something?"

"That's right," Sabrina answered. "I wanted to talk about my grandson, Santos's son, Joselito."

"Is he here?"

Sabrina spoke in a tone that reflected grandmotherly pride, as well as deep anxiety. "Joselito is far from here. He's one of the most talented boys I've ever seen, and I'm not speaking as his grandmother."

"That's right, every grandmother is objective," Arthur teased.

"You're wrong," Sabrina countered. "When you meet Joselito you'll change your mind. He's not typical; he's an atomic reactor. His energy could melt steel. He's a good person who can't abide injustice anywhere. No! In my whole life I never met a person with the integrity of Joselito. When he was a young boy in school, he made the teachers' lives miserable if he saw any injustice in the classroom. There was a time when he pursued the teacher all the way home for several days, because he'd chosen to punish a weak student who didn't have a strong father to protect him, the way another father had protected his son who had done the same mischief. That's Joselito."

"Okay, you called Shmuel from Yerushalayim so he could hear you brag about your grandson?" Arthur asked incredulously.

Sabrina pierced him with her glance. The weak, hesitant widow who had fallen so easily into the missionary's snares had long since vanished, swept away in the flood of tears she had shed over the years. Too late, a strong, unyielding personality had taken her place.

"Shmuel," she said, the emotion in her voice all the clearer because of her rigid control, "I called you because I believe in you. You will save my grandson and bring him back."

If the lovely plaster ceiling had fallen on his head, Shmuel could not have been more stunned. "Are you talking about *teshuvah*, or conversion?"

"My grandson is a Jew," the old woman said, playing her winning hand. "My daughter-in-law, his mother, is a full-fledged Jewess. I insisted that both my sons marry Jews; it was my small but sweet revenge against the cursed Church and Yehoshua Cohen, may his name be blotted out."

The last words were said with such venom that they seemed almost able to sear him out of existence.

"If he's not here, how will we help him?" Shmuel asked, once he had absorbed her words.

The door burst open. Zerach Britman jumped in, as white as the marble patio tiles. His cell phone was shaking in his trembling hands. "The old man just called," he shouted, his voice on the edge of hysteria. "Mario Paluta. Four armed men were there and the old coward sent them directly here. They'll be here in minutes."

# 27

*Rome, 5761 (2000)*

Three days in Rome had enriched Kareem Nisadov's knowledge of the city, and particularly of the Vatican. He would attach himself to groups of tourists exploring the area and listen intently to the explanations of the experienced guides. The city had many ancient buildings but Kareem showed little interest in the vast Coliseum, where Roman stalwarts of yore had clashed, where early Christians had been thrown as prey to the jaws of ravenous lions, much to the delight of the blood thirsty crowds. He strolled on the banks of the Tiber and crossed the oldest of the bridges spanning it, the Ponte Sainte Angelo. With a group of tourists, he gazed at the Arch of Titus, with its bas-relief sculpture of the Jews being exiled from Jerusalem carrying the looted Temple Menorah and other vessels. He climbed up to the lookout area on the Forum, a not-to-be-missed sight, and wandered through the Pantheon. He threw a coin into the famed Fountain of Trevi and fed the pigeons in the Piazza San Pietro. But most of all, he studied the state within a state, the Vatican.

He knew exactly how he would infiltrate the tiny state. It was not that difficult. It merely needed considerable daring, coolness, and nerves of steel.

The main churches in the Vatican, the Basilica with its famed Sistine Chapel, interested him like yesterday's news — not at all.

What did interest him were the men of the Swiss Guard, those soldiers in their elegant uniforms that harked back to Renaissance days, armed with swords and sabers, who were in charge of Vatican security.

After one trip through the Vatican, Kareem saw that Selim Yagudayev had done his homework properly. There were one hundred men in the Swiss Guard, hand picked. All were Swiss citizens, Catholics, between the ages of 18 and 25. Selim had been correct in one other important detail: None were less than six feet tall.

When he had discussed with Selim why he, Kareem, had been chosen, Selim had explained that he was the only one among all their guerilla band whose height met the requirements: Kareem was a towering 6'3".

Four times he changed his clothing and his sunglasses; four times he took the tour of the Vatican, scrutinizing the Swiss Guard's faces with the care of an inveterate tourist. Finally he chose one of them — one among one hundred whose build closely resembled his, and whose face was not unlike Kareem's, once he shaved his mustache.

Kareem was satisifed. The first breach had been uncovered. But it was not enough: a second breach, and a third, were still to come. He would be opening that airplane door for his friends.

✧

*Caracas, 5761 (2000)*

They stood, panic stricken. Four armed men! They could hardly face even one killer. None of them were armed.

The echoes of Zerach's frightened cry had hardly died down when Shmuel announced, "We've got to get out of here while there's still time."

Sabrina gave him a chilly look. "Do you think so?"

"Yes."

"I managed to deal with them with empty hands, no guns," she said proudly. "I beat the murderer with a can of olives."

She burst out laughing, ignoring the dangers of the moment.

Shmuel stood up. "If you want to stay here it's your business. I don't know how many men will be coming this time, and we have no guarantee of another success."

"You're right." Sabrina stood up from the bench with one swift movement, hardly indicative of her advanced age. She called out loud, "Santos, come here."

"Yes, Mother, what do you want?"

She spoke rapidly and he nodded his assent. Arthur whispered to Shmuel, "She told him that they want to kill him just as much as they want to murder her. Apparently he wants to stay alive."

Zerach turned to Sabrina, who was walking swiftly toward the door. "Where is the rest of the family?"

The old woman paused for a moment. "My daughter-in-law is on vacation in El Litoral."

"What's that?"

"The beach," Arthur explained. "Probably they went to the resort village Macuto, very popular among Caracanios — the nickname given to people from Caracas."

Sabrina corrected him. "No. She went to the village of Nyguata. My grandson, Joselito, is far from here. I hope he doesn't decide to return suddenly; he's an unusual young man."

They raced toward Arthur's roomy car, that fit them all in comfortably. Sabrina and her son crouched down; suddenly they seemed terrified. They urged Arthur not to waste a moment.

The car raced away.

Only a few minutes separated the departure of the car carrying the family from the arrival of a large Land Rover, that drove in with the screeching of tires and stopped in front of the Lombardo family villa.

"Assassins!" a woman in the adjoining yard screamed, collapsing in a faint.

Four men with venomous faces jumped out, frightening rifles clutched in their hands. They raced to the door and banged on it with their fists.

When it stayed shut they pressed the triggers and sent a hail of bullets throughout the courtyard, destroying the furniture. Two bullets smashed the door's lock, and then the door was opened with the kick of a dark boot. When they saw that the place was abandoned they began a frenzy of wild shooting: at walls and lamps, the refrigerator, and the pantry. Everything was irreparably damaged or destroyed. Their bullets pierced the beds, ripping through blankets still warm from human contact. Five minutes sufficed for them to take a lovely home and leave it a ruin. When they had completed their work of destruction they ran back to their car, where a driver was waiting for them.

The car raced wildly away. Diego pulled the black mask off his face. His broken nose sent waves of pain through him, and he was trembling. He was afraid as he had never been afraid before. He had taken three friends with him this time to ensure that the mission went well. But there was no one left to kill. When Don Juan and Julio would hear that their prey had vanished, they would be furious. Julio would keep his promise.

He just had to find Sabrina Lombardo — and stay alive.

Arthur sped down one of the city's long streets, Avenida Bolivar. "Where are we going, Mrs. Lombardo?"

"To Gonzales, my other son's house. He also moved very recently. No one knows his new address. In the meantime, we'll figure something out."

"Where does he live?"

"Keep driving down this road," the old woman directed him with impressive aplomb. "Until you get to Placa Diego Ibara. From there you take a left to Road 8, until Placa Miranda. There you go left again to Avenida Baralet. Drive straight down until I tell you to stop."

"These names will drive me mad," Zerach groaned. "Placa and Avenida, Avenida and Placa, Bolivar with everything. He's competing with our Rabin. Is it against the law to call streets by normal names? Chazon Ish Boulevard. Maggid of Mezeritch Square. Baba Sali Street.

Now those are names!"

Shmuel glared at him and he subsided.

Santos sat, drawn into himself, cut off from all the activity around him. Through an earphone attached by a long black wire, he listened to a small black radio that sat in his pocket. Mrs. Lombardo wiped a stray tear from her eye: "Those names hurt my heart. There are street names like those in Yerushalayim, particularly in the Beis Yisrael neighborhood: Besht Street, R' Chaim Sonnenfeld Street, R' Yosef Karo, R' Leib Dayan. How I would have loved to live on streets with such names."

Shmuel looked at her with interest. "How do you know so much about it?"

"I grew up there, in Beis Yisrael," the old woman said. "Did you think I was born in Katamon? My father was R' David Simchah Goldberg, one of the most respected figures of Jerusalem, known as Simchah the Milchiker, Simchah the dairyman. He would sell minimal amounts of milk every morning and spend the rest of the day learning in the shul. How I loved to go to him in the evening with the sandwich that my mother, may she rest in peace, sent him. I would stand in the courtyard of the shul and hear his sweet voice. See what his grandchildren have become." She pointed at Santos, who was listening intently to the radio, and she burst into stormy tears. "Not only did they take the next world from them, those savages, but they took this world as well. What does he have in his life? To get up before dawn and empty garbage cans? He spends every leisure minute listening to the sports on the radio, or watches television until he falls asleep on his chair. What kind of life is that?"

"Things will get better, Mrs. Lombardo," Shmuel tried to calm her.

"Easy for you to say. You'll go safely back home, Caracas will be a fleeting memory. And we'll be mired here in the swamp until our last day on earth." The old woman sighed in pain.

The atmosphere in the car was heavy. Arthur decided to turn the conversation to lighter things.

"Shmuel, I'm afraid you'll go back to Israel and slander us, tell people that Caracas is a city of criminals. It's not true. We have a wonderful *kehillah* here, under the leadership of Rabbi Rosenblum. We have yeshivahs and seminaries, excellent schools, and a vibrant Jewish life. You haven't seen all that because of the strange events that brought you into contact with our lowest strata. Did you know that Venezuela is a tourist's delight? The highest waterfall in the world is here, in the Guiana region. It's called the Anchal Falls, and it reaches a height of 3212 feet. It empties into the Cavra River, a tributary of the Caroni River, which is itself a tributary of our great river, the Orinoco, that crosses all of Venezuela."

"I know that," Shmuel shrugged him off. "I've also heard that though it's high, the waterfall is not one of the most beautiful, and it can't compete with Niagara Falls. With the exception of its impressive height it's nothing special, very narrow with a small amount of actual water falling."

"How do you know all this?" came a disappointed question from Arthur.

"I've got a doctorate in Venezuela," Shmuel laughed.

"So let's test your knowledge!" Zerach declared war. "Doctor Shmuel, do you know where the name 'Anchal' comes from?"

The "doctor" did not respond.

"Respected Dr. Bilad, does His Honor know the roots of the word 'Venezuela'?"

Shmuel again opted for silence.

"I'll tell you," Zerach chortled, victorious. "The person who discovered the Falls was a tourist by the name of Angel. In these parts they don't know how to pronounce the sound "je" and instead say a "ch" sound. That's why the word 'Jew' in Spanish, 'Judeo,' is pronounced here 'Chudeo.' In the same way, 'Angel' became 'Anchal.' And now to the name 'Venezuela.' Columbus discovered Venezuela's beaches in 1498. But he went on to make history in America. A year later the ship of Portuguese explorer Alonso de Uchdo reached Lake Maracaibo. He and his men found an Indian village there built on the water, on stilts. This reminded them of Venice and so they called the village 'Venezuela' — 'Little Venice' in Spanish. Eventually the entire country was called that name."

"Bravo," Arthur called out. "Did you also get a doctorate in my country?"

"No, I heard it from my rebbe at his last *tisch*," he bantered.

"And speaking of Lake Maracaibo," Arthur broke in, "it was beneath their port that they discovered the huge oil deposits that turned Venezuela into one of the world's largest oil exporters. By the way, the appearance of the port is world renowned: a forest of oil rigs, from one end to the other, miles of them. Every year our country drills one hundred million tons of oil. The oil made us all lazy; only a few are willing to be farmers, under the most frighteningly primitive conditions."

"Or garbagemen," Zerach whispered, sending a glance at Santos.

Arthur, who had not heard the whispered exchange, continued. "Soon Venezuela will not be able to meet its agricultural needs, and will have to import food, though it has huge tracts of arable land."

They reached the Avenida Baralet and stopped in front of Gonzalez's home.

"Stay here; don't get out of the car," Sabrina commanded. "Zerach, give me your phone."

"What's the matter?"

"I want to be sure we don't have a reception committee waiting for us."

She put the instrument to her ear and listened. It rang twice and then a voice came on. "'Allo?'"

"Gonzales, is everything all right?" Sabrina asked quickly.

"Why shouldn't everything be all right?" Gonzales asked calmly.

She spoke to her son for a few moments and then turned to the others. "Come, let's go in. The coast is clear." She gave a slight sigh of relief.

"At least for now," Zerach said. "Clear, for now."

---

Gonzales's home was not at all like his brother's but the men were identical twins, and their resemblance was astounding. The home was very simple, the furnishings were others' castoffs. Gonzales, who like his brother was a trash collector, spent his leisure hours in a rather bohemian atmosphere. In the evenings he was an entertainer of no small ability. He was a tall man, dark haired, with a long ponytail, who sported a large assortment of silver jewelry.

He received them graciously. "*Buenos dias,*" he said.

Shmuel stared at him, feeling a heavy fist balling up within him, rising toward his heart and almost choking him. Could this be Moishy Levin, the little *tzaddik* of the neighborhood, the shining light of the *cheder* who posed questions that the teachers themselves found difficult to answer? *Yehoshua Cohen, there is none as wicked as you*, he thought, wishing he could shout the words in a voice that would frighten the entire planet. *What have you done to these two sweet children? You've destroyed them for all eternity.*

*That cursed missionary fed them pig's meat, until they themselves resembled the animal. From sweet children, whose faces reflected the light of innocence and true Jewish purity, they've put on masks, heavy, dirty, impure masks. In the place of peyos grows a ponytail; instead of tefillin, they wear earrings. Loud shirts have replaced their tzitzis.*

As if in response to his unspoken thoughts, Santos headed toward his brother and whispered something to him in Spanish. Gonzales looked at him, thunderstruck, and shook his head as if to say, "Impossible, it can't be." Santos's head bobbed up and down — "But it is true."

Gonzales hesitated, startled, for a short moment, then thrust his hand out toward Shmuel. "You're Shmulik Bilad, Dudy's friend?" he asked in Hebrew.

The Hebrew was passable, though heavily accented with its South American lilt. Forty years of Spanish had left its mark.

Shmuel was touched; he remembered him! Perhaps he, Gonzales, would remember other things as well. Perhaps his soul, his *neshamah*, would remember? Was it possible that the nearly extinguished Jewish spark might reignite?

"It's me," he said, a smile lighting up his features. His throat felt constricted, his eyes grew moist. "You're Moishy Levin?"

Gonzales burst out laughing. "You're a real sentimentalist, remembering my name from thousands of years ago."

"Your real name," Shmuel whispered. "The name you cannot ever lose or deny."

Unlike his surly brother, Gonzales was a cheerful fellow. He burst out laughing again. "Okay, it's Moishy Levin. For you, if you insist. I'm content with Gonzales."

*Rome, 5761 (2000)*

In the afternoon Kareem Nisadov visited the city's market, Porte Perteza. He bought some cheap pearl necklaces, twenty digital watches of poor quality — forgeries of the world's leading companies — a stack of alarm clocks, and pen-sized flashlights with thin beams. He rounded off his purchases with a simple piece of luggage which, with a few simple alterations, served as a display case.

It was with this case in his hand that he boarded the train's A line, staying on until the Otaviano station and following the stream of travelers to the Vatican. The indefatigable Selim Yagudayev had procured a vendor's permit for him from the Vatican office.

Kareem had already learned that this tiny state was completely self-sufficient. It had its own banks, stores, currency, postal service, and private radio station and a newspaper, "Osservatore Romano." Even the official language was its own — not Italian, but Latin, as if thousands of years had not passed since Romulus had founded Rome.

"His" guard was standing at his usual post, across from the Vatican gardens. As always he was clad in the red, yellow, and blue uniform that had been designed 500 years earlier by the great Italian artist, Michelangelo. His face was inscrutable and he did not blink at the sight of the sidewalk vendor who had chosen to ply his wares nearby.

"Excellent watches, very cheap," Kareem opened with the hawker's cries that he had studied so intently in the market. "Necklaces to surprise your girlfriends with. Long-lasting alarm clocks; your boss will love you for it. Flashlights, flashlights, to light up your life."

Tourists to the Vatican began to buy his bargains; Kareem was almost overwhelmed by the flood of customers and fervently hoped his merchandise would not be gone before evening.

"Okay, let's see your permit," a passing policeman stopped by.

"You need a permit for a few rags?" Kareem asked.

"That's right," the policeman grunted.

With a glow of triumph Kareem pulled out a laminated card and waved it before the policeman's face.

"Here, this is my official permit," he called in his peddler's voice.

The policeman went on his way.

"Razor blades," Kareem shouted. "Safety matches, shoelaces guaranteed not to tear..."

At exactly 8 o'clock that evening the shifts changed. "His" guard passed by Kareem on his way to his quarters. Kareem looked all around him. The area was clear.

"Do you want to buy something for a few cents?" he called.

"Not interested," the guard answered in a sharp Swiss accent.

"It's worth looking at," the peddler said in wheedling tones. "A beautiful pearl necklace for your fiancee."

"Thanks, but I'm not engaged. Members of the Swiss Guard must be bachelors."

"So get a gift for your mother. Go home and tell her: Momma, look what your sweet little boy has brought you from Rome. Momma will rejoice and give her sweet little boy a big kiss. Her little sweetheart brought her something."

The guard laughed and drew closer.

Kareem showed him a particularly attractive pearl necklace. The guard kept his money in a small wallet hidden in a pocket beneath his official uniform. He riffled through his clothing looking for his cash. Both his hands were busy.

This was the moment Kareem had been waiting for. He pulled out a canister of ether and sprayed it straight into the face of the startled guard. The man opened his mouth and gagged, as if he had swallowed burning kerosene. His hands reflexively reached for his aching eyes. Kareem struck his neck with a vicious blow.

The young man's eyes rolled and he fell to the ground, unconscious.

"Hasn't anyone ever taught you not to talk to strangers?" Kareem whispered mockingly into the silent body's ears as he pulled him around a nearby fence. He dealt with him with the impatience of a boa constrictor swallowing its prey. After two minutes Kareem came out of the hiding place clad in the finery of a Swiss Guard. The guard himself he crammed into a sewage drain. He, Kareem, would be far, far away by the time they found the unfortunate fellow.

Kareem walked swiftly toward the Swiss Guards' quarters.

# 28

"So let's get to the point," Shmuel said as he turned to Sabrina Lombardo. "Why did you ask me to come to Caracas?"

"Would you like something to eat?" Gonzales asked, pointing to a fruit platter. "Maybe a banana?" He gestured toward a bunch. "They're not only large, they're excellent. I know you're not allowed to eat very much, but there's no problem with fruits and vegetables."

"Thank you." Arthur and Zerach, too, peeled the sweet bananas and gobbled them down; they were ravenous. Since their morning cup of coffee they had not eaten anything.

"I called you here for two reasons." Sabrina carefully cut an orange-yellow star fruit into five pieces. She absent-mindedly chewed each star-shaped piece of the tropical fruit; she was clearly unsettled, and occasionally a spark of fear flashed in her eyes. "Do you think we're safe here?" she asked suddenly. "I have a long story, and if the past is any indication, I'm afraid we'll soon have a visit by the organization thugs."

The phone shrilled. In the next room they suddenly heard a frightened cry: "No! It's impossible!"

"Isabella, what's happened?" Gonzales yelled, running toward his wife. He returned in a moment, his face pale.

"Santos, that was your neighbor, Francesca Samolca."

"Francesca? What did she say?"

Gonzales looked at his brother with a mixture of fear and pity. "What could she say? She could hardly talk. She just regained consciousness now. The poor woman fainted, there in the courtyard. The 'organization' has been at your home."

"What?" Santos's face contorted with hatred and fury.

"They went wild, like mad animals, and shot anything that didn't move," Gonzales repeated the neighbor's report. "Presumably because they were furious they didn't find Mother and her guests. I hope you've got insurance, Santos."

"Yes," Santos could hardly speak, "but it only becomes valid next month. I've lost all that money."

He put his head in his hands and sat down mournfully.

"My house is next in line," Gonzales said, his tone more philosophical than frightened. "I haven't much to lose."

"We've got half an hour until we've got to flee in all directions," the old woman said urgently. "Let's stick to the topic. Time is short and I have to tell Shmuel Bilad everything."

The pandemonium in the room subsided. Gonzales lit a cigarette and gave his mother a questioning look. "You're going to speak of Joselito?"

"Yes. Why?"

A cloud of smoke drifted out of his mouth. "Just asking."

Sabrina said firmly, "No such thing. I know you, you wanted to say something."

Gonzales tipped the ash into a dirty glass ashtray and inhaled again. He laughed quietly. "You've remained exactly the same, Mother. You're right, I did want to say something. Do you think it would be a good idea for us to show Rabbi Bilad a picture of my dear nephew? You know why."

*Time Bomb* / 299

"Of course I thought about it," the old woman burst out. "Isabella," she cried in a tone of command. "Bring the album."

Isabella hurried to the old fashioned wooden buffet and took a thick family album out of one of the drawers. She handed it to her mother-in-law. Sabrina gently leafed through it. "Here, I found a photo of Joselito when he was 12."

"Why not something more recent, something taken now?" Shmuel wondered. But the words died on his lips as his eyes fell on the photo. He held his breath.

He saw Dudy Levin in front of him. His childhood friend, Dudy.

The same burning eyes, the same thin face and look of maturity. It was the face of a boy both wise and unfortunate. There was only one difference: Dudy Levin had a yarmulka and *peyos*; Joselito did not. But other than that the resemblance was uncanny.

The mother and her two sons carefully scrutinized his reaction. "It's Dudy!" he cried, visibly moved.

"That's right." A tiny tear rolled out of an eye that had long since gone dry. "The resemblance between them is amazing. Joselito is a carbon copy of my poor Dudy; he even has the same Jewish name, David."

"David Levin, David Levin," Shmuel's lips moved. He felt a sudden urge to weep. He saw a small boy soaking wet from the pouring rain, crying hopelessly, wandering between the stairwell and the street crying, "Shmulik!"

The tears welled up in his eyes; his lips moved. He forced himself not to burst into a bitter sob, not to let his emotions overwhelm him.

"Joselito is blessed with great powers," his grandmother declared. "In this, too, he resembles my Dudy, he should rest in peace. Did you know that your friend Dudy had enormous potential? The teachers in his *cheder* were astonished by his talents and said, during the *shivah*, that if he had merited living to adulthood the Jewish world would have been enriched with one of the great ethical personalities of the generation. Did you know that?"

She pricked his tormented conscience deliberately and well. She was no sadist; why, then, was she wounding him, torturing him? What was she trying to do?

"I want you to bring Joselito back to Judaism. I've already told you once, and now I'm asking again." Her voice grew softer. "They stole his father; why should the thief take another generation?"

"And your other grandchildren, don't you care about them?" Zerach broke into the dialogue.

The old woman lowered her eyes and was silent for a moment. "I don't have other grandchildren," she said sorrowfully. "Gonzales has no children. Joselito is Santos's only son. One grandchild, that's all I have in this world."

Santos stared at the floor, his face frozen.

Shmuel swayed back and forth as he was wont to do when learning a difficult *sugya*. His hands moved on his knees in rhythm with his body. "I want to understand," he said, turning to the grandmother. "Am I a magician? You think that if I speak with Joselito he will immediately run off to find a yarmulka and *tzitzis* and turn into an 'instant Jew,' ready in a minute — just warm up and serve? Judaism is so vast and so deep, it's impossible to cut it into little pieces. You have to know how to speak, to go into the depths of emotion and to ascend the summit of thought, to speak simply and profoundly all at once, to read the lips of the heart."

"You speak so much, like a faucet drunk on its own dripping," Sabrina retorted. "My grandson knows nothing of Judaism! Teach him a verse of *Chumash* with Rashi, an easy mishnah with a simple meaning. Nourish his soul; it's fainting from spiritual thirst. Or else he will go looking in other places, other nations and beliefs."

She bit her lip, regretting that she had said too much. All eyes in the room rested upon her.

In order to break the awkward silence, Isabella, Gonzales's wife, put a disc into the stereo. In the background a saxophone and guitar began to play a soft wail. She poured tea, assuring her guests that it was kosher. The cups were made of styrofoam; she knew the men would not dream of using her own glass mugs.

"You said you had another reason for calling me here," Shmuel reminded Sabrina.

She turned to her son. "Gonzales, do you have the booklet?"

He nodded his assent and held out a notebook full of photocopied pages.

*This has been a well-rehearsed production.* The thought was shared by Arthur, Zerach, and Shmuel. Everything had been made ready for them — album, notebook, what else was to come?

"This notebook," Sabrina said, playing with the pages. "Because of this, we've all become hunted animals. The Church is desperate to keep this information from being made public. These simple pages that I hold in my hand are a potential time bomb. Publication will raise a huge storm."

"What is it?" the three men's eyes were riveted upon the book.

"One minute," Sabrina cast a chill upon their obvious curiosity. "I have to give you a little background before I tell you what these pages contain."

---

## Caracas, 5725 (1965)

Hadassah Levin was scarred and hurting. She wandered through her new home in the alien city of Caracas like a wounded lioness. The crisis she was undergoing was the worst she had ever faced in her difficult life.

She had known troubles, so many troubles. The first was the death of her pious, scholarly father, Simchah the Milchiker, who died suddenly of a heart attack before the age of 50, leaving behind his wife and only child, Hadassah, weeping and bereft. They had never worried about making a living; Simchah had worked hard morning and evenings to sustain his family. In the mornings he would sell his milk and evenings he worked in the printing shop of a daily newspaper, not going to bed until 2 a.m. His love of Torah burned within him like a bright flame. The ten hours between his dairy rounds and his printing work were filled with the joy of Torah learning. Very little time was left for sleep. He learned with the thirst of a man finding a cool pitcher of water on a hot tropical day. It was with this gusto that Simchah would throw himself the Gemara and *Shulchan Aruch*. He imbibed the writings of the Rambam; his eyes lovingly caressed the lines of almost any holy book. "I'm drunk on Torah," he would joke, but it was partially true. Simchah the dairyman learned for the sake of learning, in the truest sense of that lofty concept. He sought no honor for his learning, never dreamed of the respect that he would earn for his devotion. He was not interested in impressing anyone with his knowledge and refused to become involved in scholarly arguments whose underlying motivation was the desire to declare, "Look at me, I'm a *talmid chacham*, see how much more I know than you." A simple man, a simple Jew.

And one day he suddenly collapsed in shul in the middle of his learning. One minute he was deeply immersed in the words of the Maharsha; the next, his hand clutched his chest and his face paled. At his funeral it became clear that the people had, indeed, recognized his greatness and true worth. Behind the visage of a dairyman clad in a gray smock stained with the black ink of the press, giving off a slightly sour smell of milk, hid a giant of Torah. The Jews of Jerusalem knew who he was, what he was. They mourned his passing and accorded the hidden genius great praise.

The widow and her daughter were struck hard. Hadassah was a young girl on the verge of marriage. Her sorrow was unbounded, but slowly after her marriage to Shalom Levin she was comforted, living with him in great happiness. With the passing of years she recovered from this, her first grief.

But the chain of tragedy would not be broken. The drowning death of Aryeh Yissachar, her firstborn son, the genius of the family, was the second blow. Dudy's death was the third, followed by the complete breakup of the household with the passing of her husband, Shalom, whose heart could not withstand the awesome burden.

But with all the terrible deaths Hadassah knew and believed that it was Hashem Who had given and Hashem Who had taken, He is the Rock Whose work is perfect. A person did not attempt to teach the Creator how to run His world. Her hatred, deep and unyielding, was directed against Yehoshua Cohen, who had tricked her for so long, who had made her believe that there was a merciful Jew who had been touched by her bitter situation, who had devoted himself to her family, bringing them food and supplies. Now she knew it had been nothing more than the underhanded trick of a missionary, a kidnapper of the lowest order. She longed to gouge his eyes out with her bare hands.

On the other hand, Yehoshua had kept one promise. He had taken care of Moishy and Ahrele and now he was taking care of Gonzales and

Santos. The special clinic for children with motor disabilities became their second home, and top doctors checked them each week for three years, until finally their arms and legs had achieved full function. The cost of such treatments was hard for even an economically stable family, let alone a broken widow with not even minimal income.

Yehoshua Cohen kept a steady connection with her home. He had placed them in one of Caracas's most devout neighborhoods, in frightening proximity to many churches. The boys were brought to church every Sunday, until they were sick of the ceremonies, but there was no escape. They were sent to a Catholic school where they received daily brainwashing.

Hadassah tried to battle the might of the Church, did everything to remind her sons of their Jewish heritage. But she was one woman, a weak and helpless one at that, against a mighty institution, and her words went unheard, a gust of wind in a barren desert. Helplessly she saw her children cut off from their Jewishness. She could not complain of neglect. The Church worried about her too, giving her the name Sabrina, changing Levin to Lombardo. "You can't fit into these surroundings as a Jew," explained the many tutors who worked with the family after their arrival in Caracas. "Anti-Semitism here is rampant; if you'll be identified as a Jew, you'll be rejected, even killed."

Yehoshua Cohen continued to bring food and small amounts of money every week. "I'm not like everyone," he would brag. "I've got a merciful heart. The other missionaries leave their people once they've decided to convert; I'll take care of you forever."

Hadassah-Sabrina felt the urge to regurgitate when she heard that kind of talk, and displayed overt anger and hostility, but Yehoshua was made of cast iron. He would maintain his composure even if she spat at him. Yet there were days when she really believed he was good hearted, a philanthropist who worked out of humanitarian goodness. Slowly she adapted herself to his presence, and eventually it was she who would call him and ask why he was not bringing them their supplies.

And one day it happened.

Yehoshua forgot himself, and casually mentioned one of his tried-and-true tactics. "I make sure that the Jew who is a candidate for possible conversion eats non kosher food. Then it all proceeds as smoothly as water. He's pulled towards Christianity and finds himself loathing his Jewishness."

*He's right*, she thought to herself numbly. *Our Sages revealed this secret to us thousands of years ago, in the Gemara. Eating forbidden foods dulls the Jewish heart and soul, cuts him off from his spiritual sources. He becomes strange, alienated from his Jewishness.*

The pain returned anew. Suddenly she understood what this rogue had done to her two sons, why their Jewish fervor had cooled, how their spirituality and innate fear of G-d that she knew they possessed had disappeared.

The blood drained from her face. She remembered how many times they had eaten meat, thanks to the generosity of Yehoshua Cohen. "Yehoshua," she said, her voice rising in hysteria, "you gave us *treif* meat?"

He realized that he had erred, but had no choice but to reveal his secret. "It was good," he said mockingly. "Deluxe pig, excellent sausages, no?"

"I don't believe it," she said in horror.

Yehoshua laughed. "I didn't worry only about your children; you, too, enjoyed non kosher hens and pork sausages, together with your sons. Don't complain to me now."

"And we thought you cared for us, you cursed villain, at the time that you were poisoning us with your filthy meats. Scoundrel! Get out of my house!" Sabrina shrieked, anger overcoming good judgment.

He did not plumb the depths of her fury and continued to tease her. "Your sons enjoyed the meat most when they knew it wasn't kosher." This was a base lie, but he was enjoying torturing her and was getting a sadistic satisfaction out of her agony.

With the fury of a wounded bear she grabbed a glass vase from the table and flung it at Yehoshua. It crashed over his head. Water poured down upon him. The water had a reddish tinge, which he first thought came from the roses that had been inside. Then he felt a wave of unspeakable pain on his entire face, and he gave a terrible scream.

His scalp and face had been slashed in dozens of places. An ambulance raced him to the hospital, where he received a huge number of stitches to repair his torn face.

From his hospital bed he filed a police complaint. Sabrina was put into a Caracas jail, where she spent the most difficult six months of her life in the company of women who had lost all contact with any semblance of humanity.

She vowed revenge.

But Yehoshua Cohen, too, had sworn vengeance. He never forgave her. From that day on he was in her way at every turn. Slowly, for no reason, her talented sons found themselves out of school, moving from one to the other, unfathomingly never kept for more than one year. They were left without even a high school diploma after four years of study. When they looked for employment all gates seemed shut before them. Only the Sanitation Department of the city was willing to take them on. They became trash collectors, walking every morning behind the garbage truck. Sabrina's heart seemed ready to burst from hopeless bitterness.

If she could she would have left everything and fled back to Israel with her children, but her bridges had been burned completely. She had no home in Israel, no job. She feared the reaction of the religious world, was afraid of their judgment, felt they would call her "apostate." In any case, her two sons had long since distanced themselves from their beliefs; she was ashamed of them.

After a long interval Yehoshua Cohen again turned up in the lives of the Lombardo family. He was afraid that she would finally gather the courage to flee to Israel; such a development would reflect badly on the faithful missionary's work. Suddenly he tried to appease her, and asked her forgiveness for the wrongs he had inflicted upon her.

Sabrina did not fall into his trap this time. Though she pretended to forgive him she harbored within an unyielding hatred, and waited for the chance to get revenge for all he had done.

Yehoshua continued his characteristic plotting. He felt obligated to know what was going on in Sabrina's head. Was she planning on leaving Caracas with her sons, thus threatening his status as one of the most successful of the missionaries?

With his snakelike cunning Yehoshua wove a special relationship with Santos, the weaker of the twins. It was a give-and-take relationship: Yehoshua gave him money, in small amounts; in return, he received from

Santos large doses of information on the family. He told the missionary everything that happened in his mother's house.

＊＊＊

Yehoshua Cohen traveled all over the world. The kidnapper of souls had one pleasure in life: converting Jews. He felt drunk with satisfaction as he saw the fruits of his labors brought to church for baptism. He was ready to invest a year or more of his life, just for the joy of the moment when another soul was lost to the Jewish people and joined him in apostasy. This was his goal in life. His playing fields spread across the globe. He knew that the Yad L'Achim and Lev L'Achim organizations had marked him and he tried to outfox them. Occasionally he would return to Caracas for several months, learning the private matters of the Lombardo family from Santos's loose tongue.

Santos often visited Yehoshua's home, located in one of Caracas's most exclusive areas. That is what he did on that visit two months before Shmuel Bilad received two letters from Venezuela.

The nameplate on the door obviously did not read "Yehoshua Cohen," the man's name before his conversion, the one he used when he appeared as a philanthropist to some new and innocent prey that he had found. Only in Caracas did he freely use his Christian name, Pedro Marciano.

Yehoshua — Pedro — was feeling good, almost tipsy. He received Santos in a light robe, gave him a warm and friendly hug and rained kisses down upon his cheeks, surprising his guest and causing him to think that perhaps this godfather of his was beginning to get senile.

During their general chitchat Pedro poured for himself cup after cup of fine wine. Santos suddenly realized that the man was almost drunk and tried to find out what was making him so happy before he lost all touch with reality.

His eyes glazed in an alcoholic blur, laughing ceaselessly, Pedro spoke. "I baptized an entire family, a father, mother, and seven children. You know what that is? Eternal Paradise, my friend!"

"*Salud*!" he courteously clinked his glass against Santos's. Santos had

had enough of Pedro's devout piety, and tales of his successes bored him. He tried to change the subject. "So what else is new?"

Pedro hiccuped and twirled the crystal glass in his hand. The cup was empty, and the level of wine in the bottle, too, was disconcertingly low. "What else is new?" A wave of drunken laughter, accompanied by hiccups and the smell of sour wine. "I have a story for you," he hiccuped. "A story and a booklet, a small one. There are men who would pay millions to get their hands on it. Do you want to see it?"

# 29

Santos did not even blink. He did not believe Pedro; he thought he was surely exaggerating. "What can possibly be in it?" he said carelessly. "The secret formula for a new hydrogen bomb? Or maybe a list of all the people you've brought into the Church."

"Santos, you've got something, I've always said so. You've hit a bull's-eye."

"A hydrogen bomb?"

"No," he snorted. "What else did you say?"

"A list of names."

"Excellent." Pedro was delighted. "This booklet contains a list of names. The names of cherished individuals who work, most of them in Israel, though some in other places in the world. Men who are thought to be good Jews, but who are really faithful emissaries of the Church. Some do their activities without even knowing who they're working for — who — they're — working —" His breath came heavily and the words suddenly stopped. His tongue hung out of his mouth and his head lolled in a drunken stupor. The booklet fell onto the floor.

Santos calmly bent down and picked it up. He was in no rush. He skimmed through the pages and read the contents with great interest.

His eyes grew larger as he realized what he was holding in his hands. He began to tremble, carefully placing the booklet on the sofa next to the drunken Pedro. Then he ran out of the house.

"I've got to tell someone," was his first thought. The only one who would be interested was his mother. He broke all the traffic laws, risked a confrontation with policemen lying in wait for speeding automobiles, and raced to her home.

Sabrina Lombardo did not hesitate for even a millisecond. "He's still drunk?" she asked eagerly.

"As drunk as Lot," Santos promised her.

"So what are we waiting for?" she shouted. "Go to his house, take the booklet, and make a copy."

Santos followed his mother's instructions. It was not easy finding a store to make the photocopies, and it took longer than he had anticipated. When he returned to Pedro's house with the booklet, Pedro's half-closed eyes watched him carefully. An experienced drinker, his liver digested the alcohol swiftly. Without moving a muscle he watched Santos tiptoe into the house, put the booklet down on the carpet, and flee.

With Santos's exit, Pedro jumped up and checked the pages. No doubt about it: The booklet was folded and flattened, as if someone had pressed it down hard. Santos had copied the material!

The wheels of his brain began turning. Santos was not smart enough to have figured out the meaning of this file. Certainly not to realize just how explosive the material was. What had caused him to run and copy it with such haste?

Someone was behind him.

Pedro glanced at his watch. Two hours had passed since he had fallen into his drunken stupor. Enough time for Santos to travel to the other end of the city and back. Why had it taken him two hours to copy the booklet?

The other end of the city. That enemy of the Church in general, and Pedro in particular, lived at the other end of the city. Sabrina!

Warning bells went off in his head. Why would Sabrina need a copy of the incriminating booklet? A woman of 80, what could she do with it?

What could she do? A lot! She must be watched.

In the coming days he played the ignorant fool who knew nothing, thus allaying any suspicions that Sabrina or Santos might have held. Two weeks later he just "happened" to meet Santos in the local supermarket, and he accompanied him through his meandering among the shelves, chatting ceaselessly. He himself bought next to nothing. Santos, bored, tried to shake him off; that was when Pedro asked him if he would like to earn a large sum of money.

Santos brightened immediately. "How much?"

"Half a million bolivars."

Santos pushed his full cart toward the checkout. "You're joking."

"Do you want to or not? I'm absolutely serious."

Santos flung two tubes of toothpaste into the cart. He watched his purchases, careful with every coin. "If you're serious, let's talk."

Pedro lead him over to a spot behind a huge stack of soda cartons in one corner, where no one could see them. He pushed 10,000 bolivars into his hands as a deposit. "I want you to keep your mother under surveillance," he said bluntly.

"No."

"Yes. Be macho. Report her every move to me."

Santos hesitated for exactly ten seconds. "Okay."

That was how Pedro learned about the letter Sabrina sent to Shmuel Bilad in Yerushalayim. Pedro's phenomenal memory could visualize the door on the first floor of the building on Bustenai Street in Katamon, the building he had visited countless times. The Levin family lived on the second floor. Passing by the first floor, one saw a small sign that proclaimed, "The Bilad Family." He dimly remembered a chubby, smiling boy with black hair and *peyos* behind his ears who would ride his bike in the neighborhood. The twins had told him that he was a friend of their deceased brother Dudy. Pedro wondered if this was the man Sabrina was now contacting. He dictated a warning letter to Santos, and gave him detailed instructions regarding from which newspapers to cut the words. Pedro was certain Shmuel Bilad would not dare show up in Caracas. In any case, why would a normal person pick himself up in midlife and travel to the end of the earth, solely due to an anonymous letter he had received?

※

"He'll be disappointed to find out I've arrived," Shmuel smiled.

"Disappointed to find out?" Sabrina laughed bitterly. "He's known about your arrival from the moment you stepped into the airport. Who organized your 'warm welcome' if not Yehoshua Cohen? I refuse to call him Pedro Marciano."

"How do you know?"

Again, the bitter laugh. "Fool! Santos," she said, turning to her son, "he asks how I know. Why don't you ask how I knew that they'd taken you to the building site?"

Zerach and Arthur exchanged glances. "The million dollar question," Zerach whispered. "Indeed, how did you know?"

The old woman pointed to Santos, who was tranquilly sipping fragrant herbal tea, and who looked, once again, completely detached. "What Yehoshua didn't know is that Santos is a lot smarter than he thought. He worked as a double agent; after he told Yehoshua my movements he came to me and confessed his deeds. I persuaded him to continue, to get a large amount of money out of the missionary, as much as he could. You were asking where he got the funds to buy such a lovely villa — that's the answer. And that's how I knew that Yehoshua had hired the 'organization' and how I guessed where you'd been taken. Yehoshua told Santos that you would be turned to concrete the next day."

There was another point Shmuel wanted to clear up. "And you, unlike Yehoshua Cohen, were sure that I would come? Why?"

It was strange to see that a woman of her age was still able to blush. Sabrina reddened in mild confusion. "To tell the truth, I was in terrible distress and searched for a way out of the mess. I pleaded and cried to

Hashem, 'From the straits I call to G-d.' I hoped that the second half of the verse would come true, 'G-d answered me with expansiveness.' I want to rescue my grandson, and I want to get this booklet away from here so that it can be used properly. I tried to think of someone who could come and help me. I knew that in Caracas there was no one who would work with me. Suddenly a light went on in my brain. I remembered Dudy's friend. Forgive me," she blushed again, "I worked on your conscience. I knew you wouldn't be able to refuse me. I found out about you, I called some old friends in Yerushalayim, neighbors from Katamon. I was surprised to see that they remembered me; my surprise grew greater when they undestood how I was feeling and told me that if I returned to Israel I would be welcomed with open arms. I wanted to find out if anyone remembered the Bilad family. Step by step I proceeded, phone call after phone call, until I found you. I was made to understand that you were an important rabbi, a great scholar, a lecturer in a yeshivah."

Shmuel lowered his eyes modestly and mumbled, "Don't pour salt into the wound; I'm unemployed. No yeshivah wants me."

"I hope that you will soon find work appropriate to your talents and honored position," Sabrina said warmly. "But that doesn't change the picture. I know that you have a very sensitive conscience and a high ethical standard. I realized that only you would agree to help me; like a drowning woman I grabbed onto you. I pray that you won't cause me more anguish. All of my life is one big chapter of sorrows and blows, terrible tortures and broken dreams. Don't destroy my last hope."

Her eyes stayed dry, but Zerach and Arthur blinked rapidly and Shmuel held his head in his hands. There was something heartbreakingly poignant in this proud old woman, disclosing the difficult life she had endured with affecting simplicity, speaking of her solitary battle in a strange and distant land, her refusal to admit defeat in the face of an overwhelming and merciless enemy. She had lost two sons spiritually, two others to death, but her spirit and will were still bright and strong.

"I'll help you," Shmuel said warmly. "I'll do whatever I can."

"By the way, where are the lists? Can we see them?" Zerach asked.

Gonzales was holding the papers. He was about to hand them to Zerach when his mother's voice stopped him. "There's no rush," she said, looking at her watch. "There's something more important. I'm afraid they'll be here any minute now. We've got to get away."

They left the house and split up: the three guests, Santos, and Sabrina in Arthur's car; Gonzales and Isabella in their silver Fiat.

The two automobiles raced off toward Arthur's house. Two minutes after they departed, earlier than expected, a large jeep came roaring toward them, with several men peering at them from its windows.

"Let's go!" Shmuel screamed in terror. "It's the 'organization'! That's the one who kidnapped me!"

Arthur put his foot firmly down on the gas pedal and the car lurched forward. The silver Fiat raced behind.

The jeep stopped with a shriek of brakes. The driver, Don Juan, stared at Julio without saying a word. Julio's eyes were filled with horror.

"We've seen a dead man," he whispered, his voice trembling. He was a firm believer in the existence of ghosts and was terrified of the spirit world. "The Jew has come back to get his revenge."

"Are you a baby?" Don Juan hissed from between clenched teeth. "He's not dead. He escaped."

"He couldn't have escaped," Julio forced the words out of his almost-paralyzed throat. "I tied him up the way I always do. The cement has hardened over his body. It's his soul, come to get me."

Don Juan opened the door of the vehicle with one swift gesture, grabbed Julio by his black tricot shirt. He pulled him out forcibly and thrust him onto a stone gate, among thorns and dried bushes. "Listen," he barked. "Big Don Juan wasn't born yesterday. You can't fool me with the face of a cowardly rabbit afraid of ghosts. I know you're just playacting. You're a traitor. You let the Jew out. You let him run away. How much did he pay you?"

Julio gave off a flash of hatred and fear combined. "Don't talk to me that way, Don Juan. Don't talk to me as if I were a traitor. You're the traitor."

"What!" Don Juan, quick tempered, attacked Julio in wild fury, giving him a harsh kick. When he collapsed in a heap on the ground, Don Juan turned around.

A bullet whizzed past his ears. Julio was crouching on his knees, shooting.

Don Juan was quick on the draw. He shot twice at Julio, who collapsed for a second time. This time he did not get up.

Don Juan spared a quick glance at his deputy, lying motionless on the pavement. Then he ran back to the jeep, ignoring the frightened eyes staring at him from nearby houses. There was no reason to go into Gonzales's home; Don Juan did not believe in locking the barn door after the horses were gone. What he needed now was to keep his cool, to calm down, to bring order into this chaos. Where should he go? These Jews were teasing him; they were always one step ahead. The best chess player was sometimes defeated by one move.

Suddenly he knew where he had to go.

The car sped toward the outskirts of the city's industrial area, passing trucks one after the other. Now he was outside the city's poor neighborhood, on barren hills slated to become Caracas's new high-tech center. Concrete frames and glass towers were going up all around. He reached a building still under construction, jumped out of the jeep, and approached the large steel gates. He was greeted by the barking of dogs; the watchman arrived soon after. "Hello," he said, giving him a crooked grin.

"Where is the concrete that's been poured?" Don Juan demanded impatiently.

"Which one? There's been about twenty places where they've poured concrete today."

Don Juan gave him a meaningful look. "You know full well what I'm talking about."

The watchman nodded and took him into the cellar, illuminating the pathway with a lantern.

Don Juan scanned the area. He noticed cut cords on the floor and he moved near to investigate them more closely. "These are the ropes! They cut them and let him escape. Just as I thought." He spoke in a whisper that chilled the watchman's blood. "They didn't even try to hide their actions. What happened here?" he suddenly yelled, brandishing his revolver in front of the watchman's horrified face.

The watchman revealed everything.

*Time Bomb* / 315

"And you let them go, just like that? You didn't protest, you didn't tell us. Why not?"

He did not bother waiting for an answer. He would deal with this fool of a watchman later. Right now he had to rush back to Pedro Marciano, the man who had hired him. The Church would be quite unhappy with the mess his organization had made of the operation. He had to explain before Pedro began asking uncomfortable questions.

He left behind him a trembling human being. The watchman knew that the clock was now ticking: his life wasn't worth one miserable Venezuelan centimo.

---

Pedro was immersed in Caracas's daily newspaper, *El Nacional*, when someone banged violently on his door. Among his large number of acquaintances there was only one who dared to strike the door like a pirate; it must be Don Juan. At first Pedro had fumed, demanding that Don Juan ring the bell like everyone else. That was before Don Juan had explained to him that generally he did not even knock — he just opened the door and entered.

"And if the door is locked?" Pedro had asked testily.

"I shoot the lock off," Caracas's quickest draw had explained. Simple and effective.

Pedro had eventually become accustomed to the brash style of the coarse mafioso. Assassins such as he were not contenders for etiquette awards. Pedro was interested in results and he learned that Don Juan's gang had the best record of neat, professional assassinations.

Don Juan had practically broken down the door during the two minutes it took Pedro to open it. He was nervous, and his face was tense and unusually angry.

"Why so angry, *amigo*?"

Don Juan decided to attack. He forced his way into the living room and practically jumped on Pedro. "Who is your spy?" he shouted.

"I don't understand."

Don Juan kicked a leather-covered stool in order to emphasize the urgency of his words, and punched the glass tabletop to better make his point. "I'm not used to this kind of thing!" he screamed furiously. "Someone is destroying us from within. Whenever we go, they know we're coming and they run away. It's not normal. Someone is telling them everything."

Slowly the picture emerged and Pedro began to understand the situation. Don Juan, in his own inimitable style, let him know of the mission's total failure. No one had been killed, Sabrina still had the papers, the secret would be out. He understood Don Juan's tactics perfectly. The man had long since learned an important and tested rule: The best defense is a strong offense. Now he, Pedro, would teach him a lesson with an offense of his own.

"You're an absolute zero!" He grabbed Don Juan by the ears. "You have ears? Let me check." He pulled the lobes down until Don Juan was screaming in pain. "I gave you $50,000 on account, so that you kill that old witch Sabrina and the Jew from Israel, and I get foolishness about spies? Do I have to teach you your business?"

Don Juan's hands flailed about. Pedro thought that he was going to try and free his ears so he clamped down even harder, practically pulling them off. Pedro did not realize with whom he was dealing; a serious error for one who was playing with a snake's tail. The snake grows angry and prepares its venom.

"Do you understand? I'm not interested, don't come to me with excuses. Put twenty of your bullies on it, use a million bullets, so that — "

The last word never was said. Don Juan had pulled his revolver with one sharp movement and shot him between the ribs. One bullet.

Yehoshua Cohen — Pedro — lost his life in the same way he had lived most of it: on the altar of the Church.

Don Juan left the house a few moments later. He tried to destroy all incriminating evidence, and carefully wiped his fingerprints off the gun. He placed Pedro on the sofa and put the revolver into his right hand, facing the wound in his chest. It would take some time for the criminal investigation squad to check the trajectory of the bullet; even if they would eventually realize that it was not suicide, Don Juan would have gained valuable time to regroup.

The cool air felt good on his burning ears. The old man had gone too far and had deserved what he got. Even Don Juan's teacher in school had never done such a thing! Since he had turned 15 no man had ever treated him like that, and lived.

He pondered his next steps. Pedro was no longer alive, but Pedro was not the only one. Cardinal Patrick Huntado, head of the Church of John the Baptist, who himself was scion of an apostate Jewish family by the name of Fradenhaus, was deeply involved in the matter; Pedro was merely following his orders. He, Don Juan, still had to go after Sabrina and the Jew from Israel. Actually, after the three Jews, if he wanted to earn the promised quarter of a million dollars.

But now he was pursuing nothing. They would not return to the houses they had been in and it seemed they had disappeared into thin air. The game of tag was over. Perhaps one or the other would return to their homes for a few minutes, but Don Juan was not going to waste money on 24-hour surveillance at the three houses, one belonging to the mother and the others to the two sons. That was not practical. So what was?

If he wanted to get the fish out of the deep water, he needed a thick, juicy worm on the end of the hook.

He smiled suddenly. He would prepare a trap. Bravo! he congratulated himself. He had an idea that would draw them out of hiding.

---

With a great effort of will Julio managed to straighten up. His shoulders ached and his right arm felt as if it were on fire. He had taken two bullets; one in the shoulder, one in the hand. The assassin had been in too much of a hurry. Julio had feigned death and Don Juan had fallen for it. But Julio had lost a lot of blood; if he did not take care of his wounds, Don Juan would prevail. He needed medical aid, perhaps even an operation to remove the bullets.

The burning sensation in his body was nothing compared to the burning of his heart. Don Juan had slammed him into a stone fence and shot him, his deputy and partner, as if he was no more than a rabid dog. He would pay!

This very night he would surprise Don Juan and take his revenge. But he needed a partner.

He needed Diego.

# 30

*Rome, 5761 (2000)*

Kareem Nisadov walked toward the white building at the end of the Via del Pelligrino in the Vatican. This was one of three that served as the barracks for members of the Swiss Guard.

He knew that though by and large the function of the Swiss Guard was ceremonial, with true security functions in the Vatican belonging to the "Vigili" security organization, still it would not be long before a serious search would be on for the missing soldier. Kareem's time was limited.

He wondered if one of the Vigili would be waiting for him. Selim had warned him several times: "Kareem, the Vigili is a small group, but strong and effective and very well trained. They're the eyes that are watching from behind the ceremonial Swiss Guard."

A dark-blue limousine drove past him. He gave a slight shiver; an official vehicle in the area might mean some unusual activity that would disturb the quiet needed for the next few hours. He continued to walk tranquilly, his gaze falling nonchalantly on the limousine. The car pulled over. The driver's window was open and he could hear him chatting into his cellular phone. "Yes, Ma, I'm going to Africa tomorrow with Luisi. What? Of course the pope is going, that's why we're traveling. When do we leave? Sorry, official secret, I can't tell you. Okay, Ma, just you. Seven thirty in the morning. No, officially the itinerary released to the papers says 9:30. Just to confuse any enemies."

Kareem let out the breath he had been holding unnaturally. Thanks to this chatterbox of a driver, chauffeur to the Vatican security chief, he learned that the flight was leaving two hours earlier than Selim had thought. So the perfect Selim was also capable of making a mistake. Now Kareem's time was really limited.

Fifty yards before the building's entrance he stopped for a moment and pushed wads of cotton into his cheeks in order to give his face the square-jawed look of the missing guardsman. He had bidden his luxuriant mustache farewell yesterday.

The keys he had taken from the unconscious guard were in his hand. He opened his fist and carefully scrutinized each key. One of them looked right; it was attached to a plastic disk with the number 228. He entered the building and quietly walked up the stairs. He found Room 28 on the second floor.

He turned the key in the lock; the door opened easily. He saw a simple, modestly furnished room with a tiny window that was shut. There was a single wooden bed covered with a flowered quilt and a small night-stand with newspapers strewn upon it. He picked up the phone and put the receiver next to his ear. He heard the buzz of an internal line.

He sat down on the bed, pulled his mobile phone out of his pocket and turned it on. When the digital display glowed its eerie green, he pushed a long series of numbers and waited until the sixth ring. An electronic answering machine demanded shortly, "Please leave a message."

"Father wants to know if you will be coming to take part in his birthday party," he said quietly. Then he hung up.

This was the code he and Selim had worked out. The first stage of Steel Fist had been successfully completed.

This had been the easy part, smooth as clear water. Now he wondered about stages two and three. Would the water turn into oil, or thick mud? As long as it wasn't blood.

*Time Bomb*

Kareem did not waste a minute. In three hours he would be leaving his room for the airport. He had to change his clothing and put on a completely different costume, with a completely different purpose.

He hoped nothing would go wrong.

### Caracas, 5761 (2000)

"I don't know how many times I will have to recite the '*HaGomel*' blessing if I get out of here safely," Shmuel said, as they sat in Arthur's spacious and comfortable home, at the end of their panic-stricken ride.

"It's clear they saw us," Zerach said. "I was sure they would get us from the other lane."

"The hunt isn't over yet," Sabrina said in a low voice. "They will come here too! I know Yehoshua Cohen; he's stubborn as a mule. And even if he eases off, there are others. There's a well-equipped Church establishment standing behind him. He's backed by Cardinal Patrick Huntado, of the Caracas clergy. They won't rest until they've made sure my body has turned cold."

"They're not the ones who decide who lives," Arthur declared. "If Hashem has decreed that you should stay alive, they won't be able to touch you."

The group's hosts, Arthur and Sylvia Taubman, prepared a large spread for their ravenous guests. The repeated chases had exhausted all of them. They hardly knew what planet they were on, and how this all would end.

They sat around a fully set table laden with tempting foods: slices of young salmon garnished with lemon and tomato wedges, Cornish hens stuffed with rice and ground beef in a sweet-and-sour sauce, an incomparable delicacy. For dessert their hosts served apples baked in wine, spiced with cinnamon sticks and ground nuts.

The twin brothers courteously thanked the Taubmans and turned to speak to each other in subdued tones. Their mother, though, was wasting no time. "R' Bilad, we've got to plan our next step. I beg you, speak to my grandson, Joselito."

Shmuel turned to Zerach, who was swaying rhythmically over his *bencher*, his lips whispering the last words. "Zerach, are you done? Can I have your cell phone, please?"

"First, the lists." Zerach showed that he, too, could be determined. "We haven't forgotten, Mrs. Lombardo. You wanted to show us some of the photocopied pages."

"Soon," Sabrina reassured him. "The conversation is more important."

Zerach handed Shmuel the phone. Sabrina recited the phone number from memory. *I wouldn't mind such an old age,* Zerach thought. *A memory like that at her age.*

While they waited for a response on the other end, Shmuel stared at his hands. He did not know how he was going to start this conversation.

---

*Chechnya, 5761 (2000)*

Selim Yagudayev's guerrilla band had completed nine grueling days of training exercises, which included a daring commando raid to take over the jet in the event that Kareem would fail. The Sheep Shearer's Cave in the Torbakov region had served as their home for these nine days. Selim had taken care of all the details. No one knew how he had managed to organize supplies under these impossible circumstances, in a swampy, almost impassable area, in a place where any unusual movement activated the attention of Russian snipers whose sights were trained there.

Magically, two generators had appeared, supplying the necessary power for the small heaters and the lanterns that illuminated the dark cave twenty-four hours a day. Powerful flashlights, woolen blankets, communications equipment, cables, and canvas tents were also available. No one asked questions, but Selim vouchsafed an explanation. "I'm not certain how we are going to get out of here. I'm preparing for the possibility that we'll have to pass through between the mountains, and I've planned accordingly." He kept the entire truth carefully secreted within the depths of his heart. Most of the equipment was simply diversionary. He had a detailed plan of how he and his men would get from the nearby

Russian air force base to the airport at Yaoundé, capital of Cameroon, where the pope was scheduled to stop after his visit to Zaire. Selim believed in no one and trusted no one. His fighters had learned that they would receive their orders at the very last minute. The case containing priests' garb he showed to no one.

They sat, fatigued and drained, in the back portion of the cave, leaning on the rock walls and drinking cups of hot coffee to warm up. A lantern flooded this part of the cave with an almost blinding light. Selim played a Chechen folk song on a small harmonica, and the others sang along. When the last strains of the music had passed, each sat lost in his own thoughts. Eyes began to close.

Sayid Mashtatov broke the silence and spoke softly to Selim. "I have a question, Selim, if you don't mind."

Selim opened weary eyes. "Please."

Sayid's voice trembled a little; it was obvious that his opening salvo was guarded. "Aren't you worried about the consequences of this project? I'm afraid that the plan will fail and in the end we'll be faced with international condemnation, if not worse. Why couldn't we make do with some small acts of terror?"

Selim shook off the last vestiges of tiredness. "Terror. You're making me laugh. Russia is carrying on a brutal war against us. The Russian army blocks access to Chechnya for journalists and photographers, and everything is all right. As long as we didn't take part in terrorist acts we had international support, but when some of our people carried out some small terrorist acts in Moscow did you see how things changed? The Russians took advantage of the situation, they portrayed our fighters as fanatical Moslem terrorists, and in one fell swoop we lost the world's sympathy."

"And kidnapping the pope will get us public relations points in the international scene?" Sayid asked in open wonder.

Selim sighed. "How many times do I have to repeat myself? Am I a parrot? The pope's disappearance will not be known by the public. When he's in our hands we'll make a gentlemen's agreement between Russia, the Vatican, and ourselves that will keep the entire affair a secret. The Vatican will certainly demand that; it prefers a low profile. Russia, too, won't want publicity. It has carried out an unprecedented slaughter against a nation and the less fanfare about Chechnya the better. And we will certainly keep our mouths shut.

"Yes," he added excitedly, "we'll have another card in our deck, besides the pope himself: keeping news of the kidnapping to ourselves."

"And the journalists, and the pope's entourage? How can we keep such sensational news from being leaked out?" Sayid persisted.

"Rely on me," Selim answered shortly.

His well-used cell phone gave a weak ring. Samil Buchatov, one of his deputies, was on the line, calling from the guerrilla's regional headquarters.

"There's a woman by the name of Sabrina Lombardo who wants to speak with you."

"Let her call in five minutes," Selim answered.

He grabbed his briefcase and walked out of the cave. Hidden by huge boulders, Selim opened the case and pulled out a high-quality communications device and a small satellite dish. Selim used this system — that was protected against all eavesdropping — for the most confidential conversations. He set up the system and waited; one minute later there was a shrill ring.

"Joselito," the voice on the other end seemed to hide a sob, "I thought you'd come and visit your grandmother sometime."

Selim answered in an angry whisper. "I've asked you not to mention that name. Call me Selim."

"So let it be Selim," Sabrina gave in. "When are you coming to Caracas?"

"When I have time, Grandma," Selim replied. "You know that there is a war going on; I can't leave comrades in difficult times."

"There's a Jew here who wants to speak with you," Sabrina blurted out hastily, handing the phone to Shmuel before her grandson could protest.

Selim made a face. *"Grandma cooked porridge."* He remembered how his father used to tickle him as he sang the children's song when he was a baby. His grandmother certainly knew how to cook things up. What did she want from him? He longed to hang up the phone, but he had deep respect for his wise grandmother, who had influenced him from childhood onward.

In faraway Caracas Shmuel prayed: "Dear Father, put the right words into my mouth; let me not fail."

He took the first step. "Selim, I won't call you Joselito, and I might not even call you Selim. I understand that your real name is David."

"What do you want?" Selim demanded impatiently. "My time is short."

"Your grandmother wants you to come to Caracas," Shmuel said. "Maybe you can come tomorrow or the next day."

"I can't. I'm busy."

"If so, give me just five minutes of your time," Shmuel pleaded. He sensed the wall of suspicion and alienation and felt a stab of grim hopelessness. What did he have to do with all this? He had a sudden urge to hang up the phone, pack his bags, and return home to Israel.

"Don't listen to temptation, to evil." He could almost hear the many *roshei yeshivah* and *mashgichim* that he had met, from high school and onward, shouting in unison. Even louder than those combined voices, though, were the stifled sobs of a little boy: Dudy Levin, standing out in the rain.

His finger trembled on the button that would have cut off the conversation, but instead he found himself speaking earnestly, telling this mirror image of Dudy Levin of the terrible suffering the Jews had undergone in Christian countries. He spoke of the Inquisition, of the religion of love and mercy that had slaughtered Jews for 2,000 years. He discussed the Church's deadly silence during the Holocaust, which had indirectly sanctioned the murder of six million Jews. Suddenly he wondered if Selim had cut the connection a long while before; perhaps he had been speaking to the wall.

He was wrong. Selim had listened carefully to every word. There was a brief silence and then his voice came on the line: "If so, I understand from your words that it is important to take revenge against the cursed Church for all it's done to the Jews in general and my family in particular."

Shmuel was surprised. He had understood from his grandmother that Joselito was not particularly enamored of Christianity, but he had not expected such a vehement reaction. "Listen, my friend, a vengeful deity is G-d, as it says in Psalms. Only G-d can pay villains back for their evil deeds. Vengeance is not given into our hands. And in any case, what can one person do to an institution as powerful as the Church? Cut down crosses? Burn their holy pictures? Stab priests?"

Strangely, Selim felt that he could trust this stranger across the sea. The words came out before he could prevent them. "What do you think about killing the pope?"

Shmuel was thunderstruck. Was this what the young man was planning, or was this merely a theoretical question? "I haven't the faintest idea of how you would go about it, but let's say you managed to murder him. What next? You've shot an 80-year-old man, so weak he can barely move."

"He is a symbol to the hundreds of millions who believe in him; I'll wound all of them at once."

"And cause an outbreak like the Crusades and maybe take humanity into the Third World War," Shmuel cried. "You've accomplished nothing. Listen to me, my friend, do you really want to take vengeance against the Church?"

His voice held a promise. Cold sparks flashed in the eyes of Selim Yagudayev, who was Joselito Lombardo, who was David Levin, standing thousands of miles away. "What do you suggest?"

"Return to being a Jew," Shmuel said simply.

Selim was sorely disappointed. "So you're also a missionary, just like Yehoshua Pedro Cohen. You also want me to accept your religion. You're selling your G-d just like all the other salesmen in the market."

Now Shmuel was given the opportunity to show Selim just what Torah learning can do to sharpen the mind, and just what the word *"lamdan"* really means:

"You're wrong. I'm not selling my G-d and I'm not a merchant of my Jewishness. Judaism has never tried to increase the numbers of its adherents and make converts. Judaism is a religion of quality, not of quantity. 'Converts are to be dissuaded' is our credo. Islam lives by 'Mohammed's justice is by the sword' and whoever doesn't accept it is judged for death. Christianity hopes to take over the entire world under the cross, in whose name millions have been murdered. I'm asking only that you return to your Jewishness — the Jewishness that belongs to you. You are Jewish, from birth; religious zealots stole it from you. If you return to being a true Jew, observing Torah and mitzvos, you're inflicting the greatest wound on the people who stole you away. All of Pedro's work, the work of forty years, will be lost completely."

Selim pondered an answer, but Shmuel was not quite done. "Your grandmother told me about your extraordinary talents and your highly developed sense of justice, which caused you to change your identity and go and fight for the cause of the Chechen nation. I ask you: What do you have to do with them? You are a Jew, they are Moslems; you're a stranger to them. Right now they love you because you're succeeding, but the smallest hint of failure and they'll shoot you down like a Scud missile. And really, of what concern is their war with you? 'Don't get involved in an argument that is not yours,' our sources say. Give your talents to your people; believe me, you are meant to do great things."

"You've told me some interesting things," Selim said, breathing hard. "I'll think about them. *Ciao*."

He quickly replaced the receiver. The conversation had gone on much longer than what was wise. It would be a miracle if the Russians' advanced listening devices had not managed to intercept his conversation. He suspected that their sophisticated gadgetry would quickly break through the Chechen's jamming devices.

Interesting. Who was this man staying with his grandmother? He was certainly sincere, and his arguments were quite logical. As the man spoke, Selim experienced emotions that he had never experienced before in his life. He was the first man to whom he had ever revealed his plan of killing the pope. That was, in actuality, his goal, but he had not even told his own people. To them he had spoken of kidnapping. That was true as far as it went, but he had planned to go one step further. If Russia refused to negotiate with him, or wouldn't accede to his demands, he would personally dispatch *Il Papa* to the next world.

Only now did the thought occur to him: Perhaps such an action would cause Chechnya to disappear off the world map forever. His hatred of priests and Christianity blazed within him like a fire. He had never forgiven the Church for what they had done to his father, his uncle, his grandmother. It had been Sabrina who had opened his eyes to it when he was just a youth, telling him of all the tragedies and misfortunes that the Church had caused his family, all in the name of the religion of love.

"I've got to meet him for a longer talk," he whispered to himself. He returned to the cave. If any of his men understood English, the language they had used, he was in trouble. *Grandma had cooked him porridge.* This kind of conversation should never take place so close to the others. But what was the difference, really? Operation Steel Fist would go on, and no power in the world could stop it.

---

Israel, 5761 (2000)

In Israel the noise of Arab gunfire continued. The Israeli media, working for its enemy's welfare, used soothing terms, so as not to arouse in the people a basic urge to survive or a desire for revenge. Thus fatal shootings became "incidents," deadly enmity was "hostility." The word "murder" was used only in connection with threats to the prime minister from the right and, of course, Baruch Goldstein and Yigal Amir.

Every day innocent Israelis were killed or wounded sitting in their automobiles, as Palestinian cars passed them or waited in ambush and sprayed them with dozens of bullets. Major roads near the capital, Jerusalem, became death traps; the media ignored it. In the beginning of a wintry week right after Chanukah 5761 (2000) the Palestinians murdered a Jewish couple in the presence of their five children, wounding the youngsters as well. Israeli blood was being spilled like water, and the so-called Palestinian leaders were only calling for more.

At the end of that very week the mirage appeared again, and it seemed that in the near future another "peace" treaty would be signed. The theater of the absurd presented the Israeli public with another show by Deputy Minister Max Landau. The more murderous the Arabs became, the greater were the Israeli concessions. Tragedy struck home after home. Funerals of victims of the Al-Aksa Intifada became daily affairs, and Landau became even more diligent in his desire to pacify the Arab murderers.

Everyone around him wept, but he was laughing. Laughing hard and loud.

Until the paralyzed nation would recover from its democratic etiquette and release itself from the bonds placed upon it by the media and the government, Max would be able to finish his work of dismantling the State. He would give in on everything: the Jordan Valley, East Jerusalem, Rachel's Tomb, the Western Wall, sovereignty on the Temple Mount. He would begin the process of Palestinian "right of return," letting them in through the back door, so to speak, by allowing in "only" the refugees of 1948 — thus opening the way to a flow of millions of Arabs. On the water supply, too, he agreed to concede: Israeli water-purification centers were also up for negotiation.

Max would sell everything.

Everything, and quickly — for a pot of beans. Read: a piece of paper bearing the scribbles of the major players. There was the American president, a lame duck who was incapable of transferring a document from one drawer to another anymore, yet who was ready to force Israel into signing a treaty; an Israeli leader who was clearly loathed by the people; and an aging Arab murderer, partially senile, who was happy to send his colleagues to kill Jews even as he spoke of peace. Every child understood that one moment after the paper was signed — the paper that forced the lamb to give pieces of its body to the fox — the bullets would fly once again. Only this time it would be missiles and rockets fired from close range.

Max was calm; he was certain no one would stop him from dismantling the State and tearing it into pieces. Three and a half months of raging holocaust, as citizens of the State became sitting ducks in a rifle range, their lives worthless, had increased his self-confidence. The General Security Service, which was under his direct supervision, kept its finger on the pulse of all potential problems and outbreaks. Leaders were being ousted, funds were being taken away in the name of "emergency regulations."

Who would stop him from fulfilling his mission? In a short time he would proudly look toward his grandfather and whisper, "I have done your will."

And Grandfather would be satisfied

# 31

*Rome, 5761 (2000)*

That night Kareem locked himself in his room. He ignored the knocks of his comrades inviting him to go out. From behind the door, his face wrapped in a towel, he explained that he was suffering from a terrible toothache and wanted to rest.

"Antoine, don't you know there is an emergency dental clinic open all night?"

*So my name is Antoine. Now what do I do? The toothache is no longer a good excuse.*

"I don't want to see a dentist now," he moaned from behind the towel. "Let me die in peace. Leave me alone."

"This isn't like you, Antoine," a surprised voice said. "Is that how you talk to Oscar, your best friend?"

*Oscar. Aha. Thank you for the generous information.*

"Listen, Oscar," the firm voice now held a pleading note. "This pain isn't like me either. I can hardly bear myself. Do me a favor, leave me alone."

Oscar, worried, left him. A few minutes later two others came, inviting him to join them for a drink. These, too, he put off.

Kareem was disturbed. He had not taken this into account: The members of the Swiss Guard were showing unexpected comradeship and anxiety for each other's welfare. Apparently, standing still all day long did something to them. These men, all alone in daylight, turned social in the evening. If even one of them would suspect something, Selim's whole house of cards would collapse.

After the last anxious friend, George, had conducted still another conversation through the closed door, Kareem lay down to rest. He found it difficult to sleep. His nerves were keeping his intense fatigue at bay. He was afraid of the future but he was even more terrified of the present. Four of the guards had already commented on his strange behavior. If they began to speak about him there was at least a chance that they would decide to break into his room. And then — farewell to all of his plans.

Fortunately for him, it didn't happen. But the tension kept him awake. *Why hadn't Allah given him an easier task in this world?*

It was 3 o'clock in the morning when he began to prepare. He sat in front of the mirror and placed a number of small bottles neatly in a row before him. He mixed various solutions, experimenting with colors and combinations. When he was satisfied with the results he washed his hair, dried it, and carefully dyed it. When he was done he saw before him a convincing gray head of hair. He emphasized the wrinkles at the edge of his mouth with a thin brush and deepened the lines on his forehead. His nose, too, received attention, giving it a fleshier look. A pair of blue-gray sunglasses shaded his eyes. At last, he inspected himself closely in a mirror and compared himself to the small picture. The resemblance was convincing, excellent. Now what was the name? Jack Harrison. *From this moment on I am Jack Harrison.*

At exactly 5 a.m. Kareem left the barracks. His house of cards, a tower actually, was now resting solely upon Selim's intelligence information. If he had made a mistake — if, for example, the Swiss Guard began its day at 5 a.m. and not at 5:15 — the error would be fatal.

Selim had not made any mistake. As Kareem left the building he could hear the buzz of alarm clocks going off in several rooms. His success was now contingent on a small margin of time between one action and the next. He took swift steps to the rendezvous in the Via Angelo.

The taxi was waiting for him. The driver sat calmly, his hands resting on the steering wheel. His thin Italian mustache turned up into a smile when he saw his passenger. Kareem had already hired him on his second day in Rome. This was a driver with connections, who possessed entry and exit authorizations to the Vatican. He had been designated to drive him on the critical day.

Twenty minutes later the cab was standing at the entrance to a typical old-style Italian home. These stewards, whose airplane was their second home, couldn't find some nicer place to live? Apparently this was what one chose, if one were an American living in Rome in rented quarters two days a week.

He pushed the doorbell firmly with his finger. Just as Selim had told him, the ring was loud, and could be heard throughout the house.

The resident raced to the door. Kareem saw the peephole grow dark, and he knew that Jack Harrison was looking at him and not believing what he saw.

The door opened a crack. This was a risk: Jack might have retreated into the house screaming, but whoever had studied the psychological profile of the steward had accurately predicted his reaction.

The door opened further. A gray head came out. "Who are you? I can't believe it. Who are you?"

"Pleased to meet you," Kareem nodded his head. "I am your twin brother."

Jack rubbed his eyes and stared at him without comprehension. "I have no twin. Who are you?"

"Mother never told you about me?" His head moved back and forth in distress. "What a shame."

His hand suddenly grabbed the wrist of the confused steward. The man felt just a tiny stab and managed to stare for a few seconds before collapsing to the floor.

"What is it in me that makes everyone fall?" Kareem hummed to himself a few words from the Chechen song, "Children of the Revolution," as he dragged Jack to his bed and tied his hands and his feet together. By the time the steward would awaken from his long sleep, Operation Steel Fist would be over.

*Time Bomb* / 333

When he left, he took the key and firmly locked the door behind him.

The driver was waiting for him patiently and quietly. His experience had taught him not to ask too many questions. "Where to now?"

"Leonardo da Vinci Airport."

Kareem boarded the Alitalia flight at 6 a.m..

---

## Chechnya, 5761 (2000)

At 6 a.m. the armored car departed toward the military airport "Yuri Andropov," fifteen miles southwest of Grozny. Visibility was poor; thick fog covered the road and the three soldiers within could hardly see a yard in front of them.

The blazing barrel blocking the poorly paved road brought the armored car to an abrupt halt. Two soldiers jumped out and approached the flames. A hail of bullets brought them both down to the ground, raising the total number of Russian casualties in Chechnya by two.

Selim and his men quickly subdued the driver and raced off with the armored vehicle toward the airport. Army trucks passed them, Selim waving cheerily at the drivers. They could be forgiven for not identifying them; even an officer would have had trouble seeing the difference between these men and the Russian soldiers. Same uniform, same hat, same rifles and arms.

They waited for a truck to catch up to them. Selim flagged it down.

The driver pulled over next to him. "What's the matter, comrade?"

"What are you carrying?"

"Routine equipment," the man answered in a bored voice. "Supplies, broken refrigerators, machine guns for the workshop. Cases and cases."

Selim waved a slip of paper in front of the driver, who was leaning out his window. "I have orders here for you to take twenty soldiers to the plane."

The driver tried to object. "I don't have room to put a safety pin in here."

"It's signed by the base commander, General Koblenko Murbaski," Selim said quietly.

"Why didn't you say so before?" the driver retreated. General Murbaski was tough, and his reputation had preceded him throughout the Grozny area.

They left their armored car and boarded the truck, settling themselves with difficulty in among the boxes. Eight fighters immediately went into boxes that were half empty, finding excellent hiding places for themselves there. One of them entered the driver's cabin for a friendly visit, and soon had parted the driver from his truck. The truck was theirs now. It would bring them to a particularly large transport plane due to take off in another hour for the city of Astrakhan near the Caspian Sea. Selim, though, had a different destination in mind. The cranes that would load the boxes, with their human cargo secreted within, would do the rest. Lengthy surveillance of the air base had taught Selim that the planes were routinely fueled up with enough gasoline for a much longer flight. After they had taken over the craft and had visited the cockpit, the pilot and copilot would undoubtedly have a dramatic change of heart and willingly transport them to Yaoundé, capital of Cameroon.

---

Diego Igoaso lay on the bed in the regional clinic, screaming in pain as the nurse took the bloody bandage off his nose and cleaned the wound with alcohol. "*Aiii!*" she said as she stared at the unpleasant sight of his broken nose. "You've got to go to the hospital. How did this happen?"

"I bumped into a wall," Diego growled. "Just bandage it and stop asking questions."

"It's terrible," the nurse said. "You bump into a wall and get such a bad break?"

She was asking far too many questions; worse, her voice indicated open skepticism. What did he care, though. Let her think it was a drunken brawl.

A shadow covered the glass door of the clinic; the door burst open.

The nurse cringed. Julio never looked his best when he was angry. His eyes turned into hostile points of black and his cheeks had a purple-black hue. "You spoiled brat," he hissed at the sight of Diego. "You get a little punch in the nose and you run to put a Band-Aid on like a kindergarten child. I'm walking around with a broken shoulder and not making a big deal. You're coming with me."

"Let me finish putting on some ointment," Diego wailed.

Julio grabbed him from the treatment table. "Stop this nonsense!" he roared. "Let's go!"

They disappeared from the clinic, Diego half-dragged away. The nurse wondered for a few moments if she should report the incident to the police but decided to do nothing. These were clearly dangerous criminals; why get involved with them?

Julio sped away. "When we're finished dealing with Don Juan you can go to the hospital and get the best doctors. We'll straighten your nose; it will be as long and beautiful as the Brooklyn Bridge."

Diego thought he had not heard correctly. Perhaps the pain was affecting his hearing? "Who are we finishing with?"

"Don Juan." Julio's voice was hard with a deadly coldness. "He broke my head on a pile of rocks and then shot me. He will pay."

"And what about the old lady?"

"Her turn will come," Julio promised. "Do you think I've forgotten about her? She and her Jew guests, they're all dead as far as I'm concerned. But Don Juan is first in line."

"Where are we going now?"

Julio's voice was measured. His words came out like bullets. "To his house, *amigo*. Don Juan forgot that once, about a year ago, he gave me his key. We'll work on his electricity a little. When he gets home tonight there will be a power outage. He'll be upset. Don Juan doesn't like missing his sports events on television. He's addicted to soccer. I know him well, I've seen this dozens of times: He comes home, puts a cold can of beer on the table, kicks off his shoes, and turns on the set.

"Tonight, when he finds out that there's no electricity, he'll run like a blind mouse to the electric box and start to fiddle with the circuit breakers. He never calls an electrician. A surprise will be waiting for him there. When he touches the main breaker he'll be fried. That's what I need you for. I don't know anything about electricity, but you're a professional electrician. You'll help me turn him into a big, juicy beefsteak."

---

Don Juan, too, was thinking about fried steak. To be more specific, he was thinking about fires. He had managed to impress upon his memory Arthur's features during his surveillance of Shmuel, when Shmuel had first come to the synagogue. Then he had seen the two of them return together from Gonzales's house.

That was enough.

Don Juan possessed a formidable memory as well as good friends in the Interior Ministry, friends from the "organization." He visited one of those good friends, who used his description to build a profile of the man he wanted. The Interior Ministry official then fed it into the computer, which included photos of most of the country's citizens. Don Juan's description was excellent and the computer ran its search. Half an hour later the clerk called Don Juan. "I have the particulars."

"Go on."

"His name is Arthur Taubman. His wife's name is Sylvia. They live in a villa in the rich Jewish neighborhood, on Avenida Konstimus 78. I put his address into the computer and found it on a city map. Right across from him is a seven-story building, the Caroni Hotel."

"That's enough for me."

Don Juan knew what he had to do. That night he would set Taubman's house on fire. Then he would wait. There were two possibilities. One, that the fire would do the job for him. Two, the mice would flee. If that would happen, he would be waiting across the street, on the second floor of the Caroni Hotel, a sniper's rifle in his hand. He would pick them off, one by one.

you're a professional electrician. You'll help me turn him into a big, juicy beefsteak."

---

Don Juan, too, was thinking about fried steak. To be more specific, he was thinking about fires. He had managed to impress upon his memory Arthur's features during his surveillance of Shmuel, when Shmuel had first come to the synagogue. Then he had seen the two of them return together from Gonzales's house.

That was enough.

Don Juan possessed a formidable memory as well as good friends in the Interior Ministry, friends from the "organization." He visited one of those good friends, who used his description to build a profile of the man he wanted. The Interior Ministry official then fed it into the computer, which included photos of most of the country's citizens. Don Juan's description was excellent and the computer ran its search. Half an hour later the clerk called Don Juan. "I have the particulars."

"Go on."

"His name is Arthur Taubman. His wife's name is Sylvia. They live in a villa in the rich Jewish neighborhood, on Avenida Konstimus 78. I put his address into the computer and found it on a city map. Right across from him is a seven-story building, the Caroni Hotel."

"That's enough for me."

Don Juan knew what he had to do. That night he would set Taubman's house on fire. Then he would wait. There were two possibilities. One, that the fire would do the job for him. Two, the mice would flee. If that would happen, he would be waiting across the street, on the second floor of the Caroni Hotel, a sniper's rifle in his hand. He would pick them off, one by one.

---

Time Bomb / 337

"How did Joselito sound to you?"

Shmuel forced a smile, followed by a look of doubt. "He believes very much in his own ideals. He's passionate on the subject. The chances of him returning from there in a vertical position are about as good as the chances of Antarctica bumping into Africa in the near future."

"It could happen," Zerach, always the optimist, broke in. "The globe is melting as a result of the thinning of the ozone layer. There are icebergs hundreds of kilometers long that are breaking off. Soon their water will be lapping the shores of African beaches."

The two brothers showed an unexpected interest in Zerach's words. Santos, too, had not forgotten his Hebrew. He seemed concerned. "Do you think that's true?" he said worriedly. "Is the globe really going to go up in flames because of the increased radiation?"

"Absolutely," Zerach said cheerfully. "It's a slow process. Every hundred years the temperature goes up half a degree. In the next few decades it might speed up, and the increase will be three or four degrees. Don't forget that we're also influencing the process through our activities. Researchers believe it will happen in two hundred and forty years."

"Two hundred and forty years?" Santos was relieved. "Even Joselito's grandchildren won't be alive anymore."

"Don't forget," Zerach continued, "that in 240 years the globe will be exactly 6000 years old. This explains the Gemara which says that after six thousand years the world will be destroyed..."

The sun set and Caracas switched on its lights. The electric lines battled against the darkness, and beams of white and blue light flickered in the dusk. Shmuel, Zerach, and Arthur *davened Minchah* and *Ma'ariv* in Arthur's house. "It's still dangerous," Arthur declared. "We have to stay hidden until we can get away from here. If saving one's life sets aside Shabbos observance, how much more so does it take precedence over *davening* with a minyan."

He had no idea how on target he was. At that same hour Don Juan's car was driving up the hill that led to Avenida Konstimus. In the trunk lay a sealed plastic bag heavy with kerosene-soaked rags. The concept of saving one's life was very real, and very threatening. Had they known what was approaching, no doubt, they would have *davened* with even more fervor.

Sabrina walked toward them after they *davened*. In her hand she held the sheaf of papers. "I think we shouldn't put this off any longer," she said. "Let me show you what this contains."

They sat around the table. "It's very interesting," Sabrina said. "Detailed lists like these. Yehoshua Cohen must have had a pretty high position in the organization to be allowed access to this information. Cardinal Huntado had great faith in him. We begin with a man by the name of Zekil Fernbach, son of a banker, Getzel Fernbach, who lived in Prague about —"

"About one hundred sixty years ago," Zerach finished the sentence.

"That's right," Sabrina said. Suddenly she froze in surprise. "How did you know that?"

"It's a long story," Shmuel said. "Let's just chalk it up to *hashgachah pratis* — Divine intervention."

"You may be up to date on part of the story," Sabrina continued. "But the remainder should surprise even you. What is clear is this: For thirty years after Getzel's death, Zekil Fernbach continued to manage the bank his father founded. The first page includes a chart of business activity between an unnamed church and the bank. It seems that the church sent funds to the Bank Fernbach regularly, on an annual basis. From 1852 on, the church had become a full partner in the bank. There is also a memo that Zekil brought to the church, listing the names of two poor families in Prague's Jewish Quarter. One of them is Asher Worms, who died in March of 1852 leaving seven orphans, the oldest of them 13. That's just the beginning. Do you want updated lists going through the year 2000?"

"What a question!" Zerach jumped up as though bitten by a snake. "We need all the papers."

The wail of a smoke alarm interrupted the conversation; suddenly they could smell burning wood.

Sylvia quickly ran into the room, panic stricken. "Fire! The house is on fire!"

Arthur stayed cool. "Sylvia, what's the matter?" he said, deliberately keeping his voice calm. He was a man of great self-control. "We've practiced evacuating the house." He turned to his guests. "Sylvia is terrified of fire; her grandmother perished in a blaze. Don't worry, my house is equipped with special fireproof exits. We'll use them to get out."

Arthur managed to calm them all down despite the rapidly thickening smoke and the flames that had begun to lap at the edges of the room. He did not lose his composure for even a moment, and he led them toward a narrow hallway, whose walls showed an orange-red glow. The fireproof walls gave some protection during the critical minutes needed to get out.

They raced toward the exit. Sabrina would not let go of the papers even now. She held them to her chest and looked toward her sons, who tried to stay near her.

From the street they could hear the wail of approaching fire engines. "My alarm system is hooked up to the fire station," Arthur explained. "The system seems to have worked well. I hope the damage will be light."

They stood huddled next to the exit, waiting to leave.

Zerach Britman was both a very suspicious man and one with a clear head. From the moment he had heard the alarm he wondered if this was a case of arson, another threat to their lives from the "organization." Suddenly everything became clear.

"Stop!" he shouted. "Arthur, do you have a back exit?"

Arthur released the door knob. "Yes, but we'll have to go through the smoke to get there."

"So don't breathe for the next minute," Zerach said. "We can't go out this way. It's a trap."

Arthur weighed his words. Perhaps he was right. But to go back into danger?

He had a few seconds to decide before the fireproofing gave way. What should they do?

340 / *Time Bomb*

# 32

*Chechnya, 5761 (2000)*

The simulation exercises on the airplane in the cave proved their effectiveness. The cranes loaded the cases of material into the belly of the Antonov, the Russian cargo plane. For half an hour none of those inside moved. After thirty minutes Selim gave the signal; they jumped out of the boxes all at once with rifles cocked and overpowered the shocked Russian soldiers. Musa Jibarov threatened them with a hand grenade whose pin he had already pulled out. The grenade was a dud but highly effective in the panic and fear that it sowed. The terrified eyes of the five soldiers attested to the success of the surprise attack. They stared at the Chechen ghosts open mouthed for a few seconds, until professional gags were placed upon them. The rest was even easier. The two pilots did not present even minimal resistance in the face of the gun barrels pointing firmly at them. "What do you want us to do?" they asked, defeated.

Selim was emphatic. "First, cut all communication with the ground; don't answer any calls. When we get close to our destination you will make contact with the ground and ask for permission to land."

"Where do you want to go?" the captain asked.

Selim did not answer. He walked toward the instrument panel of the aging plane and checked each of the gauges. His eyes fell on the gas gauge; as he had expected, it was full. "Sayid, come here."

Sayid approached.

Selim gave him curt instructions. "You're to watch the pilots. I don't have to show you the rudder, the air pressure, the flaps. If you see anything change — particularly in the compass or the speedometer" — he pointed to several gauges — "or in the altitude gauge" — again he pointed, "you blow up the side of the plane. Clear?"

That was enough for the pilots. These hijackers knew their way around the cockpit. They could not be fooled. And, indeed, Selim had learned it all. Before every mission he always did his homework thoroughly. For this he had studied the technical aspects of an Antonov, from nose to tail — not to mention the pope's 767, that was as familiar to him as his own hand. Sayid had not specialized in the details of the Antonov, but he had a general familiarity with aircraft and quickly caught on.

Selim turned to the captain. "You've heard of the equator?"

"Vaguely," he answered, his lips contorting in a shadow of a smile.

"Good. About 100 miles north of the equator, longitude 10, southeast of here, there is an African nation, on the western shore. It's called Cameroon. The capital of Cameroon —"

"— is Yaoundé," the flyer smiled again. "You want to fly there. Certainly."

He seemed almost happy to oblige him. *If I were a pilot stuck on the monotonous Grozny-Astrakhan route, flying from Red Army bases to the battlefield in Chechnya, I would also jump at the chance of visiting a land as interesting as Africa,* Selim thought wryly.

Other cargo planes of the same or similar make had crashed or been lost in Chechnya, and Russia had not made a big deal about it. *By the time someone in Astrakhan wakes up and sends interceptors into the sky, we'll be far away from here,* Selim thought with grim satisfaction.

The plane turned its nose south enroute to Yaoundé, capital of Cameroon, the second stop on the pope's itinerary.

## Caracas, 5761 (2000)

"He's right." Sabrina concurred with Zerach. Her head whirled like that of a cornered animal desperately seeking a place of flight. The smoke was getting thicker; the danger of returning to the burning house grew greater from moment to moment. "It's a trap. It's just like them. Someone is waiting in ambush near the front door. We've got to go out through the back."

"And what if they think we'll figure that out and are waiting for us at the back?" Shmuel asked.

"That's going too far," Zerach objected. "They're not masters of *pilpul*, Talmud scholars like you are. Let's go out the back."

They raced toward the kitchen, which was still free of flames. Just one door separated them from the house's backyard. The door was locked. The key was there, but, because of long disuse, refused to turn. Arthur kicked the door open; it broke with one swift motion.

They raced out of the house: Arthur and Sylvia, Zerach, Shmuel, and Sabrina supported by her sons, Gonzales and Santos. Her eyes were half-shut and she repeated ceaselessly: "Moshe and Aharon. Moshe and Aharon. You are not Gonzales; you are not Santos. Let's take it upon ourselves right now: I will be Hadassah, you will be Moshe and Aharon."

"That's what you're thinking about now?" Gonzales said in wonder, making his way among the bushes and plants, some of them quite exotic. They stumbled along, almost falling occasionally. There was no place to walk, the garden was so full of greenery. "Sylvia is a botanist," Arthur said apologetically. "She experiments here. That's why it's so overgrown."

❧

The garden was overgrown. That was what Don Juan had seen an hour before, as he carefully checked the house, looking for a place for his ambush. *Would they try to run through the back?* he wondered suddenly. But when he looked over the garden he calmed down. No way they would come here, in this overgrown mess, that was certain. The bushes made an almost insurmountable obstacle. They would leave through the front door.

## Caracas, 5761 (2000)

"He's right." Sabrina concurred with Zerach. Her head whirled like that of a cornered animal desperately seeking a place of flight. The smoke was getting thicker; the danger of returning to the burning house grew greater from moment to moment. "It's a trap. It's just like them. Someone is waiting in ambush near the front door. We've got to go out through the back."

"And what if they think we'll figure that out and are waiting for us at the back?" Shmuel asked.

"That's going too far," Zerach objected. "They're not masters of *pilpul*, Talmud scholars like you are. Let's go out the back."

They raced toward the kitchen, which was still free of flames. Just one door separated them from the house's backyard. The door was locked. The key was there, but, because of long disuse, refused to turn. Arthur kicked the door open; it broke with one swift motion.

They raced out of the house: Arthur and Sylvia, Zerach, Shmuel, and Sabrina supported by her sons, Gonzales and Santos. Her eyes were half-shut and she repeated ceaselessly: "Moshe and Aharon. Moshe and Aharon. You are not Gonzales; you are not Santos. Let's take it upon ourselves right now: I will be Hadassah, you will be Moshe and Aharon."

"That's what you're thinking about now?" Gonzales said in wonder, making his way among the bushes and plants, some of them quite exotic. They stumbled along, almost falling occasionally. There was no place to walk, the garden was so full of greenery. "Sylvia is a botanist," Arthur said apologetically. "She experiments here. That's why it's so overgrown."

❧

The garden was overgrown. That was what Don Juan had seen an hour before, as he carefully checked the house, looking for a place for his ambush. *Would they try to run through the back?* he wondered suddenly. But when he looked over the garden he calmed down. No way they would come here, in this overgrown mess, that was certain. The bushes made an almost insurmountable obstacle. They would leave through the front door.

A young, bored hotel clerk stood behind the registration desk in the lobby. "I'd like to rent a room." His sharp eyes took in the message boxes behind the clerk's back. He could see the name Goldberg on a memo placed in a box on the second row. "On the second floor, please. If possible next to Mr. Goldberg's room." Don Juan's earlier surveillance had revealed that these rooms faced the street.

"Goldberg?" The clerk checked the various boxes. "He's in Room 217. Would you like 219?"

"*Si*. We're good friends and I'd like to be near him."

"Should I tell him you've arrived?" the clerk asked courteously. His hand hovered over the house phone.

"No," Don Juan said firmly, pulling the hand away. "I want to surprise him."

He registered under the name Bendito Emanuel San Jose, paid in advance for two days, took the key, and immediately went up to the room. He held a plastic bag in his hand and a leather case whose contents would have surprised, and frightened, the clerk. After he finished the job he would get out of here; no one would know a thing. He always did his work neatly, and never left fingerprints.

Once in the locked room he opened the case and assembled the sniper's rifle. A telescopic viewfinder gave him maximum accuracy. He placed the rifle on a windowsill, with only the edge of the barrel sticking out. He then went downstairs holding the sealed plastic bag. He crossed the street and walked assuredly toward Arthur's home. Three back windows were open and dark; that was enough for him. He threw in the kerosene-soaked rags and a lit match. Then he casually walked away. The rubber gloves, which gave off the pungent smell of gasoline, went into a nearby garbage can. He returned to the hotel, went up to his room, grabbed the rifle, and placed his eye to the viewfinder.

Five minutes passed; nothing happened. He cursed quietly to himself. They were undoubtedly running around like frightened mice in the house. Why weren't they coming out? Maybe they had been overcome by the smoke? Not likely; the fire was not that bad. People got out safely from homes under much worse circumstances.

The siren of a fire engine wailed; the truck stopped noisily next to the house. The street was bathed in the flashing red lights of the truck. A crowd gathered to watch.

The firemen did not waste a moment. They surrounded the burning house and began sending a stream of water and foam onto it. One fireman jumped on a steel ladder and sprayed the top floor.

The front door was broken open as the firemen raced inside to save the residents.

Don Juan's curses became more pronounced. His eye, strained against the lens, began to tear. He felt an enormous temptation, in his fury, to shoot the firemen who repeatedly appeared in the viewfinder. Impossible. The firemen had not rescued even one person.

They had gone out the back!

He left the rifle on the windowsill and sped toward the elevators. Much to his chagrin, all three were on upper floors.

Without wasting a moment he turned to the stairwell and raced down. He joined the excited crowd, pushed through, and made his way to the back of the house, his hand firmly grasping the revolver in his pocket.

---

*Rome, 5761 (2000)*

At 7 a.m. the pope's convoy reached the airport, driving directly to the runway where the Alitalia plane was waiting. The plane was reserved for his party only. After the large entourage had boarded, the "Popemobile" was loaded into the cargo hold. This was an armored vehicle, whose windows and body were bulletproof. Its chassis was strong enough to withstand an explosion of four tons of explosives.

The passengers found their places. The entire first-class section was at the disposal of Passenger Number 1, accompanied by his chief of staff, his spokesman, his security chief, three deputies, two doctors, and two secretaries. In addition to these there was a long line of people, starting with his personal chefs and ending with the Popemobile's chauffeur, as well as the security chief's driver.

The men close to John Paul II — the official name of the man who was born Karol Wojtyla in Poland in 1920 — wondered if the time had not come to slow things down. In addition to the exhausting trip to Africa, there were other journeys planned for the near future to places such as Syria, Malta, and the Ukraine. They knew what only later would become common knowledge, that the elderly pope was suffering from various health problems, the most serious being Parkinson's disease. The more sharp-eyed had already detected many symptoms of the disease — trembling, shuffling gait, a stony look, and a tendency to slur words during speeches. Several years earlier, when rumors had begun to circulate as a result of the first signs of illness, the pope's spokesman had admitted that he was suffering from a genetic disturbance of the nervous system, but the sickness had never been called by its name.

John Paul's spirits were in high gear. This trip to Africa was, in his eyes, a most important journey. The visit to the dark continent would begin in Kinshasa, capital of Zaire, and continue to Yaoundé in Cameroon. In Yaoundé a contingent of ten African religious leaders would join him. He had recently had a fascinating correspondence with one of them, the African Cardinal Philip Morteiza. The cardinal, whom John Paul did not know personally, seemed from his letters to be a serious intellectual who had posed profound and searching questions, "just to understand, not to attack," as he had put it, questions that seemed to touch at the very basis of Christianity. John Paul wanted to work out the answers to the questions, some of which had caused even him a few difficult moments, and so he waited impatiently for the meeting.

At 7:30 the plane took off from Rome on its way to Africa. It carried 140 on board, including the two pilots and the crew.

Among the crew was one tall steward who carried a passport bearing the name Jack Harrison. His real name was Kareem Nisadov. He, too, was waiting impatiently for the emotional meeting with the ten religious leaders in the Yaoundé airport. He particularly longed to meet Cardinal Philip Morteiza.

*Caracas, 5761 (2000)*

"Where are you taking us?" Shmuel asked, as Arthur led them single file to the edge of the courtyard. The obstacle course through the thick foliage had ended, leading them to a small path which branched out into different directions. One way led to the street; the other, to a neighbor's yard.

For the first time Arthur ignored rules of etiquette and roughly clamped his hand on Shmuel's mouth. Shmuel gagged and looked at Arthur without comprehension. Arthur gestured to him to keep absolutely still.

Arthur himself did not realize how right he had been. Just a few feet away, on the other side of the yard, Don Juan was searching for them, his hand firmly jammed in his pocket. He had six bullets in the revolver; more than enough. In the general chaos of the street no one had noticed him sneaking around the fence with the measured tread of the professional assassin, a man trained to read the map and guess his victim's escape route. Don Juan was absolutely sure that they were fleeing through this backyard. But the street was incredibly noisy, and here in the yard he heard nothing at all. Confusing.

In the absolute silence he continued to wander through Arthur's neighbor's yard. The crackling of small stems breaking underfoot was the only sound he heard. This yard was four times the size of the Taubmans'. A large wooden gate hid it from the street, that still seemed to roar with the wailing of fire trucks and the shouts and murmurs of the crowd. The firefighters were hard at work. The fleeing victims could clearly hear the roar of water being sprayed at high pressure on the fire.

"I need your cell phone," Arthur whispered to Zerach.

Zerach handed it over. Arthur walked away from the gate. He pressed a number and began to speak in the quietest of tones. "Michaelo, this is Arthur. I need your station wagon. I know my house is on fire; we'll talk afterwards. It's a matter of life and death."

He waited for a minute and ended the phone call. "He's agreed," he quietly told the group, his face lighting up. "We're like brothers. Here, he's coming."

Arthur led them to his neighbor's large garage. They waited tensely for the neighbor, Michaelo Senavera.

*Time Bomb / 347*

A minute later they saw him arrive, a pleasant, round-faced man with a brightly colored yarmulka on his head. He gave a surprised grin when he saw the large group awaiting him. They were all pale, and the old woman looked on the verge of collapse. Michaelo pursed his lips, ready to ask questions, but Arthur gestured to him to keep quiet. Michaelo opened the small door that led into the garage and the group piled into the station wagon parked within. "Take us as far away from here as you can, on the most circuitous route. Get out of here; go as fast as you've ever driven," Arthur instructed him.

"I don't understand a thing," Michaelo said, shrugging his shoulders. "But for you, my brother, I'll do anything." He turned on the ignition and gunned the engine, only hitting the garage door remote control at the very last minute.

The garage door hummed open with a slowness that grated on their raw nerves. Even before it had completely opened up, the station wagon was tearing out onto the street.

They were more than one hundred yards away — far past the range of a revolver — before Don Juan noticed the vehicle speeding away. "It's them!" he almost shouted, in his overpowering rage. The speed with which a snake bit his enemy was nothing compared with Don Juan's ability to draw a gun, but there was no point at this distance.

He ran aimlessly and felt the sour taste of defeat. They had gotten away yet again, against all the odds. His arms fell limply to his sides, swinging back and forth as if made of rubber. He flagged down a cab and rode home, his face contorted with fury. The last chance gone. Gone! After the story with Julio and now this failure, his standing in the "organization" was at risk — perhaps even his life.

Despair hit him so strongly that he completely forgot about the sniper's rifle that he had left in Room 219 of the Caroni Hotel, resting on the windowsill, aimed at Arthur Taubman's door. He forgot the fingerprints he had left on the rifle. This had never occurred before, but now he felt almost as if he had lost his sanity. "I'm finished," he whispered to himself several times, "the assassin's been assassinated."

When he opened the door to his home in one of the more distant quarters of the city his anger blazed even stronger. Another power outage. The whole city government should be fired! No electricity. Like living in the Middle Ages. He flicked on the light on his sports watch. Almost 10 o'clock. Caracas's soccer team would be lining up on the field. His beloved game would be starting in minutes and he had no electricity. A scandal.

Perhaps the problem was a short circuit in his own electric box. The circuit breakers were very sensitive and cut the flow at the whiff of a problem. If the base of his electric coffeemaker merely touched a drop of water the circuit cut off.

He walked blindly toward the hallway near the door. His other neighbors had their electric boxes outside in the lobby, but his was not. Members of the "organization" had strict laws. An electric box in the house was one of them. If it was outside, someone might turn off the lights in order to lure you outside. Something might happen.

He opened the door of the electric box and fumbled in the darkness for the main circuit breaker. In the darkness he could not see the exposed wires that stuck out of one of the switches.

A blinding flash of lightning exploded in his face; then he was engulfed in a black abyss.

---

Sabrina and her sons escorted Shmuel and Zerach to the airport. Arthur and Sylvia were busy with insurance claims and discussions over compensation for the damages they would be awarded for their burned house. They bade farewell to their Israeli guests in the Caroni Hotel, where they had rented rooms. Now they knew that their lives had been saved on the evening of the fire. The hotel had been in pandemonium when the sniper's rifle had been discovered on the second floor. The police were called in, fingerprints taken. The angle of the rifle and the telescopic viewfinder told the story.

"I don't know what I've gotten from this whole affair," Sabrina managed a dim smile, her voice sounding particularly weak against the noise of the airport. "I think I just drove you crazy."

Shmuel shook his head back and forth. "You've taught me something very important in life. I will never forget it."

For once Zerach was also serious. "Shmuel spoke with your grandson, Joselito, and planted a seed. One can never know when the seed will sprout, but sprout it will."

Even Gonzales and Santos were touched. "It was good to see you, old friend," Gonzales thumped Shmuel on the shoulder.

A tear glinted in the corner of Santos's eye, shining under the terminal's bright lights. He warmly pumped Shmuel's outstretched hand. "We've lost our lives. Moishy and Ahrele were murdered by Yehoshua Cohen. Santos and Gonzales are empty beings. No past, no present, no future. Consumed forever. But maybe Joselito will dare do what I cannot. Perhaps he will go one day to Jerusalem, put on *tefillin*, and take back what was stolen from me. Adopt him as a son, Shmulik; adopt him."

His shoulders trembled. Suddenly Shmuel fell upon him and wept.

The defense mechanisms that the young Shmuel Bilad had built over many years around the turmoil in his heart were shattered. He saw a little boy standing and crying in the rain, and he, Shmuel, cried with him. *How could I have forgotten you, you forlorn and helpless little boy? How did I enjoy that book? I left you to freeze in the Jerusalem winter, to catch pneumonia and to die before you had even begun to taste the world. How could I have caused you, Moishy and Ahrele, such a terrible fate? I made a terrible hole in your home, and through that hole a sly fox walked in.*

He cried for two lost souls; two pure Jews, working as trash collectors in a strange, faraway land.

*Yehoshua Cohen, they should create a new form of Gehinnom for the likes of you. What did you want from these poor unfortunate boys? Why did you destroy them eternally?*

Sabrina turned to Zerach. "Don't forget this," she said, handing him a small cardboard file.

"The lists." It was a statement, not a question.

"I assume you'll know what to do with them," Sabrina gave a forced smile. "It's time to say goodbye, Moishy and Ahrele. Time to go."

"Yes, it's home to Bnei Brak, Israel's poorest city when it comes to money, Israel's richest in Torah and holiness," Zerach laughed happily. "Goodbye Caracas, farewell Venezuela. And goodbye to your unlucky assassins and thugs."

They waved again to the Lombardo family. An old mother and two middle-aged men. Three shattered images. A tragic family saga. But perhaps they would still know some moments of gladness in their lives. Perhaps, one day, the Levin family would be reborn.

Perhaps.

## 33

*En route to Cameroon, 5761 (2000)*

Following Selim's detailed instructions, the captain of the Antonov did not respond to the increasingly anxious broadcasts coming over the airplane's communications system. The Russian air force sent out two MIG-21's to search for the missing cargo plane; radar on navy ships afloat on the Black Sea swiveled around, but found nothing. Those first few hours had been the most critical; during that time, the airplane had managed to travel out of range.

Selim instructed the aviators to take a straight course that crossed over Iran, Saudi Arabia, the Red Sea, Sudan, and mid-Africa. They were now approaching Yaoundé, Cameroon's capital city.

"This is an Antonov cargo plane approaching at 10 degrees, at a height of 35,000 feet, requesting permission to land."

The control tower in faraway Yaoundé had received no word of a missing Antonov plane. The airport's officials heard the pilot's glib explanation of why the plane had come so far and, having accepted his words, courteously authorized the landing.

The shock of the ground crew in Yaoundé's airport was unmatched when ten black-garbed priests walked off the plane.

"We've been invited to meet the plane of His Holiness, the pope," the head of the group, who introduced himself as Father Philip Morteiza, head of the Church of Nigeria, explained.

"The plane will be landing in another hour. You won't have long to wait," the ground crew informed them. "You got here just in time."

The other "priests" in the the delegation looked admiringly at Father Morteiza, their laughter carefully concealed. What could you say: Selim Yagudayev had proved to be a consummate actor, an impresario who put on a most spectacular show.

In their excitement over the arrival of such an honored delegation, and in anticipation of the imminent appearance of the pope himself, the ground crew neglected to ask technical questions such as from where the plane had flown, and why a religious delegation from Africa was arriving on an antiquated Russian cargo plane. The smiles of the pilot and copilot lit up their faces and broadcast, "Everything's okay" — a tribute to Selim the director. No question about it, a revolver hidden beneath a priest's black cloak had a most persuasive effect.

They were brought to the VIP lounge in the terminal and served soft drinks and fruit. They were, after all, very special guests, guests of the pope himself! In another hour they would be flying with him on his personal plane. Admiring glances were stealthily cast upon these select priests sitting on leather sofas with their flowing black robes. Priestly robes, a brilliant idea of Selim's. One of the many materials of war that the Chechen freedom fighters had prepared in advance of their meeting with the head of the Catholic Church.

<hr />

Luisi Kiramonti, head of the security forces, ran thin fingers through his dyed black hair. He took a deep drag on a cigarette in the galley at the back of the plane, breathing in the smoke that clouded the small area. Something was disturbing him. This morning he had heard reports about

Antoine, the Swiss guardsman who had suddenly disappeared. His friends declared that in the evening he had acted strangely, locked himself into his room, and complained about a terrible toothache; in the morning he had simply vanished. Perhaps he had gone home without permission, but that was not like Antoine. Maybe this was just a coincidence, but Luisi did not like it.

As far as he was concerned, this entire stopover in the Yaoundé airport was unnecessary. The plan had called for the pope to speak to a large group of devoted followers in the "Heroes of Africa" Square in the city center. Two things had caused the last-minute cancellation. They had been informed that it was pouring in Yaoundé and there was no shelter for the speaker, let alone the audience. In addition, the pope had experienced mild stomach pains. The planned event had therefore been canceled. If not for this ridiculous meeting with ten African priests they could have completely skipped Cameroon and traveled straight to their next stop, Nigeria.

From the narrow window he could see the deep-blue sky enveloping the plane in endless serenity. The plane began its descent. Most of the passengers had belted themselves in but Luisi, like the stewards, always waited until the very last moment. Who were these priests? The Vatican's effective intelligence service had vetted each member of the delegation to a thorough check and had approved the meeting after the pope had demanded it. The pope was particularly anxious to meet the Nigerian cardinal, Philip Morteiza. According to his information Morteiza was a very young man and had already managed to climb high up on the clerical ladder as a result of his unusual talents.

"You look worried, sir."

Luisi shook himself out of his reverie. The gray-haired steward gave him a tentative smile.

Suddenly he felt the need to unburden himself, if only to this pleasant-faced American.

He took one last puff on the cigarette and threw the burning butt into a sink. "The world belongs to the young; you've heard that phrase?"

"Who hasn't?"

"Here's the proof," Luisi said in disgust. "I'm 55 years old. You're probably about 50. In a little while a young cardinal, 32 years old, who looks about 18 from his picture, will come on the plane. The pope is waiting anxiously to meet him. He's told me about thirty times about the incredible wisdom of this Father Morteiza, and his great desire to see him one day sit in his chair. Did you hear that? An African pope! On that day, a billion believing Catholics will go back to idol worship. The pope thinks that if he, a Pole, broke a chain of 450 years of Italian popes, an African can also do it!"

The angle of descent sharpened. The plane roared on. Luisi and the steward swiftly made their way to their seats and fastened their seat belts. Luisi did not care if they talked about him in the front of the plane. His addiction to nicotine was well known, and on every flight he spent hours smoking with the stewards.

The plane landed and slowly taxied through the airport. A few minutes later the doors were opened by members of the security team. (*Another mistake of Selim*, Kareem thought. *He said I would open the door*.) Ten priests wearing long robes came in, accompanied by two smiling stewards.

The pope's chief of staff was waiting for them, together with a security officer. They welcomed the guests and seated them, two by two, in different sections of the plane.

A few minutes later they were taking off to their next stop.

Luisi did not hurry to get up. "By the rules of etiquette I'm supposed to be the one to take Cardinal Morteiza to the pope. But I don't feel like it," he mused.

"You don't feel well?" the steward asked anxiously.

Luisi laughed. "I'm not afraid to tell the truth. I don't like him. I don't know why, but my gut tells me that something about this guy is no good."

"I don't like him either," the steward said sympathetically. (*Careful! Your tongue is wandering.*)

Luisi slowly lit another cigarette. "Why? Do you know him from somewhere?"

"No, absolutely not. (*I've only spent hundreds of hours with him*.) I just feel the way you do about these young people, how they shove us to the side all the time." He tried to cover his slip of the tongue in a wash of words.

"That's the way it is." Luisi inhaled with the enjoyment of a heavy smoker. He felt his skin begin to prickle. He was familiar with the feeling. He did not know why, but his sixth sense was sending him a red-light warning that something was wrong.

The pope's chief of staff, Pietro Medrici, waited for Luisi for several minutes, casting increasingly anxious glances toward the back of the plane. Luisi had disappeared. Someone had to bring Cardinal Morteiza into the first-class section.

He approached the cardinal. "Please come with me, Your Excellency."

Though Selim Yagudayev was tempted to break into a dance, he carefully kept himself in check, walking with measured steps and a somber expression on his face. A wave of joy washed over him. His plan had succeeded. It had been more than a year since he decided to kidnap the pope and since then he had been working at it, step by step, with meticulous precision. He had sent letters in the name of an actual clergyman, the talented Cardinal Philip Morteiza, to the pope. The letters had been faxed to a friend of Selim's in Nigeria, who had mailed them from Nigeria to the Vatican. He had given a post office box as his address, and there he received John Paul's replies to his polemical questions. After a year the pope had expressed a great desire to meet the young cardinal whose thought process was so clear, and so was born the idea of an encounter with ten African cardinals.

And now he was about to reap the fruits of his efforts.

Countless times, he had envisioned what would happen next.

The first step after the kidnapping would be to try and get Russia's agreement on a full withdrawal from Chechnya. Russia would refuse. Hopefully, they would refuse. Then he would assassinate the pope with his bare hands.

They reached the first class section. Two armed guards sat near the door; they courteously moved aside. Cardinal Morteiza looked astonishingly young, but all the staff on the plane knew that the pope held him in high esteem.

John Paul II was napping. His head hung down. His white skullcap had fallen forward on his head; his chin touched the snow-white collar of his robe. Pietro Medrici hesitated but the pope abruptly awoke and looked at them with weary, aging eyes as he adjusted his skullcap. A light suddenly flickered within them. "You're Cardinal —Cardinal —"

"Morteiza," Selim broke in, rescuing the old man from the embarrassment of his memory lapse. "Father Philip Morteiza."

Medrici seated the cardinal next to the pope and waited for the old man to give him notice that he was dismissed. Within two minutes, Medrici left, leaving the two men alone. The pope's personal secretary, Monseigneur Imrei Kabonego, had also left the area, respecting Il Papa's request. The pope's personal physician, Gianfranco Pinci, who had operated on him after the pope had broken a thighbone during a 1994 fall in a bathtub, was in constant touch with his illustrious patient and only he remained.

"I was curious to meet you, such a young man," John Paul said. "But I didn't realize just how young you actually are."

"I, too, have so wanted to meet you, Your Excellency," Selim smiled, patting the pocket in which he had concealed the plastic handcuffs. Not that he would need them; the old man could barely move.

His sharp eyes found the pope's "panic button" — a round red button resting on his knee. One light touch and his guards would be there, his doctors, everyone. He had to get him away from that button. They chatted for a few minutes of this and that. The old man found it difficult to concentrate on a serious theological discussion at this time; he apologized and said he had to take a short nap, in order to be alert for their important talk.

His head again fell forward.

The time had come to act. Selim turned to the doctor. "Can you come here for a minute?"

The doctor, busy reading an Italian weekly, lifted his eyes. "What's the matter?"

"He wants medication," Selim whispered. "I don't know which."

The doctor threw down his periodical and walked over with swift steps. He bent over the pope. Selim gave him one quick blow to the back of his neck and the doctor collapsed at Selim's feet. The old man continued to sleep.

*Time Bomb* / 357

Selim pushed the unconscious doctor to the side gently and pressed a button on his watch.

Outside, the watches of the other "priests" buzzed. The signal had been given.

Nine priests stood up from their seats and pulled out rifles from beneath their robes. "Don't move!" they shouted wildly. "One move and we blow up the plane!"

Luisi Kiramonti was chain-smoking with the steward in the back. His nervousness multiplied with each passing minute; every cigarette increased his need for more nicotine. The place was thick with suffocating smoke.

He heard the shouts and jumped to his feet. "Something's happening!"

"What can be happening?" the gray-haired steward asked, as he hit him over the head with a heavy bottle of Chivas Regal. The security chief slumped to the floor, all his worries forgotten.

The pope continued to sleep as Selim quietly stood up and strode into the cockpit, a gun in each hand. "This plane is hijacked," he shouted. "If you make a move you will harm the pope."

The hijacking was quick and effective. The security men were overwhelmed and, fearing for the pope's safety, posed no active resistance. The kidnappers busily handcuffed all of the security men, leaving no one unbound. Two of them burst through the first-class section and joined Selim in the cockpit. Sayid Mashtatov became the pope's new personal bodyguard. The cabin crew were shocked to see the American steward Jack Harrison betray them; none dreamed that this was a Chechnyan double. And not a single one of them was on hand to see the emotional meeting between Selim and Kareem in the cockpit, the hugs the two kidnappers exchanged. They pumped each other's hands. "It worked!" they exulted, laughing joyously.

Selim, though, hastily got back to the job at hand. "Arrange immediate contact with the Russian government," he commanded the pilot. "I want the deputy prime minister. No," he continued, thinking out loud. "No, absolutely not. I want the president on the line. Get me Vladimir Putin himself."

"I have no contact with the president of Russia," the pilot said dryly. "I can get through to a control tower in Russia and relay your request."

"This is not a request," Selim said furiously. "This is a command."

The captain made contact with a control tower in Chermeteyvo 2, a Moscow-area airport, and gave Selim the microphone.

"This is the Holy Rebels Organization of Chechnya. We have hijacked the pope's plane. I repeat: We have hijacked the pope's plane. We have 140 hostages in our hands, including pope John Paul II. I want to speak with President Vladimir Putin within the next twenty minutes regarding our demands for releasing the pope and his entourage. If I don't get Putin on the line in that time, we will kill a hostage every minute. You can figure out how long it will take before we get to the pope himself."

He knew that Russia, until not long ago a communist state, was not particularly concerned about the fate of the pope, but he also knew that if his demands were not settled soon, news of the kidnapping would spread throughout the world, and a mighty wave of pressure would be brought to bear on Russia to accede to the hijackers' demands.

The confusion finally broke through the pope's sleep. His face froze when he realized that he had been a victim of a terrible fraud, and that the famed Cardinal Philip Morteiza was actually a Chechnyan terrorist trying to liberate his land from the Russian occupation. He sorrowfully realized how he had fallen into the snare.

The plane echoed with the wild cries of the Chechnyan terrorists as they barked orders at the passengers. *Are they planning on attacking me?* he wondered, as he heard one of them cry, "One suspicious move and the pope pays with his life."

He beckoned Selim over with his finger. Selim approached, his face radiating impatience, his eyes filled with contempt.

"I'm not angry that you deceived me. I just want to know, why are you so angry?"

"I am a Chechen," Selim replied. "Russia has occupied our homes, our land. We want it all back. Russia is oppressing hundreds of thousands of our people and you, Your Excellency, remain silent. Just like Pope Pius remained silent while Hitler slaughtered millions of innocent Jews. Russia has captured our beloved leader, Salamon Radeyv, The Gray Fox, and is breaking his spirit in prison."

John Paul's face took on its own gray tinge. The Gray Foxes, he whispered to himself. Just like twenty years ago. Mohammed Ali Iksa, too, was a member of an organization called Gray Foxes.

Pictures began to move through his head like a slow-motion movie.

He remembered the first attack. Twenty years ago. It was on Wednesday, May 13, 1981...

# 34

*Caracas, 5761 (2000)*

Cardinal Patrick Huntado was worried. He had been pacing up and down for three quarters of an hour, back and forth, between his living room and the door to his porch. His faithful contact, Pedro Marciano, had not answered his calls for two days now. Don Juan and his gangsters had also vanished, as if the earth had swallowed them up. What was going on?

Occasionally he would break the monotony of his pacing, go out onto the porch itself, which looked down upon scenic Caracas. He stared at the distant horizons as if there he would find an answer.

The sun had set, taking its radiance away with it. Day would soon be over; another day gone. He stood outside for a few more minutes watching dusk slowly but surely overpower the remaining daylight. The streetlights came on, creating a bluish web. Sparks of white light twinkled in the blackening sky, like diamonds in night's robe covering the city.

He awoke from his reverie with a firm decision, went inside, and began making a series of phone calls.

A few minutes later his messengers, young, energetic priests who completely accepted his authority, were on their way to the homes of Pedro, Don Juan, Julio, and Diego. Another group of young priests raced to the homes of the Lombardo family: Sabrina, Santos, and Gonzales.

Within an hour the picture was complete. And it was dark and gloomy.

Pedro Marciano and Don Juan had been found dead in their homes. Pedro, it seemed, had committed suicide with one bullet; Don Juan had been electrocuted. Julio and Diego, Sabrina and her two sons had all vanished.

Cardinal Patrick Huntado muttered a string of curses that had never found their way into his prayer book; a bit of foam formed at his mouth. Furiously he pulled the necklace with its golden cross from his neck and flung it onto the table. His face was contorted with rage and in his hopelessness he lost all control of himself. He lashed out at the walls, kicking and screaming, and bit his finger so hard it began to bleed. His eyes rolled in their sockets and animal-like cries issued from his throat. His secretary, Father Camio Bertoli, stood to one side and watched indifferently. These temper tantrums were nothing new to him. The revered cardinal could work himself up into a fury that bordered on insanity.

"Have you calmed down?" Bertoli asked, when the cardinal had finally subsided. "Do you want a Valium?"

"No!" Patrick screamed, slamming his fist onto his desk. The telephone jumped into the air from the force of the blow. "The Church hasn't faced such a colossal failure in its entire history and you, you fool, ask me if I've calmed down! Everyone is gone, our best missionary has killed himself, and Don Juan has been electrocuted."

"It is a decree from Heaven which must be accepted with love," the secretary said, crossing himself piously.

Patrick's heavy hand swiped across the priest's cheek. "If an idiot like you had created the world, it would be square, just like your brain. Don't you understand that someone attacked Pedro and Don Juan, and made it look as if their deaths were a suicide and an accident? And where have all the others gone? Get me the airport now."

Bertoli, shaken, sat down by the phone and diligently punched in the numbers. He handed Patrick the receiver.

"Bolivar Airport? Get me the Border Police. Border Police? This is Cardinal Patrick Huntado, head of John the Baptist Church. I must know urgently if a man by the name of Shmuel Bilad has left the country. No, I don't have his passport number. He's an Israeli citizen."

The policeman checked the computer and found the name almost immediately. Shmuel Bilad had left Caracas and was on his way to Israel.

The birds had flown.

A feeling of helplessness washed over Patrick, but he soon regained his composure. Using a specially secured phone he telephoned a number in Israel and spoke at length to Deputy Prime Minister Max Landau, bringing him up to date on all that had happened. Shmuel Bilad's fate was now in the hands of the State of Israel.

"He's got the lists," Patrick emphasized. "You know what can happen."

"I know," Landau affirmed.

"I'm relying on you to know what to do. Take care of it quickly and effectively," the worried cardinal ended.

Landau worked frantically. His sharp brain had immediately assessed the situation. It was likely that the bearded Jew would not know what to do with the explosive lists that had fallen into his hands. No responsible journalist would dare publicize such data based on a sheaf of photocopied pages and an almost unbelievable story. But time was not on his side, and the best solution would be to quickly get those incriminating documents away from him, before he managed to use them. Without the lists he was no more effective than an old, toothless dog.

The first call he made was to his contact, a high official in the General Security Services. The name Shmuel Bilad was mentioned several times, together with the instructions: "Take care of it quickly and effectively."

"It'll be taken care of immediately. Within less than twenty-four hours we'll have those lists in our hands."

A second call was placed to His Honor, Judge Dori Talmi. The judge was relaxing, sitting on his porch, his feet encased in comfortable slippers, a large plate of watermelon cubes and salted cheese on the table next to him.

Dori promised full cooperation. The attorney-general's office would sew up a fat legal file on Shmuel Bilad, in the event that the GSS offensive did not succeed.

"I'm counting on you, Dori," the deputy prime minister reiterated.

"It'll be fine, Max."

Landau's third call was to the home of a police officer who in the past had helped in dealing with undesirable elements. Men taken into his care were released from captivity in debilitated physical condition, suffering from strange chronic illnesses; they were diagnosed, too, as suicidal depressives.

Mr. Bilad would get this treatment if he would continue in his struggle despite their efforts.

The stage was set. Now they only had to wait for the actors to arrive.

### *Rome, 5741 (1981)*

On that Wednesday, the 13th of May 1981, about 100,000 people were gathered in St. Peter's Square in the Vatican to hear the pope speak. They were crowded in the semicircle which was surrounded by the hundreds of pillars known as Bernini's Columns. The route that the pope was to take on his way to the platform where he would give his weekly lecture was clearly marked and closed off.

A dark-skinned man of Turkish extraction, Mohammed Ali Iksa, was one of those who had arrived at the area. He approached the route where the pope's vehicle was to pass. He was a member of the Gray Fox terror organization, based in Turkey, but had left the group because they had not supplied enough action, joining instead the Islamic fundamentalists in the Middle East. He had not come to listen to the speech; he had come here to kill the pope.

At 5 p.m. the open car, with its gleaming leather upholstery, began its journey. The pope was surrounded on all sides by security guards from the Vigili as well as policemen from the city of Rome. The pope passed the large group at about two miles an hour, waving to the crowd which roared its joy and crossed itself endlessly. He patted the heads of young children, much to the enjoyment of their parents, and to the chagrin of the security people, who did not appreciate the proximity of the throng, which would easily enable a potential assassin to strike.

Eighteen minutes after his trip had begun, the first shot was fired in St. Peter's Square. The pope remained standing, his hand leaning on the car seat; suddenly he slumped. The nine-millimeter bullet had torn into his stomach and pierced his small and large intestines. He instinctively grabbed his stomach in the place where the bullet had hit him as if to try and stanch the flow of blood. The second bullet was fired, hitting his right arm. The arm fell to his side, flapping weakly like a rag. Blood spurted onto his white robe, staining it a deep scarlet. The assassin, not satisfied, fired off a third shot, which again hit the pope's right hand.

The driver sat, dumbstruck. Too late, one of the security men threw himself onto the pope in order to protect him. The car continued its slow movement, until it reached a waiting ambulance. Eight minutes later John Paul had reached Gemli Hospital in Rome, where he underwent six hours of surgery that saved his life. It took many months of convalescence before he fully recovered.

It would be a long while before the authorities discovered the identity of the ones who had dispatched the assassin. At first they suspected the KGB of the former Soviet Union. Moscow, for reasons of its own, would have liked to see the assassination of the man whom it suspected would ignite the fire of nationalism in Poland. In those days the members of Poland's Solidarity workers' union were demonstrating, under the leadership of Lech Walesa, and as they flexed their muscles Moscow tried to reoccupy the country and destroy the organization. The Soviet Union very much disliked the Polish pope's clear support for his native countrymen. But after several months, Israel's Mossad discovered that it was not the Soviets; it was the hand of Iran. Ayatollah Khomeini was personally responsible for the action. The head of the largest Christian church in the world was to be the first victim in the holy war, the jihad against the west.

The pope, for his part, greatly disliked Islam. The beliefs of the Koran and the fundamentalists were harsh. On a visit to the Olivetti plant in Italy John Paul shocked the workers when he interrupted his own speech to deliver a vituperative lecture on, "the Koran, which teaches men aggression. Islam is a religion of violence. These people are very dangerous."

Time after time he told his men that the coming world hostilities would not be between East and West, nor between the United States and Russia, but rather between the Islamic fundamentalists and Christianity. He was careful to differentiate between the Islamic religion and the Islamic fanatics.

John Paul returned to the present. To his hijacked plane. He opened his eyes and saw the Chechen terrorists still wearing their flowing robes. Again, here they were, Islamic fundamentalists, fanatics.

And they had not come just to free Chechnya. They wanted to kill him.

# 35

Selim Yagudayev agreed completely with the pope's assessment. Unlike his men, who were counting the minutes until Putin would come on the line, he hoped that the Russian president would stay away, consistent with the tactics generally used when dealing with hijackers.

"You know the rules of the game," he would tell his fighters during exercises in the caves. "Hijackers give a certain specified amount of time to one country or the other. The negotiators on the ground use delaying tactics: The prime minister is not available, the president can't, the interior minister has just gotten ill, the defense minister fell down the stairs, the foreign minister is at his brother-in-law's funeral, and on and on. We know the game. Enough of it. This hijacking will be like the classic ones of old. We'll start from the end. Every minute we shoot a hostage. That's the way it will work."

If Russia would be obstinate, as always, he would have a chance to take vengeance for his father, his uncle, his grandmother Sabrina, and the other thousands of unfortunates who had been kidnapped from their

Jewish heritage and made to convert, some forcibly, others through brainwashing, through the long years of history.

But Putin did not plan on giving him the pleasure. Exactly twenty minutes from when they issued the ultimatum his voice could be heard in the cockpit.

"Vladimir Putin speaking."

Selim spoke into the mouthpiece. He felt a wave of emotion. Today he was making history.

"This is Selim Yagudayev, leader of the Chechen freedom fighters."

"Rumor has it," Putin broke in sarcastically, "that the great leader Yagudayev was not born in Chechnya at all, but in Caracas, capital of Venezuela, with the name Joselito Lombardo."

Selim did not lose his composure. "When you find the truth, even if it's at the other end of the world, you join it."

"And the truth is found in Chechnya. I didn't know that. Too bad Aristotle and Plato didn't know that either."

Selim did not flinch. "There is only one truth; of lies there are many. And I am speaking with one of them."

"Okay, let's get down to business," Putin said, ending the exchange. "I, too, have some conditions before I negotiate with terrorists. The first is that this does not leak out. If the men of my security forces tell me that the weakest radio transmitter anywhere has broadcast the affair, I will cut off all contact with you without further notice. Clear?"

"We accept," Selim said with satisfaction. Just as he had thought: Russia would maintain complete radio silence in order to avoid international pressure. They could always claim they thought it was a prank.

Selim radiated strength and charisma. His men, standing beside him, thought that they had never seen him so sure of himself and his beliefs. "We want you to evacuate Chechnya. Pull your forces out immediately."

Putin found it difficult to speak. A full minute passed before he recovered. "Let me understand. You want to fly in the air with the pope for two months?"

"Two months?"

"That's what it would take for us to take care of the logistics of evacuating all equipment, bases, and buildings, from Chechnya. Pulling out the forces would be another two months. So it seems that you want to spend four months with the pope. What will you do there, learn the Koran with him?"

Selim drew the card that he had been holding close to his chest. "I want guarantees that you will retreat."

Putin cut off the communication. It appeared that he was consulting with his experts. The pilots continued to keep the plane on course, but Selim saw the quiet smiles they exchanged. "The Russian president is a man," the pilot whispered.

Kareem Nisadov licked his lips nervously. The moment of truth was upon them.

The plane flew over the African skies in its journey to nowhere. A bright light shone throughout the cockpit. Strips of land broken up by rivers flew by beneath them. The atmosphere would have been peaceful if not for the strange ways of fate that had brought these six men into a crowded cockpit.

The microphone again crackled into life. Putin spoke with new confidence.

"What kind of guarantees do you want?"

Selim and Kareem had carefully planned this moment. "I will give you an account number in the Bank of Africa, in the Yaoundé, Cameroon branch. You will order your Minister of the Treasury to transfer $5 billion there. The transfer will take place within one hour. I will receive confirmation of the transfer in one hour and five minutes."

There was a short break; they could hear whispers in the background. Putin said to his advisers, "They're madmen. Five billion." His voice grew louder. "You want a homeland or money? It seems you want money."

Selim was firm. "I want a homeland. The money is just a means of guaranteeing that you are not lying to me. I won't touch it. It will be in the hands of a neutral state, Cameroon. On the day the last Russian soldier leaves Chechen ground it will be returned to you. Fair or not?"

"We can't get five billion that quickly."

Selim laughed. "Talk to your newspaper magnate, Gosinski, or one of your other billionaires."

"You're a bunch of imposters," Putin suddenly yelled. "You know what? Take your fantasy pope, send him my regards, and put a bullet in his head. I don't care."

Selim turned his head toward the door and commanded, in a voice cold as ice, "Get me Luisi Kiramonti."

He returned to the microphone. "President Putin, in another minute you will hear with your own presidential ears the sound of the bullet that will kill the man in charge of Vatican security, Luisi Kiramonti. He will be the first; afterwards we will kill a hostage every minute. You are hereby responsible."

There was the sound of panic in the plane as Luisi, his face white, was dragged to the cockpit. A bluish-purple welt throbbed on his neck, where he had been hit. He had just regained consciousness. Hatred burned in his eyes as he glared at the face of the steward with whom he had chatted. "Traitor," he hissed. He was placed between two kidnappers. Selim then commanded the pilot, "Describe to the president what you are seeing."

The pilot's face had a greenish tinge, and it was not from the sunshine flooding the cockpit. His voice was choked; he looked like he was about to regurgitate. "Mr. President," he said, "this is no joke. Luisi Kiramonti, Vatican security chief, is standing next to me. There is a revolver held to his temple."

"That's right," Selim said, grabbing the microphone back. "Have you changed your mind, Mr. President?"

The microphone was quiet; silence was interrupted by a Russian curse. "For my part you can shoot the pope too."

Kareem pulled the trigger.

Luisi Kiramonti screamed once and then collapsed, as if his legs had been cut off. This was Kareem's specialty: He held a gun pointed to the temple in one hand while his finger actually pulled the trigger of the revolver held in the other. He had shot a blank into a pillow held next to Luisi. Nothing had happened to the hapless security chief, but fear had done its work and he had fainted.

The pilot asked Selim for the microphone. With tears in his eyes he begged Putin to change his mind. "We're dealing with professional killers. Do you want Russia held accountable for the murder of the head of the Christian world?"

Putin asked for time to rethink his position.

Selim knew what was going on in the minds of Putin's security cabinet gathered somewhere in the Kremlin. They had been certain he would not dare do anything. Until now, most of the Chechen rebels had been found to be a bunch of fools who had never done anything more serious than place a small bomb in the center of Moscow. No one would have dreamed that they would dare to kidnap the pope.

But now they had been given a convincing argument that certainly offered food for thought.

For five minutes there was complete radio silence.

Putin's voice came over the microphone again. He sounded interested but not defeated, despite the fact that he was indeed giving in. "The money will be transferred to the bank in Cameroon within the hour. Today the chief of staff will be ordered to begin evacuating our forces from Chechnya."

The wave of joy that broke out in the airplane seemed like a fireball in the metal orb. It first engulfed the hijackers in the cockpit. They began to shout, then hugged and kissed one another. From there the rejoicing traveled to their comrades in the other parts of the plane; they, too, broke out in wild, junglelike cries. Finally — and for very different reasons — the passengers took part in the celebrations. A spark of hope had lit up the deadly darkness. The Russian president had given in, and perhaps soon they would be freed.

Thirty-three minutes later, when the celebratory revels had diminished, the confirmation came in. The money had been transferred to the account in Bank of Africa.

"Now," Selim told the Russian president, "once we've been informed that the money is in Yaoundé, I will free the pope. I want a plane with two pilots to wait for us in the airport in Abuja, Nigeria. There we will free the pope and most of the passengers. We will take five hostages with us, who will stay with us until we reach a safe haven."

For the second time in two hours the Alitalia 767 landed in the airport in Cameroon. The head of the pope's office explained to the ground crew that there had been a minor change in the itinerary; they were to let the steward Jack Harrison off the plane and wait for him to return in about an hour. "He's attending to an important request of the pope's. In the meantime you can refuel the plane," the chief of staff added pleasantly. He cut off the communications device and, with a furious look at Selim, asked, "Was I okay?"

Selim pulled the revolver away from the official's forehead. He smiled but did not answer. The man was angry. No wonder. He had every right to be.

Kareem Nisadov was Selim's messenger. He left the airport and returned after a tense hour. His round face bore a triumphant smile. In his hand he held the bank confirmation. Selim carefully checked all the copies of the documents. The confirmation had been signed; the astronomical sum was there, with all its zeroes intact. At Kareem's request the bank manager himself had signed the papers.

"The transfer has been made," Nisadov shouted. "Long live free Chechnya!"

"Long live free Chechnya!" the plane seemed to shake from the roar of the ten happy men.

John Paul's face contorted in disgust. "Animals, not humans," he murmured to himself.

---

The large entourage landed in Abuja, the Nigerian capital, a few hours behind schedule. The plane's doors opened but first only a small group of fifteen people came out: ten black-robed priests who walked very near to five others. Everyone smiled pleasantly at the ground crew. The group rushed toward an Iberia Airlines airbus that was waiting for them, the engines at ready; within minutes they had taken off.

Only afterwards did the papal entourage emerge from the Alitalia plane. Though the ravages of the past few hours were clear on their faces, no one spoke of the hijacking. Selim was right. It was not only Russia that wished to avoid publicity. The Vatican was even more concerned that no word leak out. The pope's spokesman, Monseigneur Jean Magii, gave a short briefing to journalists, declaring that the pope had felt unwell during the journey from Cameroon to Nigeria, and he had therefore been forced to return to Cameroon for a short while. He would have to rest for a few hours before continuing the trip.

Selim and his group returned to Cameroon with the airbus. There they freed the five remaining hostages and the pilots, once they felt themselves relatively safe. Their hideout had been prepared far in advance. They carefully made their way there: a rented apartment in the capital itself. That night they celebrated their victory.

The next morning, while the exhausted group was still sleeping, Selim went to the Bank of Africa. He wanted to make sure that everything was all right.

With his tailored suit, fashionable sunglasses, and elegant briefcase in his hand, Selim resembled dozens of other young businessmen in the bank. But when he left half an hour later he did not look like them any longer. He looked like a person who had been slammed on the head with a heavy hammer. A man who did not even have one dollar in his bank account to help pay for the damage!

"The transfer was not carried out?" he choked out the words. "Impossible. Here is the bank confirmation." He waved the documents in front of the manager, who had made time for this client who claimed that he had $5 billion dollars in his account.

The manager looked carefully at the papers. He lifted his head and burst out laughing. "Young man, go and find some better business. This document in your hand is a complete forgery, and not a very good one at that. No stamp, no computer confirmation, and if you look carefully at the fine print you'll find a dozen other details. I never signed any such order. Not yesterday, never."

Selim left the bank, thunderstruck.

The bank manager looked after him and nodded. The asylums were full of well-dressed men.

Selim returned to the rented apartment and his sleeping comrades. He violently pulled up the shades, filling the place with sunlight. The men awoke, startled, rubbing red eyes.

"Let us sleep," Sayid grumbled. "We've been working for a whole year on this operation."

"Quiet," Kareem yawned. "Don't wake me."

Selim walked toward him and pulled the blanket off him. Kareem jumped up angrily. "What's the matter with you?"

"What's the matter? I'll tell you what's the matter. You're a traitor," Selim screamed. "You fooled us yesterday. The papers you brought back from the bank are forgeries. The Russians have tricked us and you helped them."

The words filled the apartment, heavy and suffocating as thick smoke.

Selim repeated his words again and again, until their import grew clear to all. The sounds of angry words grew louder.

Kareem recovered quickly. "You call me a traitor. You should be ashamed. I endangered my life for my country. I could have gotten shot in the head when I left the airport for the bank. I did all the work and you call me a traitor? At least we're Chechens from birth. You're just a kid who came from Caracas to have some adventures at our expense. You're a stranger."

He turned to his shocked comrades. "I knew this would happen. He's been fooled. Putin has made a fool of all of us! We followed this stranger, put our lives in danger, so that Selim — no, Joselito — could have some fun!"

Selim felt his face grow scarlet. He stared at Kareem, saw the wolflike delight in his eyes. *He's betrayed me, betrayed Chechnya. He knew this was a forgery. He's been working with them all along.*

The room filled with murmers that soon escalated into shouts. Kareem had with him eight men who had gone to sleep drunk with victory and who had awakened to a totally different reality. They had fallen from the summit of success to the abyss of failure. Someone had used them.

All of Selim's charisma seemed to have left him and been transferred to Kareem. They repeated his words; the shouts turned into slogans:

"Joselito the liar, Joselito the traitor."

He stood before them with a face carved of stone. His eyes were opened wide. Impossible! This was how they repaid him for what he had done for them? Yesterday they would follow him through fire and water; today they surrounded him like dragons spewing forth fire and hate.

Sayid grabed his shirt collar. "You'd better get out of here, before we kill you. Get out!"

Kareem and Sayid grabbed him and kicked him mercilessly down the stairs. Selim felt as if he had broken into pieces. His body bruised and throbbing, he painfully stood up and left the place.

---

He who laughs last laughs best. *You thought you would get rid of Kareem when you didn't need him any longer, but he beat you to it.* He had been a stranger among them from the first moment, accepted only because of his powerful charisma, but in the end even the charisma had not been enough. As soon as it became clear that the daring coup had failed, failed utterly, he had been cast out.

He had relied too much on graphology. When he had studied Kareem's handwriting he had never expected this. Too late he realized what Kareem had done to him. Apparently he had contacted someone on the Russian side, an army or intelligence officer, and had revealed the plan. He had offered to cooperate with him, no doubt for a profitable deal: the promise of protection, a hefty payment, and, perhaps, the position of puppet president of Chechnya, under Russian control.

Alarm bells seemed to go off in his head. Yesterday he had had the strange feeling that everything was going too well. Everything was so smooth. No one had tried to fight them off. Putin was a good boy. The bank could have made problems. Now he understood.

President Putin had not been surprised; he had just pretended beautifully. He knew all about the hijacking even before it happened. Kareem had not missed hurting Luisi just for fun; he wanted to come out clean from the affair. The main thing was, he had managed to completely fool Selim, and turn all his comrades against him.

Chechnya was not liberated and would not be liberated. Kareem had managed in one moment to destroy Selim's position, to remind them that all he really was was a student who had come looking for some action in Chechnya, while he, Kareem, was a true native.

A true native, that cursed traitor.

With freedom fighters like that, was it any wonder that Chechnya was trodden beneath the pitiless Russian boot?

And these are the men you wanted to befriend?

Suddenly he thought of the words that the wise Jew had said, the one visiting with his grandmother. *What do you have to do with them?... Don't get involved in an argument that is not yours... Right now they love you because you're succeeding, but the smallest failure and they'll shoot you down like a Scud missile...*

And that was what had happened. The missile had been clad in the figure of a kicking foot.

# EPILOGUE

"You know something, Shoshana?" Shmuel laughed. "I think you've lost a client. I don't need Bach herbal essences. You were right. The trip abroad refreshed me and set my priorities straight. Now I know what I'm going to do. I've decided to spend my life in *kiruv rechokim*. I'm starting tomorrow, *bli neder*."

It was evening. Shmuel had returned from the airport in the cab that afternoon, tired and drained from the long flight, but feeling happy and uplifted. "Welcome Home, Abba" signs greeted him, covering the door from top to bottom. He looked joyfully at them all — from the computer-designed sign of his eldest, Yanky, to the crayoned "Welcome Home, Abba" drawing of an airplane by their youngest child, Tzila.

"Abba, what have you brought us?" the children asked, unashamed. "The golem of Prague," Shmuel joked. What a miracle that Zerach had suggested at the last minute that he buy a few things; otherwise he would have returned empty-handed.

After the homecoming he went to take a nap. The rest of the family tiptoed through the house in order not to disturb him. But he could not close his eyes. He was too excited to sleep. He remembered a *Minchah* that he had *davened* not so long ago, *davened* moments before dusk after a nightmare that had almost driven him mad.

A few minutes later he went to shul for *Minchah* and *Ma'ariv*. He walked back home feeling almost giddy with joy. How many good things had happened to him on this trip! One of the best was his close friendship with the smiling chassid, Zerach Britman. He had said goodbye to him only a few hours ago, and already he missed him.

It was on his return to his home that he noticed the small bottles of herbal essences arranged neatly in a row and informed his wife that he no longer had any need of them.

Shoshana was not quite so sure. She placed a small vial on his desk. "I think you should take a few drops. It will help calm your fears."

"I have no fears." he said with a small smile.

"Shmuel, forgive me, but I have to get back to work. Three women are waiting for reflexology treatments."

"No problem."

Shoshana went to her "treatment room," the important-sounding name for what was actually just a closed porch where she had placed a special reflexology table. Next to the table stood a desk and a stool which she sat upon during treatments, and where she spoke with clients who came for advice on using the Bach herbs.

After Shoshana had left the room he poured himself a cup of juice and opened the briefcase he had brought back from Caracas. He had been waiting for this moment. He now held the notebook with the photocopied sheets in his hand.

The first pages he knew well; the story of Getzel and his son Zekil were very familiar. But the next pages were full of new information. Here was a list of Zekil Fernbach's grandchildren, living in many different countries, but particularly in Israel.

Could he find the Fernbachs of Katamon? Yes, they were here too; they had apparently left Israel and were now living in Chicago. He was more interested in them than the others, but when he got to the next page the blood drained from his face. Judge Dori Talmi was a direct descendant of Zekil Fernbach. The researcher Dr. Ofir Gal was his nephew.

The next line hit him like a ton of bricks.

Deputy Prime Minister Max Landau.

Now the man's behavior was easily understandable. When had Israel ever given so much to a bloodthirsty, brutal enemy who had turned the people's lives into a nightmare? When had an Israeli government ever been ready to give up everything, to give all into enemy hands? If Max Landau was Zekil Fernbach's grandson, everything became clear.

The list included journalists, top media personalities, judges, and government figures. Their beliefs were not just those of enlightened people trying to look at the enemy through a humane perspective, leaving behind primitive emotions. This group of grandsons was a cancerous growth in the body of the nation of Israel. After all, a malignant tumor was only a group of cells bent on self-destruction, for with the death of the body came the death, also, of the cancer itself. But unlike cells, which had not been entrusted with the power of choice by their Creator, these progeny of Getzel Fernbach had sworn allegiance, it seems, to the destruction of the Jews from within.

From here came those "enlightened" legal judgments, those strange verdicts that extracted the teeth from the nation's security forces, that placed nail after nail in its coffin. From here came the media reports that groveled in the most revolting way before the cruel enemy that wished to destroy it, yet incited endless hatred against its own yarmulka-wearing citizenry who wanted only to live in peace. The left knew how to hate, loved to hate. This was the Israeli left, described by one of its own leaders: "If our fanatics were left in a room with a deadly snake, — the snake would die first." The feelings of the left, cut off as it was from its own Jewishness, had turned to hatred. From here they got the perspective that enabled them to look at the knife-wielding enemy as a friend, and a yarmulka-wearing Jew as the greatest danger. Looking at these papers, Shmuel realized that the left's fears were, in a sense, true. The Jews with the head coverings were the ones who would destroy the generations-old dream of all anti-Semites to wipe the Jewish people off the map.

---

He heard the doorbell ring. Shoshana could not get it, the little ones were napping, the big ones had gone out to play.

He took another look at the lists; he would go back to them in a minute. He went to the door.

Two women were standing there, apparently a mother and daughter. Something about them seemed strange, but he could not figure out what. The wigs they were wearing looked like they came from a carton of theatrical costumes.

"Does the reflexologist Shoshana Bilad live here?"

"Yes, but she's very busy. Do you have an appointment?"

"No. But I need treatment urgently," the older of the two declared. "I have terrible pains. I just can't stand it."

Without waiting to be invited the two walked into the house.

The phone rang. He headed toward the closest extension, in the kitchen.

He did not recognize the voice. "Is this the Bilad family?"

"Yes."

"This is Nitzan from the Meroz company. We're conducting a poll about consumer usage. Would you be able to answer some questions?"

Shmuel tried to get out of it, but he was loath to just hang up or be rude to the young person who was so pleasant on the phone. It took him a full five minutes to get rid of the pollster.

He finally hung up the receiver and went to see if the two women had found their way to the treatment room. Shoshana came out when he motioned to her, but she had no idea what he was talking about. No one had come in or joined the women waiting for their turn.

"Strange." His brow wrinkled. "The older woman complained about terrible pains. She said she needed treatment urgently."

Shoshana did not share his anxiety. "So maybe she decided to go to the emergency room. It happens."

It happens.

He returned to his study and looked around. Someone had been here! The file was gone; the notebook had vanished from his desk.

Shmuel turned over the contents of the room, but found nothing. "The two women," he fumed. He gave a shout for his wife. "Shoshana! Those women were interested in me, not you. They've stolen something."

He raced outside. A normal Jerusalem evening. Nothing strange out here. No one rushing, no one running away.

"They've disappeared." Now he realized what had been so strange about them. They were not women at all; they were men, disguised. Not only the wigs, but the dresses, too, were part of a production. A successful production. They had come into his house, apparently after having kept it under surveillance, knowing that no one was there except for him and Shoshana. With perfect timing they sent the pollster to call him, keeping him away from his room, and making off with the file.

Who were they?

Who?

Shmuel grabbed a few drops from the vial his wife had given him earlier. Shoshana was right. He would need a double dose to keep him calm.

He poured the liquid onto a spoon, then stopped. Wait. Who knew if this vial had not been tampered with?

His hands began to tremble. The spoon fell from nerveless fingers and its contents spilled onto his desk.

His eyes goggled as he watched the liquid begin to sizzle and crackle. Within minutes it had burned a deep hole into the Formica finish in a haze of suffocating orange smoke. Droplets fell onto the floor, leaving a tiny hole.

It was, it seemed, some virulent acid, of a sort that one did not normally encounter. He suddenly remembered someone in yeshivah telling him about Jordan's King Hussein, who was always a prime target for assassination. Many times he miraculously escaped death. Once, Shmuel's friend told him, the king had a cold. His physician had prescribed nose drops. Hussein possessed razor-sharp reflexes, as a result of the many attempts on his life, and he was suspicious of everything that surrounded him. The young king took the nose drops and spilled a little out into a sink. In front of his eyes he saw the drops bore a hole in the porcelain surface.

Shmuel fell onto his bed, trembling. "Nothing will help you, Shmuel Mordechai ben Tova Gittel. You're a marked man."

Two weeks passed.

Shmuel tried to fulfill the vow he had made that night in the construction site in Caracas, but from the day those two agents disguised as women had turned up in his house he was afraid to set foot outside. Every sound frightened him. He refused to answer the phone, and only other members of the Bilad family answered the door. Even they were prohibited from opening it unless they knew exactly who was on the other side. Life in the house had become one long nightmare.

The ring sounded like any other. Shoshana walked to the door. A minute later she was in Shmuel's room. "An older woman wants to speak with you."

"Help me," Shmuel groaned. "It's not a woman, it's a man in disguise. A GSS agent."

Shoshana gave him a grave look. "Maybe you'll let me finish," she flared out at him. "She says you'll be happy to see her. Her name used to be Sabrina Lombardo, now it's Hadassah Levin. She's not alone. She's got a young man with her, wearing a black yarmulka and *tzitzis*. His name was Joselito Lombardo; now he's called David Levin."

Shmuel slowly ventured toward the door. His knees trembled like those of an old man.

A dream.

Sabrina gave him a teary-eyed smile and looked at him hopefully. Shmuel stood, paralyzed. They had come to Israel. Sabrina, Joselito — a double of Dudy Levin.

"Dudy," he said, bursting into tears.

The young man answered with a smile. "That's right, I'm David Levin," he said in a pronounced South American accent. "Not Joselito Lombardo, not Selim Yagudayev, not Philip Morteiza."

"What are you talking about?"

"It's a long story," the young man said, his eyes dancing.

"Shmuel, is that how you greet guests, leaving them standing in the doorway? Please come in," Shoshana said graciously.

Shmuel radiated joy. He remembered the words of the verse: "There is a reward for your work." One short telephone call, and see who was here.

They sat with their visitors. Shoshana served refreshments and chatted with the tough old woman. Shmuel spoke with her grandson, trying to find out what had brought him to fight with Muslim Chechen rebels.

David told him everything.

---

"I was a boy who cared fiercely about justice; I couldn't bear injustice, it didn't matter where, when or by whom. My motto was the opposite of what you said, 'Don't get involved in a fight that is not yours.' I would get involved in any argument, once I identified who was being unjust. I suffered greatly because of this trait; it didn't make me very popular. But I wouldn't change. I have a kind of measuring scale within me; I was always weighing and balancing who is unjust and who is not. By the way," he said, with a mischievous grin, "my grandmother can vouch for that. I'm the one who was 'guilty' of getting you to Caracas."

"Meaning?"

"When I was still a young boy your name was mentioned in the house. Grandmother spoke very angrily about you, blaming you for the tragedy that destroyed our family."

Hadassah lowered her eyes but nodded assent. "That's right," she said, tight lipped. "Joselito changed my mind."

"What Joselito?" The young man burst out. "Joselito Lombardo is dead. I'm David Levin."

He continued quickly. "My grandmother very much respected my opinion, from the time I was young. I said you were no more than a messenger of some Divine Providence. A little boy who forgot that his friend was waiting for him for a key was not a murderer. I caused Grandmother to change her mind about you.

"Two years ago I became absorbed in the story of the Chechens. The injustice disturbed me. The Russians occupied a land, slaughtered its citizens, and the whole world was silent. I changed my identity; that's not hard to do. I traveled to Moscow under the name Oleg Telushkin.

I enlisted in the Red Army and was sent to Chechnya. There I befriended the Chechen rebels. My comrades in the Red Army were futilely searching for the underground fighters, but I knew where to find them, and eventually joined them. They knew the truth of my identity but they accepted me as one of them. I was a more patriotic Chechen than they were. I was looking for a place to put my enormous sense of justice."

"And your energy," Sabrina added. "You have a lot of energy, and you were putting it into the wrong place. You had to get a good strong kick from your 'friends' in order to understand that a Jew has nothing to look for among the non-Jews, and even if you give everything to them, they will blame you for the failure."

"The main thing is you've returned," Shmuel said with a smile.

"In his merit I am here," Hadassah concluded. "I often thought about returning to Israel, but I didn't want to come empty-handed. I vowed only to return with at least one family member. Also, I didn't want to leave Caracas until I'd taken vengeance on Yehoshua Cohen. It took forty years, but I finally lived to see him punished. One thing, though, hurts me terribly: I wanted to take revenge upon the Fernbach family, who gave us into the hands of the missionary, and so I gave you the file. Now I hear that it's been stolen."

Shmuel extended his arms in a gesture of hopelessness. "But," she answered after a moment's thought, "perhaps it's for the best. Our powers are small against theirs. The end of this will come only when *galus* ends as well."

"Maybe they are what's stopping the redemption," Shoshana mused aloud.

"Who knows?" Shmuel sighed.

Shoshana turned to Hadassah. "What about your sons? Why have you given up on them?"

Now it was Hadassah's turn to sigh. "My sons have, much to my sorrow, lost their sense of self. Christianity destroyed their desire to do something good, their joy in life. The moment they converted they became like lifeless dummies. Not Jews, not gentiles. Cut off from everything, not belonging anywhere. They won't come here, even for a short visit. Nothing. They're gone."

She seemed on the verge of tears. Tactfully, David changed the subject. He turned to Shmuel. "Your words to me during our conversation, that the greatest revenge I could take against the Christians was to return to being Jewish, have been haunting me ever since. I decided to come and learn about Judaism in Israel. Everything you told me has been echoing in my mind. 'Don't get involved in an argument that is not yours.' 'They don't really love you.' Much later I saw that you were right. Kareem Nisadov was jealous of me, that I, the stranger, was more successful than he was, the patriot from birth. He looked for any way to get rid of me, and finally succeeded."

"His success is yours too," Shmuel interrupted. "In his merit you returned to the land of your fathers."

"But we also had sweet revenge," Hadassah continued. She told him of the death of the missionary Yehoshua Cohen, who paid for his actions with his life, and of the series of assassinations within the "organization" that had resulted in a gang war that had not yet ended.

When they left the house at a late hour, Shmuel felt that a heavy stone had rolled off his heart. The circle was closed. Dudy Levin no longer was following him. He had appeared in a new form, as David Levin, to return to the Levin family their stolen Jewishness.

"I think I'm free now," he told Shoshana that night. "It looks like the GSS or someone else wanted those pages from me. Now they have no reason to be frightened of me. I'm just small potatoes."

---

*The next evening*

The offices of Yad L'Achim in Jerusalem were used to many visitors, but those such as Shmuel Bilad and David Levin were still unusual.

The men in the office sat around them and listened to Shmuel's fascinating tale. With tears in his eyes he recited all of it, beginning with that wet, wintry day when Dudy Levin had taken ill, until this moment, as he sat with David Levin, Dudy's nephew, who wished to return from the long road that had taken him from Caracas to Moscow and Chechnya, and, finally, here to Jerusalem.

The director of the organization, R' Aryeh Lipsker, broke the silence that reigned when Shmuel finished his story. "There is a reward for your efforts," he told Shmuel. "You've been permitted to come full circle, from uncle to nephew." He sighed. "But it's an old story. That's how they operated forty years ago. Today they're much more up to date. They look more modern, and they use their financial incentives differently. They infiltrate charity funds, get their lists. The recipients are given generous sums and promises of even more funds if they do one small thing, join their activities. That's how they entrap innocent Jews."

Shmuel was silent. He could see a man with a reddish beard dropping coins into the home of an impoverished family, slowly and furtively cutting off the branches from its life-giving tree, the tree of Judaism.

"The threat from these 'Messianic Jews' today is far worse than it was then," R' Lipsker continued. "They have an excellent propaganda apparatus. Like Yehoshua Cohen, they concentrate on the weaker elements, on the naive and unlearned. They sell themselves in a most persuasive manner, and make all sorts of trouble. Their chutzpah is unbounded. They even opened a missionary center in Bnei Brak! Jews and non-Jews come to an apartment on Esther HaMalkah Street for 'prayer' ceremonies and fervent sermons about the merits of 'that man,' from the top clergy, and are given support and funding from mission societies in Finland and Germany. Another group, called 'Witnesses of the Name,' are no less dangerous. These are nothing more than missionaries, but the State of Israel recognizes them as a valid religious organization, and when our workers try to stop their destructive activities they put themselves at risk of jail sentences, since they are 'disturbing the religious sensitivities' of the missionaries.

"David Salimonoff, for example, a member of the 'Witnesses,' filed a complaint against some wonderful men, our workers, who three years ago filmed his activities for twenty minutes. He claimed that they also insulted him publicly by calling him a missionary, something which he claimed could have negative effects on his work. They might go to prison for this —"

"Yehoshua Cohen was proud when they called him a missionary," Shmuel laughed.

R' Lipsker gave him a serious look. "The world has changed, the methods have improved, but the goal remains the same: to take as many Jews as possible away from their beliefs. The number of missionaries in Israel increases day by day. The enlightened State of Israel has no serious laws to stop them, and they take advantage of this.

"David Levin has returned to his rightful place —" R' Lipsker's eyes fell on the young man, "but many, many are going on the opposite path, and leaving us, in the way that Moishy and Ahrele were turned into Gonzales and Santos Lombardo. We need help."

"That's why I'm here," Shmuel declared. "I have come here to fulfill my promise."

"The men in the division that fights missionaries will be happy to have you join them," R' Lipsker said with satisfaction. "As a learned man you will be able to help us in the field but, even more, in transmitting Jewish beliefs through Torah lectures. We have branches all over the country where more than 1,500 people, mostly from the Soviet Union, come daily, to hear words of Torah. You will be teaching in a way you've never done before, giving these people a chance at eternity."

❦

*The next evening*

They were sitting and eating a light dairy meal. Shmuel had not felt this good in a long while. His fears were gone; life had new meaning. Now he would be able to combine his desire to teach Torah with his new activities.

Shmuel's son Yanky, sitting with them at the table, told them about a left-wing Jewish journalist who wanted to help the poor Palestinians in Gaza, giving them bread and food. Ungratefully, the Arabs were not impressed with the charity and had held her for an entire night in a bug-infested hole with a bag over her head. She had almost died there, until she was liberated the next morning at the direct intervention of the top echelon, who were afraid of what the incident would do to their image.

"What was her name?" Shmuel asked, buttering his bread.

Yanky looked at the newspaper in his hand. "Nufar Talmi. It says here that she's from a very important family. She's the daughter of the well-known leftist judge, Professor Dori Talmi."

*Time Bomb* / 387

Shmuel's hand froze. Dori Talmi, one of the names on the lists.

What had our Sages said? "Whoever has mercy on the cruel will end up being cruel to the merciful." He thought about those who felt sorry for murderers, instead of dealing with them as the Sages advised: "Whoever comes to kill you, kill him first." At the same time, to their own brethren they were cruel and unfeeling.

The telephone broke his reverie.

"Yanky, please get it."

Yanky picked up the receiver. "Abba, it's for you."

"Who is it?"

"R' Michael Pankovaski of Yeshivas Meoros Elimelech. He says it's urgent."

Shmuel's face was startled as he took the phone. What could R' Pankovaski want?

"R' Bilad?"

"Yes?"

"How are you?"

"Thank G-d."

"R' Bilad." The voice held the hint of suppressed excitement. "You won't believe this. I have a job for you. I want to give you the position you used to hold: to be a lecturer in our institution."

"I don't believe it."

"You must," R' Pankovaski laughed. "You can start tomorrow. We're in the middle of *Perek 'Lo Yachpor,'* in the *sugya* of *'rov and karov.'* Can you come?"

"Let me sleep on it," Shmuel said, still in shock. "It's hard for me to take this in. What happened? My beard grew black again?"

R' Pankovaski laughed. "Why should we care about your age, Shmuel? For my part, you can be 90, with a long white beard."

He said a warm goodbye. Shmuel found concentrating difficult. What should he do? Return to Meoros Elimelech?

But, "I shall repay my vow."

*I promised to give my life to kiruv rechokim. Yad L'Achim and Lev L'Achim are waiting for me.*

The telephone rang again.

This time Yanky picked it up. "Abba, it's for you again."

"Who?"

"R' Isser Zalman Samet of Yeshivas Masuos Avraham. He says it's urgent."

Shmuel did not say a thing; a wan smile appeared on his lips. His eyes were twinkling as he put the receiver to his ear.

"R' Bilad, how are you?" the hearty voice came over the line. "If you knew what I was about to tell you, you'd be dancing in the street."

"*Nu*, let's hear."

"We've discussed your taking a position in our yeshivah," R' Samet said, enjoying every word. "I wanted to be the bearer of good news and let you know we have something for you. In the top class, as we discussed."

This time he did not say, "I don't believe it."

"What are you learning?"

"We're in the middle of *Perek 'Lo yachpor,'* in the *sugya* of *'rov and karov.'* So, you'll be coming?"

"Let me sleep on it."

"Sleep well, and come in tomorrow refreshed and ready to give the class. The boys are waiting anxiously for you."

*I will repay my vow.*

"I could put together the lectures and give them in both yeshivahs tomorrow. But I'm not going to," he told his surprised wife and son. "I have made a promise and I will keep it."

"Abba! They're running after you!" Yanky said.

Shmuel smiled. "Let them run."